Books by Tracie Peterson and Kimberley Woodhouse

All Things Hidden

Beyond the Silence

THE HEART OF ALASKA

In the Shadow of Denali

Out of the Ashes

Under the Midnight Sun

THE TREASURES OF NOME

Forever Hidden

Endless Mercy

Ever Constant

THE JEWELS OF KALISPELL

The Heart's Choice

With Each Tomorrow

Books by Tracie Peterson

LADIES OF THE LAKE

Destined for You

Forever My Own

Waiting on Love

WILLAMETTE BRIDES

Secrets of My Heart

The Way of Love

Forever by Your Side

BROOKSTONE BRIDES

When You Are Near

Wherever You Go

What Comes My Way

GOLDEN GATE SECRETS

In Places Hidden

In Dreams Forgotten

In Times Gone By

HEART OF THE FRONTIER

Treasured Grace

Beloved Hope

Cherished Mercy

PICTURES OF THE HEART

Remember Me

Finding Us

Knowing You

For a complete list of titles, visit TraciePeterson.com.

Books by Kimberley Woodhouse

SECRETS OF THE CANYON

A Deep Divide

A Gem of Truth

A Mark of Grace

TREASURES OF THE EARTH

The Secrets Beneath

Set in Stone

For a complete list of titles, visit KimberleyWoodhouse.com.

With
EACH
TOMORROW

With EACH TOMORROW

TRACIE PETERSON
KIMBERLEY WOODHOUSE

BETHANYHOUSE

a division of Baker Publishing Group
Minneapolis, Minnesota

© 2024 by Peterson Ink, Inc. and Kimberley R. Woodhouse

Published by Bethany House Publishers
Minneapolis, Minnesota
BethanyHouse.com

Bethany House Publishers is a division of
Baker Publishing Group, Grand Rapids, Michigan

Printed in the United States of America

Library of Congress Cataloging-in-Publication Data
Names: Peterson, Tracie, author. | Woodhouse, Kimberley, author.
Title: With each tomorrow / Tracie Peterson and Kimberley Woodhouse.
Description: Minneapolis, Minnesota : Bethany House Publishers, a division of Baker
    Publishing Group, 2024. | Series: The jewels of Kalispell; 2
Identifiers: LCCN 2023053578 | ISBN 9780764238994 (paperback) | ISBN
    9780764239007 (casebound) | ISBN 9781493446537 (e-book)
Subjects: LCGFT: Christian fiction. | Romance fiction. | Novels.
Classification: LCC PS3566.E7717 W584 2024 | DDC 813/.54—dc23/eng/20231120
LC record available at https://lccn.loc.gov/2023053578

Scripture quotations are from the King James Version of the Bible.

Cover design by Dan Thornberg, Design Source Creative Services

Cover images from Shutterstock and 123RF

Baker Publishing Group publications use paper produced from sustainable forestry practices and postconsumer waste whenever possible.

24 25 26 27 28 29 30   7 6 5 4 3 2 1

This book is lovingly dedicated to the
Christian Mommy Writers Group.

For all the Woodhouse Easter eggs
and screaming peaches. Thank you
for all the smiles, laughter, and encouragement.
I just wanted you to know how much
I adore every one of you and absolutely
love being your honorary den mother.

Dear Reader,

This series features three beautiful historic landmarks in Kalispell. First, the Carnegie Library (*The Heart's Choice*), which is now the Hockaday Museum of Art. Then the Great Northern Railway Depot (*With Each Tomorrow*), which is now the Chamber of Commerce. And finally, book three will feature the grand McIntosh Opera House, which is located above what is now Western Outdoor on Main Street.

Though based on real locations and, at times, real people, this book is a work of fiction.

The railroad was the life and death of a town in the 1800s and early 1900s. It provided a way in and out of the town, and the promise of well-maintained telegram lines (as these inevitably followed the railroad tracks). Towns fought over who would get the railroad and petitioned the various railroad companies to come through their area. In other cases, towns were created as railroads built their lines. They often called these end-of-the-tracks towns. In some cases, they never grew larger than a so-called whistle-stop, where the train would blow its whistle as it passed through and snag the mailbag from a high pole alongside the tracks while throwing out the incoming mail onto the platform. Usually, these towns were also the water stops, since the early steam trains used thousands and thousands of pounds of water per hour of operation.

When a railroad designed their tracks to sidestep a town, it wasn't at all unusual for that town to pick up and move. Buildings were put on pallets and dragged by teams of draft horses. Wagons and skids were loaded with whatever could be transplanted and the entire town went to where the railroad was going to be.

That's how important the railroad was in the old West.

For a time, Kalispell was a regional headquarters for the Great Northern Railway. Farmers relied on the railroad to transport their crops, and ranchers to move their cattle. The town employed a great many men for the railroad. So imagine the distress when it was announced that, because the mountain grade was too dangerous, the railroad officials were moving their regional headquarters from Kalispell to Whitefish, Montana. The people of Kalispell were devastated and feared it would mean the end of their town. After all, they'd seen a nearby community reduced to a ghost town when the railroad bypassed them.

When we discovered this story in our research, it was too interesting to pass up. The citizens of Kalispell are today, as they were then, incredible people who know how to fight for their town and for the benefits they need to continue moving toward the future. Our story is a work of fiction, but we thought it would be interesting to put our characters into the middle of a real historical crisis and see what might happen. We worked to be accurate with the details regarding the railroad and its move, and hope you enjoy the ride.

Kim and Tracie

Prologue

Watching the person she loved most in the world die was the absolute worst experience ever. Nothing could be as dreadful. Not even dying herself.

Ellie bit her lip and commanded the tears in her eyes to stop.

They didn't listen.

They puddled in the corners until they spilled down her cheeks in great streams of salty liquid. Licking her lips, she swiped at her cheeks. "Mama? Tell me what to do . . . how can I help you?"

Another wail escaped the woman on the bed.

A woman who no longer resembled the loving mother who'd given birth to her and raised her. Gone were the rosy cheeks and brilliant smile. The plump bosom and curvy figure had shriveled into the gaunt frame that couldn't weigh more than ninety pounds.

Ellie tightened her grip on Mama's hand, willing the pain away.

But another scream tore out of her fragile mother. Ellie clenched her eyes against the sound. She hated cancer! Hated the doctor for not being able to help. Hated God for allowing this.

Just an hour ago Mama had talked to her. With ragged breaths, she'd pleaded with Ellie to trust God and have faith that all would be well. That His will for her life was perfect.

Ellie had nodded and lied. Anything to make Mama feel better.

She might only be fourteen years old, but she'd witnessed too much suffering, too many horrors to believe that God's will was perfect. Or even good. No matter what Mama said. No matter what Ellie had believed as a child. No. Not anymore.

Maybe back when she was little, she'd been gullible enough to believe. Back when Mama was well and whole. She'd been so proud that her daughter had placed her faith in the Almighty.

Her mother had been the strongest woman of faith ever . . . and *this* was what God allowed to happen to her?

It wasn't right.

It would never be right again.

What would she do without Mama?

The hot tears started in earnest again.

Mama's wails dimmed to moans, but she continued to writhe as the stomach cancer ate at her body.

Doc had said it wouldn't be long now. Why couldn't he fix it?

It didn't make sense. Mama was fighting for life, for each breath. If she was still fighting, why couldn't the doctor?

Mama stilled.

The silence was worse than the wails.

"Mama?" Ellie scooted closer.

Waited for her mama's next breath.

She counted to ten before it came.

Mama's body lay limp beneath the thin blanket. Sweat dotted her forehead and Ellie wiped it away.

"Jesus!" Mama's voice sounded with sudden strength. "Take me home!" The cry crackled from her throat.

"No . . . Mama, please . . . I need you. You need to stay with me." Great sobs racked Ellie's frame and she gripped her mother's hand and squeezed.

Mama's face pinched into a grimace again. An agonizing, guttural sound filled the room.

And then . . .

Mama's face relaxed into a smile. Her body lay limp.

Ellie counted.

Mama didn't take a breath.

"Breathe, Mama." The whisper choked its way out. In Ellie's mind, she started counting again.

When she reached five hundred, everything stopped. The counting. The pleas.

The hope.

Everything inside her shattered. Never to be put back together again.

Why would God do this? Why would He take such a beautiful soul? How could God's will be for those so faithful to Him to suffer so much?

She shook Mama's thin hand. Nothing happened.

All color was gone from Mama's face.

No writhing. No moaning. No wailing.

No grimace wrinkled her brow.

No life.

Nothing.

Ellie jerked her hand away. *"No!"*

AUGUST 10, 1895—KALISPELL, MONTANA

"Owner of the flour mill." Dad grinned and gripped Carter's shoulder tight. "I'm proud of you, son."

Carter Brunswick stood a little taller. He'd worked hard and saved his money for years to get to this day. It was perfect. And his twenty-first birthday to boot. "Thanks. I couldn't have done it without the Lord and, of course, you and Mom."

The smile that stretched across Dad's face was broader than any he'd ever seen. "Let's get on home. Your mother is preparing a celebration."

"A celebration? She shouldn't have gone to the trouble." Even still, he allowed the excitement to build. If he were still a kid, he'd be skipping down the street.

"She wanted it to be a surprise, but you know me . . . I have a hard time keeping secrets." His father's step had a definite bounce to it.

"I won't tell her that you gave it away, but I need to make a stop first. I've asked Pastor Woody to pray over this new venture so I can dedicate the business to the Lord. Mom won't mind, will she?" He stopped in the street. "I was hoping you would join me."

"Your mother won't mind one bit." Dad's jaw quivered for a moment as he pinched his lips together. "And I would be honored."

They walked in silence to the church, and Carter took the time to calm his nerves. All the nervous energy he'd carried around the last few days was a jumbled mess inside of him. But now that the papers were signed, the flour mill was his—and the depth of what lay ahead was sinking in.

He would be responsible for the mill and its workings. A huge undertaking. Then there were all the employees. Their families would depend on him to make good decisions and keep the business growing. The town needed the flour, as did surrounding areas. One day he'd even branch out and send their delicious wheat flour across the country.

His shoulders dipped a bit under the weight of it all. Had he bitten off more than he could chew?

Dad and his partner—Fred—had started their wheat farms ten years ago. They'd even helped another man who'd been through hard times get the mill started because neither one of them could manage their farms *and* a mill. But when the mill owner's wife died, the mill went up for sale.

Carter fasted and prayed for three days and knew without a doubt that he was supposed to purchase the mill and run it.

But in the back of his mind, doubts niggled at him. Was he old enough? Was he wise enough? Would the workers respect him? What if he had issues? Financially. Or with equipment or distribution?

They reached the church steps and Dad stopped at the bottom and turned. "Carter, I know you. I can see the worry crisscrossing your face." He placed his hand on Carter's shoulder again. "You've taken on a massive job, but God will see you through. Just like you said, God has provided and opened the door. Keep Him first, and He will guide you."

"Yes, sir." He inhaled deep. "That's why I wanted to come here. It's important to give my work over to the Lord."

"Then, let's go." Dad headed up the steps and Carter followed.

Twenty-one. He couldn't believe it. He was the owner of the flour mill at twenty-one! When he was younger, he'd had lots of dreams. Most of them centered around their wheat farm and the mill. But when several of his school chums courted and got married, envy began to seep into his heart and mind.

His *biggest* dream had been to get married, have a family, and carry on the legacy his parents and grandparents gave him. But finding the right gal proved harder than it was to dream it.

He'd done his best to set that part of his dreams aside, but inside, his heart yearned for it no matter how much he tried to quell it.

Taking two stairs at a time, he followed Dad. All in good time. God had given him this part of his dream, He would supply the rest. If it was His will.

Man, he hoped it was. Pastor Watkins opened the double doors as they reached the top step. "Welcome. So good to see the Brunswick men today." He clapped his hands together. "And what a day it is. Am I looking at the new owner of the flour mill?" His eyebrows wiggled.

"That you are." Dad patted Carter on the back.

"Wonderful!" He held out an arm toward the sanctuary.

"I asked the elders and deacons to pray with us—just as you asked, Carter."

"Thank you, Pastor." As they walked into the space, the smell of lemon oil filled his senses. Someone must have polished the pews recently.

"Let's head to the front. If you'll kneel, Carter, the rest of us would like to surround you and lay our hands on your head and shoulders as we approach the throne of Grace."

Carter nodded and walked forward.

Now that the time was here, everything else fell away. Silence filled the room and he stepped to the altar and knelt.

Surrounded by godly men whom he'd known half of his life, Carter dipped his head and closed his eyes.

Lord, into Your hands I give my life and my business. May I bring glory to Your name . . .

One of the elders began to pray, and a rush of warmth filled him as tears streaked down his cheeks.

1

Tuesday, May 10, 1904—Montana

E very last bit of patience Eleanor Briggs once claimed as her own had disappeared about two hundred miles ago. This train trip used it all.

But why? It wasn't like this was any different from any of the last hundred journeys with her father. This was her life.

She flipped through the pages of *Century* magazine, trying to find something that would occupy her mind.

When would they arrive at their destination?

Mile after mile of endless prairie had left her feeling rather empty and—dare she say it?—lonely. Thank goodness they had finally reached the mountainous region with its magnificent scenery, but even the views out the windows couldn't change the fact that she was bored. And tired.

Of trains.

Of living out of luggage.

Of the same conversations, articles, and lectures on conservation.

Horrid thoughts really, but as long as no one else heard

them, she could be honest. She used to love traveling with her father. His work in assisting his dear friend George Grinnell in seeing to the formation of a new national park in Montana was a worthy cause. Still, there was a restlessness inside her that, at twenty-four years of age, she couldn't quite explain.

Patience was hard to come by, but she couldn't allow others to see her inner turmoil. Especially not her father.

No matter what, she couldn't damage his work or reputation.

So here she sat. On a train. Bored out of her mind.

The train took a steep incline, and it jerked and tilted on the tracks. Oh, she did not like the looks of the curve ahead. Several passengers gasped, and another woman squeaked and gripped the man's arm next to her.

Never in her life had Eleanor been on such a ride. Heavens, if this was how the railroads were built in Montana, perhaps Father and Mr. Grinnell should address that before attempting to bring scads of people out for a national park.

Her heart jumped at the screech of the train's wheels.

The conductor walked through the car, with a calming voice. "We're going over Marias Pass. Don't worry. This is all normal and the train is perfectly safe."

Forcing herself to look down in her lap, she blew out her breath slowly. Normal. Sure. Hadn't her father said that the rail lines *west* of Kalispell were the worst? Over Haskell Pass? With tight curves and bridges the railroad had a headache keeping maintained?

She closed her eyes against the turmoil in her stomach. Haskell Pass was worse. This was Marias Pass. They were fine.

They were fine.

They were fine.

All she had to do was think about something else.

Anything.

The train jerked again, and a small child whimpered and then cried.

Eleanor turned the pages in the magazine and found the article her father had encouraged her to read. It was written by Mr. Grinnell and spoke of the great beauty held by Montana's mountainous regions. He referenced it as the "Crown of the Continent," and given his vast travels all over North America, she supposed he could be trusted as the expert.

The views so far were lovely, even if the journey here might kill them all.

Wincing, she pushed the dreadful thought aside and made herself read the article.

By the time she reached the end, the tracks were straight and level again.

With a sigh, she laid the magazine back in her lap and allowed her gaze to roam the landscape. For years she had listened to her father and George Bird Grinnell speak of Montana and the grandeur of its mountains and the unspoiled wildness of its vast forests. Grinnell had been instrumental in the creation of the Lewis and Clark Forest Reserve. As was his usual approach, he sought Congress to set aside lands in a forest reserve and then went to work convincing them to do more. In the case of Montana, he wanted a great national park to be created. Her father wanted that too.

So did she.

As a conservationist, Stewart Briggs was well known for his belief that the vast, majestic lands of the United States should be preserved for everyone to enjoy. For years, her father had touted the perils of farmers and ranchers owning thousands and thousands of acres of land, especially when it encompassed large areas of land best preserved by the federal government. She'd heard him speak to more than one group about the unjust practice, and the idea made sense to her. Although—she smiled—every once in a while her mind liked to argue the other side. Even though she didn't understand it and hadn't researched it. What would it be like to own a large ranch or farm? What if the land was passed down from generation to generation? Questions flourished. But it was best to agree with her father. He'd done plenty of research over the years.

Of course, he was violently opposed to the Homestead Act of 1862 that gave millions of acres of land to settlers who were willing to improve it. *"Why improve what Nature has perfected?"* was Father's motto.

This also made sense to her.

Still, in their travels through the country she'd seen many family farms. That was a piece of the puzzle she wished to understand. Obviously, they needed food to eat, but did one family need so much? It was not a topic she could bring up with her father.

Grinnell often used Father to raise money for his causes, and the two were determined to see land ownership limited in America.

"Did you see George's article?"

She glanced up to see her father return to his seat from the smoking car.

At least some conversation would pass the time. "I did. I must say he intrigued me with his comment that this area is the Crown of the Continent." She glanced out the window. "It is impressive, but I could compare it to the Colorado Rockies . . . say, Estes Park. Surely that place could also be called a Crown of the Continent. And what about some of the scenery we've seen in photographs of Alaska? Photos never do justice to an area, but it is easy to see that Alaska holds many great views. Perhaps it could also hold the title." Not that she necessarily *wanted* to argue with her father about the same things they'd already discussed at length, but something inside egged her on.

"You are simply in a disagreeable mood. If Grinnell says it's the Crown of the Continent, then I doubt we shall be disappointed. Already the scenery has changed from prairie to mountains."

As if she couldn't see that for hersel—

Stop it, Eleanor. She blinked away the disrespectful thought.

Her father took out his pocket watch and frowned. "This thing isn't keeping proper time at all. I just inquired of the porter, and it was completely off." He shook the watch a bit. "Remind me when we're in Kalispell to seek a repair shop."

"I will." Eleanor set aside the magazine and picked up her journal. Just like Father to change the subject and shut down a conversation when he didn't like where it was headed.

Oh my. She *was* in a disagreeable mood.

She dug a pencil out of her pocket and made a note to herself: *Watch repair in Kalispell.*

She put the pencil back and closed the journal. "How much longer for this trip?"

"Not all that far. Four hours at the most. The mountainous terrain will slow us considerably, but hopefully we'll soon be able to glimpse the full glory of Montana."

After days on the train, four hours wasn't all that much. So why did it seem an eternity? She picked up the magazine again but tossed it aside almost instantly. There was nothing in it to hold her attention.

Why was she so . . . restless? Unsatisfied?

Every bit of this feeling was unsettling. She and Father had gotten into a comfortable pattern. Why couldn't she just go on with the way things had been?

She released a sigh.

"I hesitate to mention it"—Father brushed lint off his trousers—"but before we left Chicago, I had a letter from New York."

She turned to him and schooled her features. Father expected her to listen—no matter how mundane the topic. No need to react until he said exactly what the letter was about. Since New York had once been their home state, it was anyone's guess what information the letter might contain.

"It was from the Brewsters."

She tipped her head ever so slightly, keeping her eyes on her lap. The mention of the family threatened to twist her insides. But she willed her heart to slow and kept her mask of indifference. "And how are they?"

"They offered a bit of news. It seems their eldest son, Andrew, is marrying in August. They invited us to attend. A formal invitation will be sent later, but they know how busy I am and wanted to give some warning."

"And do you plan for us to attend?" Every bit of her hoped against hope Father would say no. A long time ago, when she and Andrew were still young, they had been considered a couple. She found him compatible enough, handsome, and even intelligent, but he was also self-focused and rather greedy. She'd put an end to their relationship long before anything official was declared. It didn't seem prudent to attend with such a history.

Still, Eleanor knew the family meant a great deal to her father. If he wanted to go, she would travel with him. Just as she always did.

"Are *you* of a mind to attend?" He rubbed his bearded chin. "I am not opposed if that is your desire."

"Not at all. I have no interest in his wedding." She smoothed her hands over the cover of her journal. "Seems rather senseless to go all the way back to the East Coast when our summer plans clearly have pointed us west." She had no desire to go anywhere back east after this horrid train ride.

Her father relaxed a bit in his seat. Had he been concerned about her reaction? "I'd rather hoped that would be your conclusion on the matter."

"Would you like for me to send a gift when the time is right?" She picked up her journal.

Her father's expression grew thoughtful. "I suppose that would be a kind gesture. What would be appropriate, Ellie?"

Her chest tightened. Why couldn't he remember she wasn't Ellie any longer? Not for ten years. Mother always called her that . . .

And the nickname died with her.

Over the years, Eleanor insisted Father call her by her full name. But every once in a while, he forgot.

Best not to make an issue of it. She smiled at him. "Knowing them as we do, I might suggest crystal. Waterford, of course."

"That sounds sensible. Pick out a piece and let me know when it's ready. I'll pen a letter to send when the time is right."

Eleanor jotted a note, then glanced at him. "Anything else?"

"Nothing of importance." He settled back and closed his eyes. "Your mother would tell me to use this time for a nap despite the growing beauty outside. I believe I'll heed her advice and try for a bit of rest before we arrive in Kalispell."

Mother.

The band around Eleanor's heart tightened even more. They had mentioned her less and less as the years passed, but for some reason Father had mentioned her more and more since heading out west this trip.

Was Mother on his mind that much? Even after all these years? Perhaps in his older age, he was simply recalling fond memories of her.

Father's soft snores filled the space. Didn't take him long, did it?

Eleanor turned back to the window. Although, instead of Montana, she saw the last few weeks of her mother's life. Heard Mama praying for death to come quickly . . .

Even now, it ripped Eleanor's heart in two.

That had been her first experience with death. It was horrible. How could Mama say that if this was the will of God, they would bear it with grace?

The will of God? For a woman to bear such wretched pain that she could scarcely draw breath? The will of God for a fourteen-year-old child and her father to watch their dearest on earth suffer for weeks on end? Where was *grace* in that?

Mama's words washed over Eleanor until she couldn't bear it. She closed her eyes and squeezed them against the barrage.

Pray for understanding and peace of mind.

God will provide comfort.

He's a good and loving Father who watches faithfully over His children.

Trust Him. Trust Him. Trust Him . . .

Rebel tears slipped out from underneath her lashes no matter how much she commanded them to stop.

No.

Eleanor blinked and swiped at her cheeks. No more. She couldn't deal with it.

She frowned and cast a glance at her father. He was still asleep. What would he think of her rambling thoughts?

While Mother was alive, Father had been by her side, at church every time the doors were open. But after her death, he lost himself in his conservation work and the new scientific discoveries of the day, and bit by bit, little was ever mentioned about spiritual matters. That suited Eleanor just fine.

Every once in a while, her mother's teachings drifted through her mind, and a great swell of the faith she'd felt as a child would overwhelm her. But it was easily pushed away.

They traveled so much that their friends and family had no idea if they attended church or not. What did it matter anyway? Most people assumed someone was a Christian if they acted with kindness and bowed their head for the mealtime prayer.

Eleanor propped her chin in her hand, watching trees

and mountains swim together in a dizzying palette of grays, browns, and greens. This was what really mattered, wasn't it? Conserving the land. Making sure generations after them could enjoy the splendor and beauty the western frontier had to offer.

There was enough to do without worrying about faith.

Besides, Father's work and writing had garnered him a small measure of notoriety. People didn't seem to care what he believed since he was making the world a better place. As far as she was concerned, the less said about God, the easier it was to ignore His existence.

Plain and simple.

He'd taken away her mother. He deserved no better.

"We'll reach Kalispell in about twenty minutes." The conductor's voice reached the fuzzy edges of Eleanor's brain.

Opening her eyes, she straightened and looked across the way to where her father sat, his gaze fixed out the window. When had she fallen asleep?

"This is amazing country, Ellie."

She shook the haze from her mind, smoothed her traveling suit, patted her hair, and leaned toward the window. Now that the train had slowed, she could make out the complex details of the landscape. Majestic mountains rose in snow-covered glory against a brilliant blue sky. Forests of pines, thick and lush, pointed ever upward across the green valley floor, scaling the mountainsides like Alpine climbers.

"It's most impressive."

"I can see why George wants part of this state set aside as a national park. We shall have a wonderful time on this trip." He clasped his hands together and grinned like a

26

schoolboy. "Already I have a feeling of great consequence. It's almost as if I'm meeting my destiny head on."

Eleanor stared at him, a chill washing over her. Pulling her gaze away, she shifted it to the window. What had Father meant by that? She had no desire for this trip to be one of great consequence. Normalcy and peace were all that she longed for. Putting aside a momentary sense of panic, she drew a deep steadying breath.

"Maybe we should think of settling down this way, Ellie."

Ah. So there it was. *And* another use of her nickname. What was going on with him? "But why here? I've never heard you *once* speak of settling down. You said there was too much work to do." She hated that she sounded accusatory, but at least it was honest. They'd promised to always be honest with each other.

"Yes, but I am fifty-five years old. I won't be able to continue this life indefinitely."

Since when did Stewart Briggs talk of retiring from his conservationist work? Why would he start now? He was still young and able-bodied. Fifty-five wasn't all that old. She'd seen him climb mountains and raft rivers with the strength of a man half his age.

"We no longer call New York City home, and I truly have no desire to return there. The only thing we left behind was your mother's grave, and certainly she would admonish us to disregard that matter. As much as I loved her with my whole heart, I know that she never wanted us to spend our days at the cemetery mourning her passing."

Panic rose further in her chest. She wasn't attached to Mother's grave, and what Father said was true. Still, the direction of this conversation was unnerving. "No. Indeed not. Mother was clear about that."

"It seems we should probably give some thought to where we might like to settle." He leaned back in his seat. "You're at the age where you should take a husband, not continue traipsing around behind your father."

What? Eleanor turned and faced him, placing her hand on his sleeve. "Where is this coming from?" She shook her head. "You've never been one to push me to marry."

Father's face tightened and he refused to meet her gaze. "I suppose it was that news about young Andrew. Sometimes I think about your sacrifice to work at my side and wonder if it was the wisest choice I might have made to allow it."

Eleanor stiffened. "Have I disappointed you? Have I failed in assisting you?"

"Of course not." As the train slowed, Father leaned closer and covered her hand with his, giving it a pat. "My thoughts were only that I may have kept you from the life you should have had. You might have married and had children by now. Most of your friends have done so."

That last sentence sliced through her middle like a knife. "I do not regret my choice to work at your side, Father. I hope you don't regret it either." She slipped her hand from his grasp and lifted her chin, giving him a pointed look. If ever there was a time to change the subject, it was now.

He didn't take the hint. "I don't. I just think perhaps it's time for an . . . adjustment. For now, however, let us explore the area around us and see what George has to say about his strides toward getting the president's ear on this matter.

President Roosevelt is a tremendous supporter of preserving the lands. It would be the perfect end to my career if I should share in the creation of a national park."

Eleanor clenched the arm of the seat as if she might suddenly be thrown to the floor if she loosened her grip. She forced her hand to relax. Everything would be all right. Father was just having a moment of reflection. He hadn't really had time to think things through. He wasn't going to give up his conservation work. He wasn't going to insist they settle down in one place.

But . . . why did that bother her so? Hadn't she just been abhorring the length of yet another journey?

She was simply tired. Not herself. She squared her shoulders and glanced at her reflection in the window. Her hat was on straight, and her coat lapels lay perfectly flat against the simple collar of her blouse. She was ready for Kalispell and whatever fate it had in store.

The train came to a stop. She stood and collected her bag.

If she was feeling addled and stressed from the treacherous trip the last few hours, then Father might be as well. Maybe that's where all the retirement conversation was coming from. Too much time to think on the train ride.

But then to bring up marriage! He just *had* to remind her that she was a spinster.

Tingles ran up and down her right leg. Then her hat took that moment to come undone, and it flopped down over her eyes.

Reaching a hand up to right it, she fiddled with the cantankerous object until her hand came back full of feathers and ribbon. She took a long, deep breath and refrained from stomping her foot.

All right, so she wasn't ready for this. Not in the least little bit. In truth, she was a frustrated, overtired spinster with a numb backside and leg, and a hat that was no longer decent or presentable.

2

Carter Brunswick leaned against the wall, arms crossed, hat in hand, and listened as one of Kalispell's leading citizens voiced his opinion. The topic—one that was enough to stop his heart for a moment—the Great Northern Railway's plan to pull out of Kalispell in favor of making Whitefish, Montana, their divisional headquarters.

Carter had owned the mill for over eight years now. In three months, it would be nine. But if the railroad moved? He might not make it there.

Panic wasn't going to solve anything. Hopefully the Judge and mayor would have some new information regarding a decision from the owner. He prayed they would. Because the way the discussion was going, it seemed they would need a hefty dose of heavenly intervention for things to not get out of hand.

Jerod McVey had been chosen to speak on behalf of some twenty local sawmills. "First, I've been commissioned to address the fact that Great Northern Railway lied to us.

Initially, we were told that the railroad wasn't rerouting. They were just looking for a route north to coalfields. In Canada. Now that the truth has come out, we don't appreciate what is happening. We ship a lot of lumber out of Kalispell. It's imperative we have a railroad for our business.

"We can't afford to freight our goods by wagon to Whitefish to catch the train. Our prices will double, perhaps triple, and that will ruin us. The railroad brought the town here and we all established businesses based on that. Whoever is in charge should probably understand that we've conferred with legal representation and are not opposed to suing the railroad if they continue down this road."

Several of the other mill owners agreed. With loud voices. And with more abrasive language than Jerod.

Judge Milton Ashbury stood and motioned for everyone to quiet down. The Judge—as most called him—was a fair man who had no problem letting each man speak his piece, but he did require it be done in an orderly fashion.

"I believe we all understand how important the railroad is to Kalispell." Judge Ashbury's words brought instant silence. "Jerod, it might help our cause with the railroad's owner, Mr. Hill, if you were to put together all the facts and figures related to the timber business."

"We've already done it, Judge." McVey held up some papers. "It clearly shows our usage and need for continued service. And how much money the railroad makes off us. Lumber and grain, not to mention cattle, are shipped out of here on a regular basis. Lumber is by far and away the most productive since the other two are more relegated to certain times of the year. But lumber is shipped daily. It's the heart of our town. We *need* to be able to freight our goods out of here in an easy manner and the railroad is the only means to provide that."

The man made a good point.

Carter's family came to Kalispell in 1885, along with his dad's best friend, Fred Owens. The two men immediately went to work buying up as much farm ground as they could afford, and little by little the acreage grew from several hundred acres to over twenty thousand. A lot of work had gone in to clearing that land and preparing it for growing wheat. As a result, his father now co-owned the largest wheat farm in the area.

Carter remembered those days with a mix of fondness and disdain. It had been the hardest work he'd ever done. His father always reminded him that one day he'd inherit the lion's share, so in many ways he was working his own land. But he hadn't had pride in it like Dad. How he would smile at the fields full of ripened grain. The land was everything to Jacob Brunswick. Well, that and the crops it produced.

Even now, as Carter approached his thirtieth birthday, his father planned to gift him with two hundred acres, reminding him of the importance of land management. Carter had just built a small house in town near the mill with the hopes of building a larger home for a family on his own land one day. He wanted to expand the mill . . . but now those ideas needed to be rethought. Having two hundred acres seemed unnecessary when the town could possibly die.

The more he allowed the thought to tumble around his mind, the more troubled he became.

No. Doubt and fear were not from the Lord. He shook his head and watched the crowd.

Drooping shoulders, sullen faces, and disgruntled murmuring filled the room.

Losing the railroad would hurt him. He had a great many customers to whom he shipped flour, and like the sawmills, he would have to raise his prices if he lost the ability to move his wares by train. But would the town die? If it did, he'd have to move the whole mill. But where?

A ruckus started down near the front, drawing Carter's attention back to the meeting. Several men protested to the judge that there had to be some way to stop the Great Northern from making Kalispell nothing more than a stop near the end of a spur line.

"You're the great legal mind, Judge," one of the men yelled out. "Why can't you think of a way to stop them?"

"We're gonna lose over three hundred jobs when the railroad goes!"

"We'll end up a ghost town!"

Even more men joined the fray. They'd seen what had happened to Demersville, a once lively town about three miles to the southeast of Kalispell. Once there had been more than a thousand people with a post office, town hall, saloons, and a weekly newspaper. Not to mention soldiers temporarily assigned from Fort Missoula. It was the place to go if you wanted supplies or a good time, and now it was all but dead. And why? Because the railroad didn't build into it. They skirted it altogether and Demersville died as Kalispell thrived. Would the same hold true for Kalispell when the railroad moved the main line to Whitefish?

Judge Ashbury motioned for the crowd to calm down as the mayor took the stage.

"Now folks, I know you're worked up and worried. Believe me when I say we are doing our best to get the correct information to you in a timely manner." The older man pulled out a large white handkerchief and mopped his brow. His voice was barely audible over the angry crowd.

Someone in the back of the room let out a shrill whistle, and a hush fell over the crowd.

"Thank you." The mayor cleared his throat. "Now, we haven't settled on an exact date, but Mr. Louis Hill will be coming to Kalispell in the next few weeks. That gives us plenty of time to put your questions and concerns together. Submit them to my office and I will make sure they get to Mr. Hill. Let him know what this railroad means to you, to Kalispell."

"He says it like that railroad man actually cares about what happens to this town."

At the muttered comment behind them, Carter exchanged a glance with his dad. It was true. The trail of railroad ghost towns through the Midwest showed what happened when railroads up and left. He appreciated what the mayor was trying to do, but there was little comfort—or import—in writing a letter. The railroad people were unlikely to change their minds.

Irritation rippled through the mass of people again, voices getting louder and louder. The cacophony was giving Carter a headache.

Someone shouted and shoved another man close to where Carter and his dad were standing. The shoved man started poking the other man in the shoulder.

"Watch where yer goin'," he growled, pushing his hat back on his forehead.

The taller man glared at his opponent. "Get outta my way, and maybe I wouldn't have to watch anything."

Growing anger and fear were palpable. Livelihoods were on the line and the men in the room knew it. It was a perfect recipe for violence. Carter had no desire to be in the middle of a fight, nor to have to help stop one. He had his own problems to pray over with the news from this evening. He moved toward the door.

Dad stopped him. "Moving out before the rabble can riot?"

Carter gave him a grim nod. "Something like that."

His father always seemed to know what he was thinking.

"Me too." He motioned his head toward the door. "Come on. I'll buy you a cup of coffee."

Not that coffee could fix the anvil-sized weight that had landed on their shoulders. Was Dad just covering up his own worry over the matter?

They headed out from the meeting and made their way to a small café at the end of the block. Carter's father ordered not only coffee but two pieces of apple pie.

"We might as well enjoy something sweet with our coffee."

Of course. Carter had never known his father to pass up a chance for dessert. The man had a terrible sweet tooth and was even known to walk around with candy in his pockets. It made him very popular with the children.

Apple pie wasn't an answer to their dilemma either, but Carter slapped on a smile and played along. "So long as it doesn't spoil your dinner. Mother wouldn't be happy if that happened."

His father grinned. "Have you ever known me to miss a

meal?" The robust man patted his stomach. "I do just fine. Now, what do you think about our situation?"

There it was. Carter placed his hat on the chair beside him. "It's bad news to be sure. A lot of folks are reliant upon that railroad."

"There's not a businessman in the area who doesn't need it. Remember when we first got here? Getting up here was a peril at best. Bless your poor mother's heart, she was a brave soul to be sure. Coming by train from Kansas was hard enough, but then to have to take wagons and that long steamboat trip across the lake and then more wagons . . . well, she earned my deepest respect on that trip."

Carter shook his head. "Like she didn't already have it."

"True enough. She's always been a brave soul. She wanted to settle in Demersville, but never said a word. And I pretended *not* to know, which worked to our benefit in the long run." Dad took a sip of his coffee, his eyes distant for a moment, as if back on that difficult ride out west. He shook his head and set down his mug. "My point is, however, the route wasn't easy. You were eleven, and it was hard enough on you."

"I remember it well." He swirled the coffee in his cup and stared at him. "Truth is, I doubt we can change the minds of anyone based on how hard it is to get in and out of here. Usually by the time the lowest folks hear about changes, plans are already set in motion. I would imagine James Hill has already signed our fate and has his new route completely planned out. I don't know what good a visit from his son is going to do. Except maybe create more trouble."

The chipper demeanor his father had worn faded. "I'm afraid that's probably true. He's probably none too pleased with the judgment against him handed down by the Supreme Court regarding his monopoly." Dad shook his head. "If anything, it has probably motivated him to take control of whatever he can."

The waitress arrived and put two pieces of pie in front of them. "It's fresh from the oven, so it should still be warm." She refilled their coffee before heading off to take care of other customers.

Dad picked up a fork and offered a blessing before digging in.

Taking up his own utensil, Carter cut into the dessert. "I've tried to figure out how we'll move forward at the flour mill once the trains aren't running. Granted, I haven't had much time to think about it, so my math could be wrong, but"—he shoved a bite into his mouth and chewed, not really wanting to say it aloud—"it doesn't bode well. The roads north are barely passable so there will have to be a great deal of improvement to them before they are reliable. The roads south to Ravalli and the rails there are better but take longer."

Carter chased the pie down with coffee while his father did the same.

"I know. It'll be the same for grain shipments. Unless I leave it all with you to turn to flour. But that doesn't make sense for our customers far away. Their mills need the business too."

Dad finished his pie and leaned back in his chair. He stroked his chin with one hand, the frown on his face deepening. Then his eyebrows lifted and he raised a finger. "Maybe . . . maybe we need to go into the freighting business."

"Or road buildin—" Carter stopped himself. Sarcasm wasn't going to help. "We don't know the first thing about either and would need a great deal of capital to get started."

"True." Dad grimaced. "Wheat has been my whole life. There has to be a way to keep Hill from doing this." Dad lifted his cup to his lips. "Jerod McVey suggested we all file a lawsuit against them, but that won't do any good until well after the fact. We'd have to show the damages they did us and by that time a lot of businesses will have folded. People will be gone. And is that honoring to God? Even though the railroad might kill the town, it feels like too much of a nasty attack for us to sue."

Carter wrapped his hands around his coffee mug, the lingering warmth seeping into his skin. "I know." He twisted the cup back and forth between his hands. "There are a couple of questions that still need answered, though. Will we still have the spur line to Somers?"

Dad arched an eyebrow. "Hmm. Good point. What are you thinking?"

"If we still have that spur, we could use the steamboats—at least for everything going south. Then we'd have to figure out something once it's across Flathead Lake." Carter rubbed his face, exhaustion starting to weigh his mind down. There was so much to consider. "I also wonder if we will have a spur or branch line here off the main line? If so . . . how often will it come to Kalispell? You heard the men—the biggest fear is that we'll end up like Demersville." Anxiety burned in his chest, but he took a deep breath. *Lord, help me stay calm.* "God brought us this far, but for the life of me I can't figure out what He has in mind."

"I know, son." Dad scraped the last bits of pie from his

plate. "It's hard to believe they'd cut us off. With more people moving into the Flathead Valley and the battle cry to make a national park near here, you'd think the railroad would be expanding rather than cutting lines." He tipped back the last of his coffee. "Not to mention the Czar just created his Whipps Block. He'll be needing to ship in all sorts of goods. So let's presume that we'll still have the spur lines."

Ah yes. William Whipps. The man actually seemed to like being called the Czar. True, he'd served as mayor several times. And he founded The First National Bank in Kalispell. Of late, he'd formed a mercantile business with his son and built one of the largest and most modern buildings in the area to house it. And then there was his Kalispell Liquor and Tobacco Company. Neither of which the Brunswicks had any use for. But there were plenty in town who did.

With all those accomplishments, perhaps the moniker was appropriate.

Carter leaned back in his chair. "All right, we can be hopeful about the spur lines and that the railroad tracks will still be in place. Maybe we can encourage them to find a way to make the tracks safer—especially headed west. Hill's protest hasn't been about lack of usage, but rather the dangers of the grades and what it takes to keep the tracks in good working order. Anything coming from the east is still going to have to go over Marias Pass to get to Whitefish rather than here. The pass to the west is even worse and what they're trying to avoid. Maybe the folks in Kalispell could hire someone to survey the situation to the west and make it safer? At least help the Hills see why it's necessary for us to keep a train coming into Kalispell?"

"Now that has some merit." His father leaned forward.

"I'll mention that to the Judge. Could be he's got some friends who could figure out the particulars and make a presentation to Hill's son when he gets here."

Carter exhaled a breath he hadn't realized he'd been holding. The anxious energy in his chest lessened. His shoulders relaxed. Amazing how much better he always felt after talking things over with Dad. "So we have some options. We need to help the railroad see how important it is to still come into Kalispell. But we should probably be ready for any outcome. Even if they can figure a way to make the route in and out of Kalispell less dangerous and convince Mr. Hill, it'll take time." Carter grabbed his hat. "Speaking of time . . . I'd best get on over to the depot. I have a much-needed repair piece for the mill coming in on the train and"—he checked his pocket watch—"it's due in any minute."

He said a quick good-bye to his father and hurried out the door, then drew back a step.

Just as he'd feared, pandemonium had broken loose.

Men from the town meeting had brought the *discussion* out into the street. Only, no one was listening and everyone was yelling. Men were nose to nose, arguing about anything and everything.

Carter made it halfway through the crowd when the pushing and shoving began.

Great. Just what he needed. A brawl.

Not that he could blame the guys for getting up in arms over their livelihood being threatened, but he didn't need to be in the middle of this mess. He moved as quick as he could to get out of the crowd.

Smack!

A punch from his left landed square in his eye. He ducked

and suppressed a grunt just in time to catch a punch from the other side, directly in the mouth.

It knocked him sideways, and he crashed into another brawler, who turned and rallied to return what he perceived as a push.

Carter ducked again from his crouched position and ended up falling on his chin. Pebbles and rock bit into his face. He touched his bottom lip, the metallic tang of blood on his tongue.

Wonderful.

Growls, grunts, and the sound of flesh smacking flesh filled his ears. He pushed to his feet, shoving men away as they barreled toward him. He was in no mood to put up with this ridiculous and senseless act of aggression.

He dusted himself off as he walked, noticing a tear in his favorite shirt. He narrowed his eyes and released his own growl to the crowd as he pushed through, careful to not get blindsided again. Once he was free from the crowd, he glanced over his shoulder. The fighting men looked like one big, confused ant hill.

Carter turned and made his way to the depot, his heart heavy. *Lord, this town needs Your help. Desperately.*

He placed his kerchief to his mouth and sopped up the blood. This was no way to walk through town in the middle of the day. Disheveled and bloody. Good thing the people around here knew him well. He ran a hand through his hair before plopping his hat back down. He must be a sight. But there was no time to go home and clean up. He had to get that part today.

Wiggling his jaw from side to side, he cringed. At least it didn't *feel* broken. But he was sure to have a shiner. He swiped at his face again with his kerchief. That would have to do. Hopefully he sopped up all the blood and dirt.

As he walked, his head just didn't feel right. He didn't have time for this! Those fool men! What had they thought they'd accomplish? Other than blackening each other's eyes and dishing out bruises.

Whipping his hat off, he rubbed at his forehead and ran a hand through his hair again. No sign of blood. But when he glanced down at his hat, his heart sank.

He gritted his teeth. This was the last straw.

Not only had they ripped his favorite shirt, but now his favorite hat was ruined.

It had taken three years to break in that hat and get it to where it molded perfectly to his head.

He eyed the misshapen head covering and released a sigh. This day couldn't get any worse.

3

TUESDAY, MAY 10, 1904—KALISPELL, MONTANA

Marvella Ashbury took a sip of her lemonade and watched her husband peer at her over the top of his newspaper.

"Yes, my dear?" His bushy eyebrows lifted. "Was I not listening?"

With a chuckle, she winked at him. "I appreciate your interest, but I hadn't said anything." He'd just returned home, and they'd settled in for their customary teatime. It was best to catch him now, before he was completely engulfed with whatever the newspaper detailed.

As expected, he set the paper down and wiggled his mustache. Clearly amused. "Yet. You haven't said anything *yet*, my dear. But I know that look on your face all too well. You do *have* something to say. And since I know that, you have my rapt attention."

It worked every time. And why not? She was a master

after all these years. Smiling her sweetest smile, she offered him a tea cake. "I'm concerned about this railroad business."

His amusement faded. "My dear, it is out of our hands. The best thing I can do is help our community through this time."

"I respect all that you've done, Milton. Truly, I do. But we can't allow our town to die." Sometimes she had to be a bit more forceful to ensure her opinions were heard.

He sighed. "I don't believe Kalispell will die."

"How can you be certain? We know what happened to Demersville." She sat up straighter and leaned forward. "Perhaps I need to get my ladies involved. Rally the troops, so to speak."

"There is still much to be seen. But I'm certain the citizens of this town will do their best to keep everything running. Forgive me, but the meeting this afternoon was enough on the subject for me. We should pray about it and keep our attitudes positive. If you believe your ladies' groups can be of a benefit, I've never stood in your way before and I shan't begin to do so now." With that, he picked up the paper. He clearly had no desire to continue this conversation. And why would he? It was depressing.

A yip from the right side of her chair tore her attention away from her husband. Smiling down at the little white ball of fluff, she stroked the dog's silky hair. "Sir Theophilus . . . I believe you and I have our work cut out for us." She glanced at her husband one more time. "If you'll excuse me, dear."

"Of course, my dear." The words were slightly muffled by the paper.

Marvella stood and picked up her little companion. If no one else was up to the task, she would not shy away from it.

Someone had to save Kalispell.

"Train just got in." Carter's friend had his gaze focused on the sheaf of papers on the counter he was flipping through. The tall red-headed man often had his head buried in papers after a train arrived. "But your part was the first thing I checked on. It's being unloaded as we speak."

Carter started to nod, and winced. His whole face hurt but he didn't have time to worry about that now. "Glad it made it in, Gus. That machine at the mill has been down for over two weeks. Slowed our production something fierce. I figure we'll be back to grinding on a stone if we don't get that part."

Gus chuckled as he shuffled another stack of papers. "I can just see it too. We can't let that happen, now can we?" He looked up . . . and frowned. "Whoa. What happened to you?"

"Town meeting riled everyone up."

"So you thought it was a good idea to shove your face into the middle of it?" Gus released a low whistle. "I had a feeling it wouldn't be pretty. Just didn't know it would be your ugly mug that would take the brunt of it."

Carter laughed and then moaned. "Don't make me laugh."

"You really should go take care of that." His friend pointed at his mouth and cringed.

"The part is more important. I'll deal with my injuries later." He needed to change the subject, so he leaned in. "Doesn't look good for us, does it?"

TRACIE PETERSON and KIMBERLEY WOODHOUSE

"Nope." The man looked around the room and then leaned forward as well and lowered his voice. "Don't tell anyone, but we've already been told we'll need to move to Whitefish. Things are really hopping up there and they intend to have everything done by August."

The news was like a blow to Carter's gut. "I was afraid that was the case. Does the mayor know?"

"I don't know. If he doesn't, he will when Mr. Hill gets here. It's kind of funny. You know the Hutchinson and Baker logging companies used to float their logs down here for processing. Now our mills are gonna have to find a way to get theirs *up* to Whitefish."

"Jerod McVey spoke on the mill's behalf at the meeting, he said it will ruin them. Maybe triple their prices and put them out of business."

"I suppose it was inevitable." Gus shook his head. "I've been on the route into Kalispell over the Salish Mountains. It's not for the faint of heart. It's a laborious chore to be s—"

"Excuse me, but are you the freight master?"

At the feminine voice behind him, Carter turned—and felt his eyes widen. A beautiful young woman dressed in a dark green traveling suit stood there. Her hat appeared to be missing something from the top, but it was perched in a fashionable manner atop a nest of blond hair. Her blue eyes glared at him in a most unnerving way.

"I'm the assistant." Gus's tone was polite enough, but Carter could tell he didn't appreciate her interruption. "Be with you in just a minute."

Her gaze darted between the two men, her eyes narrowing. "But it really can't wait. I'm here with my father and we're meeting a very important man. I need to arrange for our luggage and my bicycle." She stepped closer.

"When I'm finished with Mr. Brunswick, I'll get right to whatever you need." Gus turned back to Carter and gave him a knowing look.

It took everything in Carter to keep from snickering at his friend. So he kept his face turned away.

The woman cleared her throat. "You two have been talking for some time now. I have tried to be patient, but you seem more caught up in your conversation than doing your job. I need to arrange for our things to be delivered and I insist you help me."

Who *was* this woman? Carter turned. "Where are you from, Miss?"

Her blue eyes widened a fraction. She took a step back and clutched her bag to her chest. "I don't see what that has to do with anything."

"I was just curious as to where it is folks like you come from."

Her trepidation vanished at his tone. She stiffened and one eyebrow arched high on her forehead. "Folks like *I*? What do you mean?"

"Well, most folks are taught manners . . . to wait their turn. It would seem wherever you come from . . . well . . . that apparently wasn't important."

Oooh, she did *not* like that.

"I am *not* without manners, even though it appears you are, sir. Dripping blood all over the place and looking like you just came from a saloon brawl."

He cringed and opened his mouth to respond, but she plowed on ahead. "I simply am in a hurry and figure your

48

chitchat and hometown gossip could wait. My father is inside even now meeting with his friend and I'm certain he's concerned about my delay."

In truth, her father was probably grateful for a break from this demanding young woman. "Perhaps he'll consider that you weren't the only ones on the train and that maybe you had to wait in line." He motioned to the numerous people milling about the platform behind her, then pulled out his handkerchief to dab at his lip.

"Or maybe he'll hope that a *polite* gentleman will see my need and attend to me." She lifted her chin. "Or are we too far west for that type of man?"

Carter narrowed his gaze. If she wanted a gentleman, she'd get a gentleman. "I do apologize. I'm Carter Brunswick, m'lady." He tipped his hat and gave a sweeping bow, ignoring the throbbing in his eye. "And you are?"

Gus laughed, but when she pointed a stare at him, he swiped it away.

She gave both men a curt nod, a frown fixed on her face. "Miss Eleanor Briggs. My father is the famous conservationist Stewart Briggs, and we're meeting the even *more* important George Grinnell. Perhaps you've heard of him."

Rubbing his chin, Carter shook his head. "Can't say I've ever heard of either of them, and certainly not you, Miss Briggs. But I will point out, you've stood here arguing your point and wasting my time as well as Gus's. If you'd just practiced some manners and waited your turn, I would have been long gone."

"And as pleasant as that sounds, instead I'm stuck here waiting for you to make your point and attend to whatever it is you've come to do." She crossed her arms.

Gus chose that moment to walk away.

Smart man.

She huffed. "Very well, Mr. Brunswick. I will wait."

"See. That wasn't so hard."

Gus came back to the window and slid a sheet of paper toward Carter. "Sign here for the part. It's out back near the rear loading dock."

Normally, Carter would have rushed off his signature. *Normally.*

However, the meeting today, getting hit in the face not once but *twice*, and now Miss Briggs's attitude left him feeling rather ornery. He carefully signed his name, giving attention to every detail. When finished he just as thoroughly perused the paper before handing it back to Gus.

"Ellie! Are you all right?" Two well-dressed men approached.

Carter grinned. "Ellie?" Now that wasn't near as stuffy as *Eleanor.*

"It's *Miss Briggs* to you!" She turned to the two men. "My apologies. I'm just fine. It's just taking a *long*"—this time she pointed her glare at Gus—"time to arrange things, Father."

Carter tipped his hat and looked at the gentlemen. "You must be the famous conservationist Stewart Briggs." He heard Eleanor give another huff.

The older man looked a bit confused. "I am. Are you all right?" He pointed to his own eye.

"Rest assured. I'm fine."

Mr. Briggs turned to his companion. "This is my friend and fellow conservationist, George Grinnell."

Grinnell tipped his derby hat at Carter. The man's bushy

mustache twitched with a fascinating rapidity. Whether it was with amusement or irritation, Carter couldn't say. Most likely the latter.

"Pleasure to meet you both. Carter Brunswick. Hope you'll enjoy your stay in Kalispell." He touched his fingers to his hat. "Nice chitchatting with you . . . *Ellie*."

With that Carter left them, smiling to himself at the look of shock on Miss Eleanor Briggs's pretty face.

"Wish I had better news, Grant."

Grant Wallace pressed his lips together, unable to look his boss in the eye. He'd hoped the Great Northern Railway would keep him in their employ in Kalispell. But from what his supervisor, Collin Hoffman, just told him, that wasn't to be—at least not in the position he'd worked up to. "I've been with this railroad for over six years now. Been a good worker too, and they're just gonna let me go?"

Collin's forehead creased. "Not necessarily. You have as much a chance to work in Whitefish as anyone."

"But I'd hafta start at the bottom again, right?" Grant glanced up at Collin.

His boss nodded. "I'm sorry, Grant. It's the way things are right now. I'm sorry . . . but I'm being transferred to Whitefish and will be assistant foreman in the shops."

Ah. The knife wedged itself deep in his gut. Collin—the boss—had been forced to take a lower position up at the new location. Probably everybody would have to.

The only problem? That lower position was *Grant's* position. The position he'd worked six years to attain here.

There wasn't much hope for him staying here and no chance to transfer to the same job.

"You can probably hire on as a section hand. If you volunteer now and help with laying the line into Whitefish, you'll be ahead of some of these other men." His boss's tone was encouraging, but it didn't help.

Grant picked at a hangnail on his thumb. He'd already done his time as a section hand when the railroad was being built west. His brother, Alvin, was a section repair worker. He went out with other men to fix the track whenever rockslides, snow, or wear and tear altered the line. It was hard work, especially in the mountains, and Grant had no desire to return to it.

It was clear—for now the options were limited. He pulled his cap low over his eyes. "Maybe I'll see what other work is available."

Collin shrugged. "Well, keep in mind Kalispell will probably be nothing more than a widening in the road in a few years. There are worse things than moving to Whitefish and starting over with the railroad."

There might be, but at the moment Grant couldn't think of a single one. He gazed out across the shop. So many men were going to lose their livelihood.

Maybe it *was* time to move on. Maybe head down to Missoula. He heard that was quite the place now.

Hoffman was still talking. ". . . besides, you're a good tracker. I hear tell that the push to get a national park up in the mountains is going well. You could probably be hired as a guide. You'd probably like that a whole lot better than working here anyway."

Grant *was* good at tracking. It was something his father

taught him when Grant had been just a boy. He hadn't really thought of it as a full-time job, but hearing Collin suggest it caused him to give it serious thought. "I'll keep that in mind."

Collin pulled on his coat. "You'd probably have to move to Whitefish for that as well. Or even farther into what they call the Forest Reserve. Hard to tell, but I'm betting that the officials who have the final word on making a national park will probably go there rather than Kalispell."

"Yeah . . ." None of the ideas made him feel a lick better.

"Grant, you have to let your men know that by the end of July we'll be closing everything out and moving it to Whitefish. They can talk to me if they're interested in moving with it. The railroad is bringing in a few outsiders for choice positions, but for the most part they're going to need a lot of the men here."

"Just not in the positions they are currently working." He grumbled the words.

Collin sighed. "Look, this change is affecting everyone. Some won't have to change their jobs because they're still at the bottom, but they'll have to move. Those of us who've worked longer end up paying the price. I'm sorry you have to be one of them. You're a good worker. I'll see what I can do to help you."

"Thanks." But he didn't feel thankful about anything. Not one good thing had come out of this.

He watched Hoffman head out. Grant might not have to work as a section hand, but he would have to go back to being an underling. Which was unfair. He had more experience and time in with the Great Northern. Why didn't they value that?

Of course, Collin was being demoted too. Which should make him feel better.

But it didn't.

He liked the position he was in. It was tolerable and he knew the job well. Every day he worked inside, out of the elements, and managed parts and supplies. It was easy compared to what his brother had to do. And now, just because someone got a wild notion to move the line, he was losing his job.

He pulled out his pocket watch, his thumb running over the etched pattern on the front. It was the only thing of value his mother had given him before she died. Pushing the sentimental thought away, he popped it open. 4:45. Nearly quitting time. He still needed to round up his men and let them know the news.

He walked into the loading area and put two fingers to his lips and gave a loud whistle. Most of the fellas heard him, and those that didn't were rounded up by the ones who did. The men came to stand in a semicircle around Grant.

"Is it as bad as we thought, Boss?"

The respect and the title helped him shake off the feeling-sorry-for-himself cloak he'd wrapped up in. These men needed him. "'Fraid so. We've only got to the end of July. I'd hoped it was all still in the planning stage and that maybe we had a chance to change their minds. But apparently old man Hill wants to move fast on this."

"They've been thinking toward it for a while now. At least that's what I heard," a voice threw out.

"Yeah, well, you'll need to let Mr. Hoffman know if you want to move to Whitefish and remain employed with the railroad. He says most everyone will retain their jobs if they want them. There are a few who won't, myself included. I'll likely have to rejoin your ranks."

Murmurs rippled through the crowd at that news. These men, his friends and coworkers, had been his companions for several years now and watched him come up through the ranks. They respected him and never failed to do the job he asked for. He knew he'd be accepted right back into their numbers, but that wasn't what he wanted. The urge to go pout in a corner was strong.

Keller clapped Grant on the shoulder. "You're always welcome, Boss. A bunch of us have already talked about it, and some don't plan to move to Whitefish. Some of us are heading out to Missoula."

"Yeah, I'm considerin' a move there myself." Grant pulled his leather gloves out of his back pocket. "But for now, we have a job to do. Make up your minds about the move, and tell Mr. Hoffman as soon as possible."

One by one the men went back to their stations.

All except Alvin. His face was black fury.

Grant steadied himself for his brother's reaction. Out of all the workers, he worried about Alvin the most. He was unpredictable most days, but this . . . ?

This might just set Alvin off in a bad way.

And that wouldn't be good for anyone.

The carriage approached a three-story, red-brick home, and Eleanor smiled up at the beauty of it. White columns gave it a stylish and moneyed look. The lawns were mani-cured and lush looking. Pink and white rose bushes lined the front of the house, softening the harsh lines of the red brick.

She hadn't expected such elaborate architectural design in the middle of frontier Montana. The mansard roof with its white-trimmed dormer windows set it apart from other houses in the neighborhood.

Architecture had always intrigued her, and this home seemed to be of the Second Empire styling. Perhaps she could go to the library and do a bit of research in her spare time. She'd been told the Carnegie Library here was a charming building in its own right. Anything to get her mind off her tedious thoughts of late and these unsettling feelings.

"I know you'll enjoy staying here with the Ashburys. They have a most excellent cook and spare no expense with the meals. Marvella is an exceptional hostess." George Grinnell faced her and her father. "Although she's opinionated and not afraid to speak her mind."

"Ellie is the same way." Her father patted her knee. "They should be satisfactory companions for each other." His mischievous grin made her want to roll her eyes, but she squelched the impulse.

Had Father decided to just use the forbidden nickname all the time now?

With her mood the way it was, it might be better if they were to camp out under the stars. Dealing with a cantankerous woman wasn't going to help matters. Not until Eleanor figured out whatever it was that plagued her.

Mr. Grinnell droned on. "They definitely support the idea of a national park. Mrs. Ashbury is in charge of a women's group and has been instrumental in getting them to write letters to President Roosevelt. Judge Ashbury is also supportive. He will be a great advocate for our cause."

The carriage came to a stop in front of the mansion. The driver immediately jumped from his seat to help them from the carriage as a boy came to take hold of the horse.

Eleanor could barely contain her need to escape the conveyance—and the conversation. She jumped to her feet, laid her hand on top of the driver's gloved hand, and descended the step of the carriage. It was a bit unorthodox, but she walked right up to the rose bushes and took a deep inhale.

Heavenly. Nothing smelled quite like roses. And the air here was so clean and fresh.

"Good for the soul, isn't it, my dear?" Father held out his arm for her.

Time to pull herself together and follow etiquette.

Grinnell led the way, but the door was opened by a uniformed butler before their party reached the door.

"Good day, Mr. Grinnell. Won't you all come in?" The tall man bowed and held out a welcoming arm.

"Tobias, I've brought Mr. Briggs and his daughter." Mr. Grinnell waved a hand at them.

"Very good, sir." The butler took their hats and gloves and placed them on a nearby marble table. "If you will follow me."

"After you, Miss Briggs." Mr. Grinnell nodded at her.

As Eleanor stepped into the marble foyer, she made a quick study of her surroundings. A grand staircase. Tasteful decorations. And the scent of something marvelous baking wafted through her senses.

The butler knocked on a tall wooden door.

Then something yipped.

What in heaven's name was *that*? These people had an indoor pet?

Eleanor darted her glance at Father, whose smile had turned into a frown.

A woman's voice called from the other side. "Come in."

The butler stepped inside.

"What is it, Tobias?"

"Mr. Grinnell has returned and brought your guests, ma'am."

Father shoved Eleanor with his hand on her back and in the trio went.

A white ball of fur raced toward her and then jumped up and down at her knee.

What *was* it?

Eleanor stiffened and backed up, but the tiny thing was tenacious. Then it yipped again, and a little face looked up at her with adoration. Tongue hanging out. Eyes alight with excitement.

She'd never been a fan of dogs or cats. Or any indoor pets, for that matter. Probably because her father didn't believe animals should be domesticated and that's what she heard her whole life. Only one time she'd questioned him, about horses being domesticated and his response had been that horses were different.

But now, staring down at the little face that begged for her acknowledgment, she wasn't sure what she thought. She took another step back, trying to get the dog's paws off her dress, and studied those mesmerizing black eyes.

"Sir Theophilus, get down and come here." An older, thick-waisted woman strode over, took the dog into her arms, and smiled at her. "You must forgive him. He simply loves company and gets so excited at the prospect of making new friends."

Grinnell smiled and offered a slight bow. "No harm done, of course." He turned to Eleanor and her father. "Mrs. Marvella Ashbury, may I introduce Mr. Stewart Briggs, my dear friend and colleague. And his daughter, Miss Eleanor Briggs."

Mrs. Ashbury fed her pup a treat and gave his head a stroke. Her smile was wide and welcoming. "I'm so delighted that you've come to Kalispell."

"Thank you for having us, Mrs. Ashbury. We are grateful for your hospitality," Father replied. "You have a lovely home."

"Thank you, Mr. Briggs. And please, since you will be staying with us for a while, I insist that inside our home you call me Marvella." With the dog still in her arms, she went to the bell pull. "You must be exhausted. I'll have you shown to your rooms for a rest."

Eleanor was tired, but the magnificence of this room was captivating. Floor-to-ceiling shelves held hundreds, possibly thousands, of books. At the other end of the room was a large fireplace with windows on either side. It looked like the perfect place to curl up with a book and a cup of tea. "Thank you for the offer of rest. However, we are waiting for our things to arrive from the station."

Mrs. Ashbury shifted the dog's position. "Well, perhaps you would join me for tea then while we wait. Supper will be at seven so it might be well for you to have some refreshment now."

It was as if her hostess had read her mind. "That sounds delightful."

A woman appeared at the door. She looked to be in her fifties and wore her hair in a tight bun. "Yes, ma'am."

"Mrs. O'Neil, our guests have arrived, but their luggage has not. I believe we'll take tea in the large parlor. When their things get here, please show them upstairs so they can freshen up and rest before the evening meal."

"Very good, ma'am. I'll see to everything."

This household could clearly pass for one in New York City's society. A bit shocking, since they were out on the frontier in Montana. But impressive, nonetheless.

The biggest difference was that it wasn't . . . oh, she should go ahead and admit it. The home wasn't stuffy. The mistress wasn't snooty and trying to show everyone she was wealthier or better than anyone else.

It was refreshing.

And made Eleanor feel . . . at home.

"Let's move to the parlor. I think you'll appreciate the artwork there. The Judge has just received a shipment from back east, and the paintings were hung this morning."

The men moved on ahead, while Mrs. Ashbury waited for her at the door. "My dear, you are rather lovely, but older than I imagined. What is your age?"

What? Had she just been insulted? The warm feelings she had a moment ago vanished. Eleanor blinked. "Um . . . I am twenty-four years."

"Goodness, and still unmarried. Well, that's all right. Your work with your father has kept you traveling and busy, no doubt. Are you at least engaged to be married?"

Eleanor stopped. Did the woman mean to be imposing and rude?

She checked herself. Really, this was no different from many matrons in New York society. Maybe too many months on the road had thinned her usually thick skin to society's pressures. "No, ma'am. I am not."

"Did you leave some special fellow pining for you at your last location?"

Eleanor worked hard to hold back the sarcastic comment that wished to fly. "No. There is no one in my life other than Father."

The older woman's eyes seemed to light up. "How wonderful!" At her exclamation, the little dog began to wiggle and yip. Mrs. Ashbury laughed and released the dog to the floor. "See"—she straightened—"even Sir Theophilus is excited."

Eleanor eyed the white fluff ball. What could it possibly be excited about besides treats? "I'm afraid I don't understand, Mrs. Ashbury."

"It's Marvella." The look on her face suggested she might be up to something. "Since you'll be with us all summer, I'm certain to find you a husband."

Her stomach began to churn. Why was everyone concerned about her marital status all of a sudden? She glanced into the parlor to see if Mr. Grinnell or Father had overheard the nosy woman's comment. But no. They were engaged in their own conversation. Eleanor looked back at Mrs. Ashbury and shook her head. "I assure you that won't be necessary. I have no interest whatsoever in finding a husband."

"*Tsk, tsk, tsk.*" There was such sadness in her hostess's face. "You've been out in the sun too much, and it has affected your mind. Never fear, my dear. I'll handle everything. You just wait and see." She patted Eleanor's arm, a confident smile turning up her lips. "Your time in Kalispell will be a great success. I just know it." Marvella glided into the large parlor, leaving a confused Eleanor in her wake.

Affected her mind? If anyone were to ask Eleanor right then, she'd say it was the outgoing Mrs. Ashbury whose mind was affected. Because hers most certainly was *not*.

4

Grant didn't mind most things. But waitin' on his brother when he wasn't sure what was goin' on in that fool's head was one something he did mind. A lot. He had been sitting on a bench outside the railroad depot for a half hour now with no sign of his little brother.

The rest of the afternoon had gone just as bad as he'd imagined. Men were out of sorts. Arguing about anything and everything. Several went home early and said they weren't coming back.

Then there was Alvin. Soon as he heard the whole story, he clamped his mouth shut and stormed off.

Never a good sign.

The whole situation was messed up. They didn't have the whole story, which bothered a lot of the men who had families to feed. It'd be different if all the men were single and could just pick up and move to Whitefish. If there were homes and businesses already built and established.

But no. The railroad had been shady, saying they were

just looking to establish a new route into Canada. Grant scoffed. He shoulda known as soon as the townsite in Whitefish was surveyed and dedicated in June of last year. Rail yards were already constructed. Why, he wouldn't be surprised if the rail line wasn't already half built to Eureka. They'd probably kept that a secret too.

He slapped his hat against his knee and looked around. Kalispell had become home.

He liked it here. Liked his job.

But that was already gone.

Hadta face facts . . . he couldn't do a single lickin' thing to change it.

"Hey, Grant." Gus called to him from the door. "Alvin left a while ago. Said to tell you that he wouldn't be back for a couple days."

"What?" He jumped to his feet. Alvin never went anywhere.

Gus shrugged. "Sorry, that's all he said." He closed the door to the depot.

What was his brother doin' takin' off like that? Grant flexed his fingers, fighting the black mood building in his chest.

Nothin' he could do 'til Alvin got home. But when that happened . . .

They'd be havin' words.

Carter marched up the stairs to the Carnegie Library. Hopefully his friend Mark would have some time to talk some sense into him.

As he entered the beautiful building, the silence washed

over him and calmed his racing heart. Between the meeting, the brawl, and the run-in with Miss Eleanor Briggs, his adrenaline was still pumping.

"Carter." Mark walked around from behind the counter and greeted him. "What brings you to the library?" He winced as Carter got closer. "And good grief, what happened to you?"

As Carter relayed the story of the meeting and brawl, Mark cringed several times and covered his mirth with a hand.

"I know. Go ahead and laugh. Leave it to me to walk straight into a fight. But wait until I tell you what happened at the train depot." He launched into the story of the part for the mill, his discussion with Gus, and the interruption of one Miss Eleanor Briggs. "I've never met anyone so high and mighty." When he got to the part about him and Gus egging the woman on, he was smiling.

"You enjoyed it!" Mark laughed and smacked him on the back. "Not that I encourage that kind of behavior, but it sure is good to see you out of the mill and actually talking to a woman."

"What is that supposed to mean?" Carter crossed his arms over his chest.

His friend chuckled and grabbed a couple books. "It *means* that you say you want to settle down and have a family, but you sure don't seem like you're trying. You work long hours. You don't speak to the women at church." He walked over to a shelf and placed the books there.

"I'd rather it be me working the long hours than any of my men that have families. Since I'm single, it doesn't take me away from a wife or children."

"And that's commendable. But Carter"—Mark gripped his shoulder—"we've known each other for a long time now. I've never known you to pursue a woman even though you've always wanted a family. I hate to say it, but if you're expecting God to just plop one down in your lap one day, that's not how He usually works."

"It'd definitely be easier."

Mark laughed and shook his head. "But not near as much fun. Just look at me and Rebecca."

Carter studied his friend. He and his new wife were the perfect couple. Carter couldn't compete with that. Besides, there weren't any women in town who struck his fancy. Definitely not any in town who shared any common interests with him. "Yeah, but you two have books in common. You could probably discuss them the rest of your lives. Who wants to sit around and talk about milling wheat and"—he was hesitant to mention his one and only hobby—"fishing?"

"That's it, then." Mark's face turned grim as he walked back behind the counter. "Guess I'm just going to have to tell Marvella to pray for a woman who loves fishing."

"Don't you dare."

Eleanor dressed in the only gown she'd brought that was acceptable for a formal dinner. It wasn't as fashionable as she would have preferred since it was several years old. Still, the lavender gown was good enough for a Montana affair. With its high neck and long sleeves, Eleanor felt amply covered and not at all showy. It was a far cry from the form-fitting fashions of the day. Her society friends back east would probably be amused by her modesty. Not that she had seen or heard from any of them in years.

And not that she cared about having a new wardrobe created each season. Goodness, at this point, she simply cared that everything she owned be practical and modest.

It wasn't as if they didn't have the funds to supply her a new wardrobe. Not only did her father come from family money, but Eleanor's maternal grandfather had been a wealthy shipping magnate and had given his daughter a home in the most fashionable part of New York City as a wedding gift.

Eleanor grew up in society, was taught etiquette and rules, and participated in all the grand events and activities. All while her father traveled and spoke around the Eastern Seaboard about conservation.

That was, until Mother became ill.

She swallowed the sudden lump in her throat. They'd always had money to buy whatever they wanted. Except the one thing they desired most.

A cure for her mother's cancer.

Everything changed after Mother died.

Oh, every time they were back east, she slipped back into the role, but her so-called friends only spoke of money, the latest fashions, and who wore what to which party.

Losing Mother changed her perspective.

About money.

About God.

About what she wanted out of life.

Eleanor sighed. What *did* she want out of life? She had no one other than Father to talk to about her restlessness, but she couldn't share it with him when she didn't even know what was at the root of it.

She glanced at the mirror, smoothing out the wrinkles in her bodice. She'd wasted enough time dawdling over her appearance.

Even though her mood hadn't lightened, she pasted on a pleasant expression and headed downstairs to the large parlor where everyone was gathered.

"There she is." Father held out an arm to her and escorted her to the dining room.

"We are privileged to have you with us, Mr. Briggs, Miss Briggs." Judge Ashbury dipped his chin at her. The stately older gentleman appeared at ease and not at all stuffy. His eyes even twinkled. "George has told us all about you, Mr. Briggs, and your charming daughter."

Charming? Eleanor couldn't remember the last time the word had been used to describe her. But the compliment seemed sincere. And the Judge was so hospitable and congenial it was easy to relax.

"Thank you for having us." She curtseyed.

Father pulled out a chair for her. "Please call me Stewart. George and I go way back."

The table was set with fine china, crystal, silver, and linen. Impressive. For a moment, she wanted to giggle to herself. To think that when Father first announced they were headed to Montana, she had imagined meals at hand-hewn tables with simple dishes. Wouldn't Marvella be shocked to hear that?

Almost as shocked as Eleanor was to realize she was the one underdressed for the occasion. How presumptuous of her to assume that Montana would be filled with backwoods, uneducated, poor people.

The footmen served the main course as conversation

filled the room. Rack of lamb with oven-roasted potatoes and carrots. A delicious sauce of cherries and currants was offered as well. Eleanor's mouth watered. It smelled absolutely delicious.

"What about you, my dear?"

Eleanor glanced up. Uh oh. She hadn't been paying attention. "Oh, please excuse me. I was captivated by this delicious lamb."

"Our cook, Mr. Jefferies, has studied abroad." Marvella's pride at this made her cheeks glow. "He's good, and I seldom have anything to say against his dishes, although there was that one time when the pork roast was tough. He blamed the pig, but we couldn't be sure." She speared a piece of roasted carrot. "We were speaking of the magnificent scenery you passed coming into and through our area. What was your impression?"

The change in subjects made her head swim. Eleanor sipped her water to give herself time to follow her hostess's train of thought. "It was incredibly beautiful. Scene after scene of snowcapped mountains, crystal lakes, and a riot of colors in the moraines where wildflowers grew. It is a gorgeous section of the country."

Marvella's enthusiastic nod sent the hair on top of her head bobbing. "I agree. I agree. Such majesty. One can't help but think of God and the radiance of His creation reflecting His beauty."

She bit her tongue. She was *not* going to discuss God and matters of faith. Her hostess wouldn't care at all for her opinion should she do so. She sliced off a piece of the lamb and took another bite, eager for the subject to change.

George Grinnell rescued her. "I'm sure that all of America

is certain to see the value in preserving more and more land for public viewing and use. We must do this now and minimize westward expansion."

"Once the battle cry of businessmen and politicians back east . . ." Apparently it was her father's turn to put in his two cents. Eleanor withheld a sigh. She'd heard this a hundred times. "'Washington is not a place to live in. The rents are high, the food is bad, the dust is disgusting, and the morals are deplorable. Go West, young man, go West and grow up with the country.' Horace Greeley said it, yet gave no consideration to the land grabs we would see because of it."

Mr. Grinnell tapped the table. "It was wrong to encourage a nation of dreamers to take up vast tracts of land and fence them in to keep the world out."

"Hear, hear." Father added his hearty approval to Mr. Grinnell's statement. "I will only add that massive tracts of farmland or ranches disrupt the natural terrain they take over. There should be designated spots for farming and ranching. The acreage could be predetermined by the government, setting up plots for anyone who wants to take on those enterprises. Land allotment then benefits both as intrusion upon the land is kept to a minimum, and what is not claimed is able to be preserved. It would also keep harmful incidents like the Land Rush of 1889 from happening again."

Eleanor studied her father for a moment. His cheeks were red, and his eyes were sparkling. It was the most animated she had seen him in quite some time.

Judge Ashbury cleared his throat. "Yes, the Land Rush was quite the mess. But as I recall, it was a mess created by the federal government's failure to create an orderly process by which people could claim their one hundred and sixty acres."

Father dabbed at his lips with his linen napkin. Eleanor held her breath. It wasn't often Father or Mr. Grinnell were challenged outright like this.

"The government did do a poor job in organizing the assigning of land," Father finally said. "But the principle was sound. One hundred and sixty acres is more than enough to establish a flourishing farm and still preserve vast segments of our great nation for all to enjoy."

"Land ownership is not the problem, as I see it." The Judge cut into the lamb, his voice calm in contrast to the strident opinions of the men she knew and respected. "Land ownership and settlement has done wonders for isolated territories, where no one would venture if left untouched completely. There is no reason land ownership and nationally preserved lands cannot stand side by side."

Oh dear. That went against everything her father had said for years. Eleanor had always agreed with him . . . but she hadn't considered what the Judge was suggesting.

Eleanor leaned forward. "Might I inquire why a single man needs hundreds if not thousands of acres of land?"

The Judge smiled at her and his mustache twitched. "Our world has a growing population. If men don't own a great deal of land, they can't produce the food that population requires."

Even though she didn't agree with his opinion, she liked him.

The Judge speared a piece of lamb. "Our own Jacob Brunswick owns twenty thousand acres of farmland."

Marvella gave a firm nod. "Oh yes. The Brunswicks' farmland simply ripples with the most impressive crops of wheat. And they are so generous. They sell their wheat at a fair price, and I know for a fact they have helped their fair share of down-on-their-luck families. I believe their farm alone supplies enough wheat for three counties. And they ship to Canada." Marvella's pride in her community shone through her prais—

Wait a minute. "Brunswick?" Eleanor frowned. "I met a man today named Carter Brunswick."

"Why, my dear, that is Jacob's son. His *unmarried* son." Marvella raised a brow.

Oh, for heaven's sake!

The Judge took a sip of water. "Carter owns the local flour mill and his father farms those twenty thousand acres I spoke of. Jacob plants it mostly in wheat, which Carter grinds to flour." The Judge pointed his fork in Eleanor's direction. "Why, that very dinner roll you have on your plate is made with Brunswick flour."

"But twenty thousand acres owned by one man?" Father's eyes widened. "That's excessive."

Marvella tipped her head. "Well . . . he co-owns some of it with a partner."

As if that made a difference. How could these intelligent people not understand? Eleanor shook her head. "It doesn't seem to me that any one man should own that much land. The government could own it as a public farm and lease it out to be managed. That way it would be accessible to all. They could still arrange roads through the farm so that the public could make their way to the forest preserves and national parks. I just don't see the need for one man to own so much." And it wasn't just because she'd had a run-in with the rude Mr. Carter Brunswick earlier.

"Well, we will simply have to open your eyes to the truth while you are here." Marvella lifted a buttered half of roll to her lips and smiled.

The truth? Did she really believe she was in the right and they were in the wrong? How could she?

The Judge cleared his throat again as Father set his fork down. "My dear, there are families in the West who have tended the land since it was wild. They have worked generation after generation to clear it and cultivate it to grow this nation's food. The government can't be depended on for such things. There is far too much already for the government to manage."

Father opened his mouth as though to say something, but the Judge went on.

"And without the farms this nation would suffer. Montana produces large numbers of cattle for beef, lambs for the meal you're enjoying this evening, and pigs for the bacon and ham you will enjoy at breakfast. Animals require large acreage of grass to feed upon, not to mention the hay that must be planted and cultivated and baled for winter, when the snows are too deep for grazing. That is why farmers and ranchers need a great deal of land."

Eleanor glanced at her father. Why was he so silent? She had heard him argue the same topic many times with great passion and vigor. Did he not wish to offend his hosts? She pushed ahead anyway. "But what happens when we start to run out of land? If only a small portion is set aside for parks, and the rest is ranched and farmed, we run the risk of citizens and future generations inheriting a sparser, less beautiful America than when it was first settled. Right, Father?"

He started a bit, as though he had been lost in his thoughts. "My daughter is correct . . . If Mr. Brunswick owns all the land surrounding the area where we would like to see a national park preserved for the people of this great country and others as well, how would they gain access to it? There must be some compromises. Twenty thousand acres is too much."

Eleanor nodded. Exactly so. The land must be preserved. But the look on the Judge's face made her wonder. He wasn't angry or upset. Simply . . . contemplative.

"And how would you decide, my dear, how much land is needed to grow enough wheat for your dinner roll?" Marvella snatched up another dinner roll and held it up. She looked at each person at her table. "Without wheat there would be no dinner rolls at all, and what a pity that would be." She sniffed the roll and put it on her plate. "Mr. Jefferies's rolls are some of the lightest and most delicious in all of Montana—perhaps I could dare to say the entirety of America."

Eleanor smiled in spite of herself. Marvella was a force to be reckoned with even if she was on the wrong side of the argument. Mr. Grinnell hadn't been exaggerating when he'd said their hostess was unafraid to argue her point of view.

"As I said earlier, vast private ownership is unnecessary. It is not only an issue that impacts us now, but our future as well. Vast holdings that are private are passed from generation to generation. Not only can the public not access them, but it gives a small group of individuals an excessive amount of control over land that could be preserved with all its beauty and natural resources for years to come. If it was given over to the government, it could be kept in public trust and leased out, along with the general population still maintaining access to the public lands. Or, as we discussed earlier, much smaller parcels of land given away by the government until none are left for that purpose." Father's emphatic words accompanied the dip in his brow.

The Judge studied Father. Eleanor could see why Mr. Grinnell extolled the older man's virtues as a judge. His expression was impenetrable. "You've never owned a large piece of land, have you, Mr. Briggs?"

"No. I haven't. I once owned a place much the size of this one in New York City. We had gardens and a stable just as you do. It was sufficient for all our needs." Father jerked his knife through his slab of lamb and shoved a chunk of meat in his mouth.

Eleanor studied him. Was that a sheen of sweat on his brow? But why?

Judge Ashbury nodded. "And for us it more than meets our needs. But we also are blessed with the money to *buy* all of our produce, wheat, and meat. From people who own land. Did you grow your own food on your property in New York?"

Father did something she'd never seen him do. He sputtered! Could it be he'd never heard or considered what the Judge was saying?

Father lay his fork on his plate before speaking. "Well, no. We didn't have room for anything other than my wife's flowers. We were so seldom there after my wife died that Eleanor and I agreed to sell it and rent lodging as we had need. We own *no* property currently. And we manage just fine."

"Yes, but because of your lifestyle, you have the ability to purchase food wherever you go." Marvella smiled at her guests. "That means that those who farm do so not only to feed their families, but ours as well. I agree that land preservation is a necessity, but I think there should be careful consideration given to where and how much land is conserved and the impact of that conservation on those who work by the sweat of their brow to help provide food for us."

The room fell silent. Knives and forks clinked against the fine china as they ate their meal. Eleanor's shoulders were beginning to hurt. Her throat felt dry no matter how many sips of water she took. She had never considered that aspect of conservation before. Rationally she knew that food had to be grown somewhere. But never had she truly thought about the people who grew wheat and corn and vegetables. Eleanor chewed the corner of her lip. The conversation was moving so quickly, it was almost impossible to remember what her own argument was.

Or what she actually believed.

Eleanor glanced around the table. Only Marvella seemed to not mind the tension that had descended over them. She was smiling down at her little puffball of a dog, who was dancing for his fair share of meat.

Finally, the Judge wiped his mouth and looked over at Father. "I'm sure you find traveling the country with no permanent address a perfect way of life. But most people aren't of a mind to move about all the time. Many came to this country because land ownership in their home countries wasn't a possibility."

Eleanor plucked a dinner roll from the basket in front of her and sliced it open. She spread a pad of butter over it, her thoughts jumbled. She'd never considered how other countries controlled the freedoms of their citizens to have a spot of their own. But America was so vast and wild. Couldn't the Ashburys see the need to protect the precious resources of their country without allowing people to purchase absurd amounts of land?

Mr. Grinnell joined the discussion as the Judge paused to take a long drink of water. "Surely you are not suggesting that we parcel out land to everyone who enters our great country simply because they were refused that luxury at home."

"That would be absurd." The older man raised an eyebrow. "I'm saying that America has always attracted those who wanted to own their own farms, ranches, orchards, and vineyards. Those things require land and many acres of it. Some have managed the same acreage for generations and do so with great pride. In turn, we are the beneficiaries of their hard work."

At least Mr. Grinnell had the fortitude to look a bit embarrassed at his ridiculous assertion. The Judge folded his hands on the table in front of him.

"As I've mentioned, I am supportive of making national parks and all that they have to offer. I support state lands and federal preserves that will see the beauty go on unspoiled. *However*"—he cleared his throat—"I am also in support of private land ownership and will remain so. I would be a hypocrite to say otherwise. Especially if it limited the number of dinner rolls served at my table." He grabbed another roll.

"Well said, husband." Marvella held up her glass, and the little dog dancing around her chair yipped. She pinched off a piece of a dinner roll and tossed it to the pup. "Sir Theophilus agrees as well."

The men chuckled, and the tension eased as the discussion shifted to other topics.

But Eleanor kept thinking about what the Judge said. On a small scale, his points made sense. Yet she still couldn't agree with large-scale land ownership and never would. The land belonged to everyone. Americans, no matter their social status, should be able to experience the awe of Yosemite, with its sharp mountains and lush pine trees. To see the beautiful Half Dome rock jutting into a sky painted with a pastel pink sunrise. Vivid memories of geysers gushing forth water from the ground and bighorned sheep prancing across rocks and streams filtered through her memory. It was as near a sin to fence it off solely for personal use as it would be to steal paintings from the great art museums and take them home for private adoration.

She pressed her lips together. No wonder that Carter Brunswick should be involved in such a thing.

Carter Brunswick.

Just one meeting with the infuriating man and he'd infiltrated her thoughts, no matter how hard she'd tried to keep him out of her mind. Her mouth tipped down as she recalled his reprimand of her manners—or lack thereof. She sniffed. If there was anyone in that argument who needed to learn manners it was him. His familiarity in using her nickname, his teasing her when they didn't even know each other—unconscionable! And did the man think she hadn't

78

noticed how deliberately he'd signed his name and looked over his papers?

Some men would do anything to make a point.

She would consign all thought of him to the deep . . . if only that smiling, handsome—albeit bruised—face would stop invading her thoughts!

Wait. *Handsome?* Oh good heavens! He was decidedly *not* handsome. And even if he was, *she* certainly wasn't attracted to twinkling blue eyes framed by laugh lines, and light brown hair tousled by the wind—

Heat crept up her cheeks and she closed her eyes. *Eleanor! Collect yourself!*

She sipped her water, then lifted her fingers to smooth her furrowed brow. Such a line of thought simply wouldn't do. Even if Carter Brunswick *was* handsome, he was on the wrong side. A ruffian to boot.

She lifted her chin. It was decided.

She simply would not tolerate him. Or further thoughts of him.

And that was final.

"Mother, that was a mighty fine supper." Carter stood and walked over to where his mother was seated and kissed her cheek. "But I need to get back to town before it's dark."

"I wish you could stay longer. I do so enjoy hearing about all that's happening."

"Well, Dad can fill you in more about the meeting."

"I wish those men would learn how to control themselves. There is no sense in brawling in the streets." She laid down her napkin and crossed her arms over her chest. "Just look at your face."

"Well, it's a weighty subject." How did he get himself out of this one? "Oh, I did meet some new folks today. The men are conservationists and there's a young lady with them. The daughter of one of the men is a sassy little thing. Blond hair and blue eyes. Stands about yea tall"—he pointed to his shoulder—"and rides a bicycle."

"A bicycle? How interesting." His mother began to clear the table. "Sounds like she made an impression."

Carter rested his elbows on the table. His change of subject could prove to be worse than the first. But Ellie was becoming the first thing that came to mind. He needed to tread carefully, or Mom would have them married with kids in no time. "I suppose she did. She was rude and a little on the obnoxious side of things. I was talking to Gus and trying to find out if my part came in and she just sashayed up and interrupted us. Thought her needs were more important and wasn't afraid to say so."

"And did this sassy young woman have a name?" The cheer in his mother's voice as she scraped the plates was almost comical.

Carter groaned. His mother had been less than subtle in recent months about him settling down. It wasn't as if he was avoiding marriage. But it hadn't been a priority. Not with figuring out how to run his own mill. All his time and attention had been focused on making the mill successful. And with the railroad trouble now, he didn't have time to seek out a wife. Mark's assertion that he'd been waiting for God to plop the right woman in his lap probably wasn't too far off the truth. Not that he would admit it.

"I'm heading out to take care of a few things before bed." Dad headed for the kitchen door. "Good to have you here, son. See you tomorrow."

"Good-night, Dad. Love you."

Dad turned around and grinned. "Love you too. But you better escape while you still can." His loud whisper from behind his hand gained him a swat from Mother's kitchen towel.

"All right, all right." Carter turned back to his mother. "Her name is Ellie—actually *Eleanor*—Briggs. *Eleanor* is rather stuffy though and her father called her *Ellie*. I like that better, don't you?"

"Doesn't much matter what I like. It does seem strange that you should have such an opinion on a first-time encounter." Mother scrubbed at the skillet.

Carter shrugged. "Just saying I like the name Ellie better than Eleanor. Don't go trying to marry me off to her."

His mother made a face at him. "The thought never occurred to me! Just wondered why she made such an impression."

He leaned against the counter. Why *had* this woman made the impression she had? It wasn't as though he didn't know a number of women in town, some almost as audacious as Ellie. But none of them had come to occupy his thoughts the way she had. Hmm . . . "Probably because she didn't back down." Yes, that was it. "For such a little thing, she didn't have a lick of restraint in stating her opinion." His response to her came back to him and he cringed a little.

"What?" Mother put her hands on her hips. "Carter Brunswick, what did you do to that girl?"

He chuckled. "Nothing. It's just that . . . well, she stated

81

her emphatic opinion right after I was punched. So I might have been a bit . . . sarcastic with her."

"Might?" She shook her head. "I do hope when you do decide to settle down with some girl that she will understand that side of you."

"Well, if she doesn't, then she won't be right for me. My wife will need to be able to hold her own with me. Just like you do with Dad." He kissed her cheek one more time and headed toward the door. "See you later."

"Ride back carefully. I don't want to hear that you were blazing down the road at a full gallop."

"Only if there's a grizzly—or my irate mother—chasing behind me." He tossed the comment over his shoulder then skedaddled before she could respond.

5

THURSDAY, MAY 12, 1904—KALISPELL, MONTANA

Brunswick Flour Mill was running at full capacity again now that his machinery was purring like a kitten. Amazing what peace that gave Carter. Nothing had felt right since the railroad dropped their announcement. He looked over the list Jack Gustafson had given him and signed at the bottom. Jack had been his right-hand man for over four years now. He had come from the Pillsbury mills in Minnesota and offered expertise that had gone far to teach Carter everything he needed to know.

"Thanks, Jack. I appreciate your attention to detail."

Jack took the papers and gave them a shake. "Devil's in the details some say, but for me the details are more of a divine concern. Seems to me the devil's all about chaos and disorder. God's the one who sees to the details."

"True enough. Well, I think it's important you know that I appreciate that detail."

His friend quirked an eyebrow at him. "That shiner's getting more colorful as the day goes on."

Carter narrowed his gaze, wincing as his eye started throbbing. Again. "Let's just not even talk about it, okay?"

Jack chuckled and sat behind his desk, opposite Carter's. "Sure thing. You're the boss."

"Why don't you catch me up on Miriam and the boys? I've been praying for them since you told me about the scarlet fever. I'd say that's a bit more harrowing than me walking into the wrong end of a fist."

"I appreciate your prayers." All signs of laughter left Jack's face. "The boys pulled through all right, thank the Lord. Poor Miriam was up with them around the clock. The youngest is just two and he seemed to suffer the most. On Saturday I intend to load up all four boys and get them out of the house for the day. Miriam needs a rest. I need to figure out what we're going to do."

Carter laced his fingers together behind his head and leaned back. "Why don't you head out to see my folks? My mother would love to see the boys. She misses getting to spend time with her grandchildren back in Kansas."

"Really? That would be great."

"Sure. They've got some new lambs and a calf, not to mention the horses and chickens. I'm sure the boys would burn off plenty of energy running around the farm. And knowing Mom, she'd probably force you to let her oversee them while you and my dad had a nice long talk."

Relief relaxed the worry lines around Jack's eyes. "Sounds pretty good to me. You sure they wouldn't mind?"

"Not at all. I'll send word out to them to expect you. I can well imagine this will make you a hero in Miriam's eyes, and I'm all about supporting that." He smiled at his friend, happy he would take him up on his offer. Jack and Miriam were two of the hardest working people he knew. And they loved their boys, but those little guys had endless energy. Carter didn't know how Jack and Miriam kept up with them.

"Well, thanks, I know she'll appreciate it. I'd best get back to the inventory." Jack folded the papers and grabbed a pencil before exiting the office.

Carter jotted a note to his mother. She would take matters in hand and keep those boys busy. It would be a win for everyone.

At noon, Carter called in one of his newest workers. Bill Preston was just seventeen and Carter wanted to encourage him. Jack said the boy lacked a lot of confidence, and he'd heard around town that Bill's father was an overbearing drunkard who had condemned his family to poverty. Maybe Carter could help Bill change things for him and his family.

The young man was ashen faced as he approached the door.

"Come on in and sit with me a moment." Carter ushered the tall, skinny boy into his office.

"Did I do something wrong?" Bill's voice was barely audible.

"No. Just the opposite. You're doing a great job. Jack tells me you've been handling bagging the flour like you were born to it. He said we've never had a better worker on the machines."

Bill straightened a bit. "Thank you, Mr. Brunswick."

"I believe in rewarding folks for their good work. You've been working hard. You're here early every morning and never hesitate to stay late if you're asked. I appreciate a man who gives his job his all. It's time I give you a raise."

His eyes widened. "A raise? Truly? My family needs the money bad. My ma has a hard time making ends meet." He pushed back his sandy hair. "I was afraid you were going to fire me."

"No chance of that if you keep at it like you've been doing." Carter picked up the note he'd written his mother. "I wonder if you would do a personal task for me?"

"Of course. Anything you need." The boy looked almost as excited by the prospect as if it were his birthday.

Carter grinned. "I figured I could count on you. I need this note run out to my mother. You know where my parents' farm is, don't you?"

"Of course. Everyone does."

"You can take my horse, Mercury. He's over at the livery. Just deliver this note to my mother, and she'll feed you. It's one of her favorite things to do. Then I'd like you to take the rest of the day off. All I ask is that you return the horse before nightfall. Which gives you a few hours given our longer and longer days."

The boy looked stunned. "You mean, I can just ride around if I want to?"

"Absolutely. Just don't overdo it. Don't go too far up into the mountains and wear Mercury out. I might have use of him tomorrow."

"No, sir. I wouldn't do that. I wouldn't go that far."

"Well, take care of the note and then you've earned a break." He handed the paper to Bill.

"Should I tell your mother that you said for her to feed me?"

Carter chuckled. "You won't have to tell her anything. She'll insist. I promise."

The boy tucked the letter into his shirt pocket. "Thanks, Mr. Brunswick. I ain't never had an afternoon to myself."

Carter stood and extended his hand. "Well, it will be just between us. No sense worrying your family about the details. You're still on the clock as far as I'm concerned. Just doing something other than bagging flour."

"Yes, sir!" Bill pumped Carter's hand up and down. He turned and ran from the office, crashing into someone outside the open doorway as he exited. Carter heard his muffled apology, figuring he'd probably run into Jack. Instead, he heard the voice of none other than Miss Briggs.

Carter's gaze snapped up and he straightened. There she was. With her big, beautiful blue eyes.

He shook off the shock and stood. "Well, hello, Ellie. Come on in." He suppressed a smile as she stalked into his office.

"It's *Eleanor,* but for you, it's Miss Briggs, if you don't mind."

Make that, big, beautiful, *fiery* blue eyes.

He chuckled. "But I *do* mind. *Miss Briggs* makes it seem that we don't know one another very well, and you and I have a history."

"We've only just met." Her eyes flashed, but if he wasn't mistaken, there was a hint of a smile hidden there.

"Yes, but in that meeting we learned a great deal about one another." This was too much fun. When had he become such an instigator?

She tipped her head to the side, eyebrows drawn together. "Is that so?"

"Absolutely." He ticked his list off on his fingers. "I learned that you are the daughter of a famous conservationist named Stewart Briggs. You hail from back east and own a bicycle."

"I said nothing about being from back east. How did you surmise that?"

Carter folded his arms over his chest and shrugged. "Because we're very nearly as far west as you can go. Just about everything is east of here."

"Oh. I see." She nodded, a bit of a twinkle in those expressive eyes. "Go on, then."

Carter lost no time. "You are confident and of the opinion that your affairs are of the utmost importance. You are careful with your appearance, but not so stuffy that you don't consider comfort."

She stopped him once again. "How do you suppose that?" She mirrored his stance, crossing her arms against her serviceable brown jacket.

"I noted that you were wearing well-worn walking boots. Seems to me a woman of means with such boots keeps them for their comfort. I know that's why I continue to wear these boots of mine."

She smiled at that. Barely.

But he'd count it. "See. I was right."

"You are good at deducing. That's all."

Carter offered her a chair. "Won't you sit and tell me why you've come today, Ellie."

She sat on the edge of the chair, hands folded in her lap. "Stop calling me that. You're giving casual consideration to a relationship that doesn't exist. Only my parents use my nickname."

"But I like it so much better than Eleanor. Eleanor is stuffy and formal."

"Which is what I prefer to be with you."

He leaned against the edge of his desk and watched her

look around his office. It probably wasn't as fancy as offices she'd seen in businesses back east. But it served the mill well. It was clean and the large windows set in the brick eight feet above them let in enough light to warm the room. "Stuffy and formal? You want to be considered as stuffy? That's hardly a flattering characteristic."

She rolled her gaze heavenward and sighed. "You, sir, are one of the most exasperating men I've ever encountered."

Carter laughed. "My mother has often said the same thing. But she loves me dearly."

"Well, you needn't fear the same reaction from me."

He rubbed his chin as he studied her face. "I don't know, Ellie. I might grow on you."

"I highly doubt that." Those eyes flashed at him.

But her lips tipped up ever so slightly. It was a perfectly charming response. She was enjoying this.

"Maybe not today—"

"Maybe not ever." She pointed to his face. "How's your eye?"

"It hurts, but I'll live." At least the bruise was fading to a greenish-yellow rather than the bold purple from a few days ago.

"Too bad." Her growing smile softened the sting of her retort. "I didn't hear at the train station how you came to be so bloody and bruised."

"The railroad had just made an announcement at a town meeting. People weren't too happy about it. I happened to walk into a couple punches."

"Interesting story. Are you sure you weren't the initiator? You don't seem to have trouble starting arguments." She held his gaze.

His jaw dropped. She could definitely hold her own. "I can assure you that I am not a pugilist."

It was her turn to appear surprised. "I'm impressed that you know the word, Mr. Brunswick."

"You give me far too little credit."

She waved a hand. "Never mind. I recently heard about your father's massive acreage. I'm told that he owns twenty thousand or more acres of land. I want to know why a man would believe himself in need of that much land."

It took him a moment to catch up to her abrupt change in subject. Why was she asking about his family's land? "You'd have to ask Dad."

"You mean you don't know *why* your father bought up all that land?" Her tone was sharp. Her chin tipped up.

Who was the instigator now?

"I suppose it was because he needed it for the farm. He and his friend Fred Owens are wheat farmers. They wanted to grow enough wheat to feed Montana and a few other states."

"But why so much land?"

This conversation was far from the lighthearted banter they shared when she walked in. He didn't much care for it. "It takes a lot of acreage to produce a lot of wheat. And it takes a lot of wheat to produce flour." He met her disapproving gaze without flinching. "Is it the wheat you object to, or the land being farmed?"

Ellie brushed at her skirt. "I disapprove of private land ownership. Especially in vast quantities. Land such as there is out here should be open to the public, for all to enjoy."

"Then where would you get your bread? Or don't you eat bread?" Carter shook his head.

She looked ready to throw something at him. "Of course

I eat bread. Honestly, Mr. Brunswick you are one of the most difficult men I've ever met. I'm trying to have a simple conversation about the land, and you try to make it about me. I am not the focus of this discussion."

He pondered that. "You could be. I have a few questions I'd love to ask."

She pressed her lips together and shook her head. "I want to know about the land."

"Then come out to the farm after church Sunday, and you can talk to my dad over dinner. I'm sure he'd love to meet you and answer your questions." Carter could see it now. That would liven up the dinner table for sure. "You might even come to like me after all."

"I assure you, Mr. Brunswick, that will never happen." She rose from her seat and headed for the door.

"Ellie!"

She turned and glared at him.

What *was* it about that glare that tickled him? "I just wanted to say that it's not a good idea to say never. I find when I do that, it's almost like a challenge for God to show me that I'm not the One in control."

Her eyes snapped as a frown covered her face. "First, Mr. Brunswick, I would have to believe that God took an interest in mankind for that comment to mean anything to me. Second, I *am* in control of my destiny and the choices I make, whether you are or not."

Ouch. He shouldn't have been so flippant. Her anger at God was palpable. "I'm sorry. I shouldn't have teased like I did."

She met his gaze and held it for several seconds. "No, you shouldn't have."

Eleanor got on her bicycle and rode as fast as she could back to the Ashbury house. Her hands trembled and her insides felt all flipped upside down. What was the matter with her? Better still, what was the matter with *him*? How dare he make comments about God being in control and never say never? She'd never heard of anything so ludicrous. She didn't even know what to believe about God anymore.

God seemed, *if* He did exist, to hold His creation in complete disregard. Why would Eleanor want to have a relationship with a God who let her mother suffer and die?

Just like God, Carter Brunswick both attracted and repelled her. As a child, she'd felt so drawn to God and wanted to know more about Him. But now . . .

It was as if God was dangerous.

Carter had the same effect on her. He screamed of danger. Why, she didn't know. But she couldn't allow herself to be attracted to him. No matter how much he drew her in.

Neither Carter Brunswick nor God had a place in her life.

A shiver raced up her spine and she almost fell off her bike. Slowing to a stop, she took a couple deep breaths. What was wrong with her? Everything had been unbalanced for days.

Eleanor got off the bike and walked beside it. No sense taking a tumble. It was a perfect summer day. She took a deep breath of mountain air—it seemed fresher than any she'd ever known. Chicago air had been full of coal smoke and odors too numerous to count. New York wasn't much better.

But here, the entire sky suggested a purity that couldn't

be had anywhere else. And why? Because man had not been allowed to spoil it with overpopulation and large processing plants or factories. There had to be a way to keep men from coming here to tear apart the land and ruin what was so naturally stunning.

Her mother's voice echoed in her mind. *"God made the world perfect and beautiful. It is man who has wreaked destruction upon it. Man, who destroys it to serve his purposes. God gave the earth over to man to be tended in a loving and productive manner, not to damage it beyond use and then move on to the next place and do the same."*

Mother had loved Father's conservationist beliefs. She wanted mankind to be taught to nurture and care for the land. She wanted to see the earth thrive and blossom as it surely had in the Garden of Eden. Mother believed that man could co-exist with creation, but only by drawing closer to God to better understand Him.

Oh, for pity's sake! For so long, she'd pushed away any thought of God. Why was He now coming to mind over and over?

And why did she feel a strong desire to go back to Him? To understand the heavenly Father her mother loved. Perhaps . . .

She nodded. The only way to resolve this confusion was to do her research. Ask questions.

It seemed that the Ashburys were God-fearing people. Perhaps she could have a conversation with Marvella and gain some sort of insight into what the older woman thought about God. She'd undoubtedly be as expansive on her thoughts about Him as about the other topics she discussed.

Eleanor approached the Ashbury mansion and started

up the long circular drive, compelled to press on toward the answers she needed. Father said each man was responsible to make his own destiny, so she supposed it made sense that she would desire to speak to the older woman or anyone else who might afford her understanding.

As for this ridiculous sense that she had no control whatsoever over her life?

Well, that was absurd. And she'd soon prove it.

Grant stirred the pot of beans and bacon, then put the lid back on. He added wood to the stove, then took a seat, hands circling a cup of coffee. The melancholy and gloom at work still pressed in on him. Many of the men had bought houses in Kalispell and were now faced with selling them and moving to Whitefish, where they'd probably have to live in tents for a time. The housing was so limited in the smaller town that no doubt the influx of two or three hundred men would stretch the available resources well beyond the ability to provide.

Houses would go up in rapid order. They already did. Most would be slapped together at first. Probably little better than shanties.

But here in Kalispell, the town had grown . . . nice. Nicer than anywhere else he'd ever lived. There were well-manicured lawns and tree-lined avenues. Stumptown, as many of the railroad workers referred to Whitefish, wasn't at all pretty. Grant had been up there a couple of times on railroad business, and they had a long way to go to make something out of it. With all the stumps left behind from felling the abundant varieties of evergreen trees no wonder folks called it Stumptown. Those stumps were being pulled, but the land was still so unsettled.

Alvin finally showed up saying he'd found work on building the rail line from Columbia Falls to Whitefish and beyond. He came back on his days off to the small apartment he shared with Grant, but things weren't the same. His brother was moody and unhappy with the prospects of moving north. Especially since he'd just found a girl he liked to spend time with and she called Kalispell home.

Grant glanced up at the clock. Alvin should be home any minute. Not that he was looking forward to listening to his brother's grumblings all night. His own attitude was bad enough. He didn't need to be worrying his brother would go off and do something stupid.

Alvin had always been a complainer, but of late, he seldom did anything else. Still, he'd bring news from the line, so Grant would face his brother's ire to find out what was happening. Anything to know what was being discussed among those planning out the death of Kalispell.

He rubbed his pounding temples. He'd been left to care for Alvin when their ma died. At twelve, he had done what he could to keep his five-year-old little brother from harm, but there'd been only so much he could do. He'd been a kid himself.

Alvin grew up with a mean streak and sense of dissatisfaction. It was a wonder he'd found a girl to put up with him. But he'd probably made grand promises and was pouring on the charm. For now.

The door opened and the object of his thoughts—filthy as usual—stomped through. The stench of him filled the kitchen. Grant couldn't disguise his distaste.

"I know. I know. I need a bath. And I intend to have one before I go see my gal, but right now I'm starvin'. You can live with the smell. What's for dinner?"

"Beans and bacon. Cornbread." Best not to argue over something as unimportant as a bath. "I'll dish it up. Go ahead and sit down. Any news?"

Alvin was already halfway into the seat. "A few of the boys and me have been talkin'. We figure the only way to get Hill to listen to reason is to threaten what he cares about."

"What are you talking about?" Grant spooned their dinner into bowls.

"Keepin' the railroad in Kalispell, you idiot." Alvin frowned. "We figure if we threaten Hill's son that we can get him to change his mind or at least keep both lines open. We haven't come up with a plan yet, but Hill will be in town soon, and we figure that'll be the time to strike."

Grant stopped what he was doing to give Alvin a hard stare. "You could go to jail for the rest of your life if you do something like that."

Alvin shrugged. "*If* I get caught. Either way, it'd be better than living in Stumptown."

6

THURSDAY, MAY 12, 1904—KALISPELL, MONTANA

Driven by her thirst for answers and some way to rid herself of this weird melancholy and restlessness, Eleanor parked her bike on the porch and entered the Ashbury mansion, hoping it was time for tea. Perhaps a conversation with her hostess would help ease the weight in her chest. She needed to talk to someone. Her thoughts felt like a tangled ball of yarn. Every string she pulled seemed to make the tangle into a knotted mess.

The butler bowed ever so slightly. "May I take your things, Miss?"

She removed her gloves and hat. "Is Mrs. Ashbury in? I'd like to speak with her."

Tobias shook his head as he held out his hands for her hat. "My apologies, she's not available at the moment."

"Well, this is a fine kettle of fish."

"Pardon, Miss?"

Eleanor plopped her hat back on her head. "I'm sorry,

97

Tobias. You've done nothing wrong. I appreciate your help, but I'm going to take my bicycle out again."

"Very well, Miss." Another bow and then he opened the door for her.

Once she was astride her two-wheeled conveyance, she pushed her legs to the limit in all hopes of working out the frustration. But frustration with what exactly? And why couldn't she put her finger on it? Never had she dealt with these kinds of feelings before.

Almost like she didn't even understand herself anymore.

The more she pedaled, the more it built. In all her years, she'd been a lover of research and facts. To not have the answers annoyed her.

Father had said and done a few odd things lately as well. Maybe they were both simply going through a season of . . .

She couldn't find a name for it. Yet another question without an answer.

With a shake of her head, she focused on the streets before her. She needed to pay attention or she would get lost.

People milled about, strolled the sidewalks, and walked in and out of businesses. Kalispell really was a quaint little town.

All the news in town was about the railroad. Since Kalispell was the economic center of the whole area, it made sense that the railroad was here. But she also understood why the railroad was moving their main line division point up to Whitefish. If the rails west of Kalispell were worse than what she endured on the way *here*, then she, of course, was in full agreement. It would also be better for the creation of a national park.

Winding her way through Kalispell's streets, she turned right on Third Avenue East and headed for the depot. Not for any particular reason, but it was on her mind. At the end of the road, she found herself facing the tracks. She turned left and rode up to the building.

The two-story depot was clean and neat. No grand piece of architecture, but it was welcoming and practical as it bustled with activity. Something she'd come to appreciate more the past couple years. She parked her bike outside the door and saw the same man behind the counter. The man who obviously knew Carter Brunswick well.

He hadn't seemed all that impressed with her after her first arrival, but he'd been nice enough. Maybe she should smooth things over. Since things weren't busy for him at the moment, she walked up to the counter. "Gus?"

He glanced up from his paperwork and blinked several times. The hesitation in his eyes couldn't be mistaken. "Miss Briggs. How may I help you?"

"I was simply riding my bicycle about town and found myself curious about the building here."

"Oh?" He went back to his papers and scribbled something else on one.

"It's an excellent depot."

He continued to write. "Yes, it is. We are pleased to have it."

"May I perhaps look around?"

"What for?" He frowned. "Forgive me. It's just a train depot. Built in 1892. Had a fire in 1899 and we had to rebuild the interior."

She blinked, then shrugged. Why *did* she want to look around? This strange boredom of hers was leading her nowhere. "Just curious."

"You're welcome to look here on the main level, but up-stairs are private quarters. And the basement is off-limits. Too much equipment down there. Wouldn't want a lady to get injured or covered in dirt." He shifted his gaze to her but didn't really appear like he cared what she chose to do.

"A basement?" How very intriguing.

"Off-limits." He drawled out the words. "It doesn't have lights and is pretty scary if you ask me, so a lady of your station wouldn't care for it." Going back to his papers once again, he released a little huff when she made no move to go. "Anything else, Miss?" His tone had lost what little patience it had held.

Maybe because she hadn't been very nice their first meet-ing. She swallowed. Carter had been correct, her manners had been lacking that day. "I apologize, Gus. I was in quite a fret when I first arrived, and I didn't treat you well. I'm afraid you received the sharp edge of my tongue, and I'm sorry."

He chuckled a bit and shifted the papers in front of him. "If I recall, Carter received the worst of it, but he's got a thick skin. Don't worry about me, Miss Briggs. I've dealt with worse than the likes of you. All's well."

She felt lighter even though his comment stung a bit. "Thank you for that, Gus. And thank you for your assis-tance the other day." A bit more of the cloud in her mind lifted. "I'll leave you to your work."

Back on her bicycle again, she stared at the pretty brick building before she rode toward the other end of town. It had been a long time since she had simply conversed with people she didn't know.

And, for that matter, since she'd taken time to converse

with people she *did* know—other than Father and his friends.

Their work took them all over the place and most of her activities included meetings with her father's friends and fellow conservationists. There was always a list of things to accomplish. Papers to write. Correspondence to send. And, of course, all the travel.

Now that she thought about it, it had been a while since she'd had luncheon or tea with another female her age.

Had her skills become dull in that area? Was she so used to the blunt speech of the men she worked with that she didn't even know how to be . . . *normal* anymore?

As her thoughts spun in circles, a grave revelation sunk in. Perhaps she was a spinster after all.

And a rude one at that.

FRIDAY, MAY 13, 1904

After an awful night of tossing, turning, and reviewing her life, Eleanor was sure about one thing.

She had no idea who she was anymore.

She'd so poured her life into assisting Father with his work that his beliefs and opinions became hers. His conversations, her conversations.

It had been drilled into her that the work was paramount, so whatever they did, whatever idea they championed, it was more important than whatever anyone else was doing.

Now that she thought about it . . . wasn't that rather arrogant?

Her mother would roll over in her grave.

This wasn't how she'd been raised. Mother was kindness, goodness, and love. It didn't matter that she was wealthy, she shared with others. Listened to them.

Respected them.

Many times as a child, Eleanor had assisted her mother with various charities. Mother never treated anyone as someone of less import than she was.

Eleanor cringed. For some time now, she'd demanded attention because their work was important, and they were important people on an important mission. They were trying to preserve the beauty of America for generations to come! They were doing something of substance and meaning. Those facts had been the anchor of her work the last few years. Now . . .

They rang hollow.

Perhaps *that* was the cause behind her melancholy.

That and the fact that she'd simply been going through the motions without thought to others. At all.

Well. That was going to change.

She headed to the dining room for breakfast, only to pause when she saw that Father and Mr. Grinnell were the only ones seated at the table. She'd been hoping for some creative discourse with the Judge and his wife.

"Good morning, Ellie." Her father looked so relaxed as he lifted his coffee cup to his lips. "I hope you slept well."

She'd stopped trying to correct him about using her old nickname. For whatever reason, it relaxed her.

Gracious. That ornery Carter Brunswick was right. She *was* stuffy. "Not the best, but I'm sure I'll rest well tonight." A footman held out a chair for her. "Where are the Ashburys?"

"The Judge had an early case to hear, and Mrs. Ashbury had a meeting. They said to enjoy ourselves and the cook would prepare anything we liked for breakfast. We've already ordered." Father flipped a page in his newspaper.

Bother. This was putting a kink in her carefully-thought-out plan. She'd hoped to ask several questions over breakfast to help her figure out who she really was. Well, she would simply have to wait for lunch. Or dinner. "What are we doing today?" She took up her linen napkin and placed it on her lap.

"George and I are working on a paper to present to President Roosevelt." Father never even looked at her over his paper.

"Will you need me?"

"No. Feel free to explore town or stay here and enjoy the day." Another sip of coffee. Another flip of pages. "After Mr. Hill arrives, we will be discussing the railroad and the national park. I'll want you to take notes at that meeting."

"Of course. What time should I be ready?"

"He's supposed to arrive today, but our meeting won't be until tomorrow." Mr. Grinnell answered the question and at least glanced at her. But then his attention was back on his own newspaper. "After we hear him speak to the town, we'll set out on our expedition to see some of the southwest areas of the land I believe should be set aside for the national park. We'll be gone for a couple of weeks."

"I know we discussed getting a new tent"—Father folded his paper—"and George suggested an outfitter that might have what we need."

The footman was at her side. "What would you like for breakfast, Miss?"

"I'd like a cheese omelet and toast." She gave her order and then looked at the man. "I'm sorry, I don't know your name." It was high time she started taking notice of more than just landscape details. People deserved her respect.

"Clarence. I'll put your order in with the chef, Miss."

"Thank you." Ah. There was the cream. She poured a generous amount into her coffee and looked back to her breakfast companions. "I'll get the name of that outfitter when we conclude our meal, Mr. Grinnell."

"Of course."

It wasn't but a minute or two before another footman brought in steaming plates of food. Ham steaks and eggs for the men. Toast in silver racks shaped like swans. An assortment of jams, jellies, and plenty of butter. Then Clarence returned with her omelet.

For several minutes the silence continued except for the occasional clank of silver or buttering of toast.

It brought her thoughts back to what kept her awake last night.

Boring indeed. No wonder she was restless.

There had to be more to life than this.

There had to be more to *her* than this.

If only Mrs. Ashbury hadn't left. More than anything, Eleanor needed another woman to talk to. The mistress of this home had something in her eyes that Eleanor longed for.

Peace.

The Judge had it as well. Mrs. Ashbury was jovial and full of life. No matter how opinionated she might be, or that she was determined to marry Eleanor off, something in the woman drew Eleanor like a magnet. And the Judge was full of wisdom and yet calm even when he disagreed on a subject.

Mr. Grinnell set his fork on his empty plate and interrupted her thoughts. "Have you had a chance to ride your bicycle around town?"

"A bit. It's a delightful place. I rode past the Carnegie Library—which I still intend to visit—and the Brunswick Flour Mill. Yesterday, I went back to the train depot. It's an inviting building. The town seems to be bustling."

"That, of course, is about to change." Grinnell shook his head. "What with the railroad pulling out. Such a shame. But it will be to our benefit." He stood. "If you'll excuse me, I must get ready for the day. The letter to the president is our top priority." He handed her a slip of paper. "Here's the information about the outfitter."

"Thank you." But his words made her stomach sour. Is that what she sounded like to others?

"Do you think you could enjoy living in a town like this, Ellie?" Father's voice was low and warm.

She blinked several times, still pondering Mr. Grinnell's careless words. "I'm not sure I understand. For a few weeks? Months?"

His eyebrows shot up with his smile. "Permanently."

Permanently? In Kalispell? That was a large jump from what he said to her on the train just a few days ago. She grappled for a response.

"I am wearying of all the travel, and you know I hope to write a book one day."

She thought it through. What if they *were* to settle . . . to give up their nomadic existence and stay in one place? "I don't know a lot about Kalispell yet, but it seems like a wonderful place to live. I love the mountains. And Flathead Lake isn't far." The first time she'd seen the Rockies, she'd talked about them for days, until her parents finally asked her to stop. There was just something about the mountains and water that . . . nourished her soul.

"We can talk about it later, I just thought I'd ask while we were alone." Her father stood. "Oh, my dear, would you drop my watch off at a repair shop?"

"Of course, Father, I already had it on the list. I just need the watch."

He left, and Eleanor lifted her chin. It seemed she had some errands to run. Might as well make the most of it.

After fetching her hat and gloves and Father's watch, she asked for her bicycle to be brought around. Bart, the stable-boy appeared moments later with the bike at his side. He seemed enthralled by it.

"Thank you." She took the bicycle in hand and grinned at him. "Have you ever ridden?"

The boy shook his head. "It looks too complicated."

"It's just a matter of balance really. Oh, and keeping the pedals going. If you don't do both at the same time, you will fall over."

"Wow. Have you ever fallen over?"

She grinned. "Several times in the past. Especially as I was learning. But that's all right. You just get back up and start again."

His eyes were wide as he watched her hop on the bicycle. She gave him a little wave and pedaled down the street.

The ride to town was brisk, with the crisp mountain air in her face. Eleanor dropped off the watch at the repair shop and then made her way to the outfitter Grinnell had recommended. She had to ask for help locating it, but recognized some of the places she'd passed the day before and felt that perhaps she would soon have her bearings. And then, all at once, she had arrived. *Johnson's Outfitters*, the sign announced.

Seeing no good place to leave her bicycle, she leaned it against the front of the brick building and made her way inside. Immediately she had the attention of the clerk.

A middle-aged man with a balding head and bushy mustache offered her a slight bow. "May I help you? We carry all of the most up-to-date supplies for outdoor needs."

"I would like to see what you have available in tents."

"Of course. Come right this way." He turned and headed toward the back of the store.

Eleanor followed him. Canteens, wool blankets, hatchets, and a large display of new duck canvas shoulder packs caught her eye.

"These are our very best tents." The clerk came to a stop in front of rolled and bagged tents. He released the drawstring on one end of a tan-colored bag and slid the tent out. "The canvas is waxed to keep out moisture and although you can't see it, the wooden tent poles fit into each other with a clamping mechanism to tighten it down and hold it in place. It keeps the tent steady and secure. And instead of just six stakes, this tent has eight. Makes for a very comfortable stay. I've used one like it several times myself."

She examined the cloth. It did seem to be a quality piece. "Is it large enough for two or even three people?"

"Oh, yes. This is the deluxe model. If you need something smaller or bigger, we have those as well."

He showed her a couple of other styles and talked about

their benefits and failings, then left her to go and help another customer.

"The best tent is the one he showed you first . . . if you have the money to spare."

Eleanor whirled around to find a man a little taller than she was.

A bit grubby in appearance, he gave a shrug. "I've led a few folks out into the wilderness and have tried a few tents in my time."

Did all strange men out here feel free to speak to women they didn't even know? How disconcerting. Still, no need to be impolite. "Thank you. I appreciate your . . . advice. We've done a great deal of camping ourselves, all across the United States."

She turned back to the selection, hoping the man would get the hint that she wasn't interested in having him help her.

"The name is Grant Wallace." He moved to her side.

Eleanor glanced his way again. He seemed harmless enough. But she would keep her guard up, just in case. "I'm Miss Briggs."

"What brings you to Kalispell, if you don't mind my asking?"

She frowned. She did mind, but she'd promised herself to do better. Mother had always stressed it took very little to be kind. "My father is here with Mr. George Grinnell. Perhaps you've heard of him? He is working to see that a national park is developed not far from here."

The man frowned. "I've heard of that, but not the man."

Something in his expression drew her attention. "You don't seem very happy about it."

"I don't see the need for it one way or the other." He

crossed his arms over his chest. "Especially if that has something to do with the railroad pulling out."

Grinnell's words from earlier whispered in her mind about the railroad's move being to their benefit. She ignored the little warning bells in her mind, her passion for the subject coming to the forefront. "But you should. Preserving our lands is most important. If we stand by and do nothing, it won't be long at all until all the illustrious landscapes are overrun with settlers and those who will do nothing to maintain the beauty. You should see things back east. Many a picturesque area has been overpopulated and destroyed."

He shrugged but the lines in his forehead deepened. "I suppose you could have a point, but I know Mr. Hill of the railroad supports a national park, and I can't be for anything that man wants."

Well . . . how odd. "And why is that?"

"He's hurting a lot of folks around here by moving the main line. I work for him, and it ain't right that one man should have so much power as to leave hundreds of men out of work just because he doesn't like the route he made. Says it's too dangerous and steep and demands it be altered."

"Safety should be an important issue to everyone." Why was the man so set against a less dangerous set of tracks?

"Safety is important, but so is keeping a town alive. A lot of people are going to lose their jobs, me included."

Oh. That explained his reaction to her mention of the railway. "I am sorry for that, but maybe if you worked to support a national park you could get a job there. You appear to know something of the outdoors."

For a moment, she thought he was considering the idea. But then he shook his head. "I've worked for the railroad for a long time. It's what I know. What I'm trained to do. You can't go around telling people to get a different job just because it suits your opinion."

"Perhaps if you considered mankind's greater good and how preserving the scenery could benefit and bless them, you might find that a national park job would suit you better." Oh dear. Once again, she'd allowed her opinionated self to spout off. She peered over his shoulder for the exit, willing to abandon the purchase of a new tent for now if she could simply walk away.

"Mankind has never considered *my* greater good." His laugh was rough. "I'm not sure I care to worry about their greater good."

Another man ambled up to stand alongside Grant, his demeanor less than congenial.

She really should be on her way . . .

The first man nodded to the second. "This is my brother, Alvin. He cares even less than I do about the greater good of mankind. We do well to see to our own good. We'd be just as happy if the rest of the folks in this country just stayed where they are and left Montana alone."

The darkness in the brother's eyes sent a chill up her spine. What had she gotten herself into? She had nothing to say in response, but it didn't matter. The men turned and walked away.

Releasing her breath, she put a hand to her chest and her limbs relaxed. Goodness, when had she grown so tense?

It was impossible to understand these Montanans. Owning thousands of acres of land. Mad at the railroad for wanting a safer route. Surrounded by all this incredible beauty and not willing to do what needed to be done to preserve it.

She turned back to the tents just as the clerk returned. She pointed to the tent in front of her. "I believe I'll take this one."

Perhaps staying in Kalispell wasn't the best idea after all.

7

WEDNESDAY, MAY 18, 1904

The exact arrival of Mr. Louis W. Hill had been kept a secret.

Mainly because after the town meeting turned into an outdoor brawl, the railroad didn't want to risk any danger to the owner's son. Eleanor and her father had been sworn to secrecy so that the railroad tycoon could arrive at the Ashburys' without event. She didn't mind. The poor man would probably be bombarded the whole time he was here.

Putting a hand to her stomach, Eleanor took several breaths. She'd barely had time to change from the split skirt she wore to ride her bike into her lavender gown. There'd been no time for a bath, so she felt rather unkempt. And now she had to meet this new man, whom Father had been anxious to meet.

The Judge stood in the front parlor with his hands in his vest pockets. The man portrayed wisdom and confidence and yet quiet humility all at the same time. How did he do it? She'd only known him a few short days, and already she respected him far more than any other man she'd met. "The peace and quiet of our little town will be interrupted for a bit. Let's pray for calm heads to prevail."

"Excellent suggestion, my dear." Marvella shifted on the settee. "I can't say I'm in agreement with the railroad on this matter."

Mr. Grinnell grunted from the window.

What a rude thing to do!

Marvella, of course, was the picture of courtesy and ignored the man.

Time to redirect the conversation. For all their sakes. Eleanor inclined her head to Marvella. "Do you know Mr. Louis Hill, Mrs. Ashbury?"

Her smile was broad. "No, but the senior Mr. Hill is a dear friend. He and his wife have been our guests on many other occasions. They love to travel."

"They own the railroad so I would expect as much." Father smiled. "I'm looking forward to meeting their son."

At that moment, Eleanor heard the front door open and Tobias's low, calm voice. Their guest must have arrived. A hush fell over the room and Eleanor held her breath. What would he be like?

After the butler announced Louis Hill to the room, Father stepped forward. "Stewart Briggs, at your service. I'm pleased to meet you, Mr. Hill. I've heard a great deal about you and your father."

"And I've heard a lot about you." Goodness, such a gracious man. "George has kept me apprised as to your work and support of our dream of another national park in Montana. Although in fairness Yellowstone mostly resides in Wyoming."

"It is amazing how vastly different the two places are." Father moved back to his seat. "My daughter, Eleanor, and I spent an entire summer in Yellowstone a few years back. There are a great many differences and that will entice people to want to conserve this area as well."

"Yes, these American Alps, as I like to call them, are worthy of being set aside, especially for their glaciers. Certainly as worthy as last year's addition in South Dakota."

He must be referencing Wind Cave National Park. Eleanor loved that area.

She opened her mouth to reply, but Mr. Hill continued.

"Of course, they've done nothing with it to actually establish viewing, but the area is at least set aside."

Mr. Grinnell stepped closer, apparently not wishing to be left out of the conversation.

As he put in his two cents about South Dakota, Eleanor licked her lips and shared a look with Marvella, who picked up a scone and took a bite. It seemed neither of them was needed for this introduction to the important Mr. Hill, after all. Marvella didn't seem to mind, but had Eleanor known she wouldn't be needed, she'd rather have taken that bath.

Hill clasped his hands behind his back. "Mark my words, it will be years before they are able to set up a proper way to explore the area, while our glacial lands beg for visitors and will have a proper railroad running through it."

Eleanor picked up her own scone and nibbled at it. Judge Ashbury came and sat down beside his wife. He hadn't said a word, but it was clear he'd been listening to everything the men had to say on the matter.

She'd love to ask him his thoughts, but the men rambled

on about how the nation's citizens needed to see these national lands. Then Hill's dominant voice took over again.

"President Roosevelt should have little problem motivating Congress to set this land aside. It's already perfectly arranged. With the exception of a few changes and additions. I have great plans for concessions and hotels throughout the park. We'll talk about it tomorrow, of course. When I can show you the plans I've had drawn up."

Eleanor almost choked on her scone. She lifted a cup of tea to her lips and prayed the bite would go down. *What* had the man just said? Concessions and hotels?

Didn't that defeat the purpose?

Swallowing her tea, she lowered her face to study the carpet lest the others see her frown. What good was setting aside the land so that it remained in a natural state if a person was only going to turn around and build a lot of hotels? And something so intrusive as concessions?

The more she thought about it, the more she fumed. All these years . . . all this time spent on conservation. Every statement she'd made on the subject, every debate she'd had with people who dissented so that they could understand. And then it all came down to this? What were they even fighting for?

She eyed her father, but he was smiling. How could *he* be all right with this?

"The benefit of a national park here in this great state is two-fold, Mrs. Ashbury." Mr. Hill's voice invaded Eleanor's thoughts. "I am as passionate as Mr. Grinnell and Mr. Briggs in seeing our great country preserved." He flashed the group a smile. "But funds and investors are needed. Congress likes to see that these national parks have support to help them continue. While Father has no use for a national park personally, he was pleased to hear that it would be possible for the southern boundary of the park not to cross his plans for future tracks. And that it will obviously drive up the number of passengers."

The unsettled feelings that had plagued her now made her world feel completely upside down. If money and profits were the direction they were headed, she didn't know what to believe anymore. Didn't know what to feel. Didn't know what to stand for.

Nothing made sense.

Without a word, she fled the room and ran up the stairs to her chambers.

If only she could go back to simpler times, when her mother was still alive and could guide her through this mess.

But no. She couldn't do that. Because God had taken her away.

She had no one to turn to.

No one.

❧

Carter leaned on the railing of his porch and listened to the sweet sounds of Kalispell.

This place had been his home for twenty years. It was hard to imagine that it could soon dwindle and die . . .

Perhaps he was getting ahead of himself. They were only at the beginning of this journey. He doubted any of the other businesses in town wanted to pack up, leave, and start over.

Besides, he'd come here with his family long before there was an actual town. They survived then. They would survive now.

*God, just don't let me get too big for my britches. It's impor-
tant that we listen to one another and help each other through
this new trial. I pray that You will guide me and all the leaders
in this town.*

He gulped the last of his coffee and watched the kids
across the street playing tag.

A longing for a family of his own rose up within him as
their joyful laughter filled the air. What would it be like to
have a family? To teach his own children about the land
and God's creation?

A bit of sadness rolled over him and he shook it away.
The Lord hadn't provided an open door in this area yet.
Mark's words came back to him and made him laugh. Yeah,
he had been kind of waiting for God to just plop the right
woman in his lap. Which was ridiculous. It was probably
time to take action. Pray about it. Ask the Lord to guide
him and then get up off his duff and do something about it.

So rather than wallowing, he should get out there and
play with those kids.

Carter set his cup down and jogged across the street.
"Need an extra player?"

"Sure, Mr. Brunswick!"

"Be on my team!"

"Come play with us!"

He laughed at their exuberant welcome. "I'd love to play,
as long as you call me Carter."

"Mama won't let us do that." The littlest of the group
chimed in. Her hands were clasped in front of her. "You're
an adult so you hafta be a mister."

"All right. How about Mr. Carter, then? Will that work?"
Each kid nodded.

"Good. Okay, so let me guess . . . I'm it?"

Squeals of delight filled the air as he chased the kids. In the slowest motion he could. Which only made them giggle more.

After half an hour of tag, he was plumb worn out. Leaning over his knees, he worked to catch his breath. But the kids just kept on running.

A sweet little girl stood next to him. He smiled at her. "Where'd you get all this energy?"

She shrugged. "I dunno. But Mama said we had to get it all out before we came inside."

Carter chuckled. "Yeah, I can imagine she did."

"Look!" Little Charlie waved his hands. "It's the new lady on her bicycle."

All the children stopped and watched as Ellie headed down the street toward them.

Carter had never been on a bicycle before and wasn't sure he would ever want to try it. But she handled it with ease. Seemed pretty good at it, too.

Honk! A horseless carriage careened around a corner right into Ellie's path. *Honk! Honk!*

She rang her bike bell several times, but the car continued on its path. Straight for her. Ringing the bell some more, she swerved and barely missed the car, but the tilt was a bit too much for her and she flew into Mrs. Sidler's bushes. "Ah!" Her strangled cry was muted by the thick foliage.

Carter raced down the street and pulled back the shrubbery in which she was ensconced. "Miss Briggs! Miss Briggs?"

Moaning was her response.

"Miss Briggs . . . are you all right?"

The horseless carriage disappeared down the road. What on earth? Who *was* that?

An arm poked out of the greenery. "Help, please."

He tugged on it, but she was stuck on something. "Is perhaps a piece of your clothing attached in there somewhere?" He couldn't see through the thick branches, but her stockinged feet stuck out by his legs.

A few unladylike grunts and groans escaped the shrub. "I'm in need of your assistance, Carter Brunswick." The voice was a bit more agitated this time. She stuck her hand out again. "Just pull as hard as you can."

"You got it." He grabbed onto her arm with both hands and tugged.

It took a couple of hard yanks, but she came loose, and he flew back onto his backside with the momentum.

"Oomph." Miss Briggs fell in a great heap down at his feet, covered in pieces of Mrs. Sidler's bush. Ellie pushed her hair, which was in disarray, away from her face and stared at him. Then she burst into laughter. "Thank . . . you."

"You're welcome." He attempted to stand, and pain in his backside made him go down on one knee. "Ow!" He rubbed the offending part of his body and grimaced.

She covered her mouth, but her laughter only increased. He joined in, and pretty soon, they were laughing so hard, tears streaked down both of their cheeks.

Carter finally calmed and took a deep breath. He found purchase with his feet and kept a hand on his backside. His tailbone was gonna be sore for a while. "You sure you're all right?" He helped her to stand.

"Oh, other than some scratches and a million pieces of shrubbery attached to me, I believe I'm just fine." She began to pick each piece off one at a time. "Thank you for your assistance. That car came out of nowhere! Heavens, I'm used to seeing them in Chicago and the other big cities, but I wasn't expecting to see one out here in the wilds of Montana. Especially not aimed right for me! They must not understand how to steer yet."

"You handled yourself just right. If you hadn't swerved when you did, you'd probably be badly injured." Who could have been driving one of those contraptions here? Perhaps Ellie was correct, and it was someone learning how to drive. Carter hadn't taken time to really see who'd been driving. His focus had been on Ellie.

The neighbor children surrounded them.

Eleanor stiffened and blinked several times. "Well, hello there."

The kids stared. Then the oldest piped up, "Is your bicycle all right?"

"My bike!" She jumped and looked around for it.

But two of the children had already pulled it out of its shrubbery cocoon.

She put a hand to her chest. "It appears to be in working order." Crouching down, she examined the pedals and wheels. "But I do seem to have a flat tire." She put her hands on her hips. "Bother."

"Anna! James! Caroline! Michael! Charlie!" The children's mother called from her doorway. "It's time to come inside."

"Gotta run, Mr. Carter. Thanks for playing tag with us." Anna squeezed his hand and then ran off with her siblings.

Ellie peered around him as she watched the kids. "I guess it's a good thing you were out here playing tag. I might not have been able to extricate myself from that bush without you." When she glanced at him, her blue eyes shimmered with the remnants of her laughter. "Thank you, again. I truly needed the laughter. It's been a trying afternoon."

"You're welcome." He cleared his throat. Funny. It seemed she was opening up to him, and he had no idea how to respond. "Why don't you allow me to walk you back to the Ashburys' since your tire will need fixing."

She looked around. "I appreciate it. Especially since it is getting a bit later."

Carter took charge of the bicycle and wheeled it between the two of them. Neither one of them said anything and the awkward silence grew.

They'd walked two whole blocks before he couldn't stand it anymore. "I didn't think you were the silent type."

"Pardon me?" She turned her face toward him. Little pieces of shrub still stuck out from her hair .

"You just always seem to know what to say." There. Maybe that was nicer. But it was hard to concentrate on being nice when every step made him wince. Could a man break his tailbone? Or had he done some other sort of damage?

"You know, Mr. Brunswick—"

"Carter."

"Fine. Carter." She huffed. "I realized that I was partly responsible for us getting off on the wrong foot. I apologize. I apologized to Gus as well. Neither one of you deserved my irritation. It was rude of me."

His eyebrows shot up higher than he knew they could reach. "That's awfully kind of you to apologize, Ellie—"

"Eleanor."

"Fine . . ." At least for now. "*Eleanor.* I believe I owe you an apology as well. It wasn't right for me to take my frustration out on *you*. I wasn't exactly planning on getting sucker punched that day."

She stopped and turned toward him. Then she stuck out her hand. "I forgive you."

He took her hand and shook it.

She narrowed her eyes. "What is that wry grin for, Mr.—er, I mean Carter?"

"I told you, one day you just might like me."

The most unladylike groan he'd ever heard accompanied her swat to his arm. "You, sir, are incorrigible."

"I will take that as a compliment."

"You would." But she laughed and he laughed with her.

For the first time, he glimpsed behind the facade and great walls that had surrounded Miss Eleanor Briggs. He'd thought she was a snobby little thing, albeit attractive and feisty. But now? There was a different side to her. Something deeper.

They walked several paces before he dared to dive in. "You said it had been a trying afternoon. I've been told I'm a good listener, and we've got a good walk in front of us . . ." He let the invitation hang in the air, hopeful she'd respond without snapping at him.

She clasped her hands in front of her and took in a loud, long breath. "I'm examining my life."

He kept his features neutral. But who said things like that? He blinked several times and tried to figure out how to respond.

"I see I've perplexed you." A smile tipped up the edges of her lips. "Do you not ever sit and ponder your very existence?"

He stopped walking for a moment and stared into her eyes. Her candor was refreshing, though a bit surprising. On the other hand, he *had* asked. And she deserved an equally honest response. "I do. Every time I watch the sunrise or the sunset. When the winter wheat first sprouts up out of the ground, all green and lush, then snow covers it. It goes for months in dormancy and then it continues on again in the spring. Or when I sit in awe of the mountains, Flathead Lake, or see a baby for the first time. I thank God for these miracles and can't fathom His love for little ol' me."

The longer he talked, the farther her face dipped into a frown.

What had he said to displease her?

"You really believe that, don't you?" Her face was so hard, like flint.

"I do." What on earth had caused the hurt that swelled in her eyes?

"Good for you." She yanked the bicycle from his grasp. "Thank you for your help, Mr. Brunswick. I'll take it from here." With rapid steps, she marched away, the weight of the world seeming to lay on her shoulders.

Carter's jaw dropped.

He'd seen the full gamut of emotions in Ellie in the short span of half an hour. His heart ached for the pain he'd seen in her eyes. There was so much more to her than he'd ever imagined. Now, more than ever, he wanted to spend time with her. Get to know her.

But his gut held him in check.

Eleanor Briggs was clearly wrestling with God. Carter wasn't about to get in the middle of *that* battle.

Still, the one thing he *could* do was get down on his knees and pray.

⟞⟝

Marvella took her time ascending the stairs before she headed to Eleanor's room. After watching the girl storm out of the parlor earlier, then race out not half an hour later to ride her bike, *then* return covered in foliage with a tear-streaked face and looking madder than a hornet, Marvella knew it was time she took matters in hand.

She rapped on the door.

"I don't need anything, thank you." The forced cheer was clear even through the door.

Marvella knocked again.

"I don't wish to be disturbed. Thank you." The tone was a bit more clipped this time.

Third time was always the charm. She persisted once more and leaned her ear against the door. While the thick wood kept her from deciphering anything, she did hear what sounded like huffs and a good deal of grumbling.

Perfect.

The door whipped open, and Eleanor stood there, mouth wide, about to speak her mind. But as soon as she spotted Marvella, her lips clamped shut. Her shoulders relaxed a bit. "My apologies, Mrs. Ashbury. I thought you were one of the staff."

"Not a problem, Eleanor. And please, call me Marvella."

"Yes, ma'am." She held tight to the doorknob.

"I do believe it's time we had a chat." Marvella wriggled her way around the girl and walked into the room. "Woman to woman."

Eleanor closed the door behind her. "What is it you'd like to chat about?"

She took a seat in one of the chairs positioned in front of the fireplace. It was really a cozy room. Marvella smiled. Oh, how she'd loved decorating each room in their beautiful home. She patted the chair next to her. "Come sit."

"All right." But the rigid set to her shoulders was back.

"Why don't you start with what put you in such a snit this afternoon after Mr. Hill arrived."

Eleanor gasped and sputtered. "I . . . I . . ." She cleared her throat. "I wasn't in a snit."

Marvella leaned back in the chair and crossed her hands under her bosom. "There's no need to get defensive. I've been known to be in a snit myself . . . from time to time. You should ask Milton." She put her fingers to her lips as she laughed. "But, dear, it isn't good to bottle up all your feelings inside. The storm clouds have been chasing themselves across your face ever since you arrived."

Eleanor wilted and blinked several times.

"Now, now. No need for tears. Unless you really need to let them loose, then I won't stand in your way. But I'm here for you. Just as I've been for countless other young women over the years." Marvella gripped the girl's hand and squeezed.

And then the floodgates opened. Tears fell from Eleanor's big, blue eyes, dampening her cheeks. She gripped Marvella's hand like it was a lifeline.

"I don't know what's wrong," the young woman sniffled. "Everything seems to agitate me. Even those who are trying to help me."

Marvella nodded, pressing a soft handkerchief into Eleanor's lap. "I know it's hard to believe since we've only known each other a short while, but Milton and I care about you, and your father."

Eleanor let go of Marvella's hand and pressed the white square to her face. "I can see it. But I can't understand why. I've not been pleasant. For heaven's sake, both my father and I argued with you and your husband about Father's work." She shook her head, her blond hair shining in the afternoon light.

"Oh tosh." Marvella laughed. "That was not an argument, dear. Just a good, old-fashioned exchange of ideas. Conversations like that help us grow and think about things differently."

"That's just it." The words burst out of her guest, seeming to catapult her from her chair. She began pacing her room. "After that conversation, and the one this afternoon with Mr. Hill, I don't know what to think anymore. For years I've believed what Father said. What he's taught about conserving the land. But now I can't stop thinking about farmers and ranchers and food." She let out a huff. "And all this God talk. You, that Carter Brunswick, the Judge . . ."

Marvella studied Eleanor Briggs for a moment. Her heart broke, seeing the consternation and fear so plain on the young woman's beautiful features. But in her experience, not many entered the kingdom of God without a fight. And that's exactly what Eleanor was doing. Fighting God. "I know it's not easy figuring out what you believe." She folded her hands in her lap and arched her eyebrows. "But it's worth it in the end, especially when you come to Jesus, finally seeing that He was the one drawing you close the whole time." She stood and crossed the room to Eleanor and slipped an arm around her waist.

Eleanor didn't stiffen at the contact, but she refused to meet her gaze. "You sound like my mother."

Marvella smiled. "She must be a fine woman."

Grief flashed across Eleanor's features. "She was."

Ah.

Marvella squeezed her tighter. "Go on."

Eleanor shook her head, sobs choking her throat. Then the tears came in earnest, a wild tempest of sorrow. Marvella kept her thoughts to herself, not wanting to push her young friend too hard. Grief wasn't something that was easily dealt with. Marvella knew that all too well from her own mother's passing years ago.

Finally, Eleanor pulled away and wiped her face again. "I am sorry," she whispered.

"No apologies needed, my dear. Sometimes a good cry sorts out a multitude of issues."

"Not this time, I'm afraid."

Marvella tipped her head. "What is it?"

"I just . . . I wish I understood why my mother had to die. Why didn't God hear my prayers to keep her alive?" Her eyebrows dipped, and her jaw tightened. "I don't understand why God hates me."

Well, that was unexpected. Marvella sent up a prayer, asking for wisdom, when she was interrupted by Eleanor.

"I'm sorry. I'm usually not this emotional." She stepped back, threading the soggy handkerchief through her fingers. "Please disregard what I just said."

As if she could forget it! Marvella shook her head. The Lord had sent her a hurting young woman who needed His love and truth. "Thinking God hates you isn't something that is easily forgettable, Miss Eleanor. But"—she tapped her foot—"I can see right now you don't want to discuss it."

Relief visibly swept over Eleanor. "Thank you."

Marvella arched both of her eyebrows. "However, don't you think you've gotten out of another discussion about this. At some point, you are going to have to patch things up with God, my dear. And we will most assuredly be having *that* conversation soon." Marvella gave Eleanor a firm hug. "And I'll be looking forward to it. Now, ready yourself for dinner. I'll see you in an hour or so."

Marvella swept from the room and shut the door with a firm click. Eleanor's confession still ringing in her head, she made her way to her room and sat down in an overstuffed chair. For a moment, she clasped her hands together and prayed for the Briggs family. Then she plucked the Bible off the side table, searching for verses about God's love.

The next time Eleanor Briggs said God hated her, Marvella would be ready to show her just how wrong she was.

THURSDAY, MAY 19, 1904

Even after using cool washcloths over her eyes for more than an hour this morning, Eleanor still had puffy eyes. But Father insisted she attend another discussion in the library about the national parks. Not that she'd said one word last time.

It had been nice to get everything off her chest last night with Marvella. The woman was an incredible sounding board. And while she had strong opinions about Eleanor's need to "patch things up with God," she'd been relatively quiet and even offered her shoulder when the tears were the worst. In fact, she hadn't given a lick of advice then, which shocked Eleanor. But told her they would talk some more later.

Of that, Eleanor had no doubt. Once the woman set her mind to fixing something, she usually did it.

With a deep sigh, she entered the library.

Mr. Hill was talking. He seemed particularly excited about his ideas for accommodations.

"I told George that I would like to see all the park buildings done in chalet fashion, including the depot. I believe it will accentuate the setting in a most beneficial way and remind visitors of the Swiss Alps."

"That does sound fitting." Mrs. Ashbury came to Eleanor's side, cuddling her little dog. "Don't you think, Eleanor?"

Since she'd been so deftly invited into the conversation, she offered her opinion. "I believe we should blend into the scenery as best we can, with as few buildings or alterations to nature as possible."

"Of course, my dear. We are all in agreement there." Her father looked from her to Mr. Hill. "My daughter is devoted to securing as many national parks as we can in our lifetime."

Why would Father say that? She'd never said or implied that was her goal. Was he trying to impress the railroad man or Grinnell? She cleared her throat. "I would like to see more land made public and left untouched, but that would include *not* building hotels and concessions to further damage the area."

"Wealthy folks aren't going to always be willing to spend

their time traveling and living in tents." Mr. Hill's expression showed a kind of bored amusement. "At least not for long. It can be a great novelty and attraction for many, and those types of guided tours will be offered. We would hire men familiar with the area to take guests into the wilderness, away from the comforts of hotels and dining rooms. My wife and I enjoyed a trip like that in Yellowstone. We lived in a tent for a week and ate around campfires. It was an experience, to say the least."

The men chuckled, then Grinnell stood and paced. "This is exactly what we need—for Americans to *experience* our national parks. There are a great many dangers to be sure, but that is why we need to carefully plan the routes and pathways. We can post rangers to watch over the camping areas, where the guests can go to enjoy getting away from the routines of life. And we can have luxury lodges for those who would rather enjoy the beauty in comfort."

"I have already designed two depots, both with defined Alpine features." Mr. Hill's excitement grew as he talked. "I believe visitors will be completely enthralled. We will have lodges as well as cabins to accommodate everyone. We will offer indoor plumbing and electricity as well."

"More development and destruction on the land." Eleanor bit her lip while the Judge made some comment that thankfully left her outburst unheard.

Then the room went silent.

Whatever Judge Ashbury said had the men's attention.

He paced in front of Mr. Hill. "The problem of the railroad is uppermost on the minds of folks here in Kalispell." He sighed. "I appreciate that you've taken time to come and speak to them personally, but I fear you haven't come to hear them out."

Mr. Hill shook his head. "It can't be helped. There are too many problems with the current line. The grades can't be reduced, and the dangerous twists and turns have caused derailments. Loss of product and life is unacceptable, and my father is adamant that the problem be resolved."

The Judge's chin lifted. He did not look pleased. "Well, I must give my attention to other matters, gentlemen." He left the room, but the men continued to talk.

Marvella stood. "I need to tend my roses. Would you like to accompany me, Eleanor?"

As much as she wanted to say yes to Marvella and escape the tension of the room, she couldn't. "I promised to take notes for Father."

"All right, dear." Their hostess left as well.

"I thought perhaps you two could write up pamphlets that we could sell to the tourists who come and want to explore on the hiking trails and walkways. Perhaps create some type of reference to the plants and trees, as well as the wildlife." Hill had unrolled some sort of plans that all the men hovered over.

"Walkways?" Eleanor couldn't believe her ears. "What kind of walkways?"

"Wooden. Probably about four feet wide—enough to allow two people to pass each other on the trail without needing to step off and damage the tundra." Mr. Hill didn't seem to appreciate her question.

She didn't care. "Won't the walkways do a fair bit of damage?"

"There will be initial damage, of course, but we will do

what we can to minimize it." The man spoke to her as if she were a child in need of calming down.

Which only served to incense her more. She glanced at her father, who frowned. Whether it was because of her questions or the idea of walkways, she wasn't certain.

Grinnell studied the prints. "I could see these walkways making it easier for less-active people to enjoy the scenery."

Hill unrolled another set of prints. "Further in the mountains, however, there will be natural paths to hike. We can plan those out when the time comes."

"If they're planned out, they'll hardly be natural." The words were out before she could think. All gazes swiveled to her.

Hill glared at her and then continued. "The lake is just over here, and I figure we can put in a boathouse and a fishing outfitter."

"And is this a roadway?" Father asked. Why did he sound . . . supportive?

"It will be one day. I foresee making great roads into the depths of the park so that a person could tour to the north and south of the rail line. We wouldn't need to put the roads completely through from one end to the other. After all, that's what the railroad is for. There's money to be made here, my friends, and a glorious national park to share with the world."

Eleanor could stand it no longer. "It sounds like an awful lot of changes for the delicate balance of nature this area supports. You want hotels and concessions, boathouses, and walkways. And roads. This isn't leaving the area in a natural state at all."

Hill straightened and looked at her. "Miss Briggs, with

each national park we've seen the addition of accommodations. It's necessary to allow the visitors some comforts. You can't expect a person to come from hundreds of miles away and not eat or rest. There also needs to be ways for the park to be self-sustaining. Toll roads are necessary and perhaps one day even park entry fees."

That wasn't how it was supposed to happen. "But that isn't making it free for the public. People should be able to visit at no cost. I thought that was at the very heart of creating a national park and setting aside public lands."

"For Congress to be willing to set these places aside, they need to be self-sustaining." Grinnell's look to her was almost scolding.

Why was she all of a sudden the bad guy? She was only speaking of the very things this man and her own father had taught her.

Hill crossed his arms over his chest and stepped toward her. "To convince people that a trip to a national park is worth the trouble, one must provide certain amenities. And of course, those amenities can't come for free."

"Of course not. It's a great moneymaking opportunity." Eleanor didn't even try to hide her disdain. This man was impossible.

"Ellie, perhaps you could leave us to discuss the particulars for now."

She started and looked at her father. He was dismissing her?

"We won't be needing you to take notes until perhaps this afternoon."

So. She'd gone too far and this was her punishment. Getting to her feet, she smiled. "Of course. Mrs. Ashbury wanted to show me her roses, and this would be the perfect time. Good morning, gentlemen."

It was hard to hold her tongue. Hard not to tear up. How could her own father betray her so?

This trip had changed him. First the talk of settling down and now this conversation about making money through the national park lands. It wasn't like him at all.

Eleanor made her way outside and wandered around until she heard Mrs. Ashbury chattering about new bushes that should be arriving any day and where she intended them to be planted. The woman had endless energy as she moved back and forth amidst her budding bushes.

Sir Theophilus came running and yipping. He jumped up and seemed so eager to be in her presence that she picked him up. He immediately licked her face.

"Well, at least someone is glad to have me around." Her mumbled words earned her another lick.

"You are a welcome sight for my poor little dog. I'm much too busy to pamper him while tending to my roses." Mrs. Ashbury stepped over to her. "I'm so glad you could be spared from the discussion inside. I'm sure those men can be preoccupied with their plans. And just look. For mid-May, it is unseasonably warm. It will do wonders for my roses."

Eleanor didn't feel much like touring a garden, but she did her best to pretend pleasure.

Marvella showed her bush after bush, explaining the names and colors of each. Then without so much as a pause she straightened and looked Eleanor in the eye. "I want to know you better, Miss Eleanor Briggs."

Eleanor hesitated.

"Come now. After baring your soul last night, there's no need to be shy. I know you're a very well-educated young woman. Did you have a garden when you were growing up?"

Oh good. A neutral topic. "My mother kept flowers and herbs." The memory warmed her heart. "She showed me how to care for the plants as well, but I lost all interest after she died when I was fourteen."

"Such a young age to lose one's mother. I was in my late thirties when mine passed away and that was still too young. But we are only a vapor, after all." She barely paused to take a breath. "So you took up your father's interests in conservation after she was gone." Mrs. Ashbury stated this more than questioned it.

"Yes. I went to college and studied what I could that might aid him in his work. I learned to type and take a style of shorthand so that I could assist him with his notes and records. We've traveled, and he's spoken on so many occasions that I've lost track of the number of events."

"And you enjoy this life?"

"To a degree. I worry about Father, however. I know he's tiring and has started to talk of settling down." Why on earth had she shared that? Something about Marvella seemed to provoke confidences.

"Yes, as we grow older, we tend to want to plant roots and feel a sense of belonging. You could be happy settling here, my dear. You should suggest that to him. Despite what is happening with the railroad, Kalispell will survive. I've no doubt. We ladies have met and discussed it. We have no intention of seeing this town fall to ruin. We just got a new library, after all. We have banded together, and we will do whatever is necessary to see that our town thrives."

"And how will you do that?"

Marvella gave her a conspiratorial smile. "Well, God hasn't exactly told me yet, but He will."

8

Marvella stretched out on the fainting couch with a box of bonbons and Sir Theophilus in her lap. Eleanor Briggs was a challenge. Not only did the poor thing seem to have been in the company of men much too often since her mother died, but she also was cold toward God.

And that simply wouldn't do.

Perhaps Marvella could introduce her to Rebecca Whitman—now Andrews. The two would probably hit it off. Especially since they were both from big cities.

She bit into another bonbon and chewed, her thoughts swirling. The Lord was so good to bring another young woman across her path. Rebecca had been a challenge, as well. Brilliant and determined to be her own woman. The day she'd come to the Lord lived fondly in Marvella's memories. What a wonderful day that had been.

But Eleanor. Marvella sighed. Eleanor was the very definition of a lost sheep who'd wandered away.

Not that she pitied the young woman. Heavens, no. That girl didn't need pity. She needed the guidance and love of a mentor. Someone to draw her back into the fold. Eleanor would benefit immensely from having people around her to help her grow into who God had created her to be. Rebecca might also be able to help her guide the lost conservationist's daughter back to the Lord. The idea took deeper root. Yes. The new Mrs. Andrews might be key to the next step in her plan to help the young Miss Briggs.

Marvella popped the other half of her bonbon in her mouth. She wiped her fingers on the linen serviette on her lap and put the box of sweets on the table beside her, a smile playing on her lips.

Whatever the case may be, Marvella had found her new protégé.

TUESDAY, MAY 24, 1904

It turned out Mr. Louis Hill's arrival in Kalispell was the worst-kept secret since his family's plan for the railroad leaked. Carter didn't know who had let the railroad baron's arrival slip, but it was all over town mere hours after his arrival. Tensions among the townspeople had been simmering for weeks. But now they were like a kettle about to whistle—hot and full of steam.

To make matters worse, young Mr. Hill had contracted a summer cold. Any meeting with him had been out of the question until he was well.

Unable to voice their anger and frustration with the young man, people were starting to take their stress out on one another. Fights broke out at saloons in the middle of the day. Three days ago, Carter overheard two women bickering over a five-pound bag of sugar in the general store. Their voices rose to the point that the manager asked them to leave until they could behave in a decent manner.

Yesterday a group of railroad workers quit a half hour before their shift and marched to the Ashbury home, demanding a meeting with Mr. Hill. The Judge, calm and unyielding as ever, had dispersed the crowd with the promise that Mr. Hill would be well enough to attend a town meeting the following night at the McIntosh Opera House, seven o'clock sharp.

Word spread faster than a forest fire in summer.

Now hundreds of men and women poured into the opera house, waiting to hear what Mr. Hill had to say. But judging by the murmurs of the crowd and the number of frowns on faces, the townspeople seemed more than ready to give the railroad man a piece of their mind.

Lord, please, let everyone stay civil.

The opera house was at standing-room-only capacity. If a fight broke out, it would be mighty difficult to stay clear of it. Especially for those up on the second floor.

Carter and his father took front-row seats. It would be good to finally hear what Hill had to say. Dad had hoped to meet privately with the man, but so far Hill had not responded to any of his missives. Not that Carter was surprised. But he wouldn't burst his dad's optimistic bubble.

Judge Ashbury took to the stage, and to Carter's surprise, so did Ellie. She was accompanied by her father and Mr. Grinnell. Carter leaned over to his father and told him who they were.

"I've heard of Grinnell. You say the men are conservationists?"

"That's right."

Just then, Mr. Hill joined the others on the stage. They all took seats behind the podium.

The Judge stepped forward. "It is my pleasure this evening to introduce you to several important men. Mr. Louis Hill, as you know, is the son of James Hill, owner of the Great Northern Railway."

No one clapped. In fact, someone might well heckle or boo the man. But better sense prevailed, thank heaven.

"Our other guests are conservationist and naturalist George Grinnell and Stewart Briggs. Mr. Briggs's daughter, Eleanor, is accompanying her father on his work here. I'll let them explain later what they have been working on. For now, however, I will let Mr. Hill speak on the plans he has for the railroad."

Hill took the podium and looked out at the crowd. The bearded, mustached man wore glasses and looked like a younger version of Mr. Briggs. It was uncanny how similar the men were in appearance, only Briggs didn't wear spectacles.

Hill looked out over the people gathered there. "I am glad for the opportunity to address you this evening. I know that many of you have questions regarding the railroad's planned changes, and I hope that I can explain in a precise manner why these changes are necessary.

"First of all, most of you know how dangerous the line from Columbia Falls to Kalispell has become. The grade of the line itself is a serious matter. We hired a team of experts to explore ways to lessen the grade with perhaps more

TRACIE PETERSON and KIMBERLEY WOODHOUSE

tunneling or switchbacks, but in the long run, none of those were viable possibilities."

A low voice muttered behind Carter. "They'd have been viable enough if it meant the end of *his* livelihood."

Hill explained that rerouting the line through Whitefish would prevent further accidents and deaths, making the expense and labor more than worth the cost.

"I know that you are all concerned about losing jobs here, as well as the ability to transport your goods and people. It is something that I have given a great deal of consideration. I will concede that there wasn't an easy answer. We will, from time to time, schedule train service into Kalispell, although I cannot say how often that will be. Again, the dangers create a risk I'm simply not willing to take. Future discussions with engineers and those who can best judge the matter will take place. It is even possible that in time we will build a spur line down from Whitefish to Kalispell, and that will relieve you of your worries."

"*In time* won't help us now!"

Mr. Hill looked toward the man who'd shouted from the back of the room. "And I understand your concern."

"You *should* understand it. You're taking away over two hundred jobs," another man called out.

"Yes, but there are jobs to be had in Whitefish. Most of you can simply transfer up there."

"Our homes are here!" a woman countered.

Others started yelling their comments, and soon the entire room exploded in voices. Hill stepped aside as Judge Ashbury came to the podium and pounded on it with his fist. "*Order*, if you please. We must have order." Things began to quiet down, and the Judge continued. "Mr. Hill has graciously traveled here to speak with you tonight, and you will afford him the respect he deserves. We are not a band of banshees to be howling in such a disrespectful manner." This settled the room for the moment.

Hill finished his speech and surprised Carter by offering to take a few questions. The first man up was one of the local ranchers.

"Kalispell has a lot of farmers and ranchers. How are we supposed to ship our product without train service?"

Hill leaned forward, adopting the posture of a confidant. "You pose a good question and I have an answer. The gentlemen who have joined me on this stage are instrumental in seeing that much of the area to our north and east is set aside for a national park. I'm sure you've read about it in the newspaper.

"Yellowstone National Park has seen tens of thousands of visitors each year. The numbers continue to climb. At the park's inception the numbers were much less, of course, but once the railroad came to them in 1883 the numbers increased dramatically. Our proposed national park here will already have the railroad. In fact, the park is being planned in such a way that the railroad will bring people directly in without the need for additional transportation.

"The national park will employ dozens of people and provide hotel services and restaurants for the vast number of visitors who will come to the area. Your products will have no need to ship when that happens. Meat and grain, other foods grown here will meet visitors' needs."

"But we'd still have to get them up there. To Whitefish. On top of that, there *is* no national park at this time." The man's bushy eyebrows dipped deep over his eyes.

"That's true, but the men who are with me today intend to supply all the pertinent information that will allow President Roosevelt to move forward on the park's creation. We believe that after receiving this information, the president will make a request for the national park by the end of the summer. Our plan is that the railroad will be finished with its new line in August, and this will of course be a benefit in that the president will see there is already a fully functioning railroad in place, ready to bring visitors into the park."

"August!" several voices shouted at the same time. The comments began flying once again.

Carter looked at Dad. "I didn't realize we had so little time."

"I thought the matter was still open to discussion. I guess we know better now." Dad shook his head. "You and I and Fred need to get together and talk about this in detail. We very well may need to buy up a bunch of freight wagons. I know I've mentioned it before, but we may need to start a freighting aspect to our businesses."

"As to your other point"—Hill's raised voice quieted the crowd a bit—"with increased visitors because of the park, the railroad will be able to make the train available to Kalispell more often. Perhaps some of the tourists will even want to come here."

The crowd burst into all sorts of responses.

"So it's all about money!"

"You make plenty of money off of us, already!"

Judge Ashbury pounded on the podium once again. "Ladies and gentlemen, if you do not control yourselves, we will put an end to this meeting."

The man who'd been speaking before stood on his chair.

"Judge, there's no possible way to get a national park up and running by the end of August, and so that won't solve our problems at all. It will take years to get a national park set up, visitors to come here, and for our products to be needed. In the meantime, we will have to find a way to get our goods to market, as well as get product delivered here."

"I sympathize and understand." Judge Ashbury folded his hands on the podium. "I have no desire to be without train service in Kalispell. I'm on your side when it comes to wanting regular service to continue. However, I've never known a riot or free-for-all to result in any positive conclusion, so I'm asking everyone to take their turn speaking and do so only when addressed to come forward."

Carter glanced around and locked eyes with Ellie. He grinned up at her.

Her cheeks flushed, which was a good sign. But then she quickly looked away.

The Judge finally got everyone who wanted to speak to line up on the side. Order once again resumed as he motioned the next man forward.

"Name's Grant Wallace. I've been working with railroads all my adult life. This job's all I know. I've lived in Kalispell since the Great Northern came here. I've spent years workin' up to assistant foreman in the shops supply department. My brother is a section hand. We don't wanna have to move from Kalispell to Stumptown and even if we did, I wouldn't be able to get the same job I have now because someone else already has it. I'd have to settle fer a job with less pay and pay fer my move to boot. The railroad ain't givin' any thought at all to us loyal workers."

Mr. Hill stared down at the man, red streaking his face. The room was silent as everyone waited for his response.

Grant shook his head. "Doesn't the railroad have any responsibility for its people?"

"I'm not without feelings for the workers." Hill cleared his throat. "However, the railroad can hardly afford to pay to move everyone north. There are plenty of men who will come west and take up jobs with the railroad, so if you don't wish to move, no one is forcing you."

Grant's face darkened. "But I need my job. Seems to me that you and your pa haven't even considered the workers, much less what losing the railroad is going to do to the good folks in this town. You haven't thought about the people who'll be hurt by this. You only think about the money you'll save and make."

"And the dangers." Hill looked over those gathered. "Let's not forget the *dangers*. We have thought of our workers and the people of this great town. We can't have a railroad line that kills them off because of the dangerous route. This decision wasn't made lightly. After all, it's going to cost us a great deal of money to move an already established railroad."

Grant shook his head. "Just seems to me if you really cared about more than the money, you'd be findin' a way to keep Kalispell as the division line." He shoved his hands in his pockets and walked back toward the doors.

A man close to Dad stormed to his feet. "Just last March, the Supreme Court ruled against the Northern Securities Company your pa co-owned with J. P. Morgan and Northern Pacific's E. H. Harriman. They were named guilty of monopolizing railroads in the Northwest. No doubt this caused problems for all of you. I'm inclined to think that you and your pa have given little thought to the trouble you're causing to the good people of Kalispell. I mean, why would you? In light of the magnitude of the court's ruling, you're just trying to make up for all the money you lost by breakin' the law."

The man stared down Hill and the crowd came to its feet. Words blasted from every corner of the opera house.

Someone threw a rock at the stage, and it narrowly missed Miss Briggs. Carter came out of his seat ready to rush the stage and protect her, but pandemonium broke loose. He and his father were pushed and shoved as the crowd went wild. Two men tackled the man who'd thrown the rock.

Carter's gaze stayed locked on Ellie. Her face was pale, her fingers locked in her lap so tight her knuckles were white. Marvella wrapped an arm around Ellie's shoulders, glaring at the man being taken from the room. Carter eased back into his seat and blew out a breath.

What was his town coming to that they thought it respectable to show their frustration by throwing rocks at innocent women?

A couple deputies rushed the stage, bully sticks drawn, prepared for more trouble. Judge Ashbury took front and center. Yanking a whistle off one of the men's necks, he blew loud and long as he pounded on the podium.

"Everyone. Sit. Down. *Now!*" His glare penetrated the room like a warm knife through butter. "Unless you want to sit in jail for a night and then come see me in the courthouse in the morning and pay a hefty fine, I suggest you all act like the civilized citizens of Kalispell I hope you are. Otherwise, you can leave."

The room hushed to complete silence. Then the Judge nodded at several men who stood sentry throughout the large room.

"I will have these men arrest anyone—and I do mean *anyone*—who gets out of line from now on. Understood?"

Murmurs floated around the room.

"Good." He adjusted his vest and took a deep breath. "Now we are going to have a civilized conversation about the railroad and the national park and how that can benefit our town and keep us here in our homes."

The Judge motioned George Grinnell to come forward. The conservationist immediately went into what seemed a well-rehearsed speech about national parks in general. But no one could miss the nervous shake in his voice or the way he refused to look at the crowd for any length of time. Clearly the night's proceedings were taking their toll on everyone. Still, Carter respected that the gentleman persevered. Focusing especially on Yellowstone National Park and Yosemite, Grinnell shared information about their creation and the benefit they'd been to the surrounding towns.

From everything he said, it sounded good for the area. But the area for the park was a good distance away from Kalispell. How would that be helpful to them?

He wasn't opposed to a national park being created. It was important to preserve magnificent places of God's creation and make them available to the public. But after another fifteen minutes of discussion and questions, no one seemed to care much. The weight of losing the main line of the railroad had sunk in.

And it was devastating.

Judge Ashbury ended the meeting. Nothing positive had

been accomplished for the welfare of Kalispell, but at least everyone knew where they stood.

"Well, that was some evening." Dad let out a sigh and glanced around the opera house. He looked back at Carter, his expression tight. "Let's get together sometime this week. We can look at options for shipping up north." Dad stood as the crowd dispersed.

"Sounds good." Carter's gaze turned to the stage. Ellie and her father were in discussion with the Judge and Marvella. Ellie's cheeks were pinker, but her lips were tight and pinched. "Hey, Dad. Come with me for a minute. I want to introduce you to Mr. Briggs and his daughter."

They made their way through the sea of people and waited. Marvella spotted them and held out her arm to welcome them into the circle.

"Carter and Jacob Brunswick. I hoped we might meet up tonight. I understand you've met our house guests." Marvella patted Carter's arm.

"Yes, at least I have." Carter smiled at Ellie. "We encountered each other at the train station."

"That's what Miss Briggs told me." Marvella lifted her lips just a touch. That twinkle in her eye said more than she let on. "I hope you are as impressed with them as we are."

"Of course." Carter kept his features neutral. "I wanted Dad to meet them. He was eager to meet Mr. Hill as well."

Hill had been speaking to the mayor but turned at the sound of his name.

Dad offered his hand to Mr. Hill. "We met some years back to negotiate wheat shipments. Guess we're going to have to remake our agreement."

"Ah yes, Mr. Brunswick." Mr. Hill took the proffered hand and shook it.

Dad turned to Carter. "This is my son, Carter. He also has a contract with the Great Northern for Brunswick Flour—he owns the mill. Guess we'll both have to figure out a new way to transport our commodities."

"Ah, I see."

At least Hill had the decency to look a little uncomfortable.

Mr. Grinnell held out his hand. "Mr. Brunswick, it's a pleasure to meet you."

Mr. Briggs did the same. "Pleasure." They shook hands and then Dad turned to Ellie. "And it is a delight to meet you. Carter, you didn't tell me just how beautiful this young lady was."

Ellie's cheeks flushed and he had to suppress a grin. He raised an eyebrow at his dad. "I suppose I was just keeping that to myself for fear of the word getting around." He winked at Ellie. The pale pink bloomed to a darker red, and Carter paused. She'd had a rough night. It was probably not right to tease her so much.

"The Briggses and Mr. Grinnell are getting ready to trek out into the mountains." Marvella's eyes brightened. She rapped Carter's forearm with her folded fan. "However, I just had a marvelous idea. When they return in three weeks, I would like to host you all at dinner. Would you and Mrs. Brunswick be able to join us?"

Dad replied before Carter could. "Of course. We'd enjoy that very much."

Ellie leaned over and whispered to her dad. Carter watched their interaction from his periphery. Mr. Briggs waved a hand at Ellie and turned away from his daughter. Ellie's shoulders curled, her head dropping slightly. It wasn't his place to interfere in family affairs, but the lack of care Mr. Briggs was showing Ellie after her scare tonight set Carter's teeth on edge. He was about to ask her if she needed something, but Marvella interrupted him.

"And what about you, Carter dear? Would you enjoy an evening with the captivating Miss Briggs as your dining companion?"

Carter snapped to attention. With any luck, his observation of the pretty Miss Briggs had gone unnoticed. But no. The gleam in Marvella's eyes told him it had not. He swallowed, resisting the urge to tug his collar. "I'd be happy to be there. Miss Briggs is always a pleasure to talk to."

Marvella smiled, looking like a cat with fresh cream. Heaven only knew what was happening in her mind. "That is the correct answer, Mr. Brunswick. Now"—she turned to her husband, who had just joined the group—"what are you going to do about that miscreant who almost injured Miss Briggs?"

The Judge buttoned his coat, his eyes trained on Ellie. "You can be sure that they will be dealt with, Miss Briggs. I hope it doesn't color your opinion of Kalispell. Folks are having a difficult time adjusting, but that's no excuse for violence."

"I appreciate your kindness, Judge." Ellie gave the older gentleman the first genuine smile Carter had seen all evening.

Marvella slipped her arm through her husband's and gave the group a firm nod. "The Judge is right. Our town is in a difficult spot. But we will find a way through, with the Lord's help." She glanced at Carter and Ellie, a smile blooming on her face. "And maybe along the way see a little happiness come to fruition."

"Now, Marvella, you let these young people be. They don't need to be hustled down the aisle." The Judge patted his wife's hand. Marvella shook his hand away, giving her husband a look.

Carter chuckled. Marvella and the Judge were a pair, and for the first time since the evening began, he felt some of the stress leave his shoulders. The Ashburys had a way of doing that. "Don't you worry, Judge. I've no mind to get into any schemes. If the Lord has a wife for me, He'll lead me to her."

An eyebrow arched high on Marvella's brow, and every ounce of stress immediately returned to Carter's shoulders. He'd done it now. Marvella Ashbury would not rest until she'd matched him with Ellie. Him and his big mouth.

"How interesting that you mention marriage." Her gaze flicked to Ellie and Carter's followed. The poor woman looked like a startled deer. "You're right, however, Mr. Brunswick. I'm sure the Lord will provide just fine. Like the Bible says, it's not good for man to be alone."

"Grant, it just ain't right that the Hills don't care about their workers! I think we might hafta do something drastic. Threaten Mr. Hill or his son. Maybe even shoot one of them."

"You always want to jump from doing nothin' to going

way past reasonable, Alvin. What's wrong with you?" Grant didn't really care about the answer. This was his brother.

"I'm a man of action, Grant. You know I'm not one to sit around doin' nothin' at all."

"But shootin' someone? That's downright drastic, don't you think?"

"Sometimes drastic measures are called for. Sometimes when you got a bad thing to deal with, you have to throw out something even worse to get a fella's attention."

Grant kept walking. Sometimes there was just no reasoning with Alvin. Grant wanted the Hills to change their mind as much as anyone, but he didn't want violence and murder. After all, what good would it do if they changed the Hills's minds but ended up in a hangman's noose?

"You know, we could get some dynamite and blow a whole stretch of that new track. We always have a bunch of it on hand."

Great. Alvin was getting excited.

"If we blew out the new track it would buy us time."

Grant snorted. "Time for *what*? You heard Hill. They've made up their mind. The route from Columbia Falls is too dangerous and causes too many problems. They've already put money into the solution and if you blow it up, they'll just rebuild it. You might buy us more time, but time for what? It ain't gonna change anything."

Alvin wasn't listening. "I'll talk to some friends of mine. We're all thinkin' that something needs to be done. They ain't squeamish like you."

Grant shrugged. "Do what you want to, but I'm not promisin' to be part of it."

Alvin chuckled. "You'll come along with me on it once

you think about it. Doin' nothing for sure won't keep your job. Trust me."

Trusting Alvin was akin to trusting a stick of dynamite. Once their fuse was lit, both were deadly . . .

And could go off without warning.

9

WEDNESDAY, MAY 25, 1904

I 'm glad you made it." Marvella ushered Rebecca Andrews into her small parlor and shut the door. "We have our work cut out for us."

The mirthful grin on the new bride's face was telling. "Us?"

"Yes, *us*." Marvella winked and pointed to a chair. "We are in a dire situation, and I need your help. Now wipe that cheeky grin off your face so we can get down to business."

"Dire, you say?" Rebecca's brow crinkled, and even though the young woman tried to hide her sarcasm, it wasn't lost on Marvella. "Which young man in our community are you attempting to match to the conservationist's daughter?"

"Carter Brunswick." Marvella waved a hand. "But that doesn't matter at the moment. I'm more concerned about Eleanor's faith. She walked away from God when her mother died."

"Oh dear." Rebecca put a hand to her throat.

"Never fear. I have a plan."

"I would expect nothing less." She folded her hands in her lap.

"We don't have much time, as our guests are getting ready to depart." Marvella leaned forward and filled Rebecca in on the pertinent details. Rebecca then offered to pray for Miss Briggs, for healing and restoration.

Armed for the next step in her plan, Marvella led the way up the stairs. At the rooms designated for Eleanor, she stopped at the open door. The young woman flitted around the room, neat stacks on top of the bed.

Marvella cleared her throat. "Miss Briggs?"

Eleanor's gaze darted toward them, and she pushed some escaping blond hair behind her ear. "My goodness, I didn't realize I'd left the door open. Please come in."

"Thank you, my dear. I'd like to introduce you to Montana's very first female court reporter, Mrs. Rebecca Andrews."

Eleanor moved away from her packing, her demeanor frazzled. "It's nice to meet you. I apologize for the upheaval, but I must finish packing for our camping trip, and my father isn't the most patient of men."

Rebecca stepped forward. "How can I help?"

"It's all right, you're—"

"Nonsense." The other young woman approached the suitcase. "It's clear to see that you have a great deal to do and not enough time. Put me to work. I'm excellent at packing."

Eleanor glanced at the clock, bit her lip, and then nodded. "Thank you. When Father moved up the time to leave, I became a bit frantic. It takes a lot of planning for this kind of trip."

"Well, it looks as if you are organized." Rebecca's hands were on her hips. "Just tell me what to do and I'll do it."

"I try to pack as light as possible, and in such a way as to keep water out in case we have to cross swollen rivers, which happens a great deal." Eleanor gave instructions to Rebecca and the two packed.

Marvella watched for several moments. "I'm so excited for you to see the area that is so special to us. Milton has taken me up there several times. He knows how much I love to see glaciers. They are impressive and glorious."

"Mhm." Eleanor darted to the closet and then dashed back with several items in her hands.

"It's the most wonderful thing to sit under the great big sky and simply stand in awe of God's creation. The mountains, the glaciers, the trees, the water"—she released a long sigh—"it's simply magnificent."

When no response came from the young woman, Marvella caught Rebecca's gaze. The young wife shook her head.

She didn't like to think of herself as the pushy sort, but the urgency of the moment spurred her on. "'The heavens declare the glory of God; and the firmament sheweth his handywork.'" She stepped closer to the bed. "That's from the Psalms."

"Yes, ma'am." Eleanor finished up her packing and glanced up. Blowing a lock of hair off her forehead, she faced Marvella. "My mother used to love reading the Psalms to me."

Perfect opening. "Well, I took the liberty of writing out some of my favorite verses about the glory of God's creation for you." Marvella stepped forward with the envelope. "I'd love for you to read them under the myriads of stars, or beside the pristine waters."

Eleanor's shoulders drooped a bit. "Mrs. Ashbury, this is very kind of you, but I've already shared where I stand with God." She didn't take the envelope.

Marvella stepped closer. "Where you stand at the moment doesn't mean that's where you'll be standing next week."

Eleanor wrapped her arms around her waist. Her lips clamped tight.

Rebecca sat on the trunk at the end of the bed. "I understand you've been through a great loss. Pain and grief can cause us to shield ourselves from more hurt. Fear and doubt keep us even more closed off to the beauty and truth of love around us. It took me a long time to understand God's grace—"

"Please. I appreciate both of you coming to help." Eleanor snatched the envelope from Marvella's hand. "And I appreciate you caring about me. I'll read this later, thank you. But my father is surely waiting for me, and I don't wish to hold him and Mr. Grinnell up any longer." She marched over to the bell pull and gave it a good yank.

Marvella stood. At least Eleanor took the envelope. "I pray you have a blessed and fruitful time, dear. We look forward to your return."

"Thank you, Mrs. Ashbury." Eleanor's smile was tight. "It was a pleasure to meet you, Mrs. Andrews. Thank you for your assistance, it was greatly appreciated."

"My pleasure." Rebecca took Marvella's arm and steered her toward the door.

SATURDAY, MAY 28, 1904

A few days later, Eleanor pulled the envelope out once again. It was the third time today she'd read it.

Marvella's loopy and perfect script filled the page. Eleanor's hands shook as she read.

Dear Eleanor,

As I think of our great God—Creator of the Universe—I can't help but be in awe of all He has done. I pray as you see His handiwork—His fingerprints—all around you, that you feel ensconced in His love, grace, and mercy. These verses are some of my favorites, I hope they bless you today and always.

Love, Marvella

Psalm 147:4–5, 8 He telleth the number of the stars; he calleth them all by their names.

Great is our Lord, and of great power: his understanding is infinite.

Who covereth the heaven with clouds, who prepareth rain for the earth, who maketh grass to grow upon the mountains.

Psalm 90:2 Before the mountains were brought forth, or ever thou hadst formed the earth and the world, even from everlasting to everlasting, thou art God.

Psalm 8:3–5 When I consider thy heavens, the work of thy fingers, the moon and the stars, which thou hast ordained;

What is man, that thou art mindful of him? and the son of man, that thou visitest him?

*For thou hast made him a little lower than the angels,
and hast crowned him with glory and honour.*

*Psalm 19:1 The heavens declare the glory of God; and
the firmament sheweth his handywork.*

*Colossians 1:16 For by him were all things created, that
are in heaven, and that are in earth, visible and invisible,
whether they be thrones, or dominions, or principalities,
or powers: all things were created by him, and for him.*

*Psalm 95:4–6 In his hand are the deep places of the
earth: the strength of the hills is his also.*

*The sea is his, and he made it: and his hands formed
the dry land.*

*O come, let us worship and bow down: let us kneel
before the* Lord *our maker.*

Each time she read the words, she felt like her heart was cracking. As if the hard shell around it—which she hadn't even realized was there—was slowly crumbling.

Though she was more than a little tired after trekking into the mountains, she felt lighter. And could even breathe better.

The men's voices around the horses brought her attention back to her surroundings.

Mr. Grinnell had hired a guide, as well as a couple of men to handle the set up and break down of camp and the cooking. Which took a lot of worry off her shoulders. However, being in the saddle for nearly fourteen hours . . .

She could scarcely walk!

Once she was able to stretch and move around a bit, she felt better, although her backside would be sore tomorrow. Thankfully, Marvella sent them with a great deal of food that needed only to be warmed over a fire. Eleanor had been delighted to find that those stocks included some of the delicious chocolate cake they'd had the night before.

After enjoying a thick slice of roast beef between two pieces of bread, she took her piece of cake and settled down by the fire. She glanced to where her father sat across from her on a stool. It was getting harder for him to sit on the ground like the rest of them. She stared into the fire. Was he hurting? Was this trip too much for him? She wanted to ask but didn't want to embarrass him in front of his friend.

George Grinnell was the same age as Father, but somehow, he seemed younger. Her father had been changing over the last year or two. He was slowing down. More than she'd allowed herself to consider.

Two years ago, when he'd been invited to make a trip to South America to explore various places along the Amazon River, he had declined. She hadn't questioned him about it because his schedule had been so tight, but now . . .

Had he refused because of ill health?

She ate another bite of cake, though now it tasted like sawdust. What if Father had a disease of some sort? Something terminal like Mother had had. What would she do if she lost him?

All of a sudden, her stomach didn't want any more cake.

Besides his suggestion they consider settling down, he had talked about selling family items that he'd put in storage. Paintings and ancient rugs he'd acquired over the years, as well as other bric-a-brac. He'd even arranged for some of his pieces to be given to various museums. Were all of these clues of what was to come? Had she not picked up on the fact?

She snuck another glance at him. He seemed all right, aside from being tired. He was eating well and not complaining about any particular troubles. Not that he necessarily would. He wouldn't do anything to compromise the work he'd set out to do.

The chill of the night was upon them and even with her layers of clothing, a shiver raced up her spine. Time to retire to her Norwegian sleeping bag.

Over the years, they'd been on too many of these types of adventures not to know what was needed to stay warm and dry. Father had been dedicated to finding a bedroll or sleeping bag that would afford them the very best protection from cold and damp.

On a trip to Norway four years ago, he'd found a man who was able to skillfully produce a down-filled bag with a rubberized bottom. It was perfect for placing on the ground and even better when used in a tent. Not long after her father had worked with the man to create the bags, Eleanor saw an advertisement for them in one of the outdoor adventure magazines. The ad even mentioned that the bags had been used by the famous conservationist Stewart Briggs, although it made no mention that it was his design.

"Well, I believe it would do us all good to turn in early." Grinnell stood and stretched.

"I agree." Mr. Stanton, their guide, tossed the remainder of his coffee on the fire. "We'll want to get an early start in the morning. We won't travel as far tomorrow since we will be steadily increasing our altitude. We'll also pass through Columbia Falls so we can pick up any additional supplies we've forgotten."

Father pursed his lips. "I still think it would have been

easier to take the train to Columbia Falls and start out from there."

Grinnell chuckled. "Yes, but you would have missed out on all the things we saw today. Not only that, but I was able to show you some of the various farms and ranches in the area. You told me you wanted to know more about that."

"It was certainly an informative ride. Tiring, however. I'm not getting any younger." Father's voice was edged with humor. "I think Ellie's suggestion that I settle down and write my book is becoming more and more appealing."

Eleanor glanced away and frowned. *Her* suggestion? What was going on with him? And why had he asked to see the farms and ranches?

"We've long been awaiting a book from you, Stewart. I think your daughter is right. The world has need to hear from you."

She looked at her father once again. He caught her gaze, then looked away. She chewed on the inside of her lip. They needed to talk. Maybe not tonight, but soon.

Clearing his throat, he stood. "Well, Ellie girl, are you ready to retire? Looks like the fire is dying down."

"You go ahead. I'll help with the dishes and clean up. We don't want to attract any wild animals."

"Very well. I'll head to our tent and see you later. I'll probably read for just a bit."

The dishes were all gathered and put into a tub of soapy water that one of the men had prepared. Mr. Stanton stopped her as she reached for a towel.

"You don't need to help. We're well paid to provide these services. Feel free to just head on to bed." He took the towel from Eleanor. "Slim and Dusty can manage. They've been running bigger camps than this for some time. They know what to do."

Eleanor let her hands fall to her sides. "I just felt like I should do my part."

"You're doing your part. Enjoy the trip as best you can. Tomorrow night we'll camp near a hot spring. I think you'll enjoy the opportunity to have a nice long soak."

"That does sound pleasant, thank you." The hot springs might benefit Father as well. "Well, good-night, Mr. Stanton."

"Good-night, little lady." He tipped his felt hat and turned to say something to one of the men.

The tent was just a little way across the camp and when Eleanor reached it, she gazed heavenward before going inside. The inky black sky was dotted with thousands upon thousands of stars. Once, when she was a little girl, they'd traveled away from New York City and had stayed with friends who lived out in the country. The utter darkness there was so very impressive, but even more so was Mother pointing out that God had once compared the stars to the heirs Abraham would have.

What must Abraham have felt when God told him that?

Mother's voice enfolded her. *"We're represented up there, Ellie. One of those stars is set in place just for you. And just as God knows each star by name, He knows you by name as well. He will never forget you."*

Her throat tightened and tears burned at her eyes. If only she could believe that the God of the universe knew she existed. Cared about her. But how could that be? How could an all-powerful God even begin to care about a little girl staring at the stars with her mother? Or a young woman staring at the stars alone?

Ellie pressed a fist against her tears. For so long, she'd told herself that believing in God wasn't important, and yet . . .

Mother had said it was the foundation of everything.

As Ellie released a shuddering sigh, Marvella's words before they left came back to her.

How *could* she look at all this and not see the fingerprints of the Creator?

Her breath caught in her throat as she looked up at the vastness of the sky above her. Each star seemed to dance, almost as if inviting her to join them in their celebration. Her mind swirled as she was overwhelmed with an undeniable truth.

There *was* a God.

Yes, she believed that.

Mama said He truly cared about each one of His children.

Tears blurred her vision. "Oh, Mama . . ." How could Eleanor believe that? When Mama loved Him so much and yet He let her suffer and die?

"Mama, I wish I understood," she whispered to the sky. "I wish I could believe like you did. Have the faith that you had. You weren't afraid to die because you believed in God's mercy and love."

A tightness filled her chest and she lowered her gaze. If only she could believe in those things as well.

Carter stood on his parents' porch staring up at the night skies. The heavy stillness of a farm at rest engulfed him—cradled him as one might cradle a sleeping child. He'd always liked this time of night when the livestock and humans were asleep and a man could stand and take an account of his day . . . his life.

Right now, his life seemed to have endless questions, complications that weren't of his own making, nor his own ability to fix.

"Lord, I don't know what to do. I don't know what's going to happen to us now that they're taking the train from Kalispell. Things will have to change in a big way, and that won't be easy. I'm not even sure it will be financially prudent."

It was a big mess. One with no easy answers.

He rolled his shoulders, trying to work out the tension building in them. Earlier that evening he'd come to the farm for supper and a discussion with his father. They were no closer to a decision on how to ship their grain and his flour than the night of the town hall meeting. He needed to trust the Lord. To have faith that He would lead them as He had before.

Carter rubbed his jaw. It wasn't the first time his family had faced a tough decision. This time, however, a practical solution that didn't raise their prices sky high wasn't presenting itself. And August felt like it was tomorrow instead of a couple months away.

"God, I trust in You alone. I know You have all the answers I need, but I'm gonna need them soon."

Carter heard the front door creak open and looked over his shoulder.

Dad stepped outside. He moved forward to the banister and leaned against it with a sigh. "I knew I'd find you out here."

"I figured you'd find your way out here as well."

Dad clapped him on the shoulder, giving him a brief squeeze. "Glad you decided to stay the night. I never like you making your way back in the dark."

It didn't matter how old he got, Dad would still worry. "I wanted a night out here. Besides, I'm tired."

For several long minutes they stood in the silence, staring out into the darkness. They shared a companionship that went deeper than any other relationship Carter had known. He was close to his mother, but in a completely different way.

Dad gave a deep sigh. "You come up with any great solution?"

"Nope. You?"

"Nope."

Carter shifted and leaned back against the railing. "I don't think we have any other choice than to put together our own transportation. We can buy wagons like you suggested and hire men to drive them. Maybe rent them out when we aren't using them. But I figure we'll probably be using them most of the time."

Dad leaned against the railing. "It's going to really cut into the profits. Won't be able to give as much away."

"I've always admired your giving and tried to do the same." Carter sat on the rail. All of his life his father and mother had been committed to giving away their profits after giving to the church, paying the bills, and saving a little bit back for emergencies. Mostly, they liked to help area folks who were down on their luck. Countless widows had been saved from losing their homes or children by his folks' generosity. Few knew it came from them apart from

Carter, and likewise for his own giving. They hadn't even confided in Carter's sisters.

"Still, I have to believe that because it's something we do for the Lord, He'll see it through. He'll provide the money needed. I must believe that. It's not a selfish thing we're doing by buying wagons and hiring men to drive. Fact is, we'll be able to help a few of those railroad men who don't want to leave Kalispell for Whitefish. That makes me feel good. Of course, it isn't about me feeling good." Dad went to one of the rockers on the porch and sat down.

"God's got a plan for even this, Carter. We must remember that. I think about a dozen stories in the Bible where God went ahead of folks and caused things to happen in such a way that it served His purpose. He's never caught off guard, even when we are." The chair creaked as his dad began to rock. "I think of Proverbs sixteen, verse nine, 'A man's heart deviseth his way: but the Lord directeth his steps.'"

"I keep reminding myself of that." He couldn't really see much but his father's outline in the shade of the porch, despite the moon being three-quarters. Still, he could imagine his father's calm countenance and gentle smile.

"Things could be a whole lot worse. We've seen it bad and know what it is to really suffer. This is difficult, but not suffering. Others will suffer, though, and that makes me want to do whatever I can to help them."

"I know. This will likely hit our community hard for a good while. Like you said, God has put it in us to give what we can, and we'll go on doing that. If He wants us to do different, He'll let us know one way or another."

The chair creaked for a few minutes before Dad spoke.

"There's an exceptional wagon maker down in Missoula. He also repairs and sells used wagons. I'll send a telegram and see what's what. Could be he has what we need."

"How many do you think?"

"I'm guessing at least ten wagons to begin with. We'll need to buy horses too, but there's a few draft teams for sale in the area. And what's not here we can probably pick up in Missoula as well. If we plan it right, you and I could go down after we harvest the winter wheat and get it shipped out. Can Jack manage the mill for you a couple of weeks?"

"Jack could take over the mill and not miss me at all. And Bill Preston is becoming a big help. It will be a good chance for him to learn a bit more about running the mill. Jack can teach him." Carter grinned.

"Bill Preston, huh?" Dad leaned back. "He seems like a good kid. Shame about his dad."

Carter nodded. "Bill takes good care of his sisters and mother. He's a hard worker and doesn't complain, no matter what he's asked to do. I've gotten the better end of the bargain." Yes, this plan was coming together. Why had he been so worried? "I came out here to pray and it feels like God has answered before I've asked. Guess we've got work to do."

"*I've* got some sleep to catch up on." His dad rose and gave a stretch. "Come on, son. You need your rest too."

"I'll be right behind you."

"Don't stay out here too long. . . . I know you have a penchant to overthink things. Leave it in God's capable hands." The door creaked again as his dad entered the house.

Carter turned and gave the night sky one last look. A verse from Psalm 121 came to mind. "My help comes from the Lord, the Maker of heaven and earth," he whispered, peace washing warmth over him. It reminded him of the day his pastor and elders had prayed for him when the mill opened.

Thank You, Lord.

The Lord would help them get through this.

10

Thursday, June 2, 1904

Grant stepped out into the scorching heat of a record-hot June day. There was no relief inside or out. Sweat dripped down his temple, adding to the moisture already gathered around his collar. A good shock of cold water would help clear his mind and cool him off.

He followed the worn path to the water pump at the side of the building, trying to sort his thoughts. He needed to decide about moving to Whitefish soon. But like he'd told Mr. Hill, a move for him and Alvin took money they didn't have. Which was why he hadn't cleared out yet. If he could stretch his time at his current position until the last minute, every cent of that pay would help them get north or keep him and Alvin going until they figured out what they were gonna do.

Alvin.

Even thinking his brother's name made his shoulders tighten. He was getting crazier with his ideas to stop the railroad leaving Kalispell. Alvin's frustration and anger were understandable. Grant felt that way too. But the mayhem his little brother was scheming . . .

It was crazy.

Lately Alvin's rage had turned against the national park. After hearing about all the fancy plans for Whitefish and the opening of the park, Alvin decided Mr. Hill and those conservationist fellas—Mr. Grinnell and . . . was his name Braggs? Briggs?—were on his list for troublemakin'. Kept sayin' the two went hand in hand. That the people supportin' the national park must be in cahoots with the railroad.

Grant grasped the handle of the water pump and worked it a few times until a stream of water spilled from the spout. He bent over and stuck his head under. Water poured down his neck and soaked his shirt. After a minute he stood and slicked his hair back off his forehead. He pumped a couple more times and cupped his hands, drinking in the cool water. It felt good racing down his throat. Settled him down.

"Is that his carriage over there?"

Grant stilled. Was someone talking to him? He glanced around. There was no one he could see. He swiped his forehead and turned to head back to the depot when another voice stopped him in his tracks.

"That's it. But keep your voice down, dummy. Want the whole town to hear ya?"

Grant stifled a groan.

Alvin.

Grant backtracked a few steps and peeked around the corner of the back wall of the depot. Alvin and a young man Grant didn't recognize were crouched low, several large rocks in front of them. Grant's jaw slackened. They couldn't be this dumb, could they?

"Now, Tom and Horace are waitin' for us to make the first toss. Once we do, the hor—Hey!"

Grant yanked his brother to his feet and dragged him away from his hiding spot. Alvin struggled against his brother's grip, but Grant held sure. Finally, when they were back by the water pump, he let Alvin go. The shorter man stumbled backward, landing in the wet grass with a thud.

"Grant! What'd you go and do that for? We were just about to send a strong message to that Hill fella!" Alvin glared up at him.

Grant rubbed his face. "Are you an idiot? You're in broad daylight! If the marshal catches you, it's jail for sure."

Alvin pushed himself into a sitting position and brushed the grass off his sleeves. He picked up his hat and plunked it back on his head. "So what? We aim to get our point across. If you don't like it, fine. But you leave me to my own business." He stood and poked a finger in Grant's face. "You're goin' soft."

"No." Grant slapped Alvin's hand away. "I'm goin' *smart.* Throwin' rocks like brats ain't gonna change anything. It's—"

A scream and a horse's loud whinny split the air. The two brothers exchanged glances and ran back to where the kid had been sitting. He was nowhere in sight. Neither were the big rocks they'd had piled.

Grant glanced down the main street, his eyes growing wide. Mr. Hill's carriage was rolling at a fast clip down the street. Two men bounced back and forth on the bench seat. A derby hat flew off one of their heads and tumbled in the dirt. They rounded a corner on two wheels and disappeared from view.

Alvin chuckled. "Guess young Johnny's got some grit after all. They must've pelted the horses good."

"Other people might be hurt, Alvin." Grant nodded toward the crowd gathered on the other side of the street still staring at the spot where the carriage disappeared.

"Just a bunch of busybodies over there, brother. Everyone's fine. 'Sides, I can guarantee you there are plenty of men you'd consider to be upstandin' gents as mad as us about this whole railroad business." Alvin pulled the brim of his hat low over his eyes. "You'll see. The folks of Kalispell won't take this layin' down. If you don't fight with us, you're against us." Without another word, he crossed the street and disappeared behind a building.

Grant sighed and rubbed his hands over his face. His gut churned.

This wasn't gonna end good.

FRIDAY, JUNE 3, 1904

After nine days on the trail, Eleanor's exposed skin had browned. She wore a wide-brimmed straw hat to shade her face but figured it too had probably grown darker. It wasn't really all that important. It wasn't like she had anyone to impress after the trip. If she was tanned, so be it.

The ride, though arduous, had been glorious. Her horse, Ulysses, was as good a horse as she'd ever ridden on a camping trek. The landscape was truly magnificent as they climbed narrow trails of loose shale and rock. They never wanted for fresh, cold water, as tiny waterfalls seemed to appear at every turn as they moved higher into the mountains.

At night when they camped, Eleanor found herself listening for the various animals that Mr. Grinnell and Mr. Stanton pointed out. Coyotes yipped in a relentless fashion as if desperate to tell their story. Occasionally a wolf let out a lonely howl and from time to time they had heard a mountain lion's scream, leading Mr. Stanton to share tales of encounters he'd had the year before when one of the beasts had actually stalked him.

On the fourth day they camped by a wide stream. Several men came down to fish for trout, and more than one of them widened their eyes to find her already there with a string of trout she'd caught.

One of the men whistled. "Never seen a woman outfish us afore."

She shrugged. "Hope you're hungry." Her smile seemed to come from deep down inside her.

Yes, this land had a calming effect on her. And the more she reflected on the note from Marvella and the Scripture the older woman enclosed, the more Eleanor's inner restlessness abated.

Mr. Stanton and his men fried up her fish for supper that night and compliments abounded. Fishing might not be the most ladylike hobby, but she did love it.

She got to be good at catching sight of black bears too. They seemed curious about the visitors, but not aggressive. Of course, Mr. Grinnell told them the black bears were more inclined to avoid people, whereas the grizzlies didn't fear anyone or anything. They were to be avoided at all costs. She trembled at the thought of an encounter with a grizzly. Mr. Stanton had told a story just a few nights back about a grizzly mother who attacked an entire camp of people because her two cubs had wandered into that area. He told them that if something like that happened, they were to get to their horses and vacate the camp as quickly as possible. Stanton and his men had firearms, but none of them wanted to kill a bear unless it was the only way to survive.

No wonder her father and Mr. Grinnell wanted to see this place become a national park. The longer they were there, the more she fell in love. She could only imagine what might happen to the place if they failed to see it protected. No doubt people would come in and kill the bears or push them farther west and north as they had back east. They would build houses and industries and tear down the trees and even the mountains themselves to put in roads and other marks of ownership.

But then she remembered hearing Hill speak of his chalets and depots. What was the difference between what he wanted to do to the land and what others might do if it *didn't* become a national park?

Still, she couldn't fault the idea of living in such a place. She didn't know that she would want to live right in the mountains as they were just now, but perhaps Kalispell might be a pleasant town to settle in. In fact, when her father mentioned a couple of times that he really had a heart for this area, she began to think she could be happy here. She certainly didn't want to return to a big city. Neither she nor Father were happy living that way.

And the society in Kalispell was much friendlier than out east. The West lacked the upper-crust pretension her group of acquaintances displayed in New York. Though there were struggles and futures were uncertain, the townspeople in Kalispell seemed to genuinely care for the well-being of their neighbors.

And with people like the Ashburys and Mr. Brunswick— well . . . the *older* Mr. Brunswick. Not Carter—

Eleanor frowned. *Carter?* When had he become Carter in her mind? His familiarity was rubbing off on her. That simply wouldn't do.

And why in the name of all that was good and decent did she think of him?

Of course, he had helped her out of the shrubs. They'd managed a halfway civilized conversation. Didn't end all that well . . . but . . .

Heat filled her face just thinking about it.

Perhaps she might concede to liking him after all. But just a little bit. And only to herself. Marvella could *never* find out. Her comments the night of the town hall meeting and the grin on Carter Brunswick's face caused her chest to tighten even now. She could only hope no one had noticed!

Still, *Mr.* Brunswick was handsome enough. She liked the way his sandy brown hair fell over his right eye sometimes. She liked it too that he seemed unpretentious, not at all needing to impress her. He was almost casual in his appearance and manner. Many times when she and Father had been in mixed company, young men would go out of their way to impress her. Not so, Carter Brunswick. If anything, he was the total opposite.

A smile crept to her lips. She liked that about him. He seemed so genuine. Somehow she knew if she spoke with his most intimate friends and family members she would learn that this was exactly who he was and how he functioned.

"Well, Ellie girl, I hope you're feeling less taxed than I." Her father brought his stool to sit near her at the fire.

She studied him in the fire's glow. "Are you in pain, Father?"

"A little. My back is not in approval of all this riding. I should have known better."

"Why is that?" She almost feared his answer.

He put the stool down and took a seat. He held his hands out to the fire. "I'm not young anymore. Try as I might to be just as limber and active as I was ten years . . . even five years ago, my body is less inclined to cooperate with me."

"Is that why you've been talking about settling down?"

Her father gave a sigh. "That and other reasons."

He glanced around, causing Eleanor to do likewise. Mr. Stanton and the boys were seeing to their final check on the horses, and Mr. Grinnell had already gone to his tent. From the illumination shining through the canvas flaps, it looked like he was probably reading or writing.

Eleanor looked at her father. "Is something wrong?"

He sighed again. "Not really, and yet . . ." He said nothing for several minutes. "I haven't wanted to say anything, but I received another telegram as we left." He sighed. "It's best to just come out with it. We've had some bad investments, Ellie. We're not without funds, so don't worry overmuch, but we need to be reasonable. I think it would be wise for us to buy a little house before there are any more financial downturns. And I do want to write. I've had several offers from publishers in New York, and one in London. I could make a decent wage and perhaps make up for some of the loss."

Finally, an explanation for his strange behavior. Why hadn't he shared this burden sooner? "Are you worried, Father?"

He leaned forward, resting his elbows on his knees, his expression impossible to read. "Only for you. I have done you no favor in keeping you from a normal life of marriage and children."

Eleanor picked a leaf off her skirt. Father's concern made sense in light of his confession, but still. Why was everyone so fixated on her marital state? "You haven't kept me from that. I've chosen to delay it, but I haven't given up the idea of a family of my own. I'm only twenty-four."

"I suppose it was your former beau marrying that gave me pause."

When Father sat back, Eleanor got a good look at his face in the firelight. Her breath caught in her throat. The lines around his eyes seemed deeper, making him look wearier than she'd ever seen him.

"My child, I want to see you happily settled with someone and feel that perhaps you've told yourself that you can't do that just yet. Because of taking care of me . . . working at my side."

She took his hand and gave it a squeeze. How could she help him understand that these years with him were treasured memories that she would always hold dear? "Traveling and enjoying the chance to experience amazing things?" She laughed and let go of his hand. "Father, I've had a wonderful life with you. When I think of all that I've had a chance to do and see, I know that I'm blessed beyond what most people experience."

"Blessed." He whispered the word like a prayer. "Your mother always used that word. She talked all the time of how blessed she was. Even on her deathbed."

That had never made sense to her. "I couldn't understand how a woman in such dire pain could call herself blessed."

"I'm beginning to think that perhaps she had the secrets to it all, Ellie. Perhaps I've been blind. Blinded by my own desires and ambitions. I didn't want there to be any restrictions to what I could or couldn't do. Having a relationship with God definitely restricts."

Another memory of her mother made its way to the forefront of her mind. "Mama said it was liberating to belong to God. I never understood her logic and reasoning. After she was gone, it was hard to grasp. It seemed that, if you accepted God's ways and rules, you were bound to a regimen that required constant scrutiny and precision."

Father nodded. "I felt the same. I must admit we had many discussions about it, but your mother never got angry. I've seen grown men come to blows over religious views, but your mother was at peace. I told her once that I had trouble believing there was a God, and she only promised to pray harder for me that God would help me in my unbelief. She wasn't oppressive or difficult. Never threatening as some could be." A smile played at the corner of his mouth, and his gaze fixed on some far-off spot in the sky.

Eleanor looked away, Father's wistful expression tugging at her heart. Even now, the love he had for Mama permeated his features. Eleanor plucked a blade of grass from the ground, threading it through her fingers. "Mama was gentle in her faith. I suppose the last few days have caused me to ponder Him all the more. Ever since Mama died, I felt He was harsh and unfeeling—unkind, and yet I always felt He was there . . . somewhere."

Father fell silent, then looked at her. "Yes. I agree. Your mother helped me to feel it too. With her absence . . . I pushed Him away. I was so angry I gave it my best to be a full-fledged atheist." He chuckled. "It didn't work. How could it when I was angry at Him? So I did the next best thing and declared that I didn't need God."

Eleanor understood those feelings all too well. Except, being here in the mountains, and reading Marvella's letter almost every day, the anger was abating. Still, her heart ached for understanding. "When Mother got sick, I prayed for her healing, but it seemed so hollow—so empty. I watched her grow worse and worse. I couldn't fathom why a good and loving God would allow for such a thing, and then . . . she was gone."

The silence stretched between them. Had she shared too much? Been too honest? She worried her lip and waited for Father to say something. Anything.

Finally, he let out a long breath. "I'm sorry I couldn't help you with your grief during that time. And to be honest, I didn't know what to do. Your mother was so good with you, helping you with your emotions and feelings. Especially about God. I was completely lost." Her father's voice was barely audible.

Thick cotton seemed to have coated her throat. Grief over her mother's death and thankfulness for her father's vulnerability sat heavy in her heart. "But you did help me, Father." Her smile trembled. "You showed me how to put one foot in front of the other and move forward, even when our hearts were breaking."

His expression softened as he gazed at her. "Have I told you lately that you grow more lovely, more like her every day?"

Hot tears sprang to her eyes. It had been a long time since he'd complimented her like that. "Thank you, Father."

"In personality, too. Your mother was sweet and loving, but she was also full of life and didn't mind sharing her opinion."

Really? Eleanor couldn't remember that side of her mother. She'd welcome a memory like that rather than the memories of Mother on her sickbed. That he saw bits of Mama's personality in her was a compliment she would cherish.

Silence fell between them again, but this time it felt a bit lighter. Eleanor closed her eyes for a moment, and the sounds of the forest came to life. The chirp of crickets was like a symphony surrounding camp. In the distance, owls hooted back and forth, their call and response echoing to the sky. The heat of the fire was waning, a sure sign they should be readying for bed, but she didn't want this conversation to end.

She looked at Father. "Do you want to settle in Kalispell? Do you think you could be content there?"

He looked up at the sky for a long moment, then back at her. "I think I could be. I kind of like the idea of sticking around to see the national park put in place. Perhaps even be more intricately involved."

There was excitement in her father's voice! That had long been absent.

"What do you think, Ellie? Could you be happy in Kalispell?"

She shifted in her seat. "I don't mind the idea of settling down. The longer I'm in this part of the country, the more I dread going back east for anything." She let out a laugh. It was true! She actually *wanted* to stay in Kalispell.

"Then let's do it, Ellie girl!" His enthusiasm was contagious.

"I'll speak to Marvella when we get home." Eleanor grinned, the idea taking root. "She seems to know everyone and every bit of news about the town. She could probably tell us about a half dozen houses for sale."

Father reached over and took her hand between his. She could feel the calluses on his palms from using the reins the last several days. "You're a good daughter, my dear. And I'm glad we talked tonight."

Happy tears burned the corners of her eyes. "I am as well."

Father gave her hand a pat and let it go. "Let's get some rest, shall we? Tomorrow will be another big day."

Eleanor followed him to the tent. Would this conversation bring a new openness between her and Father? How wonderful that would be. No more secrets. No more surprises. She let out a happy sigh as another thought hit her.

They were going to put roots down in Kalispell!

Marvella was going to be as pleased as punch at being right.

Again.

Oh, this couldn't be good. Grant's stomach sank. "What're you plannin' to do?"

"None of yer business." Alvin shoved things in a satchel. "I'm sick and tired of you standin' in the way. I told ya that you better stand with us, and I meant it."

"I can't let you do anything stupid. You're my little brother and I gotta take care of you." He stood in front of the door and blocked it, crossing his arms over his chest.

But Alvin paid him no mind. Just packed his bag and grabbed several things around the room.

"Alvin!"

The frying pan came out of nowhere. Pain flared in the left side of his head, and Grant couldn't keep his eyes open or stay on his feet.

Falling to the floor, he grasped for his brother.

But everything went black as he floated down, down, down.

MONDAY, JUNE 6, 1904

On their tenth night camping, Eleanor gasped when several visitors entered their camp.

"Indians." The whispered gasp escaped her lips.

They were dressed in regular trousers and shirts, but beneath their felt hats was their long hair either loose or braided. George Grinnell was immediately on his feet to greet them.

"*Oki*, Fisher Hat." One of the Indians extended his arm.

Grinnell took hold of the man's arm, and the native man took hold of his. "*Oki*, Jack Big Moon."

Eleanor watched the exchange as Grinnell nodded toward each of the other men and held their arm. Was *Oki* a hello of some sort?

Grinnell motioned Stewart and Eleanor to come. "Meet my friends, they are noble Blackfeet, and I've known them for a long time."

Jack inclined his head. "We are happy to meet Fisher Hat's friends. We have brought deer to eat."

"Thank you, that is a great gift to us." Grinnell took the bundle of offered meat and handed it to Mr. Stanton. "Come and we'll see it cooked. I can offer you some of the sweet cookies you enjoy."

Jack smiled. "I'm glad you sent word that you'd be here. We were glad to see you again."

Eleanor sat down on a rock and pulled out her journal to record the encounter. These men were . . . majestic. Almost regal the way they held themselves. And their English was impeccable. Every once in a while, one would speak in another language to one of the others, and it rolled beautifully off their lips. Frankly, it put her to shame. She didn't know another language.

Well, other than all her studies in Latin, but that was a dead language. That surely didn't count.

She listened as their visitors talked about their families and what had been happening in their villages as they enjoyed a long dinner together. The roasted meat was delicious.

Far too soon, the Blackfeet stood to go. Eleanor sighed. She was in the middle of sketching their party and wouldn't be able to finish now.

No sooner were good-byes said than they vanished into the woods as quietly as they'd appeared.

"Fascinating." Father pulled his stool close to her. "Such strong and impressive men. Did you hear how well they spoke English?"

"Yes! I was astonished by it as well." She kept her voice low. "It seems Mr. Grinnell has known them a long time. What a powerful testimony to the rest of us. The wild stories that still circulate about the Indians being savages and attacking settlers need to be put to rest once and for all."

"Agreed. Perhaps I should write about that in my book, Ellie."

She couldn't help it. She spoke up. "I notice you call me *Ellie* all the time now."

He turned to her, his brow furrowed. "Have I? I guess I hadn't noticed."

She smiled at him. "It's all right. It doesn't bother me when you do it."

And for the first time in ten years, it truly didn't.

The next day they were more than halfway through their trip. Eleanor slipped from her saddle and rubbed her hand along Ulysses's neck. He tossed his head, black mane waving with the motion. She smiled and fished a sugar cube out of her pocket. For all her travels with Father, she'd never really taken a shine to horses. But this gentle giant had carried her miles and miles without throwing her from her seat.

A sugar cube was the least she could give him.

She tugged his reins and led him to where the others had tethered their horses to munch on fresh grass. Pulling her comb out of a saddle bag and tucking it in her pocket, Eleanor made her way to where camp was being set up. A fire had been kindled and men were moving around, setting up tents and pulling out foodstuffs for dinner.

As much as her backside hurt, Eleanor couldn't wait to sit on something that wasn't swaying. She walked about twenty feet past camp to a large tree. With a groan, she sat down and leaned back against the trunk. She stretched her legs out before her, digging her knuckles into her leg muscles.

Perhaps Father was right. Even at twenty-four, her body wasn't handling trips like it used to. She tugged her hair out of its braid and pulled her comb out. With quick strokes, Eleanor worked the tangles from her hair and pulled it back into a tighter braid. There. That would hold for another day or two. Or until they found a stream and she could bathe privately.

The sky was streaked with oranges and pinks, the deeper blue of evening ebbing in. A breeze rustled the leaves of the trees, scents of pine mingling with grass and wildflowers. This was why she was so passionate about preserving the land. The peace that came in the quiet of twilight. Mountains jutting toward the sky, their sharp peaks harsh against the blanket of stars beginning their night twinkle. Eleanor sighed and felt the tension of the day ease from her.

She still had to sit with Mr. Grinnell and Father to take notes regarding what they'd discovered near a large waterfall earlier in the day. Whatever it was had caused them to be in deep discussion most of the day.

"Ellie! Come closer into camp," Father called from his place at the fire. "It's getting too dark to be outside the tent circle."

"Coming." She eased to her feet, every one of her muscles protesting.

Just as she reached her tent, a loud crack echoed through the encampment. Eleanor screamed and dropped to the ground, rolling behind the large canvas.

Instantly, the men in camp were on their feet, rifles in hand.

Mr. Stanton pulled back the hammer on his weapon. "Who's there? Show yourself. We mean no harm."

Eleanor crawled to the front of the tent. Where was Father? Oh, thank goodness. He was crouched on the ground, behind a large fallen log. Mr. Grinnell was next to him.

"Consider this a warnin'!" a deep voice bellowed. It sounded like it came from Eleanor's left, but with the acoustics of the forest and cliffs, it was impossible to tell.

"A warning for what?" Stanton hollered back.

Eleanor peered around the edge of her tent. The trees looked more ominous now that evening had fallen. The trees seemed to whisper with movement and shadows. Rocks and twigs poked her knees through the fabric of her split skirt. Time seemed to crawl as they waited to see if the mystery man responded.

Finally, the rough voice cut through the darkness. "A warning for Mr. Grinnell and Mr. Briggs. No one wants your park or the railroad movin' up to Whitefish. We know you're in cahoots to make money together. So make sure you tell your friend Mr. Hill that he'll keep seein' trouble if he don't change his mind and keep the main line station in Kalispell."

Eleanor bit her lip and sat back on her heels. Thank goodness for the coverage of her tent.

"We won't tolerate no one takin' our jobs and livelihood."

Was that *another* voice, from her right? How many of them were there?

"The railroad stays in Kalispell or there will be consequences." Another shot rang out, sending everyone to the ground again.

The sound of hooves echoed through the camp, eventually fading to silence.

Shaking, Eleanor couldn't convince her legs to work.

"Fire!" one of the men shouted. "One of the tents is on fire!"

Mr. Stanton barked out orders. "Ben! Joe! Will! Secure the perimeter of the camp. We'll guard it in shifts tonight. Mr. Grinnell, Mr. and Miss Briggs, grab the buckets and fill them with water. That tent will be a loss, but we don't want the fire to spread. Needless to say, no one rides off to explore without a guard from now on."

When they'd squelched the fire, Eleanor stood on trembling legs as her father walked to her side. She touched his arm, her fingers shaking. "Are you all right?"

The firelight seemed to highlight the shadows on his face. "I'm fine, I'm fine. Are you unharmed?" Father's gaze roamed her face. "To think you were so close to where the shots rang out. If you hadn't come back to camp in time . . ."

Eleanor slipped her arm around his waist and squeezed him tight. "I am safe, Father. I promise."

He wrapped his hand around hers. "My dear girl. If anything happened to you . . ." His voice trailed off.

Tears stung Eleanor's eyes as they sat. It was the most care he'd shown her in years. Of course Father loved her, but the distance between them had grown as they grieved Mother's loss in their own way. This trip had been good for them in so many ways.

Mr. Grinnell sat down next to Eleanor and her father, his hair in disarray. The waxed points of his mustache shifted from side to side. "Well, this is a fine situation to find ourselves in. What on earth are we supposed to do now?"

11

Carter studied the ledger and read the figures listed. Losing the train service was causing headaches for everyone, but trying to create a viable solution that wouldn't eat away all the profits was making for a bigger one.

Freight service costs had gone up overnight. And no wonder. Roads would have to be worked on. More wagons were needed. The costs of hauling freight had to figure in the difficulty of the terrain, the speed in which the supplies needed to move, and the type of product being shipped. A freighter might have asked for anywhere between eight and ten dollars per hundred pounds. To move the same freight over land?

Those prices doubled and, in some cases, tripled.

His and Dad's plan was strong. It was a huge investment, but the right one. Not just for them, but for the community. Everyone would have to rally together to keep Kalispell alive. Brunswick Farms and Mill would do their part. God had blessed them with so much, they could afford the wagons and teams. Things would be tight for a while, but they'd make it.

They had to.

Carter leaned back in his chair. It was nearly three o'clock. He might as well ride out to the farm and let his father know all the numbers. He grabbed his hat.

"Jack, I'm heading out to the farm." He passed through the receiving room. "You have everything you need?"

"Everything under control. No problems. And I've got Bill here to help." Jack nodded at the young man standing to his left.

Bill ducked his head, but Carter didn't miss the way his chest puffed out a bit. It was good to see him growing in confidence around the mill. And to have someone to help Jack when Carter was away. "Well then, I'm definitely not needed." He chuckled. "And before you remind me, I'll check and see when Dad thinks he'll be harvesting, and let you know tomorrow."

Jack gave a nod, then turned back to instruct one of the men regarding something. Thank the Lord for Jack. The man had never let him down.

The walk to the livery wasn't far, but the wind was chilly. June had come in with hotter temperatures than anticipated. But now things were cooling off with a little rain. Not enough to make trouble, however, and the spring melt was going slow due to the cooler days and nights. Hopefully the slow thaw wouldn't result in flooding.

One day recently had gotten up to the seventies, but for the most part the temperatures stayed in the sixties during the day and forties at night. He grinned. How was Ellie Briggs enjoying camping up in the mountains? Her days and nights were no doubt a whole lot colder. He hoped they had planned accordingly.

Carter had heard at church that they were due back in a day or two. Mrs. Ashbury had told him that there would be a formal dinner held very soon after that and that he and his folks were invited. He really didn't care much for dressing up, but the thought of seeing Ellie in all her finery gave him cause to look forward to the event. Mrs. Ashbury promised they would be seated together, too.

Carter smiled. The Judge's wife loved to matchmake. And this time, he really didn't mind. With any luck at all, maybe he'd get a chance to know Ellie Briggs and find out if she'd realized yet that she liked him.

WEDNESDAY, JUNE 15, 1904

"It's so good to have you back under our roof." Marvella handed Eleanor a teacup and saucer. "You take it without cream, don't you?"

"Yes, please." Eleanor glanced around the room. It was lovely to be back in Kalispell. Though she would cherish the trip in many ways, it was a relief to have a private bathing space, her own bedroom, and even her serviceable skirts and blouses.

"So tell me everything. Was the trip worth the time for your father and George?"

"I believe so." Eleanor held her cup steady while Mrs. Ashbury poured tea.

"And what was the most interesting thing that you discovered?"

Marvella took her seat and then poured her own tea while she waited for Eleanor's response. Eleanor took a sip, savoring the rich flavor of the black tea, then rested the cup on the saucer. She wanted to bring up her father's decision to remain in the area, but how to start?

Marvella held out a plate. "Cookie?"

Sir Theophilus, who had been sleeping in a most contented manner until that moment, perked up. He came bouncing across the room to jump and yip until Marvella emptied her hands and could take him in her arms.

"Before I talk about the trip, I did wish to speak to you about something else." Eleanor took another sip of tea. "Father is considering settling here in Kalispell. He wants to get on with writing a book—his life's work."

"That would be wonderful!" Marvella seemed more than a little excited. "Oh, my dear, you could not ask for a better place to call home. Kalispell is picturesque, as you know, and the people are so kind. I know there are worries about the train services being removed, but between you and me, there will always be a way to come and go, and such things do not worry me. Once Louis Hill realizes the money to be made with a spur line between Whitefish and Kalispell, we'll have regular service again. Until then, our men are capable of figuring a way to keep us moving. Never fear."

"That wasn't a real concern of mine. What I have seen of town seems pleasant and, like you, I don't believe the people here will allow Kalispell to become a ghost town."

"Mercy, no. We shall continue to thrive. And if you remain, it will be very beneficial to finding you a husband."

"I wasn't really concerned about that either." She needed

the older woman to focus on real estate for the moment. "I was hoping that you might have some properties in mind that we could consider for a home."

"Oh, I surely do." Marvella's expression grew thoughtful as she considered the matter. Theophilus settled into her arms as if concentrating with her.

"There are three properties that come to mind right away. They aren't very far from here. In fact, I could arrange for you to see all three as soon as you'd like. It will take nothing more than a word to the owners. They're all good friends."

Eleanor smiled. Perfect. Marvella would pave the way for them to settle and help take the panic out of trying to find a house to suit their needs. Normally, people who took control annoyed her, but in Marvella's case, she couldn't find fault. The woman enjoyed helping people, and even though her own agenda was often benefited, it was not done with any sort of malice or self-focus. "That sounds wonderful. I'm sure Father will be able to take a few hours to consider the possibilities."

"All of the houses are spacious and have gardens and a carriage house. Of course, you'll need a carriage and horses."

"Of course." Eleanor chuckled.

"However, if you are soon to marry, your father might not prefer a large estate." She frowned and tapped her chin. "I don't know of any smaller houses."

"That's all right. I don't have a plan to marry right away. Even if you managed to find a good match." She added the latter to keep the older woman from launching into a soliloquy regarding why Eleanor should be looking to wed immediately.

Marvella's gaze fixed on Eleanor for a moment, as if she

were about to do that very thing, then she seemed to think better of it. "The larger places are also far more fitting when considering company. No doubt you'll be having plenty of visitors as your father writes his book and continues to help George with plans for the national park. At least for a time, he will want to be able to host guests and probably fundraisers."

"Yes, you are right on that fact." Perfect. That would keep Marvella's focus off her marital state. "Father will want to have George come to stay, as well as others. There are many who have been helpful to him over the years, and I'm sure he'll want to invite them to visit once we are settled."

"You know, I just thought of the perfect house. It's only two blocks away and has a little more land than most places. Given your father's love of the land and plants and such, it would be perfect. The Hennessys own it, and she told me only two days ago that her husband's health is failing and they need to move to a warmer climate. Let me get in touch with her immediately and arrange for you to see the place."

"That sounds like just the thing, thank you! I'll let Father know." She got to her feet, which prompted Sir Theophilus to take notice. He lifted his head and wagged his tail, no doubt hoping for a little attention.

"Before you go, my dear. There's one thing that has greatly troubled me. I'm generally not so remiss in my duties, but there were a variety of things that took my focus."

Her tone seemed odd. "Whatever is wrong?" Eleanor reclaimed her seat. Having been gone for three weeks, she couldn't imagine that she'd done anything to offend the poor woman.

"It's just that, well, it is apparent that you and your father are struggling with your faith, and I believe that must be fixed straightaway."

Eleanor almost choked on her tea. It was obvious? To whom? Why? "Well . . . that is to say . . . I . . ."

Marvella gave her a worried look. "I assure you that you can tell me about it. I'm the soul of discretion."

"I wasn't . . . worried . . . that you wouldn't be." Better choose her words carefully. "I won't speak for my father, although I can say that he does believe in God. My mother was a strong believer."

"Yes, you've told me that. And her loss is why you walked away from God?"

Straight to the point. An admirable trait. If there was anything Eleanor couldn't stand, it was people who beat around the bush. "It was. I watched my mother suffer a terrible death, and yet her faith in a loving God never wavered."

"You found that appalling."

Heat rose in Eleanor's chest. Stay calm . . . "Of course I did. I saw nothing loving or kind about the way my mother died. It was stomach cancer, and she was in extreme pain. Even the medicines given to her by the doctor couldn't help much."

No doubt Marvella would now scold her for her tone. Or, even worse, defend God. Instead, the older woman fell silent, and when she raised her eyes to meet Eleanor's gaze, tears glimmered there.

"That must have been so hard for you . . . just a child."

It took every bit of Eleanor's self-control not to burst into tears herself. When she finally managed to speak, her voice was rough. "It was the worst thing I have ever known." She shook her head. "Mother was so faithful to God. She told me there had to be a reason for her suffering . . . but what reason could God have had to make a loving woman suffer such pain and misery?"

Marvella's tender gaze brought Eleanor's tirade to an end. After a moment, Marvella sighed. "Life in this world is full of sorrows to be sure. There is not only pain and suffering physically, but emotionally and spiritually, as well. Still, when we belong to God, we do not bear those things alone."

But *she* had. "Mother said her faith was liberating, but I cannot see how that was true. She wasn't spared the burdens of life, nor was she kept from the bondage of death." Eleanor struggled to continue speaking. "How was any of that liberating?"

"Perhaps she spoke of the liberty that comes through knowing you will never truly face anything in life alone. Ellie, Satan has been given certain powers over this earth. Sin entered into a perfect place God created through the devil's interference and mankind listening to his lies. The struggle has been going strong ever since. Satan even attempted to turn Jesus away from the truth through his temptations. Satan worked to turn Job away from God by taking everything Job loved. No doubt Satan would have loved to turn your mother away from her faith in God."

"But why should Satan care?"

Marvella didn't even pause for breath. Her words were fierce. "Because he hates God. He hates that God is love and shows mercy to His children. He hates more than anything that God gave mankind His Son to save us from eternal death. Folks tend to forget that there is a very real spiritual battle going on for your soul."

What was she talking about? None of this made sense. "My soul? Why would Satan even care about my soul?"

"Because it's one less that God gets if he wins it."

"But I haven't given my soul to Satan." It was time to end this disturbing conversation, and yet . . . she couldn't. "The truth is, I haven't given it to anybody."

"By refusing to accept God's free gift, you make a choice, my dear."

Eleanor swallowed. How could that be possible? If she didn't want to choose God, she was choosing the devil? What a horrible thought!

She needed to escape.

Her cup and saucer clattered as she put it on the table and stood. "Thank you for your help with the house, Mrs. Ashbury. I'll let you know Father's schedule."

The older woman smiled and selected a cookie off the tray in front of her. "And you'll consider what we discussed just now?"

Eleanor nodded and practically ran from the room.

Consider that conversation?

She raced up the stairs as if her dress were on fire.

She'd hardly be able to think about anything else!

12

Formal invitations to the Ashburys' dinner on the twenty-fourth of June went out two days later.

Eleanor was still considering her conversation with Marvella when she rode her bicycle downtown to shop for a proper dinner gown. It troubled her to think that the older woman believed Eleanor's soul was somehow the property of Satan because of her indecision toward God. How could she just presume that's how it worked?

Of course . . . Mother had said that if a person wasn't for Jesus, he was against Him, but that wasn't how Eleanor felt. God had been unfair and unkind in her mother's sickness and death, but that didn't mean Eleanor wanted any part of Satan or his ways. Did one really have to choose one or the other? Couldn't a person just remain unaffiliated with either side?

She had spotted a rather elegant dress shop on one of her outings that claimed to have a wide selection of ready-made gowns for all important affairs. Perhaps they would have something appropriate for the Ashbury dinner. She didn't know how many people Mrs. Ashbury had invited, but the Brunswicks were on the list, and that alone made her nervous.

Once again there was no designated place she could leave her bicycle, so Eleanor leaned it up against the wall of the shop and made her way inside. She was immediately greeted by a middle-aged woman. "I'm Louise. How may I help you?"

"I'm looking for a gown to wear to a formal dinner. I was hoping for something ready-made."

"I have a selection of beautiful gowns. I'm sure we can find something. When is your dinner party?"

"The twenty-fourth."

The woman nodded. "That should give me enough time for any adjustments we need to make. Why don't you come with me and have a look. Do you have anything special in mind?"

Oh dear. The last time she'd given any thought to her clothes was to make certain she had proper riding clothes and woolens that could be layered underneath to keep her warm in the mountains.

"Not really. I'll trust you to know what might look best and be appropriate. Nothing immodest, of course."

"Certainly not." The woman motioned Eleanor to follow and led her to a small room. "If you'll have a seat, I'll bring several selections to you, and you can see what you think."

Eleanor waited and at last Louise reappeared with an armful of gowns. She arranged them carefully on various hooks that had been mounted in between several large mirrors. Each gown was attractive, but Eleanor's eye was immediately drawn to a light blue silk dress with a tiered skirt and short, puffed sleeves that were banded to the upper arm. The bodice neckline was scooped but not daringly low like many of the other designs. The waist came to a point in the front and back with a delicate ribbon trim. The design was simple, understated, yet elegant.

"I'd like to try this one." Eleanor pointed to the gown.

"You have a good eye. That is one of the best we have to offer. Follow me, please."

Louise took up the gown and led the way to the dressing room. "Do you have the needed undergarments?"

Eleanor shook her head. "No. I will need those as well."

The fitting took nearly an hour. The gown was everything Eleanor could have hoped for, but it was a little large. Louise drew up the material and pinned several places to ensure that it fit perfectly.

She helped Eleanor out of the dress, careful not to stick her with pins. "I can have this ready on Tuesday."

"That will be perfect. Now I have only to find a proper pair of shoes."

"May I recommend Seymore's? I believe you will find what you need there, and they are just two doors down."

"Thank you." Eleanor finished undressing and reclaimed her split-skirt suit. She had come to all but live in these outfits when exploring or riding. Would she still have cause to use them once they were settled in Kalispell?

Tomorrow she and Father were to see the Hennessy house, but Eleanor had already ridden past the property, and it looked wonderful. The house was a mix of Queen Anne and Colonial Revival, with a tower on one side and a recessed arch under the gable. The three-story house had a porch that her father would enjoy sitting on during warm evenings. She couldn't imagine that the house wouldn't be perfect for their needs. And there were extensive gardens and trees that offered wonderful shade. They would need to hire a gardener to bring some color to the landscape, but no doubt Father would enjoy taking care of the gardens as well.

At Seymore's, Eleanor found a perfect pair of shoes. She arranged for them to be delivered, then headed outside to her bicycle. She was just about to mount when she heard her name being called.

"Ellie Briggs."

She turned. Of course. Carter Brunswick. Only he would be so bold. And yet, she couldn't hold back a smile. "Hello, Mr. Brunswick."

"Please call me Carter. I believe you've earned the right."

Her smile broadened. "Yes, I believe I have."

"Where are you bound?"

"Actually, I was thinking a little refreshment might be in order. Might I buy you a cold drink?"

He frowned. "No, but I will be happy to buy you one."

"I'd like that. Where do you suggest we go?"

"There's a nice little café around the corner. They serve a wonderful iced lemonade."

She liked the casual way he handled the matter. Even at their first meeting, she knew exactly where she stood with him, and now he was more than at ease in offering her friendship.

They started for the café with Eleanor walking alongside her bicycle. Carter glanced over and motioned to the bike. "Would you like me to manage that?"

"No, thank you. I have it." Her tone was a bit sterner

than she intended, and so she hurried to continue. "I've grown accustomed to handling it, but I appreciate that you would offer."

He shrugged. "Seemed like the thing to do. Ah, see, here we are." They had turned the corner, and the shop was right there.

Eleanor again leaned the bicycle against the building, then dusted off her gloved hands. "Please lead the way."

Carter opened the door to the small shop and ushered her inside. They took a seat near the front window at a small table for two. Eleanor pulled off her gloves and tucked them in her pockets. She could make out a bit of her reflection in the mirror, and gracious, she looked windblown.

"I'm afraid I'm rather untidy." She raised a hand to smooth back her hair.

"I think you look just fine. Have you been out shopping today?"

"I have. Mrs. Ashbury insists I attend the dinner she's giving on the twenty-fourth, and I had nothing appropriate to wear for the occasion."

"Good thing we have an abundance of dress stores where you can mull over the latest fashions."

If he only knew. Actually . . . why not tell him? "I abhor shopping. My mother did too, so I suppose that's where I get my feelings or lack of them. I picked out my gown at the first store I stopped in. Same for the shoes." She laughed. "I hope I haven't disappointed you."

"On the contrary"—he looked at her with a gaze that suggested . . . what? Respect?—"I find your confession endearing. A woman who knows what she wants and wastes little time in getting it is something I can admire."

The waitress approached and Carter looked to Eleanor. "What would you like?"

"The lemonade you suggested sounds perfect."

He glanced at the waitress. "Make it two." He waited until the waitress had gone before posing a question. "Did you enjoy your time in the mountains?"

"I did. I found it refreshing. We rode for hours each day and sometimes in the most perilous of places. Oh, and I was able to meet and talk with some of the Blackfeet. There were four different men who joined our party one evening, and I enjoyed hearing some of their stories."

"That sounds intriguing. Do you think you'll be able to accomplish all you and your father have set out to do before you leave?"

Should she share her news with him? "I . . . well . . . my father and I don't plan to leave Kalispell. Father wants to settle down and write a book on his experiences as a conservationist."

He raised an eyebrow. "And do you intend to live here?"

Was his tone one of happy anticipation or simple surprise that two people from the big cities would find contentment in Kalispell?

"Yes. Mrs. Ashbury has arranged for us to see a couple of places tomorrow. I've already ridden by one of them . . . the Hennessy house. Do you know it?"

He shook his head. "I don't believe I do."

"It's rather perfect. I think Father will like it very much. It has a large area of gardens and trees."

A mischievous smile stretched across Carter's face. "Land? You will buy a house with a large plot of land? I thought you didn't approve of such things."

TRACIE PETERSON and KIMBERLEY WOODHOUSE

Eleanor stiffened. She couldn't help it. He shouldn't tease her about something she held so dear. "I don't think you can compare a few acres to the twenty thousand or so owned by your family."

He held up his hands. "I was just teasing, Miss Briggs. But clearly it struck a chord. So I have a question: isn't ownership, ownership? What if someone wanted to come and sit in your garden as part of their visit to Kalispell?"

"I suppose they could come and ask us, and we'd probably allow for it." Really! He was insufferable!

He chuckled. "I'm not trying to fight with you over this. Just to understand where the lines are drawn. My father intends to give me two hundred acres on my birthday in August. Is that too much by your standards?"

Her standards. What, exactly, did he mean by *that*? She gave a nod. "I believe it is. What in the world will you do with two hundred acres?"

"I thought I might build a house for myself and my wife . . . and any children we might have." His tone was softer than Eleanor had ever heard it. No man she'd known back east would talk about starting a family with such honesty. "I might also expand my business and set up a second mill."

Eleanor folded her arms over her chest. "That would take two hundred acres?"

"No, but what's wrong in having the land to use as I please?"

She opened her mouth to reply but found she didn't have a ready answer to his bothersome question.

What *was* wrong with that?

"Here you are." The waitress put two glasses of lemonade on the table. "Would you care for anything else?"

Carter looked at Eleanor. "Are you hungry?"

"No, I'm fine. Just the lemonade, please." She took the glass in hand and sampled the drink. It was cold and had just the right amount of tartness.

"We won't need anything else. At least for now."

The woman smiled at him and left them to their drinks.

For a moment, silence settled over the table. Best to change the subject before they ended up in an argument. "Have you and your father figured out what you will do now that the train is leaving Kalispell?"

Carter's brows arched. "We're going to invest in our own freight wagons and teams. We'll need to hire men to run the routes as well, so at least there will be jobs in the offing."

"That sounds like it will cost you a great deal. Are you sure that's the right investment with the railroad pulling out?" She pressed her lips together for a moment. "I'm sorry. That is none of my business."

Carter laughed. "I don't mind answering your questions, Ellie. While I won't go into particulars, I can tell you it's the best thing for our town and our business right now. God has always taken care of us. My goal is to be a good steward and leave the rest up to Him."

It always came back to his faith in God. Carter was just like Mama. He thought no part of life was untouched by the hand of Almighty God.

She tucked the thought away to examine at a later time. "What about the comments Mr. Grinnell made about the national park? If they build hotels and restaurants, they will probably need all the flour you can manufacture. That should help."

He took a sip and nodded. "It will, but how does that fit

in with your ideas of land management? I thought you were all about leaving the land untouched."

She was. Of course she was. However, it was starting to seem there were other sides to the issue of national parks, conservation, and land ownership she hadn't considered. "I am. But apparently that isn't monetarily feasible."

"But you're against them building in the park and making roads and such?"

"I think so." This conversation was starting to give her a headache.

"Even if it allows people to be able to see the magnificence that is there? And provides the funds to keep the land protected?"

She weighed his questions for several moments as she sipped on her lemonade. "I probably need to examine this in a bit more depth."

"That's fair. It's always wise to think things through." He chuckled. "But then, my dad teases me for *over*thinking. Apparently, I have a knack for that."

His confession made her feel at ease. The tension slipped from her shoulders. How nice to have an intelligent discussion with a friend.

Her heart skidded to a stop. Did she just acknowledge that Carter was her friend? She began to laugh.

"What's tickled your funny bone, Miss Briggs?" He waggled his eyebrows at her.

"*Now* you use your manners." The laughter bubbled up even more and she couldn't stop. "I just thought . . ." She covered her mouth with her hand and worked to contain her giggles. "I just thought of you . . . as a *friend*." She widened her eyes.

His wide smile made his eyes even more handsome—and warmed her insides considerably.

"Watch out, Ellie Briggs. I think you just might have admitted that you like me."

"It's Eleanor, you big oaf." Though she corrected him, she actually enjoyed the sound of her name on his lips.

They continued to talk about the national park, and she asked lots of questions about Kalispell, which he seemed very happy to answer.

The information she gleaned only solidified what she'd told her father the week before. She could actually envision herself putting roots down. Getting to know their neighbors and getting involved in the community. It was a new sensation.

"Sorry, you two. But we need to close up." The waitress grinned at them and walked back to the counter.

Eleanor started. "What time is it?"

Carter checked his watch. "Nearly five."

"Goodness. These long hours of sunlight are truly deceptive. I need to get home. They'll all be worried about me. Especially Mrs. Ashbury, who now has my soul to be concerned with, as well as my physical well-being." She winced. Whatever prompted her to say that . . . and with such disrespectful sarcasm?

He stood but studied her face. "Your soul?"

"Yes." She forced a laugh. Anything to lighten the tension as they moved outside. "She's concerned because I pushed my faith aside after my mother died. She's determined to set things straight."

"Well . . . leave it to Marvella to make sure you're on the right path."

What? She stopped cold. "What do you mean by that?"

His gaze was kind, but firm. "Just what I said. There's the right path or the wrong one."

What on earth was wrong with these people? First Marvella tells her the devil has her soul. Now Carter was saying she was on the wrong path? "That's ridiculous. What about neutral middle ground? I believe in God. I just don't agree with how He does things, so it's best for me to keep my distance."

Why did he look so stricken. So . . . sad?

"Sorry, Ellie, but that's the worst decision you could ever make."

Eleanor gripped the handlebars of her bicycle. "Well, fortunately for you, Mr. Brunswick, you don't have to live my life. My decisions are just that—mine." She swung her leg over the seat and sat down. "Thank you for the lemonade and conversation."

With that she pushed off, refusing to look back and see if Carter watched her ride away.

13

SATURDAY, JUNE 18, 1904

His parents' farm offered a respite Carter didn't have in town. The change of pace was always good, and after the last few weeks, he really needed a couple days away from town. Out here, everything was less hectic. The only real worry was late-season snow or a thunderstorm with hail that blew through without notice on a summer day.

Carter gazed at the prairie stretching out before his parents' house. In the fading light of the day, the crickets were out, chirping to one another. In the distance, a coyote cried, and a moment later, another howl pierced the quiet. Carter shivered. Coyotes were usually pretty afraid of people. But their high-pitched cries still unsettled him.

Early one morning when he was about twelve, he'd heard the cries of a coyote pack close to the house when he and his family were getting ready for early morning chores. Dad had told him to stay inside, but Carter hadn't listened. He snuck out and followed his dad to the chicken coop. White feathers littered the ground. What was left of two hens lay twenty feet from the coop. His stomach turned sour, and he ran back into the house, diving into his bed and praying the Lord would keep the coyotes away.

Carter wasn't afraid of the mangy animals anymore, but he still didn't like them. He stuffed his hands in his pants pockets and leaned against the porch railing. Despite the various animals coming to life as the moon rose, the peace and quiet surrounded him. Town was convenient. Yet out here . . .

He inhaled the sweet summer scent of wildflowers mixed with the pungent fragrance of grass and dirt. Out here, he could think clearly. See life better.

Maybe, just maybe, if things worked out, he'd speed up his timeline for building a home out here.

The door creaked and Dad and Fred came out, taking their usual chairs on the front porch. Carter stayed leaning against the rail, anxious to begin this conversation. They needed to finalize details around freighting, but the two men were discussing the current winter wheat crop and how good it looked. Harvest was just about ready to begin, and his father had already started hiring extra help. Fred had brought on extra hands as well.

"You know we talked about letting the fields go fallow for a year." Fred leaned back. "We could divide the fields and fallow one and then next year fallow the other. That would cut back the amount of wheat we produce."

"We are at the point of renegotiating a contract with Pillsbury." Dad's words were thoughtful. "We're both at a good place financially."

"Agreed." Fred looked to Carter. "You could handle half the crop and we wouldn't need to ship grain."

"I'd still have to figure out what to do with shipping the flour, but at least this would solve part of the problem."

The more he talked about it, the more it seemed he thought it doable and prudent. The fields hadn't been rested in a while.

Dad gave a slow nod. "After we harvest this crop, we can put the farther fields to rest and just replant the southern acreage. That makes it easy enough to get to the mill."

Fred got to his feet. "I heard from a couple of guys in town today that there's going to be a town meeting regarding the roads to Missoula and to Whitefish. The thoughts are that Kalispell needs to get to work and make the existing roads better. That will help a lot. But for now, I'm heading home. See you at church tomorrow."

"There's a great deal to consider." Dad stretched and gave a yawn. "See you tomorrow, Fred."

Dad's partner gave a wave over his shoulder as he left the porch. He untied his horse and gave one final wave before heading off down the drive. Dust kicked up and blew across the front yard, reminding Carter that the rain had been sparse. Hopefully they wouldn't have trouble with fires. It seemed every year the rains held back, dry thunderstorms would come up to set the forests in the mountains on fire. There had been a time when fires in September had burned the summer wheat as well. Farming wasn't a risk for the faint of heart.

"I'll head to bed too." Carter got up off the porch rail. "I wish all of this could be settled."

"The Lord will direct us soon enough, son. It's our job to be ready for action."

SUNDAY, JUNE 19, 1904

Carter wasn't all that surprised when the next day's service reiterated that very point. The pastor had spoken of various times in the Bible when God called his people to readiness. There were requirements of the people, things that had to be done first, but God always came through with direction and deliverance.

It would be no different for them now.

Carter waited with the wagon while his father and mother told their friends good-bye. He saw Ellie from afar and gave a wave. She waved back in a shy sort of manner. Maybe she didn't want anyone to notice that she was responding to him.

She stayed close to her father's side. No doubt they were only there because the Ashburys made it so they couldn't refuse. The Judge and his wife could be . . . insistent. Hadn't they all been on the receiving end of Marvella's instructions?

He smiled. The old woman was pure energy and enthusiasm. If there was a queen of Kalispell, it was she. She kept watch over her kingdom and people as if she were born to it. The nice thing was that no one seemed to mind too much. Marvella was kind and encouraging. She might be a little too forward or too much into a person's business at times, but it was always done out of love.

Dad joined Carter at the wagon. "We need to get on home. Your mother invited the Briggses for lunch."

Mom gave him a wide-eyed look. "I thought it was about time I got to know Ellie better. After all, she clearly has your eye."

Carter wasn't fooled by that feigned innocence. "What do you mean?"

She laughed as Dad handed her up to the wagon seat. "You watch her all the time."

"I do not!" He climbed up to sit on the small seat behind his parents. He leaned forward to see his mother's face. "I find her interesting, but she isn't interested in me."

For some reason, he couldn't share with his parents what Ellie had told him at the café. God was obviously tugging at her heart, and he didn't want to get in the way.

"You're such a man." Mom shook her head. "We'll see what happens. . . ."

Dad climbed up and took the driver's seat. He put the horses in motion and headed them down the road for the farm. Mother waved to a couple of her friends and then turned back to Carter.

"There's something about her." She smiled. "I just have a feeling."

Carter did as well. He'd been intrigued by Ellie since they'd first encountered each other. Still, he wouldn't be foolish enough to pursue her unless she reconciled her heart to God first. Until then, they could be friends. Plain and simple.

A pity that patience wasn't one of his virtues.

The Brunswick farm was charming. The two-story log house with its inviting wrapping porch sat in the middle of a lush green yard that had obviously had some tender care. Flowerbeds burst with colors of red, purple, yellow, blue, and orange. The scent of roses teased her nose. Pink and cream hollyhocks lined the east side of the house, softening the rough log exterior with a feminine touch. Two rocking chairs and a small table sat just to the right of the front door. And on the left was a swing swaying in the summer breeze. It was tempting to skip lunch and sit in that swing, letting the afternoon slip by in peace.

Eleanor shook her head. That trip to the mountains must have done something to her brain. When did she ever want to sit and watch the clouds roll by?

When they sat down for lunch, she wasn't at all sure what to expect. Marvella set a formal table at every meal, but here there was more simplicity. Mrs. Brunswick had put out fine china, but the silver was ordinary and there was no crystal. Well-used linen napkins were set at each place and the table was covered with a matching linen cloth with an oil lantern hanging down over the table.

When Carter's father noticed Eleanor looking at the lamp he chuckled. "We don't have electricity out here yet. One day, maybe. We still light with oil and candles, but we do all right."

Carter shook his head. "I prefer the ease of electricity."

"I do as well." Father gave a hearty nod. "I also have to admit to preferring indoor conveniences and running water."

"Maybe one day." Mr. Brunswick passed her father a platter of roast beef.

The table discussion covered a variety of topics, but Eleanor remained silent. Her father and Mr. Brunswick seemed to have a lot in common. Carter's father discussed some of his farming methods, including a decision to let part of the farm go fallow for the year.

Father had shared some insight with her when they'd been camping. After seeing all the farms and ranches, he'd found it prudent to understand the true nature of how the different entities used vast acreages of land. She had to admit, her opinion about people owning large portions of land had begun to shift.

Her question to Carter about why his father felt he needed twenty thousand acres came back to her. For some reason it didn't seem all that important anymore. There was something about this farm, and the ease in which the Brunswicks gathered for Sunday dinner, that left her feeling a part of the family.

There was no need to push for answers to questions that really didn't matter.

"Eleanor, you went to college, is that correct?"

Carter's mom's voice broke through her reverie.

She looked up at her. "Yes, Mrs. Brunswick, I did. I love to learn and studied all that I could to help Father in his work."

"I think education is very important. Carter went to college, as did his oldest sister for a couple of years. She fell in love and married a young man from her classes, however, and that was the end of that." Mrs. Brunswick smiled. "Our middle daughter fell in love in grade school and married that boy as soon as we'd give permission, but she loves to read."

"Ellie always loved to read." Father patted her hand. "I believe reading is the single most important thing we can do."

"Oh, do you prefer being called Ellie?"

The innocent way the older woman asked the question made her pause.

Her heart sped up just a bit and it was difficult to breathe. She closed her eyes and then opened them again. "My mother called me Ellie. After she died, I insisted everyone call me Eleanor because it was too painful to have others use her name for me." She caught her father's teary expression and covered his hand with her own. "But I have to admit, I *do* prefer Ellie."

What was she saying? She searched her heart . . .

It was true. She did prefer being called Ellie. As she accepted that truth, another crack around her heart seemed to ease the tightness. But she couldn't look at Carter. He'd surely gloat—

Then she did anyway.

His soft smile sent a little tingle up her neck. Yes, she definitely preferred Ellie.

"Reading is valuable." Mr. Brunswick looked at his son. "Carter learned to read at his mother's knee before he was three years old. Used to make people marvel at his ability."

"Ellie read at a young age too. Perhaps not quite that young, but I remember her reading the Bible with her mother when she was only five."

She remembered those days as well. Remembered the scent of her mother's perfume and the tenderness she took with Eleanor as they worked through stories in the Bible. Especially the book of Daniel. She loved the stories of how Daniel stood fast before the king regarding rich food and drink. Mother had always been firm about getting plenty of healthy foods and exercising in the sunshine. She was a confirmed believer that rich foods led to sickness and that being indoors all the time caused one to have a sallow complexion.

"*Take a walk every day, Ellie. Get out and breathe deep. Keep a fast step so that your heart has to work a little harder. Muscles are honed by working them.*"

"Isn't that right, Ellie?"

She startled and looked at her father. "I'm . . . I'm so sorry. I was just remembering something Mother said." Taking a breath, she blinked away the tears in the corners of her eyes. "What was it you asked me?"

For a moment, he didn't speak. Just stared at her. He gave her an almost imperceptible nod, then cleared his throat. "I was telling the Brunswicks about your love of reading and how you and your mother read through the entire Bible by the time you were six years old."

Ellie nodded, catching Carter's watchful gaze. "It's true. Mother thought there was no better book to read and study."

Carter's mother gathered a couple of empty bowls. "I agree with her on that. It must have been so hard for you both to lose her. You have my utter sympathy. I lost my mother young as well." Mrs. Brunswick spoke with such tenderness. And love. "Mothers are so very dear to us that their loss creates impossibly difficult spaces in our lives. I've found that only God can fill those holes. What of you, Ellie?"

She swallowed the lump in her throat. "I don't think I ever filled them." She looked at her plate and took up the remaining piece of bread. "I doubt I ever will." She slathered butter on it.

For a long silent moment no one said a word. Ellie glanced at her father. Was he upset by her words? His eyes stayed fixed on his plate, shoulders tense.

Then Mrs. Brunswick got to her feet. "I have a cake for

dessert. Jacob always insists on something sweet at the end of the meal."

Carter's dad patted his stomach. "After we finish what I'm sure will be a delicious dessert, I'd like to show you around the farm, Stewart. You're welcome to come too, Miss Briggs, but I figure you might prefer sitting on the porch. There's something about it that just can't be beat."

The chance to try out that porch swing sounded like just the thing. "Thank you. I think I would enjoy that."

They ate the strawberries-and-cream cake that Mrs. Brunswick furnished and then made their way outside. Ellie took a seat, and Carter's mother joined her while the men headed off toward one of the barns.

"Ellie." She whispered her own name, trying it out. Rather than making her sad or annoyed, she loved it. Clung to it.

Cherished it.

Ellie settled into the swing and felt the tension ease from her as the swing began to rock. It was as though she'd done this a hundred times before. It felt so . . . right.

Like she was at home.

She gazed out across the open landscape, toward the mountains.

Carter's mother gave a sigh. "There's a peacefulness out here that I've never found anywhere else."

Ellie nodded, her gaze roaming the landscape that stretched before them. The white wheat danced in the breeze. The fragrance was sweet and earthy at the same time. She swallowed her pride and let her thoughts flow. "Growing up in the city, I never experienced anything like this. I wish everyone could."

"I'm sure that would be beneficial to the soul." The older

woman rocked at an easy, slow pace. "Sometimes people spend an entire lifetime trying to find peace of mind and heart."

Was she speaking about Ellie's earlier comment? Only one way to find out. "I hope I didn't offend you with my thoughts about never filling the hole in my heart. I'm not sure I want to fill it with something else. Her memories and love were important to me. They always will be."

"Oh, my dear, I wasn't suggesting you fill it to rid yourself of your mother's memory. To my way of thinking, the hole left behind comes from her absence, and nothing can ease that pain save God. Especially given how much your mother loved the Lord."

"How do you know that she loved Him so?"

"She spent the time and trouble to teach you to read the Bible. She took time to go over the stories and make sure you understood them, am I right?"

"Yes."

"She must have loved God a great deal and you as well. It's an arduous task to teach another to read, but having done the same thing with my children, I know it's a task of love . . . a special mission that God gives to each parent. Jacob also read with Carter and the girls. He perhaps did it less often than I did, but he knew it was important to share God's Word with them and to answer their questions. I'll bet you had a lot of questions. You look like the inquisitive type." She raised a brow at Ellie.

"Yes." The word was barely audible, so moved was she by the fact that Carter's mother truly cared about her answers.

They slowed the swing to a stop.

Ellie drew a deep breath. "My mother was always infinitely patient to answer my questions. She made it easy for me to understand."

"But then the answers you thought you understood failed you."

Eleanor turned to look Mrs. Brunswick in the eye. How did she know that? "Yes. My mother died, and all the while I thought God would heal her . . . deliver her from her pain and the cancer."

"But He did. He healed her completely."

Tears sprang to her eyes. This was the last place she wanted to cry. "But . . ." Her voice broke, so she tried again. "He took her away from me. That's not what I prayed for." A tear slid down her cheek.

"I know. I didn't pray for it either. God knew that I wanted my mother to get well and stay with me . . . with our family."

"Yes." Ellie wiped away the tear, but others came to take its place.

"It's hard to accept that a loving God would let such things happen. Allow sickness. Take a mother from her child or a child from its mother. I don't think I'll ever completely understand, but I take comfort in His faithfulness to never leave me to bear it alone. Ellie, God is there for you even now. He doesn't desire you to carry this alone. He loves you, just as He loved your mother."

Ellie shook her head. "But when will He take something else I love . . . someone else?"

"Oh my dear." She reached over and took Ellie's hand in hers. Mrs. Brunswick's hands were warm and comforting. "The Lord isn't randomly taking people out of our lives to make us suffer or do us harm. Death came into the world because of sin, I'm sure your mother shared that with you at some point."

Ellie swallowed. Yes, she understood everyone sinned. Understood her need for a Savior. That's why she'd put all her trust in Jesus as a child. But God betrayed that trust. And how was sin connected to Mother's death? Her cancer? "I'm not sure what you're getting at."

Mrs. Brunswick squeezed Ellie's fingers. "Adam and Eve's sin in the garden brought separation, death, and pain into the world. It brought sickness and many other things the Lord never intended us to experience. But even when His creation rebelled against Him, God still had a plan in motion. He was working things together to reconcile us back to Him, and though I don't always understand how or why, He brings redemption out of pain and suffering, if we let Him."

"But how can I trust Him when I don't know who I'm going to lose next? Or what He will take from me?" She sniffed.

"How can you not?" Mrs. Brunswick's voice was gentle, yet pressing. "What is the alternative? A life lived in fear of the next loss? A life of empty sorrows and holes in your heart each time someone goes away. Death is never easy to face, Ellie."

She buried her face in her hands and sobbed.

"Ellie, you are precious to God. It doesn't matter that you don't understand fully why things happen the way they do. But putting your trust in Him is so much better than anything else you can do. I assure you, Jesus is the only one who can make it right—who can help you understand and find joy in life."

Before Ellie knew it, Carter's mother had a comforting

arm around her shoulder. With a small cry, Ellie wrapped her arms around the woman and held her tight.

It was almost as if Mama had come back to comfort her for just a moment.

What was going on here?

Ellie was in his mother's arms, sobbing her heart out. He had come back from touring with the men and hoped to have a little time with Ellie while his father and Stewart were looking at the garden.

But now . . .

He backed away. He would not intrude on this moment. He whispered a prayer for Ellie. She was in wonderful hands. His mother would know what to do and how to help her. It was just . . .

He wanted to be the one to offer Ellie comfort.

He made his way to the back door. His heart ached for Ellie in a way he couldn't understand. There had been times when his little sisters broke down and their mother had held them close as she was holding Ellie. When Carter had been very little, she had done the same for him. But Ellie was strong and stubborn. She wouldn't have easily been moved to tears.

He climbed the steps to the rear porch and sat down on the railing for a moment to think. Stewart Briggs had just told them that he'd bought the Hennessy house. Maybe that was upsetting Ellie. Maybe she didn't want to remain in Kalispell.

A terrible thought crossed his mind . . .

Maybe her father was ill and that was the reason he had

chosen to settle down. Maybe Ellie knew he was sick and was afraid of the outcome.

Stop it! Stop overthinking it.

"Whatever it is, Lord, please help her. Help her to draw close to You . . . to put her trust in You. Let her see the truth." He paused in his whispered prayer, then let himself say what he really wanted.

"And if there's anything I can do to help her know You, show me what to do."

14

Thursday, June 23, 1904

Steam hissed as the giant steel wheels of the train squealed on the tracks. The sound bounced off the brick building, echoing through the platform. Seconds later, people poured from the train. Carts clacked across the wooden planks, ready to be stacked with luggage and other goods the train held for the town.

The lovely two-story depot held a dear place, and Marvella had never acknowledged it. Now, the thought of losing this heart of her town . . . She shook her head against the thought. Scanning the scene, she refused to allow any melancholy to waylay her love for Kalispell. The depot's tall windows were plentiful, giving it a welcoming effect to anyone around.

Couples embraced. A young boy and girl tugged on the suit coat of a man kissing his wife on the cheek, clearly happy their father was home. A railroad worker raced down the platform to the head of the train, a brown slip of paper flapping in his hands.

Marvella watched the scene, a smile turning up the corners of her mouth. It was a blessing to watch people reunite with those they loved. To see the relief of many travelers, knowing they were home. How empty the town would be without the bustle of life the railroad brought to it.

"Mrs. Ashbury?"

Marvella turned from the bustling platform and spied Gus approaching, a small brown box tied with twine in his hands. "Gus, you are a treasure." She smiled. "You found it."

The ginger-haired man blushed to his roots. "It was buried under a stack of papers in my office. I'm not sure how it got there."

Sir Theophilus squirmed in her arms, whining. "No, sir. You will be a good boy and stay right here. There is a treat at home for good behavior." She glanced at Gus. "No harm, Gus. I know things happen. If you'll just slip it right under my arm here and—*No!*"

The box fell to the ground as Sir Theophilus wriggled free and bounded to the ground. He danced in a circle around his mistress as she tried to catch him. The train hissed steam again, and the white dog jumped, barking at the train. The whistle blew, and Sir Theophilus took off across the wooden planks, yipping all the way.

"After him, Gus!"

The man took off after the white fluff ball, and she followed, puffing her way through the crowd. Shoulders bumped into her own. Luggage hit her shins, and she barely withheld an unladylike grunt.

Were these travelers oblivious to the emergency at hand? Why were they not moving out of her way? Breaking free of the mass of people, she paused and strained on her tiptoes.

Gus's red head bobbed only fifteen feet ahead of her. He was running toward the exit of the depot.

"No, Sir Theophilus! You stay right there, mister!" Gus's voice ricocheted off the brick building. Rough yips followed, and Marvella entered the cool shade of the depot to find Gus on the ground, papers everywhere.

Her bosom heaved. "Where?"

"Up East Avenue." Gus grunted.

Marvella turned and looked through the open doorway. Sure enough, Sir Theophilus was bouncing up East Avenue, zigzagging under a wagon and up on the sidewalk. "Naughty dog!" She ran as fast as her skirts would allow.

Several townspeople paused in the street and on the sidewalk. It wasn't every day one saw the Judge's wife run through town after a miniature canine. Tendrils of hair escaped her once-impeccable updo, waving behind her like a flag. Sweat slid down her temples into the lace collar of her light blue silk day dress. Silk! She sucked in a breath. What an impractical fabric to run in.

Marvella could feel the curious stares and knew word of her escapade would reach the Judge. She practically skipped across the dusty street, a frown deepening on her face. Her husband had warned her Sir Theophilus needed a leash when she was in town. But she had stubbornly refused. He was such a good boy and never ran away.

Oh, how she disliked being proven wrong!

Marvella slowed her footsteps, spotting the little terror. He was flipped upside down on the porch of a white house, pink tongue lolling out the side of his mouth. He rolled back and forth, body wriggling with delight.

At last! Marvella clutched her skirts in her hand, easing

her pace to a manageable stroll. She didn't need him running away again, but the dog spotted her. Sir Theophilus sat up and yipped.

"You scoundrel!" She stepped up on the porch. "Come here, pup. It's time to go home. We've had enough excitement for one day." She leaned forward, arms outstretched, expecting him to jump into her arms as he always did.

His black eyes glittered in the afternoon sun. He shifted on his haunches, seeming to measure each step his owner took toward him.

Marvella swallowed. "Please, Sir Theophilus. I am tired of running."

But he was unmoved. He barked again and bounded down the stairs, barreling under Marvella's skirts. She twisted around to catch her balance and fell with a loud *oomph* on the porch stair, landing on her rump.

Tears stung her eyes, and Marvella dropped her head into her hands for a moment, her shoulders shaking. Then she tipped her head back and let out a peal of laughter.

"Well, Lord, I must have needed a little humbling today."

Sir Theophilus ran back up the stairs and jumped into her arms, snuggling into the crook of her elbow. Marvella sighed and snuggled the dog close.

She was never going to hear the end of this.

FRIDAY, JUNE 24, 1904

One last look in the mirror and she gave herself a nod. "Well, Eleanor, you're ready for society." With that, she headed down the stairs.

She peeked into the dining room and it took her breath away.

The grandeur of Marvella's formal dinner table was not to be ignored. The servants had outdone themselves in arranging her chosen silver, crystal, and china. The table glittered under the electric chandelier where hundreds of crystal pieces reflected the light.

Fresh flowers from the Ashbury gardens were arranged in tall crystal vases. Each arrangement was lavish and full and set on risers so as to not interfere with table conversation once guests were seated. The finest of ivory linens graced the table, and everywhere Eleanor looked, things sparkled.

"I see you're sneaking a look." Marvella's voice caused her to jump and put a hand to her throat.

"I couldn't help myself." Eleanor turned. "It is stunning. It would rival the tables of the Astors and Vanderbilts. No one in high society could find fault with it."

Marvella looked at her oddly, then laughed. "Oh, my dear, someone will always find fault with something, but I never let it give me the slightest worry." She gave Eleanor a wry grin. "Like when I had to chase my darling dog through the streets of Kalispell. I'm sure several tongues wagged about that as I looked very silly. But I can't let wagging tongues disturb me."

The Judge came to stand next to his wife, slipping an arm around her shoulders. "Well said, my dear. However, you could listen to your husband when he suggests that it is best to get a leash for outdoor walks."

Eleanor giggled as Marvella waved a hand. "Oh fiddlesticks, dear husband. It was one incident."

"Whatever you say, my dear." The Judge chuckled. "I just stopped to tell you how beautiful you look tonight. And you as well, Miss Briggs. You both shine."

Eleanor dipped her head, his kind words washing over her. "Thank you, Judge. I was just telling Marvella a similar sentiment over her dining arrangements."

"And that is where I take my leave." The large man shrugged. "Enjoy your discussion, ladies."

Marvella sighed as she watched her husband cross the room to some acquaintances. "That husband of mine. What would I do without him?"

The love in the older woman's voice made Eleanor smile. "You two are a perfect match."

"We are, indeed, my dear. And we will come back to *your* perfect match in a moment. But I must say I am pleased the dinner setting is to your liking. I don't do these things for approval or for society. I do them to share what God has given us. And because I think it's important to appreciate traditions and heirlooms. I haven't used the Meissen china in ages. It dates to the 1780s, when my great-grandmother was gifted the set on her wedding day."

"It's beautiful. I've always been fond of Meissen."

Almost as much as she adored Marvella's gown. Dark plum, the neckline was modestly appointed with a slight vee that held a velvet bow at the point. The gown appeared to be silk with a very fine, sequined tulle overlay. The sleeves were long and full and fell loose at the wrist.

"I must compliment you on your gown. You look lovely in it."

Marvella gave a slight bow. "Thank you, dear. It's a bit lavish, but I found it in Paris. Milton and I took a trip to

France last year, just before Christmas, and I haven't had an occasion to wear it. Usually I'm content with our dressmakers here. They are just as talented, and I don't need to go touting around that my gown is from Paris. But the color was just too perfect to pass up." She smoothed away a wrinkle in her sleeve.

"It does compliment your figure and complexion." Eleanor meant every word. Marvella wasn't one to brook nonsense nor false praise, and Eleanor respected that enough to not even attempt such.

"As does your gown. That blue silk draws out your eyes. I believe you will charm the stuffing right out of Carter Brunswick and any other single young man who happens to see you. Now, come along. Let's go and see what the men have gotten up to. I'm sure some of our guests have already arrived and I want you to help me host. Having you at my side will be a blessing, and it will allow you to get to know all of my dear friends."

Eleanor followed the older woman to the large parlor, where she found her father and others discussing the national park. She glanced around for some sign of Carter, but he wasn't present.

She touched Marvella's shoulder. "Excuse me just a moment. I'd like to greet my father."

The older woman waved her on. "Of course, my dear."

Sir Theophilus appeared from out of nowhere and insisted on Marvella's attention as he began to dance around her and yip.

Eleanor grinned at the small pup—funny how it had grown into her affections—and moved across the room to her father, her gaze sweeping the large area. Still no sign of

Carter. Anticipation zipped up her spine. Heavens, she was actually looking forward to seeing him. Still, she needed to be careful tonight. If she showed even a sliver of interest in Carter, Marvella would spot it right away. The less interference on that front, the better.

"My dear Ellie. What a charming dress." Father studied her as she approached. "You're the image of your mother."

The compliment snatched the breath from her lungs. She warmed with his kind words. Swallowing tears, she leaned forward and kissed her father's cheek. "Thank you, Father. That is kind of you to say. And you look dapper." She turned to Mr. Grinnell and another man she didn't know. "Good evening, gentlemen."

"Miss Briggs, it's so nice to have your company once again." Mr. Grinnell gave a slight bow. He turned to the man at his side. "This is Mr. William Whipps, one of Kalispell's most celebrated citizens."

She offered the older man a nod of acknowledgment. "Mr. Whipps."

"This is Eleanor Briggs, Stewart's daughter."

Mr. Whipps bowed. "It is a pleasure to meet you. These gentlemen speak highly of you."

"I'm sure they are prejudiced." She slipped her arm through her father's and gave it a slight squeeze. "I've heard great things about you, Mr. Whipps. I believe you were the first elected mayor of Kalispell."

"Yes, and the only one to serve three consecutive two-year terms." He rocked back on his heels, chest puffed out.

Eleanor almost expected his buttons to pop off his snow-white dress shirt.

Several new guests arrived, and Eleanor excused herself.

"I'll let you men get back to your discussion. I promised Mrs. Ashbury I would help her host tonight. She wants to make sure I get a chance to meet all her friends."

She turned and ran right into someone's shoulder. Strong hands gripped her arms, helping to right her before she tumbled. "Good evening, Miss Briggs."

Carter Brunswick's voice washed over her like a warm breeze. Eleanor cleared her throat and took a step back, pulling her arms from his grasp. Gracious, when had it gotten so hot in this room? "I apologize for not looking where I was going. Good evening, Mr. Brunswick."

He grinned. "You look different tonight. Quite pretty."

"Meaning that I look terrible the rest of the time?" The retort slipped out before she could stop it. Why couldn't she graciously accept his compliment like a normal woman?

Carter let out a laugh. "I would have been just fine with you wearing that bicycle costume of yours, but I would imagine Marvella would have had something to say about it."

"You might be surprised. Our hostess seems at ease with my costume, as you call it. She probably would have dressed it up a bit with a corsage or perhaps let me borrow some jewelry. She definitely would have made me feel like a princess. If you don't believe me, note Sir Theophilus. You'll see he's wearing one of the Judge's bow ties."

They both glanced over at the small dog curled in Marvella's arms.

Carter snapped his gaze back to hers with a wide grin. "I would expect nothing less. I've never seen Marvella make anyone ill at ease. She has a kind word for each person and makes everyone feel as though they are the most important person in the room."

Eleanor nodded as she watched the older woman move from one guest to the next. She took time with each person, leaving a trail of smiles and laughter in her wake. What would it be like to be so confident? To make people feel at ease and cared for simply by being herself? "I wish I could be more like her. I think my nerves get the better of me, however. You might not believe this, but I'm shy by nature."

"You're right, it is hard to believe." He moved a little closer, his tone playful. "The woman who accosted me at the train depot certainly did not seem shy."

Her cheeks grew hot. Goodness, the last thing she wanted to do was blush like a silly schoolgirl. "I was worn from the trip that day. I just needed to get things arranged and be done with it. I am sorry for the way I acted, you know."

"I know. Ellie, I—"

"Leave it to you to already have Ellie cornered." His mother's tone was warm and teasing, cutting off whatever Carter was about to say. "How are you, my dear?" She leaned over to give her a hug.

Eleanor embraced the woman, trying to catch a look at Carter from her periphery. What had he been about to say? "I'm fine. Your son is always entertaining."

"That's one way of putting it. I must compliment you on your gown. The style is so flattering and you make it regal."

"Thank you, Mrs. Brunswick. It was a last-minute choice that I am glad to have found. After spending years traveling around with Father, I haven't bothered to keep up with my wardrobe. Mrs. Ashbury startled me when she mentioned this dinner and how she intended to introduce us to all her Kalispell friends."

"Well, it suits you perfectly. Don't you think so, Carter?"

"I do."

Their gazes met again and Carter gave her a wink.

Her face was now definitely on fire. Ignoring Carter's impudence, Eleanor turned back to Mrs. Brunswick and studied the woman's evening gown. Though her style was much simpler than many of the other women present, the modest neckline, puffed sleeves, and navy-blue silk with black velvet trim brought out the deep blue of her eyes. "You look beautiful, Mrs. Brunswick."

"Now, I thought you were going to call me Sarah."

"Oh, here you are. I see Carter has already found you." Marvella joined the trio. Sir Theophilus lifted his head to examine the group. When no treats were produced, he sniffed and snuggled back into Marvella's arms.

"How could I not gravitate toward the prettiest *unmarried* woman in the room?"

Eleanor restrained a smile. Such a wise man to qualify his statement. No woman wanted to feel she was less attractive than another. As far as she could tell, most of the women in the room were years older and married.

No doubt Marvella had planned it that way.

"She is at that." Marvella took hold of Eleanor's arm. "And she has promised to help me host this evening. However, I want to ask that you be her escort into the dining room, Carter. I've seated the two of you together so that you can get to know each other better."

Of course she had. Eleanor wasn't sure if she should laugh or be upset that the woman was so determined to marry her off.

But Carter hadn't lost his manners. "I appreciate that, Mrs. Ashbury, and will be happy to act as Ellie's escort."

She hooked her arm through Eleanor's and pulled her away from the Brunswicks. "Well, come, my dear. I want to welcome my guests and introduce you at the same time."

Eleanor enjoyed meeting each of Marvella's friends. Many of them wore expensive, tailored clothes and jewelry that bespoke their fashionable upbringing. However, none of them were pretentious nor the least bit standoffish. In most of the social circles Eleanor had been a part of in New York, the women were reserved to the point of being cold. She had been taught by her mother at an early age that women in society were the eyes and ears of their husbands and fathers. They were raised to listen carefully, read between the lines in conversations, and make open judgments of what wasn't being said as much as what was.

The ladies in Marvella's social circle seemed far less concerned with such things. They laughed and were witty and shared stories of their lives without hesitation.

What a delightful gathering!

When dinner was finally announced she glanced around to find Carter. She hadn't far to look as he was at her side.

"I'm here to do my duty." He offered his arm.

Eleanor placed her hand on his black coat sleeve. "Sorry that you had to be singled out. I'm sure my father would have been happy to escort me."

Carter shook his head. "I'm happy to be chosen."

Something in his tone assured her he spoke the truth. Carter never seemed to pretend to be anything more or less than he was. He was always simply himself.

Up and down the full length of the Ashburys' table the conversation picked up. The man on her left was deep in discussion with another man, leaving Eleanor no choice but to look to Carter. She caught him gazing at her profile, and he smiled once again when their eyes met.

"I'm glad we have this time together."

She nodded and rubbed her fingers along her linen serviette. She wanted to ask him why he was glad to have time with her. Especially since almost every conversation ended with some sort of argument. Better to change the subject. "It's such a well-set table, don't you think? Such a spread."

He glanced to the left and then to the right. "Marvella knows how to impress."

Eleanor met his warm gaze. "By the way, I very much enjoyed having dinner with your parents. Father did as well. I think he figured your father would be all about his profits and money, but said he was quite knowledgeable about conservation and land management."

"Dad has made it his goal to tend the land as he felt God had called Adam to do. We've always tried to nurture the land and care for it in a way that improves it rather than uses it up."

"I like that." Her shoulders relaxed a bit. After the stress of meeting the Ashburys' guests, it was nice to talk to a friend. A friend. Nothing more. "I still don't understand the need for one person to own so much land, but coming here has caused me to see things from a different angle. It's clear that wheat is beneficial to all, and we should be thankful for the farmers who are willing to work so hard to grow the crops."

"A great many people benefit, to be sure." He placed his napkin on his lap. "So how goes the national park plans?"

Eleanor winced. While things were certainly better between her and Father, she still didn't understand why he kept her in the dark about his work. "I'm not sure. I think I might have said some things that were contrary to what my father and Mr. Grinnell and Mr. Hill hope to accomplish. They're less than eager to have me in their conversations these days."

Carter settled his knife and fork on the edge of his plate and took a sip of water. "What in the world could you have said that would cause them to put you aside?"

"I don't like the idea of building hotels and concessions in the park."

"I agree. The area they've chosen for the park is my favorite place to go and commune with God. I can't imagine it being blemished by hotels and such all over the place." He twirled the stem of his water glass between his thumb and index finger. "On one hand, I appreciate the progress we've made in the last few decades. Trains, horseless carriages, industry making all sorts of things easier. But I'm also sad about some of the ways it is changing our country."

She pulled back and looked at him. Blinking several times, she realized her jaw had dropped. Terribly unladylike of her. "Carter Brunswick, I'm shocked that we agree."

"Over time, Miss Briggs, I hope to amaze you even more." He gave her a wide grin and turned back to his meal.

The servants brought in platters and moved around the table to offer their amazing dishes to the guests. Eleanor helped herself to baked salmon and asparagus. Carter did the same. For a time, they ate in silence, accepting or refusing other foods that came throughout the course of the meal. But soon they picked up the conversation right where they'd left off.

The more they chatted, the more Eleanor found that Carter agreed with her on a great many things.

"Attention, please."

Eleanor turned toward Mrs. Ashbury's voice, as did everyone else at the table. The older woman had a captive audience.

"I apologize for interrupting your meal. However, I have something important to say." She glanced at the Judge, and he nodded.

"I'm not sure all of you realize it, but Mr. Briggs and his daughter Eleanor plan to settle down in Kalispell. It's my hope that they will love our little town, and that was why it was so important to bring you all here tonight. I hope you will all extend friendship to them as they settle in. I believe they will become an important part of our community." She gave a little chuckle. "And, in keeping with my gifting, I've assured Miss Briggs that I am determined to aid her in finding a husband. With her beauty, I'm certain it won't take long."

There were chuckles from the dinner guests as they all turned to smile at Eleanor, who had all but dropped her fork. Still, unwelcome attention notwithstanding, she kept her features neutral and even managed a small smile at Marvella. The woman couldn't help herself. But it would be nice if the older woman would listen to her every once in a while. Surely she knew by now that Eleanor didn't like having her personal business shared for all to hear.

Besides, marriage *was* something Eleanor wanted someday, but right now she had so many other pressing matters.

Eleanor glanced at Carter, who seemed amused by the entire thing. Her chest burned even more. He didn't seem to care a whit about the embarrassment the older woman had caused. Of course he didn't. He wasn't the one on display.

"I'd say Carter has the best seat in the house," someone commented and again the crowd chuckled.

Eleanor forced a smile. If she said or did the things she wanted to do and say, she would cause a scene. She drew a deep breath and refocused on her plate. She *would* get through this.

Soon enough, the guests turned back to their dinner, and the most critical subject: the railroad services being terminated. Odd that they all seemed to see it as the end of the world. Surely Kalispell had more to offer the community than just a train depot. Albeit a lovely one.

She had to be missing something.

She turned to Carter. "I know that the train is important to Kalispell, but why are so many afraid that it will be the end of the town when they lose it? There are a great many towns in this world who haven't the service of a train."

Carter dabbed the napkin to his lips. "But Kalispell has grown dependent upon it and losing it will be costly to the community. Hundreds of families depend on the work provided by the railroad. It isn't easy to pluck up a family and move wherever the railroad decides it wants to go next. Not anymore."

Eleanor frowned. "British naturalist Charles Darwin says that organisms best adjusted to their environment are the most successful in surviving and reproducing." That made sense, didn't it? "The people only need to adjust to the moving of the train's headquarters and focus on finding something else to be known for, and they will survive. If the town can't make it without the railroad and refuses to adapt, then they must die out."

"The ability to adapt to the changing circumstances of

life is important"—Carter shifted, turning toward Eleanor and dropping his voice—"but it's not the only thing. We don't grow and change in isolation. Community, helping and loving one another in good and bad times, is just as necessary." Both of his eyebrows rose high on his forehead as he locked gazes with her. "Maybe Darwin didn't think through how his theories impact actual people with real problems and issues that can't simply be *adapted* to."

Oooh! This man! He sounded so . . . superior! She couldn't keep the sarcasm out of her own voice. "I'm surprised you're even familiar with Darwin and his theories. But I do find that most Christians take a stand against him, so your attitude isn't surprising."

Carter frowned, a muscle in his jaw twitching as if he were grinding his teeth to powder. "My being a Christian isn't the reason I have no use for Darwin. I simply believe the man was wrong in the way he viewed the world. As for my faith . . . I don't believe you know me well enough to judge me."

She stiffened. He had some nerve talking about judgment. That's all he'd done since meeting her. She shrugged. "Your Christianity clearly shows. I've no doubt about your faith."

For some reason, Carter's frown changed into a glowing smile. His eyes seemed to light up. "Thank you. That blesses my soul. I had no idea that my faith was so evident. I do try to live a life pleasing to God and to share His Gospel when I can. It's encouraging to hear you say that my Christianity shows."

"It *wasn't* a compliment."

He shrugged. "It was to me. I am sorry I've made you mad. I'm not entirely sure how we got from your questions about the railroad, to this. I suppose Marvella's earlier comments didn't help, but I had nothing to do with them."

Eleanor placed her silverware on her plate and took a deep breath. Yelling at Carter would make an even bigger scene than what Marvella had done. "Just what is *that* supposed to mean?"

Carter lowered his voice to a whisper and leaned close. "I'm not seeking you out as a wife. You mentioned my faith and have made it clear to me that you do not believe as I do. Therefore, we are not likeminded in the most important area of life. So fear not. I do not consider you wife material."

Eleanor's eyes widened. So his attention had been all for show? At least Marvella had been trying to be kind and complimentary. Her hostess's words had only been embarrassing. But Carter's?

They wounded her.

He continued, either not noticing her hurt or not caring. "As for Darwin, the man was a confused soul who struggled to deal with his father and daughter's death." Carter leaned back and took up his water. "He had faith in God and then life wounded him, so he found himself confused and troubled. I feel a great deal of sympathy and pity for the man, but not the admiration that you seem to have."

"Sympathy? Pity?" The words came out on a scoff.

"Yes. The man once had a strong relationship with God. Strong enough anyway that he planned to take up the ministry. I feel great sorrow for someone who allows the pain of this world to lead them away from God."

Oh . . . how *dare* he? Her words stuck in her throat as pain tightened her chest. What did he know about the pain of this world? He had his family and a successful business. Carter had never lost anyone close to him. He had no right to speak of such things.

"Pity, too. They blame God for things that happen." Carter toyed with the handle of his fork.

Was he trying to hurt her more? Or was he simply oblivious?

He speared a piece of meat on his plate. "Loss of fortunes. The death of loved ones. People respond by putting up a wall of resentment brick by brick until they feel protected from God's interference. And yet . . . bad things continue to happen, and sorrows continue to come, only now they bear those things on their own. They refuse the one thing that could make it all better . . . God's love."

This was too much! Had his mother shared their conversation with him? She didn't think Mrs. Brunswick would be so careless, but Carter's words hit too close to home. He *must* know her story.

It was all she could do to not run from the table to her room. As the dishes were cleared for the final course, Eleanor dabbed her mouth with her napkin and tossed it on the table. The action seemed to jolt Carter from his soliloquy.

She squared her shoulders and glared at him. "All the things you said may or may not be true"—she let her fury out in her whisper—"but until you have experienced loss of any kind, until you have had to figure out why God lets horrible, painful things happen to those who love Him, I'd keep my mouth shut, Carter Brunswick."

She pushed back her chair and got to her feet. "My apologies, Mrs. Ashbury. I'm afraid I'm not feeling well. I'll retire for the evening. Thank you for a delicious dinner." She hurried from the room. No doubt all of Kalispell would be talking about this for weeks to come.

So much for not causing a scene.

"Can I do something to help you, Ellie?" Carter's mother had followed her into the hallway.

She shook her head. "No, but thank you. I just have a headache." She hurried for the stairs, muttering under her breath. "And his name is Carter Brunswick."

15

Saturday, June 25, 1904

He was a fool. He hadn't meant to hurt Ellie. He'd only said what he had to give her a sense of relief, to know that he wasn't pursuing her. No matter how much he wanted to. And boy, did he want to. It seemed every time their paths crossed, the desire to pursue her grew stronger.

Carter closed his eyes. The look on her face last night when he'd told her that he didn't consider her wife material . . .

He'd handled the whole thing wrong. No wonder, when what he was saying didn't match what he felt! But with Marvella's propensity to matchmake, it seemed wise to state the obvious. No matter how much he cared for Ellie, if she continued to push God away, to blame Him for all the bad in her life, they could never marry.

He let loose with a heavy sigh. Marvella meant well. Her matching him up with Ellie proved the indomitable woman was working hard to help them get to know each other better.

"But I already know her." He leaned back in his desk chair.

After Ellie and Mother talked that night on his parents' porch, Mother hadn't said much about their conversation. She'd just urged Carter to be kind and encouraging. Ellie had lost her mother at a young age, just as his mother had, and it made her most sympathetic to the struggle the younger woman faced.

Still, without God, Ellie would continue to struggle. She was searching for a way to make sense of the world. She was looking to feel the love her mother had given her—a love she believed was stolen from her.

Mark Andrews tapped on the doorframe. "Figured you might need someone to talk to."

"Oh?" Oh good grief. Now *he* was defensive.

"I was only two chairs away last night. I heard your conversation with Miss Briggs."

Carter deflated. "Sorry about that."

For all that Mark had grown up working his father's ranch, he was studious and loved books. Probably why he was the director of the Carnegie Library. Never one to intrude into Carter's personal affairs, Mark was a quiet listener. And trusted friend.

He crossed over to Carter's desk and sat in a chair opposite him. His gaze was unwavering, almost stern. "I'm just going to come out and say it. You're not being a good friend to Eleanor."

"What?" Just who did Mark think he was?

Mark didn't back down. "I've never seen you act as haughty as you did last night. No matter if there was truth in your words, Eleanor was also correct. You've never faced a loss like she has. Never had to wrestle with God over a devasting disease that you can't beat. Never had to watch a person you love die a horrible death right in front of you." He leaned forward and rapped a knuckle on the thick desktop. "So I'm going to say it again, you're not being a good friend to her. Especially by telling her she's not wife material. Good grief, Carter! What were you thinking?"

That was the longest speech Carter had ever heard out of his friend. And it put him in his place. The stupidity of his behavior washed over him. He was wrong. He wasn't a fool, he was an idiot! He palmed his face and shook his head. "To be honest . . . I was probably saying it more to convince myself. Ellie Briggs attracts me like no other woman I've ever met."

"And you're worried because of where she stands with God." Mark sat on the edge of Carter's desk.

"Yeah."

"You're right to be concerned about that. When I first met Rebecca, she didn't know the Lord. Marvella went on a mission to get her saved, but that didn't stop us from being friends. Right now, you should be focused on friendship with Miss Briggs. But you've damaged whatever friendship you had with her. You hurt her too. And then you tried to beat her over the head with your faith and knowledge of the Bible?"

Wrong again. He wasn't an idiot. He was an arrogant, *fumbling* idiot! "I have a lot of apologizing to do."

Mark leaned back and smiled. "It's a smart man who can recognize when he's wrong, Carter. But it's a humble man in the Lord who can own it and make amends."

Carter nodded, his gaze locked on his folded hands. Not

only did he need to make it right with Ellie, but he needed to go to Jesus. He cleared his throat and looked up at his friend. "Thank you for caring enough about me to tell me when I'm in the wrong."

"You've been a voice of reason for me many times. It's what brothers in Christ are for." Mark stood and held his hand out over Carter's desk. "I'll be praying for you, friend."

Carter stood as well and clasped his friend's hand. "I appreciate it."

Mark left and Carter plopped back down in his chair. He was thankful the office was quiet right now. It gave him the chance to confess his behavior to Jesus and seek His forgiveness. He also prayed the Lord would give him the opportunity to genuinely apologize for hurting her.

Mark was right. No matter how attracted he was to Ellie, he had to deal with those feelings separate from being a good friend to her. It wasn't fair to lash out at her when he was struggling with his attraction *to* her. He shook his head.

What a mess he'd made.

Jack knocked on Carter's door. "Got a minute?"

"Sure. Come on in, Jack."

The older man came in and handed Carter a list. "We're going to need to order these things for the mill. I took a complete inventory and checked over some of the parts that we knew were getting long in the tooth."

Carter looked the list over and nodded. "Most of these we can get in from Minneapolis. Go ahead and order them while we still have train service." He gave the list back to Jack.

"Will do." He started to go. "Any word on when your pa will start bringing in the wheat?"

"Next week, I think. He said the dry weather and sunshine has done the crops good."

"That's great to hear."

"I've been thinking we should probably do what we can to get as much flour processed as we can before they complete the line to Whitefish. I'm putting together a letter for our major buyers and sending it out today. I want to let them know what has happened and encourage them to buy extra flour for now."

"Have you and your pa figured out what you want to do regarding shipments after that?"

"We've pretty much decided to talk to one of the local freighters and see if we can't work out a deal. We'll just need to get everything to Whitefish. If both of us go to the same freight company, they might be willing to give us a discount because the work will be consistent. We'll offer them volume and commitment in exchange for not driving their prices so high that we have to double ours."

Jack nodded. "I would think they'd be glad for the consistency. I'll keep praying for you and your pa."

"I appreciate that." Carter paused. "Jack, can I ask you something?"

He paused. "Sure."

"Were you and your wife both Christians when you married?"

Jack leaned back against the doorjamb and shook his head. "Not exactly. I thought because I went to church that I was saved. But I never wanted much to do with reading my Bible and praying. I didn't really like going to church, but it was expected." He scratched the side of his jaw. "Miriam grew stronger in her walk with God, but mine fell by the wayside."

Carter tried to conceal his surprise. He never would have thought his business partner was resistant to God. Then again, he only had to look at his own behavior lately to see no one should be on a pedestal. He'd ignored the Lord regarding Ellie, and look where his pride landed him.

Jack continued. "Of course, by then we already had our oldest boy. I'm ashamed to say the fights we had were something terrible." He shook his head, his expression pained. "Makes it hard to have unity and peace with someone when you don't both honor the same things or hold to the same values."

Carter leaned forward, resting his forearms on his desk. "How did you resolve those issues, if you don't mind me asking?"

"Don't mind at all." Jack smiled and made his way to his own desk. He sat down and clasped his hands behind his head. "At some point I had to be honest about my own heart. Those fights usually started over something little, but I can pretty much point it all back to the fact that I wasn't right with the Lord. I was a hard case, Carter. I'm not proud of that."

Wow. Jack's honesty was humbling. And thought-provoking.

Carter drummed his fingers . . . he didn't want to wrongly judge Ellie again, but Jack's words helped him understand some of her outbursts. She'd even said a few times she knew God existed, but she couldn't understand Him. "How did Miriam respond to all this?"

Jack blew out a breath and sat up straight in his chair. "I thought I'd lost her a couple of times. Had she believed in divorce, I know we wouldn't be together today. However, she was more determined to please God than me. She said if God hated divorce as the Bible said, then she wasn't going to have anything to do with it, even if it meant she had to live in misery with me."

Carter felt tears sting his eyes. He'd known Jack and Miriam for years. They were as deeply in love as his own parents, that was evident every time they were together. That they'd gone through such struggles and come out whole . . .

That kind of faith was what he needed. When was the last time he'd truly stood for the Lord like Miriam had?

"Her determination was something I had to face every day." Jack's voice cut through Carter's thoughts. "She kept teaching the boys from the Bible and taking them to church, even when I stopped going. I tell you, Carter, I was in a dark place where very little of God's light got through."

"What changed things?"

Jack gave a laugh. "God did. He allowed me to get injured. I was laid up for weeks. None of my so-called friends came to see me, but folks from the church did. The pastor came every couple of days." He shook his head. "We started talking, and little by little I discovered I'd never understood what it really meant to belong to God—to be saved from hell. I thought just because I'd been raised in the church that I was all right. The pastor helped me to see the truth, and I gave my life to God."

He let out a chuckle. "Miriam almost danced a jig. Her spirits brightened, and I swear she reminded me of when she was a girl." His expression sobered. "I hate what I put her through, but she never gave up on me."

Carter leaned his head back against his chair. If he pursued Ellie as a possible wife, it could be as bad as it had been for Jack and Miriam. Maybe even worse, considering Carter's lack of patience. Especially when he felt he was right about something. He had no doubt he was right about God, but he hadn't been right in how he'd gone about his friendship with Ellie.

"Well, I'll go get these things ordered." Jack straightened and started to head out of the office.

"Jack."

The older man turned and paused.

Carter swallowed and gave his friend a smile. "Thank you for sharing your story with me. I appreciate it."

Jack dipped his chin. "I don't ever mind sharin' what the good Lord has done for me, Carter. I'll be praying for you . . . and Miss Briggs." He winked and walked out, shutting the office door behind him.

There was no getting around it. He needed to put aside his growing attraction to Ellie. For her sake, and his own.

He rubbed his face. He should have taken time to actually *listen* to Ellie instead of trying to shove Bible verses down her throat. Maybe then he would have seen what his mom did: a young woman wrestling with hard things and big questions.

Jesus was clearly trying to draw Ellie closer to Him, but instead of helping her, Carter had pushed and poked out of his own frustration and struggle.

Lord, this isn't an easy one. I don't want to do the wrong thing. I don't want to fall in love with someone who doesn't love You. Please guide my focus. Let me be a positive influence for You. But, Lord, please guard my heart. I've never felt like this about someone.

Usually, prayer left him feeling peace. But this time he almost felt worse than before he'd prayed.

Maybe it was already too late. Maybe he was already falling in love.

Lunch had just finished when Eleanor's father announced another expedition. This one would take them back to the east side of the lands they wanted to set aside for the national park.

"We'll take the train and then make our way from there. We won't be gone long. When we're done, we'll catch the train again and return home." Father put aside his napkin. "Should be back in time for the Fourth of July celebrations."

Mr. Grinnell set aside his as well. "I'm glad we're going to do this. I believe you'll be equally impressed with the scenery and species of wildlife and vegetation. It's majestic."

"When do we leave?" Eleanor took out her journal and pencil.

"If you'll excuse me." Mr. Grinnell stood up and left them alone at the table.

Her father said nothing for a moment, and Eleanor looked up to find him wearing a pinched expression. "What's wrong, Father?"

"Well, there are several other men going along on this trip. I think it would be best if you remained here with Mrs. Ashbury and the Judge. We talked about it last night, and Mrs. Ashbury said she would be delighted to have you stay and accompany her to her ladies' group. She hopes to introduce you to more people."

"You don't want me to go?" Why did it hurt so much? Father had done many expeditions on his own when she was younger.

He took her hand. "My dear, I am anxious for this phase of my work to be over." He cast a quick glance around the room. "It is wearying to me, and I wish to settle in and live a simpler, quieter life. But I promised George that I would help. And after the threats we received on the last trip, I think it would be best for you to stay behind. Stay safe."

"I understand that . . . it's just . . . my life has been in upheaval for a while, and there are so many things I wish to discuss with you. I haven't told you about my restlessness and feelings of unease." Why she'd chosen that moment to share, she wasn't sure, but she longed for a closer relationship with him again.

He cupped her cheek with his hand. "I've seen it, my dear. And I apologize for not helping you through this. If you haven't noticed, I've been on a struggle and search for truth myself."

She'd seen it. But hadn't understood until he voiced it. She shouldn't be weighing him down with her worries right now. She lifted her chin and took a deep breath. "When you get back, we'll work it out together."

"Sounds like a wonderful plan." He pulled back. "Besides, I'm sure Marvella will love having you all to herself. She'll have you introduced to the entire town by the time I return."

It was as if the older woman had heard her name and come to see what she could do. "Greetings, all. I hope you enjoyed your lunch." She pulled off her gloves and handed them to the maid.

Father spoke up. "I was just telling Ellie that you had invited her to remain here while we men went on our trip to the east side of the park area."

Mrs. Ashbury looked at Eleanor and smiled. "I am beside

myself with joy to have time for the two of us. My ladies' group meets in two days for a luncheon, and I would like very much for you to speak to them about the national park plans and ideas. It would be such a nice thing to hear about it from a lady. Knowing you support your father's and Mr. Grinnell's ideas, I am so hopeful you'll agree to speak."

"Yes, Ellie. You could have a great influence over these ladies, and in turn they would influence their husbands. With enough support from everyone we will surely see the national park take top priority on the president's agenda."

So. The decision had already been made, and there was no use arguing against it. "I'd be happy to speak to the ladies, Marvella. Thank you for thinking that I might be able to persuade them."

"Oh, my dear, you are talented, and I know that they will enjoy what you have to say."

Eleanor turned back to her father. "When do you leave?"

"The day after tomorrow. George has already arranged everything."

She smiled and carefully folded her napkin. "Well then, I should probably see to your packing. I wouldn't want you to forget anything."

The chair seemed unusually loud as she scooted back.

Making her way upstairs, Eleanor fought back tears. She had never been one given to crying, but of late it seemed to be all she wanted to do. It wasn't helpful at all. Things were changing, and she had to accept that fact. Father had announced just before lunch that he would be signing papers for the Hennessy house later this afternoon. He had arranged to buy the place nearly fully furnished. There would be little for them to do but move in.

Father's room was next door to hers. She made her way inside—noticing shirts, shoes, and luggage strewn around the room. He'd already started to pack. Why was he leaving without her? Why were people arranging her life without seeking her opinion first? Most of all, why didn't Carter Brunswick think she was wife material just because she didn't serve God the way he did?

Bother! *Stop thinking about the man.*

Well, she'd wanted to find out who she really was. It seemed she was doing so. The flat, two-dimensional, grief-laden Eleanor Briggs had been without color and life. Now . . .

She was feeling again. What's more, her anger with God was diminishing. Oh, how happy that would make Mama in heaven! She had no idea what the future held, but she wanted to be valuable. Loved. To have true friendships.

The draperies in Father's room had been pulled back, and Eleanor went to gaze out the window. It shouldn't bother her that Carter wasn't interested in her as a wife. She wasn't looking for a husband. And even if she were, Carter wouldn't be the one she'd seek.

Yes, he was kind and handsome. Very handsome. She loved it when he smiled, especially when he was teasing her. His entire face lit up and his eyes seemed to twinkle. It was like he was keeping a joke to himself. She smiled—

Stop it!

She stamped her foot. "Why am I feeling this way? It's as if Carter is more important to me than he is. I don't want to court him. He would be far too bossy, and he'd always be judging me. I could never be good enough for him . . . or God."

256

She heaved a sigh and sat down on the window seat. Life right now was just . . .

Hopeless.

Over and over the past few months, her mother's words had washed over her, reminding her of the time when she'd had faith. When she'd given her heart to Jesus.

She looked up to the sky. As much as she'd hated what Carter said at the dinner, some of it wouldn't leave her alone. Had she done as Carter said? Put up a wall of resentment and anger to protect herself from God?

Yes . . . yes, she had. And as much as she resented admitting it, Carter was right about something else, too.

Her wall hadn't helped. In fact, now that she was being honest with herself, she had to admit . . .

It *had* done her more harm than good.

That night a thunderstorm rumbled through. A clap of thunder woke Eleanor, not that she'd been sleeping very well. Her dreams had been riddled with confusion and torment. She'd been searching for her way through a wheat field. There were no landmarks with which she could make her bearings. She just wandered and at times ran through the wheat, desperately searching.

But for what?

Lightning flashed, and she heard the rain hit her windowpanes. Getting up, she padded across the lush bedroom rug to the window. If only there were a window seat here as there was in her father's room. She pushed back the drapes and gazed out into the darkness. Another streak of lightning split the night skies, and for a moment, she saw her face reflected in the glass.

She looked scared and weary. Not just weary because her sleep was interrupted, but weary of an internal fight that she couldn't seem to win. . . .

Win? Who was she kidding? She couldn't even find a moment's respite from it.

She let the drapes fall back into place, crawled back into bed, and pulled the covers high. The room had grown chilly, and the heavy quilt was a welcome relief. Another boom of thunder sent her under the covers like a child. She shivered, then felt the quilt begin to warm her.

Maybe . . . should she pray? But what could she say? She hadn't been able to pray since Mama died. How could she pray now? Especially after she'd flung all her anger and hatred at God, blaming Him for taking Mama.

She punched down the pillow and rolled onto her side, curling into a tight ball.

She was alone. Abandoned. Just like that awful night when the doctor pronounced her mother had passed on.

Mother was gone. Father didn't want her with him.

She turned her face into her pillow and let the tears come.

MONDAY, JUNE 27, 1904

Two days later, Eleanor bid her father good-bye, and then in the afternoon, accompanied Mrs. Ashbury to her ladies' meeting. The women were gathered at the home of Mrs. Norris, a woman Eleanor had met at the party. Mrs. Norris, a thick-waisted matron with broad shoulders and a short stature, was clearly used to running things, especially in her own home. She had three different maids all hopping to do her bidding. A manned buffet was set up so that the women could merely point to what they wanted and have servers place the food on the women's plates. Once this was done, the ladies took their seats in the lavish parlor and waited to attend to various orders of business.

When it came time for Eleanor to take the floor, the women were well-fed and ready to listen.

Eleanor took a deep breath to settle the nerves dancing in her stomach. Goodness, she had spoken before crowds larger than this. What need was there to worry?

She gave the women a bright smile and plunged ahead. "I'm happy to be with you today. As Mrs. Ashbury has pointed out, my father and I are in the process of settling down here. And as she also told you, my father is the well-known conservationist Stewart Briggs. He and George Grinnell have been longtime friends and are working together to make the world a better place."

Two women seated at the front of the parlor exchanged glances, eyebrows raised.

What was that about?

Eleanor tore her gaze away from them. Best not to get distracted. "I have long admired my father's work and after losing my mother ten years ago, I joined him in his work—primarily his mission to see public lands set aside and private land ownership decreased. By seeing the land set aside for the public, we can be assured that it will remain untouched and natural for the remainder of our lives and the lives of those to come."

The familiar speech tumbled out of her, but it felt . . . hollow. As if . . .

Did she even believe what she was saying anymore?

The Brunswicks cared for the land they owned. In fact, all of the ranchers and farmers they'd met on their expedition here seemed to have that same passion about cultivating and caring for the earth's resources and beauty.

Eleanor took a breath. *Stop it! This is not the time to figure out how you feel about private and public land ownership. You are here on behalf of Father and his work.*

So chastised, she brightened her smile at the ladies. "So far there are only a few national parks. In fact, there are only six, and not even a proper department in the government to oversee them. The oldest is, of course, Yellowstone. It was created in 1872 and set aside lands in what is now Montana, Wyoming, and Idaho. The others are, in order of their inception, Sequoia and Yosemite, both in California, Mt. Rainier in Washington, Crater Lake in Oregon, and Wind Cave. Wind Cave was just formed last year and is in southwest South Dakota."

Several of the ladies turned and murmured to one another. What were they saying? Perhaps they were impressed by the growing acreage of land saved by the government.

She pressed on. Had any of her previous talks taken this long? Her cheeks were beginning to hurt with the fake smile she had pasted on her face. "We're hopeful that a new national park will be approved to protect land not far from here. Just to the northeast of Kalispell, in fact. There are thoughts to call this new park Glacier National Park after the more than ninety small glaciers that remain in the more than one million acres of land they'd like to see set aside."

"More than a million acres . . ."

Eleanor smiled and nodded at the woman who'd murmured the comment. "Yes. One million acres and over 130 cataloged lakes, and it is thought that there are more than one thousand different species of plants and trees and one hundred different kinds of anim—"

"Is any of that land being taken from ranchers or farmers?" This from a woman wearing a hat bursting with feathers.

Eleanor blinked. She had no idea and admitted as such. "However, I will be sure to talk to Mr. George Grinnell and get back to you as soon as I have that information. Speaking of Mr. Grinnell—"

"See that you do. I'll be checking in with you next week, Miss Briggs." The feathers moved with each nod of the older woman's head. "It's imperative that the government remembers it is working *for* the people. Not taking *from* them."

Several women murmured their approval of the woman's sentiment. Eleanor didn't disagree with her but wanted to finish her speech before someone else followed suit and interrupted her.

"I look forward to speaking to you again, Mrs. . . . ?"

"Mrs. Howard Brown."

"Mrs. Brown." Taking one more fortifying breath, Eleanor started again. "As I was saying, Mr. Grinnell is the architect of this latest national park."

She related the statistics she'd heard her father share over the last few years. "As conservationists, my father and Mr. Grinnell are determined to see the land kept free from factories and building projects that would corrupt the land and bring death to the animals and vegetation that exists. Back east, there are already so many problems with the air and water. We see vast amounts of damage done to the land because of people tearing it apart to build a variety of things, as well as giving little regard to the elimination of garbage and waste."

Mr. Hill's Swiss-chalet hotel design floated into her mind. Wasn't she being a little hypocritical touting conservation when he wanted to do the very thing she was saying *wouldn't* happen? Maybe there was another way to appease the demanding public. His accommodations were the antithesis of what she was sharing right now.

"In . . ." She shook the thought away. "In setting aside land to become a national park, we hope to see as little building and change to the land as possible. There are some who desire to have roads put in so that visitors can one day drive themselves through the park, but in our area, there is already a train route that passes through and is more than enough, in my estimation, to bring in viewers."

Eleanor concluded by explaining that public support was imperative and asked the women to think about all the good that could be done in saving such a magnificent part of Montana for the future. She asked them, as her father had bid her to do, to encourage their husbands to speak to their politicians and to put their support, in whatever manner they could, behind the building of national parks. In particular, Glacier National Park.

Mrs. Ashbury came forward as Eleanor ended her talk and put her arm around her. "Eleanor would be happy to answer a few questions if you have any."

One woman raised her hand and Marvella gave her a nod. The woman stood. "How can they possibly keep things natural and untouched when other parks such as you mentioned have hotels and concessions built, as well as housing for those who work for the national park? I've been to Yellowstone and stayed at their hotels. One was an abominable place painted bright yellow. They had bears that we fed and places for us to eat as well. I didn't feel that they did enough to preserve it."

Exactly what she'd pointed out—and what got her banished from the room. Still, it was good to know others felt as she did. "I can well understand. I've been to Yellowstone myself and thought much the same. However, with more and more people taking an interest in the park and voicing their thoughts on how things should be done to preserve the land and animals, I believe we will see better results."

Another woman got to her feet. "How will such places pay for themselves?"

"There have been fundraisers and donations taken up for the parks. Many of our wealthiest families in America have a heart for conservation. They realize just how quickly the natural lands are disappearing."

"Disappearing into ranches and farms?" This from a woman who looked a little less refined than the others. She was dressed fashionably enough, but her face was tanned and leathery. "My family has a ranch nearby, and we own seven thousand acres."

Eleanor couldn't stop her question. "And why do you need that much land for your personal use?"

The woman frowned. "I guess you don't know much about raising cattle. You need at least an acre per cow. Two acres for cow-calf pairs. And as a conservationist you must know that you can't run them on the same section of land for too long. We have to rotate them, move them from one pasture to another. We aren't without our own style of con-servation. No one knows better than we do about keeping the land in good order."

Eleanor had no reply. The woman was right. She *didn't* know what was needed for raising cattle or wheat. She would make sure and ask about that the next time she talked to Mr. and Mrs. Brunswick.

"It seems to me that we need both to exist to provide food for America." Marvella's tone was pleasant. "I'm sure our conservationist friends would agree, but this isn't about the farms and ranches. We need support for the national park that could soon be set aside in our own area. But now, why don't we have some more refreshments. Mrs. Norris has arranged for the desserts to be set out."

Thank heaven for Marvella. This was one time Eleanor welcomed her taking over.

Sir Theophilus appeared from wherever he'd been and came to Eleanor. Jumping up against her skirt, he looked at her with an expression that suggested he understood her frustration. She picked him up and buried her face against his for just a moment.

At least *someone* understood her.

16

WEDNESDAY, JUNE 29, 1904

M y dear, I can't help but see that you've been rather downcast since your father left without you." Marvella sat down to breakfast. "I know you're used to being with him on these trips, but sometimes it's good for the men to have time to themselves. Men need to be able to just be themselves and not worry about being overheard by the womenfolk."

She gave Eleanor a smile and then opened her Bible. "I hope you don't mind if I share my Bible reading with you today."

Eleanor shook her head. "Not at all." Frankly she was to the point where anything anyone could offer to help her make sense of her feelings and thoughts was welcome.

Mrs. Ashbury turned a couple of pages. "I'm reading Psalm 13. 'How long wilt thou forget me, O LORD? for ever? how long wilt thou hide thy face from me? How long shall I take counsel in my soul, having sorrow in my heart daily? how long shall mine enemy be exalted over me? Consider and hear me, O LORD my God: lighten mine eyes, lest I sleep the sleep of death; Lest mine enemy say, I have prevailed against him; and those that trouble me rejoice when I am moved. But I have trusted in thy mercy; my heart shall rejoice in thy salvation. I will sing unto the LORD, because he hath dealt bountifully with me.'" She looked up. "David wrote these verses, and they speak to my heart."

"They do?" Those were the words of a troubled soul. At least in the beginning.

"Oh mercy, yes. I've had times of doubt and sorrow. Times when I was sure God had forgotten me. Many times when I've been on my knees crying out to the Lord. I had people in my life who were against me and who seemed to take delight in my failings. But God always prevailed and helped me through."

How could that be so? "It's just that you seem to have everything you could ever need or want. And it's hard to imagine you having enemies."

The footman put a plate of food in front of Mrs. Ashbury and then offered Eleanor one as well. Mrs. Ashbury waited until he left the room to reply.

"No one is without someone in their life who wishes them ill. It might not be for long, or it could be a lifetime grudge. I'm fortunate in that most of my enemies are long gone. Occasionally, there are those who disagree with my nature. Sometimes my opinions and enthusiasm can overwhelm those around me."

Eleanor could certainly understand that. Still . . . "I just assumed you were always kind and loving. You and the Judge seem to have so many who admire and value you."

"We do. As David said, God has dealt with me bountifully. He's dealt with us bountifully. However, we have both had our foes to fight and our battles to be won, but God has tempered me over the years. I am a better woman now than when I was your age. As I grow in Him and yield myself to His molding, I find I become much gentler in my nature. I can honestly say that my heart truly does rejoice in His salvation. I suppose that's why it bothers me so much that you are opposed to Him."

"But I'm not!" Eleanor frowned and picked up a piece of toast to cover her frustration.

"Let me bless the food and then we can continue." Mrs. Ashbury offered a quick prayer and then gave Eleanor a nod. "Go ahead and elaborate on what you were saying."

"I'm not *opposed* to God. I'm not exactly sure *what* I think or even believe about Him anymore, but I have no desire to be opposed to Him."

"Well, that is to your benefit, but please continue."

Eleanor put down the toast. How could she explain to this woman that her beliefs made little sense to her? She wanted to understand. And be understood.

"I remember what it was like as a child to cling to God and study His word. I remember how amazing it felt to be close to God in prayer." She sucked in a breath as her limbs shook. "But it all died. All of it. When Mama was gone . . . I couldn't feel anything anymore. Nothing but grief and pain and loss. The only way to survive was to shut off that part of my heart completely." The words poured out of her, like a pressure valve had been released inside her soul. "I pushed God away, Marvella. And I don't think He'll welcome me back, no matter how much I long to be whole again. I don't deserve another chance."

So there was to be a late-morning meeting of the businessmen in Kalispell tomorrow. And others who were dependent on the railroad. Grant wanted to attend, but the railroad had him busy loading freight cars. They were shipping out parts and supplies that had been stored in the Kalispell shops and sending them to Whitefish.

With each car that was packed, Grant felt a sense of doom. He wasn't at all sure yet what he would do. Alvin was still spouting off about forcing Hill to change his mind, but how could that ever work? Several of Alvin's friends were with him on the idea of kidnapping Louis Hill from the Fourth of July town party. Grant hadn't listened to much of the details because frankly it was probably better not to know what his brother had planned. At least that way he couldn't be forced to testify against him if things went wrong.

"Boss, we crated all those boiler rivets and pipes. You want us to get them loaded?"

Grant shook his head at the worker. "Not on this car. Put them on 5124, as well as the other things we packed up yesterday. Make sure the crates are marked to match the list. We don't want to have to go searching to find parts. They'll need them almost immediately."

"Sure thing, Boss."

Grant watched the man walk away. Most of his team were moving up north to work at the new headquarters. A few were leaving the area altogether. None were staying in Kalispell, except maybe him and Alvin.

Unless, of course, Alvin landed himself in jail.

Last night, Alvin grumbled for hours. "Even if Hill won't

let Kalispell remain the divisional headquarters, he can surely let us keep a small shop and section gang. They'll need to keep up the tracks and have someone on hand for emergency repairs."

Grant wasn't so sure. So far all he'd heard was that a small staff would remain on site to man the depot and rail yard, but no one knew for how long. Maybe he just needed to move and start at the bottom again. He sure as fire wanted no part of fighting and threatening to kill someone.

"Hey, Grant." Gus took quick strides toward him. "I wanted to tell you about a job I just heard about at the outfitters. They're going to have professional guides trained for the new national park and are working with Grinnell to have Kalispell be a headquarters of sorts. They know you're one of the best trackers and campers in the area and asked to speak with you to head it up." He glanced at the clock on the wall. "If I were you, I'd get over there as soon as possible."

Grant couldn't contain his grin. Somebody wanted him and knew his value! Two hours later, he couldn't help but whistle as he dished up supper for him and his brother. Wait until Alvin heard.

But when his little brother came through the door, his scowl was deeper than ever.

Well, he could cheer him up. "Guess who got a new job today?"

His brother's eyes snapped to his.

He told him the whole story, the plan from the outfitters, the need for guides since it would take months to build hotels or other facilities up in the park once it was established, and his starting salary. Twice as much as he was making now for the railroad. "We can buy us a house!"

But instead of joy over the news, Alvin reared back and punched him square in the eye.

Grant fell to the floor, his hands over his face. "What'd you do *that* for?"

Alvin kicked him. "Yer ruinin' the plan!"

"*What* plan?" Had his brother gone crazy? "I promised Ma to take care of you and not once have you thanked me."

Another kick. This one took his breath away. "I ain't never asked for your help. I'm sick and tired of all them rich people tellin' us what to do." Another kick.

His brother's tirade muffled as Grant covered his head and ears against the blows.

Marvella closed the door to her bedchamber and tossed the cushion from the window seat onto the floor. Getting down on her knees, she stared up out the window and folded her hands. "Lord, this situation is much more intense than I ever imagined. Ellie is so hurt, and I don't know how to help her. Please, God. You're the only one who can show her how You love her. Help us to love her through this tough time so she can be brought back into the fold." No more words would come. Only tears.

But God knew the groanings of her heart. Better than she even knew them herself.

She laid her head on her arms on the window seat and sobbed for the hurting young woman in the room down the hall.

An arm came around her.

Milton groaned as he knelt beside her. "We might be getting too old for kneeling."

She laughed through her tears. "Maybe not the kneeling part. But the getting-up part, yes, I would agree."

"I take it we're praying for Miss Eleanor."

"You'd be correct."

"She's a wounded one, that girl. But no one is ever too far out of reach for the Lord."

"If only I could convince her of that." Marvella sniffed.

"It's not our job to convince her, my dear. Simply to pray for her and to show her how much God loves her. No matter what."

She needed that reminder. "Once again, my brilliant husband, you are correct."

He took her hand in his. "Why don't we pray for her together?"

"I would love nothing more."

THURSDAY, JUNE 30, 1904

Carter took a seat and waited for the mayor to address the men of Kalispell. Dad hadn't been able to make it since his harvest had started, but Carter promised to bring him all the news.

The mayor signaled for people to stop talking. "I'm glad that you could join us here today. It's become evident that the decisions made by James Hill of the Great Northern Railway are final and firm. We tried our best to reason with them and get at least a regular train in once a week, but we haven't come to a firm agreement on this. Only time will tell.

"The railroad will abandon us as the main line in August. But we are determined to keep Kalispell moving forward.

With that in mind, and after discussing this situation at length with the city council, we are happy to say that we have a plan."

Carter shifted in his chair, glancing around. He heard a few comments of approval offered from men in the audience, but most remained silent, not yet convinced that any plan could save them.

The mayor continued. "We will do whatever is necessary to improve the road between our city and the railroad in Whitefish. We'll take on as many of the unemployed men as come to us to make a solid and dependable road, and to make it quickly. We will see to it that this road is not only created but maintained to keep the flow of supplies coming in and local products moving out."

Well, good news at last. This would help Carter and his father with their plans to transport goods. A better road to Whitefish might mean the freighters would keep their prices at a reasonable rate. After all, they were about to get a boon in their business.

"We are also going to look at improving the route south to Flathead Lake where we can. That way, when necessary, we can utilize the steamboats for transportation. The good news is that the existing road to the lake is better established and will probably need fewer improvements."

"When ya gonna do this, Mayor?" someone called out from the crowd.

"We are going to send a team out immediately to determine what improvements are needed. They will report back to us as soon as possible. Hopefully by the Fourth of July celebration. Then we can take a moment at the festivities to have another town meeting and report to you. Of course, with that date just days away, the report will be cursory. Some of the men will remain to take measurements and work up more of the details needed to figure the costs, and we will hear from them after Independence Day. Thus, for the time being I am adjourning this gathering to await further information so that we may make an educated decision."

Carter shifted out of the way of some of the men who were leaving. There was grumbling here and there, but for the most part the men seemed in fairly good spirits. Dad would be glad to hear the plans for the road improvements. This was the logical choice, and it would benefit everyone.

He glanced at his watch. Nearly noon. His favorite café was just around the corner so it seemed only natural that he should stop in for lunch. He was almost to the door when he spied Ellie Briggs riding her bicycle toward him. He gave her a wave. There had been no chance to talk to her since the dinner six days ago, and he needed to clear the air between them.

She slowed and stopped just before reaching the corner where he stood. Carter gave her a smile. "Where are you off to?"

"Home. Not that it's any of your business."

Her sharp tone, while understandable, took him aback. "I was hoping I might run into you today."

Her foot fidgeted on the pedal of her bike. "I was just as hopeful that we could avoid any confrontations."

He might have laughed another time, but not on the heels of hurting her. "Ellie, I'm so sorry for what I said and how I handled myself at the dinner last week. I didn't mean to hurt you."

For the first time since he'd met her, Eleanor Briggs showed no emotion on her face. "You owe me no apology. As I said, I'd rather avoid any confrontations." She propped one foot on a pedal and moved to ride around him.

He slid in front of her, arms open wide to impede her progress. "I *do* owe you an apology. And I want to make it right." He took one more step toward her, trying to catch her eye. "Let me buy you lunch. I'm just heading to the café. We can talk over some of the best beef stew and fresh bread that you'll find in all of Montana."

Her eyes slammed into his and she shook her head. "No, thank you."

"Ellie, please." Couldn't she hear how real his desperation was? "I know I don't deserve kindness and mercy from you after the way I acted. The things I said." He pushed a hand through his hair. "Please take some time to hear me out."

She looked away and then nodded. "Very well. I will extend some kindness." She got off the bicycle and Carter reached out to take hold of it lest she change her mind.

"I've got this. I'll rest it over here." He put the bicycle alongside the café, then extended his arm to her. With what looked to be great reluctance, she finally slipped her hand in the crook of his arm and let him help her up onto the boardwalk.

They made their way inside, where already the place was filling up with some of the men Carter had seen at the meeting. He led Ellie to a table near the window so she could look out and see her bicycle.

Adrenaline rushed through him, making his hands shake. *Please help me, Jesus. I want to be a good friend to Ellie.*

After pulling out her chair for her to sit, he took the chair opposite and leaned in. "The mayor held a town meeting a little bit ago. That's why there are so many people in here now."

She glanced around. "What? Why?"

"He let us all know that because the railroad is moving out, the city plans to improve the road to Whitefish and down to Flathead Lake."

"I see." Her gaze dropped to her hands in her lap. "Well, that makes sense." She pulled off her riding gloves and tucked them in her waistband.

The waitress came and told them about the specials. Carter chose the beef stew and smiled when Ellie did too. They both ordered lemonade as well. Carter wanted to tease her about her choices, but now was not the time.

Ellie glanced at him. "So when will they start the road improvements? Will they have things ready before the trains stop coming in?"

This was not the conversation he wanted to have with her, but it was his own fault. He'd started them down this path. Might as well finish it. Maybe a lighter topic would break down some of the walls between them. "I think they'd like to. Given that first snows could come soon after that, I think the mayor would probably want to have the road work finished by then."

Ellie arched an eyebrow, a small smile appearing on her lips. "Snow in August?"

Some of the tension left Carter's shoulders at that smile. "Well, probably not, but I've seen it snow every month of the year here. August isn't as likely, but September wouldn't be that surprising. Usually, it holds off until October though. I don't want to scare you from choosing to live here."

"It's a bit late for that." Ellie glanced out the window. "Father signed the papers on the Hennessy house before he left. They move out tomorrow, and we're set to move in some time after the Fourth of July. Mrs. Ashbury insisted on having the staff clean the place from top to bottom those few days in between."

"I'm glad you and your father are staying." The words were out before Carter could stop them. Well, so what? He *was* glad.

Ellie turned back to him, pinning him with her unflinching stare. "Why?"

Carter cringed. "I suppose I deserve that after what I said, but honestly Ellie, I was just trying to relieve you of embarrassment. Mrs. Ashbury loves to put people together and then take credit for it once they're married. I felt bad that she'd put you on the spot." That sounded contrived even to his own ears. He needed to own up to hurting her. Not make excuses.

Her gaze didn't leave his face. "She'd put you on the spot as well."

"Yes, but as you might have noticed by now, I don't embarrass easily. Although I will say I was a little uncomfortable that night."

She arched one brow. "Well, of course you were. She was trying to put you with a woman who was completely unsuitable. Someone far beneath your standards."

Carter folded his hands on the table. *Lord, Lord . . . help me.* "I wish I'd never said that to you, Ellie." His voice cracked on her name. "It was not only unkind, but unnecessary. I should have shut up and apologized to you on the spot." He shook his head, and now it was his turn to look out the window. Far easier than meeting the anger—and doubt and pain—in her eyes.

The waitress brought their food and drinks, giving Carter a little bit of a reprieve. Unfortunately, once the food was deposited, she hurried away and there was nothing to do but face the music.

He looked Ellie in the eye. "I want to be your friend."

She didn't look up from her plate. "But I'm not suitable to be your wife. Not that I want to be, by the way."

He picked up his spoon and dredged it through the thick stew. "I was haughty and using my pride to make me feel better about . . ." How could he say it without hurting her feelings?

"The fact that we don't agree when it comes to God?" This time she raised both eyebrows and crossed her arms over her waist. *She* didn't have any trouble spitting it out. "Which in your mind, makes me less of a person, doesn't it?"

Oh, Father, such hurt in her eyes. And I put it there. Forgive me.

The only way he could make this right was to be totally honest with her. She deserved that from him. "No. No. I don't feel that way. Honestly, Ellie, I've been attracted to you since we first met. I just know there'd never be any peace between us if we didn't believe the same thing about God. It wouldn't be any good . . . *we* wouldn't be any good together. We'd always be opposed. I mean look at us now."

She held his gaze a moment and then nodded and glanced down, but not before he noticed the shimmer in her eyes. "Yes, I believe you're right."

For a long while neither spoke, nor did they eat. They just sat looking out the window.

Carter tried again. "I really would like to be your friend, Ellie."

He stared at her until she met his gaze. She was truly the most beautiful woman he'd ever seen. He was so tempted to put aside all that had been said and offer her everything he could give her.

But even as he thought these things, even as the temptation built almost to a point he couldn't resist, a still, small voice reminded him that this wasn't the way.

Without a word, she pushed back from the table and got to her feet. She took money from her pocket and placed it on the table. "I don't hold anything against you, Carter. You are acting purely on your beliefs, and I must respect that. However, I don't see how we can be friends."

She walked across the room and out the door. Carter gripped the table to keep from running after her. Instead, he sat glued to his chair . . .

His heart shattered.

Eleanor walked over to the watch shop. Thank goodness it was just down the street from the café. Running into Carter had almost caused her to forget to pick up Father's watch now that it was repaired.

The transaction took less than two minutes, and she was off again, pedaling with all her might toward the Ashburys' house. But exhaustion soon took over. She got off her bicycle and walked the last few blocks.

Her heart was a rock in her chest. Hard. Lifeless. And the

void inside of her was growing. The more she fought against yielding her heart to God, the worse the void seemed to get. But honestly, why would God even want her heart back? If she wasn't worthy of Carter's love, she'd hardly be worthy of God's. She hadn't done anything at all to please Him. Despite what her mother said about not being able to earn God's love, there had to be something she needed to do to gain His acceptance.

She slowed her pace, not ready to reach the house. The last thing she wanted was to have to face Marvella with her joyful spirit and wisdom. The woman seemed to know all about the void in Eleanor. And yet, she didn't make Eleanor feel bad about her state before the Lord. She just asked probing questions that were like a mirror into Eleanor's soul.

That was almost worse.

Eleanor could hardly stand the thought.

What would she see there? Certainly nothing of value.

Not to Carter.

Not to God.

17

SUNDAY, JULY 3, 1904

Eleanor accompanied Marvella and the Judge to church on Sunday. Word had come via a railroad worker that her father and Mr. Grinnell wouldn't make it back until Monday morning on the Fourth of July. They'd be there just in time for the celebration, and with them would be Louis Hill. Mr. Hill had intended to come in prior to that, but when he learned that Grinnell and Briggs were studying the eastern parts of the planned park, he stopped to join them.

The Judge said it was of little relevance for Louis Hill to come back to Kalispell. But then word had been sent that Hill wanted to talk to the people about how often the train *would* come to Kalispell. Which had given many hope.

Others thought it was all a ruse.

More than one argument had started over the tension. And until things were certain, disagreements were bound to increase. Which could lead to violence.

Something Eleanor had no desire to witness.

She followed the Ashburys to the same pew they sat in every Sunday, and Marvella handed her a hymnal. In a few moments, they were all on their feet singing songs Eleanor didn't really know. She sang along as best she could, but her mind remained on her own misery.

What should she do? She wanted to speak to her father about her feelings. She wanted to ask him about his beliefs. And maybe share how she was struggling with faith and God.

After singing, prayers were offered, and then the pastor took the pulpit. He welcomed the congregation, offered a prayer of thanksgiving for the day the Lord had given, and launched into his sermon.

"Nothing in this world happens by chance."

What? Eleanor stared at the man. How could he say such a thing? Nothing?

"Throughout God's Word we can see where everything He created was made with a purpose and order. He didn't create the plants and vegetation until the sun was in place. He didn't create fish before there was water to put them in. He had a specific plan. He created man fully formed and ready to work, but not before He had a garden to tend.

"God didn't send His prophets willy-nilly into the world. He knew where He needed each one. Knew what they would say and do and who would answer His call. He knew when He sent His precious son Jesus to the earth that there would be many who would reject him . . . kill him. And still God made His plans. He did nothing by chance."

Well, that seemed true. Despite her confusion and feelings about God, she had never been able to make sense of the idea of *order out of chaos* without a Creator working to put it all into place.

"God is a God of order. He formed the earth and all that is in it, knowing exactly how it would all fit together. God is in the details of His creation. He knows each mountain and lake . . . each person. God told Jeremiah, 'Before I formed thee in the belly I knew thee;' and in Matthew 10, Jesus tells us that the very hairs on our head are numbered." The balding pastor paused and chuckled. "Although my count changes daily." The congregation joined him in laughter.

"Nothing happens by chance. There is order. God's perfect order. We don't always understand it or comprehend the reasonings behind it, but God has a plan and purpose in our lives. He has called us to order . . . to peace of heart and mind."

What would that be like? Peace not just of heart, but of mind? Was God really calling her to that? Had He known her before she was formed in her mother's womb? Did God truly give her life with a purpose just for her?

If so, what *was* that purpose?

Maybe that's why she felt so lost. God ordered her world only to have her disorder it by closing herself off from Him. Mother had assured her that God knew all, including the choices each soul would make. If that were true, then He knew the choices Eleanor would make. He knew the pain and struggles she would have and the decision she made to push Him away.

No, not just that. She rejected Him.

Such a harsh word. Carter had rejected her, and it hurt. It hurt her more than she could say. She wasn't looking for a husband, yet when Carter made it clear he wasn't looking for a wife and that even if he were, she wouldn't be the one he'd choose, it devastated her. Made her feel unimportant.

Was that how God felt when she rejected Him?

But God hasn't been important to you. You've ignored Him. Blamed Him. Refused Him.

Eleanor lowered her head. Was her rejection of Him unchangeable? Was it too late to alter her course?

She didn't even hear the rest of the sermon. She couldn't pull her thoughts out of the abyss into which they'd settled. If it was too late, then she truly was hopeless.

After the services concluded, Eleanor felt no better than when she'd started out that morning. Was this the way it would always be?

"Marvella. Ellie."

Eleanor looked up and found Sarah Brunswick. She smiled, but it was Marvella who responded.

"Why, Sarah, how good to see you."

"It's good to see you too, Marvella. I wanted to come and extend an invitation to you and the Judge, as well as Ellie, to come to the farm for lunch today."

Just then Carter came to join his mother. Eleanor couldn't even look him in the eye. Instead, she toyed with the cuff of her blouse.

"Oh, my dear, we can't come. The Judge and I are committed elsewhere after lunch. Plans for the Fourth of July, don't you know. But I'm sure Ellie would love to join you. She was impressed with the farm, weren't you, my dear?"

She had no choice but to glance up and smile. "I was. Your farm is very peaceful."

"See there, I knew she would be happy to go."

"We came in our two-seat buggy." Sarah glanced around.

"But Carter is joining us, and I'm sure he'd be happy to rent a conveyance to bring Ellie out. Especially since he'll be returning to town later after lunch."

Eleanor swallowed the lump that had formed in her throat. She wasn't sure she could bear a carriage ride alone . . . with Carter.

To her surprise, red rushed into Carter's face! Was he actually . . . embarrassed? She hadn't known that was possible.

"Mother, that would hardly be appropriate. I wouldn't want to risk Ellie's reputation."

Eleanor stiffened. He didn't want her to come to the farm. She lowered her head.

"You are good to think of such things, Carter." Marvella bestowed a gleaming smile on him. "I tell you what. Come to our house and use our surrey and take Nora with you two. She's one of our new maids. I won't need her this afternoon. She's older and can act as chaperone. If that will be all right with you, Sarah."

"Of course. She's welcome to join us. Carter, does that meet with your approval?"

His shoulders relaxed, and he shoved his hands in his pockets. "Absolutely. It solves all our problems."

If only Carter was right. But for her, the problems were just beginning.

"Wonderful, we'll see you at home." Mrs. Brunswick smiled, and Mr. Brunswick tipped his hat before slapping the reins and moving their wagon out of the church yard.

"Ellie, you might want to change your dress."

"Yes, dear, you should." As usual, Marvella made it more of an edict than a suggestion. "We'll head home, then. Carter, did you walk to church?"

"I did."

Marvella nodded. "Then come with us. We have plenty of room. And it's the very surrey you'll be using."

Eleanor shifted in her seat to look at her hostess. "Won't you need it to go to your meetings?" There had to be a way out of the ordeal without coming right out and asking to be excused.

"No, my dear. Our meetings are close to home. We had planned to walk. Now come. Let's get you home so you can change clothes."

Eleanor sat with Marvella in the second seat of the surrey. The Judge liked to drive the carriage himself and so sat in the front seat. However, later, when Carter took the reins, Eleanor knew she'd be expected to sit with him up front while Nora would sit behind them.

"I hope you have an enjoyable afternoon, Ellie. This will be a wonderful time for you and Carter to get to know each other better." The older woman smoothed out the skirt of her dress. "I'm so glad to know you won't have to spend the day alone."

Eleanor could hardly think, let alone figure out what to say. She gave Marvella a slight smile and nod. She was almost desperate enough to try and pray her way out of the situation. . . .

"Hello, Mrs. Ashbury, Miss Briggs."

The soft voice of Mrs. Andrews floated up into the surrey. Eleanor whipped around and found the dark-haired beauty and her husband approaching their conveyance.

"Well, hello, Mr. and Mrs. Andrews," Marvella chirped. "You are both looking quite dapper this fine Sunday morning."

Mrs. Andrews blushed prettily. "You're kind, Marvella." Her gaze shifted to Eleanor. "It's a pleasure to see you again, Miss Briggs. I was wondering if you were free for lunch this afternoon. Mark and I would like to host you in our home if you're agreeable."

Eleanor's heart pounded. Had God actually heard her feeble prayer? She swallowed. It was unlikely. Yet she felt a keen sense of gratitude.

"Oh, you're too kind, Rebecca. But Miss Briggs was—*oof!*" Marvella squeaked and looked at her husband. "Now just what was that about, my dear?"

Eleanor looked at the Judge, who dropped a wink her way. "I think Miss Briggs is capable of answering for her own schedule."

She could have given the man a hug. She glanced over at Carter, who was observing the whole fiasco with a bemused smile. Eleanor tipped her head toward the Andrewses, hoping he would understand her nonverbal question.

He nodded and gave her a little wave.

Relief rolled through her. "I would be delighted to join you for lunch, Mrs. Andrews."

"Wonderful!" Mrs. Andrews smiled. "Our house is just a few blocks from here. It's a lovely day for a walk."

Eleanor turned to her hosts. Marvella's mouth was clamped shut, but her eyes still sparkled. The Judge's smile was wide and easy. "Go have fun with your friends, Eleanor."

"Thank you." She whispered and turned to get out of the surrey. Carter was there, his hand extended. She slipped her fingers into his grasp, tingles racing up her arm. Once she was on the ground, she snatched her hand back. "I apologize I won't be able to join your family for lunch today."

Carter grinned. "It's quite all right, Ellie. Mom and Dad will miss your company, but I think time with Mark and Rebecca will be enjoyable for you. They're two of my favorite people in Kalispell."

"I'm glad to hear it." Mark's voice cut into their conversation. He shook Carter's hand with a grin. "If you don't mind, friend, we need to steal Miss Briggs."

Eleanor bit her lips together as Carter held up his hands and stepped back as Mark Andrews offered his arm to her. "Are you ready?"

She nodded and rested her hand lightly on his arm. His wife leaned forward and grinned. "I'm so pleased this worked out."

"I am too." Excitement bubbled up into her voice. Maybe God *had* heard her prayer today. If so, it was the best one He'd answered in a long time.

The Andrewses's house was cozy and warm. Rebecca and Mark—they had insisted on being called by their first names—made Eleanor feel welcome. Over their delicious lunch, they asked Eleanor questions about growing up on the East Coast. Rebecca even shared a few stories about growing up in Chicago. And Mark had them laughing with incidents out at his dad's ranch when he was little.

Eleanor couldn't remember a time when she felt so full, both physically and emotionally. She actually felt like she could become good friends with the Andrewses. And she hadn't had good friends in a very long time. After the meal,

Mark waved off Eleanor's offer to do the dishes. "I do them on Sundays, and I know Rebecca has been itching to have time with you."

His wife let out a laugh. "You're making me sound obsessed."

Eleanor laughed along with the couple. "I will confess, I've been longing to get to know you better too."

"See?" Rebecca patted Mark on the hand. "She *wants* to be my friend."

Mark plunged his hands into the soapy water and let out a chuckle. "Go have fun, you two. But if my wife starts grilling you, just say the word. She can get a bit intense."

Rebecca stood. "Don't listen to him, Eleanor. We are going to have a lovely time. Would you like to sit out back with me? It's a small yard, but it is comfortable for an afternoon chat."

"I would love that." Eleanor followed her hostess out to their small yard, pleased to find a small swing close on the small back porch.

The two women sat and Rebecca ran her hand along the smooth wood of the swing. "Mark surprised me with this when we moved in." She smiled. "Living in the city, I'd never had one. But there is something so soothing about being able to sit and swing. Almost like I'm a little girl again."

Eleanor relaxed into the back of the swing. "I agree. The Brunswicks have a big one on their home porch. I think Mrs. Brunswick and I sat out there for hours, just enjoying the scenery."

"Speaking of the Brunswicks"—Rebecca glanced at Eleanor—"I felt a little like we were walking into the middle of something at the end of service."

Eleanor's cheeks burned. "Well . . ." She sighed. "Marvella got it in her head that I needed to have lunch with the Brunswicks this afternoon. She was just being Marvella, but I felt forced on them and couldn't find a way out of the situation."

Rebecca released a peal of laughter. "That sounds just like our friend. She means well. But I know it can be overwhelming from time to time."

Eleanor let out a breath, thankful she hadn't overstepped with her comment about Marvella. She didn't want to be a gossip. "It's true. And while I enjoy time with them, it's still been a bit . . . awkward between Carter and me since the dinner."

Rebecca pushed the swing forward with her toe and the gentle sway caused Eleanor to relax even further. "I know we barely know each other, but I want to be your friend." She smiled. "And if you want to talk about what happened, I'm here."

I want to be your friend. Those were the same words Carter had said to her a few days ago. She'd told him it was impossible. But was it? Even if she didn't believe in God like he did or like Rebecca did . . . *could* they be friends? "I could use a friend. And please . . ." She swallowed the lump in her throat. "Call me Ellie."

"I'd be glad to, Ellie." The other woman smiled.

"And thank you for your offer to discuss what happened at dinner. I'd rather not rehash all that. Carter has apologized and I've accepted. But . . ." Eleanor rubbed her hands on her skirts. Why were her hands suddenly clammy? "I did have some questions about this morning's sermon."

Rebecca's eyes lit up. "Oh, yes. Wasn't it just marvelous?"

Eleanor bit her lip. "It was . . . something."

"That sounds like a serious kind of something." Rebecca chuckled. "Did you have a question about Pastor Watkins's message?"

Well, there was no time like the present to see if the woman before her really wanted to be her friend. "What makes you so certain that God exists and that He is who the Bible says He is?"

Rebecca paused, then let out a laugh. "Oh, Eleanor, you sound just like I did only a few months ago. I had so many complicated questions about the Lord."

"I'm glad I'm not alone in that. And just so you know, Marvella has sung your praises. She thinks your conversion to Christianity was the most important thing I needed to know about you."

"It is, in a way." Rebecca slowed the swing and stood. "I'm going to go get my Bible. Is that all right with you?"

Eleanor nodded and her hostess disappeared inside. A few minutes later, she reappeared with a black leather book under her arm and a tray in her hands.

"Oh, let me help you." Eleanor jumped up and took the tray from her hands. She was surprised to see a small plate of delicious-looking cookies and two glasses of lemonade.

"I thought we might need a treat with our conversation." Rebecca sat back down on the swing.

Eleanor took a cookie and bit into it, sugary sweetness swirling on her tongue. "These are delicious, thank you."

"Of course. Now. You asked how I'm so certain that God exists, right?"

Eleanor nodded. "And how you know that He is who the Bible says He is."

Rebecca flipped through the thin pages of the Bible for a moment, then settled on a page. "At first, I was certain about God and the Bible because the people I loved and trusted promised me it was true. And in my unbelief, I figured that was enough. Like I could tag on to their faith." She shook her head, tendrils of black hair framing her face. "But then I started reading the Word myself. I started seeing places in my life where God made Himself too real to ignore. As my faith grew stronger, the proof grew stronger too."

Yes, she could believe that, even though it had been years since she'd read the Bible. "So you really believe that nothing happens by chance? That God ordered everything in place."

"I do. I know some might think that unlikely, but for me it rings true. And again, I take it by faith. I believe the Bible is God's Word. I have no doubt that He instructed His people who wrote it and they put down exactly what God wanted on the pages." Rebecca pointed at the open Bible. "This verse especially struck me the first time I read it. 'All scripture is given by inspiration of God, and is profitable for doctrine, for reproof, for correction, for instruction in righteousness: that the man of God may be perfect, thoroughly furnished unto all good works.'"

Eleanor leaned closer to Rebecca, reading the words again for herself. She chewed over the words for a few minutes then sat back, a frown on her face. "I suppose that makes sense. I will say, of late, when verses have been shared, they seem to speak to me."

The smile that graced Rebecca's face was gentle. She reached over and took Eleanor's hand. "That's because the Bible is God's Word, and He says it's living and true. He's using it to assure you that He's real . . . that He exists." She squeezed Eleanor's hand tightly. "But do you want to know the best thing about the Word of God?"

Eleanor's breath caught in her throat. All of a sudden, she desperately wanted to know what Rebecca was going to say. She nodded, unable to speak.

Her new friend's grip tightened just a bit more. "It's that Jesus wants you to know Him, Ellie. And better still, that He loves you."

The words cracked into Eleanor's heart and tears flooded her eyes. After everything she'd done and said . . . could what Rebecca said be true?

Could Jesus still love her?

18

Grant grimaced. He hadn't wanted to get involved with Alvin and his friends and their schemes against Louis Hill, but Alvin demanded it. Grant thought about refusing, but he was in no mood to get beaten to a pulp again.

No longer was he the older brother and in charge. Alvin made that clear. The sooner Grant could start his new job and get away from his brother, the better.

He had met Alvin at the house of one of the younger members of Alvin's association, Jimmy Hutchins. Well, it was the young man's parents' house. His mother had actually cooked them a big pot of chicken and dumplings!

Did Jimmy's parents know what their son was up to?

They were gone for the evening helping to set up some of the Fourth of July tables in the park. Tomorrow would be a big celebration, and most of the town members seemed to have their parts to play.

"Ma said to make sure your boots were clean." Jimmy, a long lanky boy, stepped back as the men glanced down at their boots and then entered the house.

Grant didn't know the boy well. He looked to be about eighteen or nineteen. Seemed a shame that Alvin had wrangled someone so young into this venture. Jimmy had hardly begun to live his life. If they were caught, it was certain to be prison for them.

Jimmy closed the door, then led them to the kitchen. It wasn't a big house, and they ate in the kitchen, like most of the folks Grant knew. The small table and chairs didn't have room enough for all six of the men who'd come, but Jimmy grabbed a stool from a room off the kitchen and handed it to Grant.

"I'll just stand. Go ahead and help yourself."

The pot of chicken and dumplings, along with bowls and spoons, were already on the table. The men lost no time in grabbing up the food. Once everyone had their bowl and had settled down to eat, Alvin spoke.

"Hill gives a speech tomorrow at noon. Sort of a farewell to Kalispell with the false encouragement that eventually we'll have service again."

Grant turned to Alvin. "How do ya know that?"

Alvin frowned. "I have my sources. Don't you worry. I know what I'm talking about." He ate a little of the soup and then continued. "We'll shadow Hill all day if necessary. We'll watch for an opportune time to grab him. Everybody wear a bandanna so you can quickly put it over your face. Grant will keep the horses for us down at the rail yard. After we get Hill, we'll take him to the old huntin' cabin on the Flathead River. The one we used last year. Everyone know where it is?"

The men nodded. Alvin continued. "While we take him there, Grant will break into the telegraph office and send a telegram to James Hill in Minnesota and tell him our demands."

Too bad Alvin knew that operating a telegraph was one of the first jobs Grant had back when Alvin was just a boy. He'd thought about staying with it, but it didn't pay as well as working for the railroad. Especially since he was just an assistant, and the head man had no thoughts of leaving the job.

"Once they have our telegram, they'll know what we require."

"And what exactly are we requiring?" One of the men helped himself to a second bowl of dumplings.

"That James Hill agrees to keep the Kalispell line operational—several times a week—as well as keep a small shop here in town. We'll demand immediate confirmation or threaten to kill his son."

"And how are we gonna keep Hill from changing his mind after we let his son go?" another of the men asked.

Good question.

But Alvin just shrugged. "We'll make it clear that they do things our way or James Hill will be our next victim. We'll threaten the whole family. Louis Hill has a family. We'll threaten to kill them all. That ought to be a good enough reason to do things our way."

How could Alvin be so casual about threatening *anyone's* life? He should just walk out—

"We'll take Hill when he's alone. We'll throw a sack over his head so he can't see us. Just in case, though, we'll have our bandannas on."

"Why don't we just knock him out when we find him? It'll make him much more cooperative," one of the men threw out.

Alvin nodded. "That's a good idea. We can sneak up and hit him from behind. That'll keep him from crying out for help. The real problem is going to be getting him out of town without anyone seeing. Grant, once you send that telegram, you should do what you can to cover up our tracks for a ways."

So much for walking out. Grant nodded. "I'll take care of it."

"Jimmy, did you get some supplies out to the cabin?"

The young man nodded. "I stole a case of canned beans and a couple tins of crackers and a bag of coffee. That's enough to get us started."

"We have no idea how long we'll have to wait it out." Alvin seemed to enjoy being in charge. "Hopefully Hill will respond quickly to our telegram."

Grant finally jumped in "How are we gonna get his reply?" Alvin hadn't said nothing about that.

"You're gonna leave instructions at the telegraph office for them to print his answer in the paper. Then you're gonna watch the paper for us. We'll take turns guarding Hill. We can't very well all stop showing up for work, or they're gonna know it's us."

"We ought to ask for a ransom," one of the men declared. "Wouldn't hurt me none to have some extra money in my pocket."

Alvin gave a hard shake of his head. "No, that's the kind of thing that will get us arrested for sure. This has always been about our jobs and staying put in Kalispell. We all have reasons for not wanting to relocate to Whitefish. All we need is for Hill to agree to keep things running here. The town will call us heroes. Nobody wants to lose the railroad."

Grant finished his chicken and dumplings. It sat heavy in his gut. He looked at Alvin and the others. "Look, if we get caught, we're all gonna go to prison. You know that. Someone might even get killed. Hill might die from the blow on the head. We should think of another way to make our point."

Alvin pounded his fist down on the table, making the soup bowls jump and broth slosh out onto the table. "I don't want to hear your worries about how we're gonna go to prison if we get caught! The point is, don't get caught. You all know what you need to do, and it's just a straightforward and simple plan. Do what I told you to do, and we will all be fine."

If only Grant could be as sure of that as Alvin was, but the truth was, Grant's job wasn't going to be easy. He had to break into the telegraph office and send the telegram and then leave word for the regular operator regarding the reply. Not only that, but the telegraph office had a large open window where people on the street could see the operator at work. He would be a sitting duck. Alvin told him no one would even notice because of all the festivities, but there was always the chance someone could wander past and spot him inside.

The chicken and dumplings in his stomach churned something fierce. Didn't matter if someone recognized him at the telegraph office or not.

There was no way out of this mess.

Ellie tied the sash of her dressing robe around her waist with a sigh. It was good to be back at the Ashburys' home, though the Andrewses were kind hosts. Tomorrow Father would return, and she'd sit down and talk to him about her thoughts on the Bible and God. But right now, she just wanted to crawl in bed.

A light knock sounded on her bedroom door and Ellie went to answer it. Marvella stood on the other side of the door and smiled. Sir Theophilus was in her arms and wiggled as he tried to move toward Ellie.

"I just wanted to tell you good-night, my dear."

"I'm glad you did." She bit the corner of her lip, then pressed forward with her request. "I wonder if I might trouble you for something."

"Why, Ellie, you know you can. What do you need?"

Ellie gave Sir Theophilus a scratch on the head. "I wondered if I might borrow your Bible. I want to do some reading."

Marvella's smile broadened. "Wait right here." She put Sir Theophilus on the floor. "I'll be right back."

The dog danced between Ellie and his mistress as if trying to figure out whether to stay or go. He finally chased after Marvella while Ellie tightened the ribbons on her robe and waited.

It wasn't long until Marvella reappeared, and in her hands was a leatherbound Bible. "You may have this. The Judge and I buy extras to give away for just such an occasion. I am so delighted that you want to read God's Word." She stifled a yawn, raising the back of her hand to her mouth. "We can discuss it in the morning if you like. We won't have a lot of time because of the celebration activities, but if you have questions, just let me know."

"I will." She took the Bible, then paused . . .

The oddest sense of peace had just settled upon her.

She blinked, then met Marvella's eyes again. "Thank you for the Bible. I'll cherish it."

"Mine is my dearest possession. But for now, I'll bid you good-night. Your father will return in the morning, and I know you'll also be anxious to see him."

"Yes. I've missed him very much. We've not been separated from each other for long periods since before Mother died."

The older woman scooped up her dog and gave a little wave. "Until the morning, then."

Ellie returned to her room, closing the door behind her. The evening was chilly, so she hurried to the bed and settled in under the covers to read.

She opened first to John and turned to the fourth chapter. She started reading about the Samaritan woman at Jacob's well. The story was familiar, she'd probably read it with Mother. But now, she wanted to read it and understand it for herself.

Tears pricked Ellie's eyes as she read about the woman—a sinner, who'd had five husbands. Yet Jesus was kind to her. He didn't shame her. Instead, He offered her living water, the chance to worship God in spirit and in truth.

What exactly did that mean? She needed to know because, in some ways, she felt just like this woman.

Confused.

Thirsty.

But eager for a living water that would always satisfy her.

"Jesus, I don't know how to have You as living water, but . . ." She sniffed, wiping her eyes with her handkerchief. "Help me. I think I want to know You again. But I'm afraid.

Afraid what I might have to give up. Afraid . . . I've run too far. Afraid You won't take me back."

What was she saying? How could she be scared of running too far when she'd all but given up her belief in God? She chewed her lip and reread verse twenty-nine: *Come, see a man, which told me all the things I ever did: is this not the Christ?*

Jesus knew that woman had previously had five husbands, yet He ministered to her. He seemed to want her to worship Him. And though she should have been ashamed that Jesus knew her secrets, she wasn't. She just ran and proclaimed to the whole town that Jesus was the Christ.

Ellie shook her head. She wasn't *quite* ready for that. But she admired the woman's passion.

Paging through the Scriptures, Ellie saw snatches of Jesus healing the blind and having compassion on those who were hungry. He helped a lame man walk and called Himself the Good Shepherd. These stories were familiar, as though they'd been sitting on the edge of her memory just waiting for her. Like puzzle pieces that didn't yet fit together to make a whole picture . . . but she knew they would.

She turned the page and scanned John 11.

Her heart stopped.

Jesus raised Lazarus from the dead.

If He could do that for Lazarus, then why not for Ma—

Ellie closed her eyes. No. She wasn't going back to those old feelings and hurts. With a steadying breath, she pressed on. Martha's questions about Jesus' absence and Mary's tears of grief resonated deep within her. But then she read two words that turned her whole world upside down.

Jesus wept.

Ellie blinked and read the verse again. Jesus wept. He stood at the tomb of His friend, and He cried. She ran her finger across those words, a warmth spreading through her. The tears she'd been holding back began falling down her face.

Jesus understood! He knew what it was to feel grief. And loss. And that meant . . .

He could handle her questions about why Mother had died and the confusion and anger she'd felt for so long. Just like He talked to Martha and Mary. He heard their questions and assured them with a truth that could not be denied.

Ellie sucked in a breath as she wept. The words blurred on the page. She pressed a handkerchief to her eyes and kept reading.

Could not this man, which opened the eyes of the blind, have caused that even this man should not have died? The question froze her. It was so similar to the question she had asked. Why hadn't God saved Mother? Helped her in her darkest time of pain and suffering? Why did Mother cling to Jesus with such unyielding faith when she could scarcely breathe?

Ellie didn't understand everything. But as she read these verses, the love of Jesus poured off the page. He'd loved Lazarus, Mary, and Martha. He'd loved her mother, who wasn't suffering anymore. According to what Jesus told Martha, Mother was more alive now than she'd ever been on earth. The thought settled in her heart, wrapping around her like a soft blanket.

And . . . Jesus understood her grief. The Son of God, who could raise someone from the dead, understood her loss.

She pressed on in her reading, her heart leaping with joy

when Jesus commanded Lazarus to come forth. She could only imagine the looks on Mary's and Martha's faces, on the faces of the people with them who had been mourning. She could see Lazarus coming from the tomb. Hear the voice of Jesus commanding the things that bound him to loose him and let him go.

As Ellie read what had happened for Lazarus, her bondage started to slip away. Her heart seemed to break and heal all at once. Peace flowed through her, filling all the cracks of hurt and confusion, restlessness and anger. She clutched the Bible to her chest, a smile breaking across her face.

Jesus.

He was the resurrection and the life!

Life.

That was how she felt right now. Like she had come to life again. More than that, Eleanor could feel the love of Jesus for *her*. The thought overwhelmed her and settled her at the same time.

"Lord, I'm so sorry for running. For being so angry." She wiped at her face with her free hand. "I remember Marvella telling me that I had to turn to You and repent for my sins and give my life to You." She choked back her tears. "I repent, Lord. My life is Yours, Jesus."

MONDAY, JULY 4, 1904

Ellie didn't know when she'd finally drifted off to sleep, but when she awoke, the sun was already up, and she could hear Marvella shouting instructions to her servants. Ellie shifted and paused. Why were her arms so heavy? Ellie glanced down and a smile burst across her lips. Her arms were still wrapped around the Bible.

Father. She couldn't wait to talk with him.

They had grown so close over the years since Mother died. Would he be offended that she'd turned back to God? She didn't want to alienate him. He was all the family she had left. Surely he would understand and see the change in her and be happy for her.

She got out of bed and pushed the curtains back. The heat of the sun warmed her face and she smiled.

It was going to be a delightful day.

Carter dressed for the day in his old bedroom at the farm. He'd spent Sunday night with his folks. He hadn't originally planned to go back to the farm, but he also hadn't really had much of a chance to talk to his mother or father about Ellie. He wanted their advice as to how he should conduct himself, what with her attitude toward the Lord changing. He was feeling drawn to her and kept praying to hear God's clear voice on the matter. But he had to wait for her. Wait like Jacob waited for Rachel, even if it took years.

Whatever happened or didn't happen between them, he continued to pray that God would draw her close and that she would stop fighting and pushing Him away.

At the same time, he had to stand back and let the Holy Spirit work. If he pushed her too hard, for the sake of his feelings, that wouldn't be right. Not that he wouldn't want to encourage her to make peace with God for her spirit's sake. However, he knew his heart for her, and it would be far too easy to focus on that instead of what mattered most.

That was why he wanted to talk to his father and mother. Although maybe the Fourth of July wasn't exactly the right time to do it. He chuckled and did up the buttons on his shirt. His mother would tell him that anytime he felt the need of their counsel was the right time.

He went to the mirror and brushed his hair into place and grabbed his lightweight tan jacket. The day promised to be warm, and he wasn't looking forward to wearing a suit, but he didn't want to appear shabby. After all, it was a celebration.

Making his way downstairs, his mother greeted him first. "Don't you look nice." She stretched up on tiptoes and kissed his cheek.

"And so do you." He took her arm and gave her a twirl.

Mother laughed and fell into step when Carter led her in a little two-step. "You are certainly full of vim and vigor today. I suppose the holiday is worthy of excitement."

"My delight in the day has more to do with something else." He released his hold on her. "I hoped we might talk about Ellie."

Mother nodded. "I've been expecting that. You love her, don't you?"

The words hit him in the face. Did he?

With all the thoughts he'd had on the matter, he hadn't admitted it. "I believe I do, or that I care for her a great deal."

His mother's expression sobered. "I'm glad you care for her. Your father and I adore her too. I've encouraged her to read the Bible. To remember those things she once knew to be true. Her mother trained her in the Word. She knows the truth, but she fears it at the same time. I've been praying for her. Your father has too."

"I've prayed for her just about every day since meeting her." He sat down at the table, where there was already a bevy of breakfast foods awaiting. "Where's Dad? I'm starved."

"He said to start without him. He had to help one of the workers with something on the number four combine."

"He should have called me. I would have helped too."

"We know that, but he said to let you sleep. He's been gone for over an hour, and I expect him to be back almost anytime. But you go ahead and eat. You'll be wanting to get into town, and we won't be headed there until closer to noon."

Carter snapped his napkin open and placed it on his lap. "Pray with me?"

"You know you don't need to ask." She took a seat beside him and extended her hand.

Taking hold of it, Carter bowed his head and prayed. "Lord, thank You for this day and for the bounty You have provided. Bless this meal to the nourishment of our bodies. Lord, please give me wisdom in dealing with my feelings. Continue to draw Ellie back to You, Father. In Jesus' name, Amen."

19

"What a glorious day. Just perfect for the Fourth of July festivities."

Marvella swept into the dining room and joined Ellie at the table, where she'd just been seated by the Judge. Sir Theophilus padded along behind his mistress.

Judge Ashbury walked around the table and helped his wife to take her seat, then claimed his own. "It is indeed splendid. Shall I pray?"

"Oh, please do." The older woman bowed her head.

Ellie did likewise, and for maybe the first time, really listened to what the Judge had to say.

"Father, we come to You today in gratitude of heart and joy of spirit. We thank You for our great nation and the freedom we enjoy here. We praise You for the beauty You have created and the hope we have in Christ Jesus. Please come with us as we go through the day and guide our hearts and minds. Bless this food, in Jesus' name, Amen." He looked up and smiled. "This day gives me great pleasure."

Marvella nodded and tossed the pup a piece of bacon. "The celebratory spirit is upon us. Ellie, my dear, how did you make out with your reading?"

She picked up her napkin and settled it on her lap. It seemed impossible to describe all she was feeling. "I . . . enjoyed it very much. It brought back a great many memories of my mother."

"When I was a boy, I loved the story of David and Goliath." The Judge passed Ellie the platter of bacon. "I used to ask my mother to read it to me every night, and then I would imagine standing there before the giant and knowing without a doubt that God had already won the battle. That gave me great courage to trust in God no matter what obstacles I had to face."

Ellie let out a laugh, picturing the Judge as a little boy going to battle. Of course, she couldn't imagine him without his bushy eyebrows and mustache. "Yes, I can see how that story would give you great courage to slay your own giants." She put two pieces of bacon on her plate and passed the platter to Marvella.

Ellie could hardly sit still, but this morning it was a joyful kind of struggle. Like she had a secret that was ready to burst from her. She'd been so eager to tell Marvella about what happened last night, but Father wasn't home yet. Before she made any public declarations, she wanted to talk to him first. *God, I hope he understands.*

She started. The prayer flowed through her mind as though she'd never stopped talking to God.

"My dear, let's not overtax the young woman." Judge Ashbury's voice broke through her thoughts, and he offered her a sympathetic smile.

"Oh tosh." Marvella waved her hand. "Ellie is perfectly capable of answering my question."

Ellie suppressed a laugh and turned to Marvella. "I appreciate your interest, but before I say too much, I want to talk to my father. I want him to hear from me where I am with Jesus. With the Bible. How my heart has changed." There. That was as close as she would get to telling Marvella. For now.

"How wonderful." The older woman reached for the jam. "We will eagerly await the full story."

The Judge smiled, his eyes twinkling. He knew. "Yes, indeed, my dear."

Marvella sipped her coffee.

Ellie gave her a smiling nod. The peace that had fallen over her last night hadn't left. So this was what Mama meant about the comfort of the Scriptures. Ellie couldn't wait to dig in and read the Bible for herself. She might never fully understand why her mother had been made to suffer, but after reading about what Jesus went through on His journey to the cross, she believed God Almighty knew her sorrow and pain. He hadn't spared His own Son the pain and suffering of death! And that it was allowed on behalf of the world whom God did not want to see perish from their sins . . .

What an incomparable love.

Maybe life wouldn't always bring the answers she wanted. Maybe the Bible would give her insight, but not necessarily complete understanding. Perhaps that only came, as Sarah had said, by growing deeper in her love of God.

The Judge glanced at the clock. "It's nearly time to pick up the men from the station. I'm going to have Jim drive today. I'll send him back with the luggage, and then he can drive you to the park, Ellie."

"Oh, I had thought to go with you to the station."

The Judge stood. "If you wouldn't mind waiting, I need a short time of meeting with the men and thought we might be able to talk at the depot."

She forced a smile. "I understand. I can wait."

"The Judge is going to drop me off to meet with my ladies on the final touches for the luncheon." Marvella gave her husband a sweet smile. "I'd like to make sure the girls have everything they need."

Ellie helped herself to scrambled eggs and toast, then held out her cup when the footman brought coffee around again. It would be a long day. She doused the dark liquid in cream and put sugar in as well before sampling it. Coffee had never been her favorite.

Marvella held her delicate teacup in her hands. "Is Louis planning to stay with us?"

"No, my dear. He's coming in his private train car so that he can attend today's festivities and then go up as far as the tracks will allow to inspect the route to Whitefish. He'll have his accommodations with him."

"Well, we can still invite him to join us for dinner each evening."

The Judge shook his head. "No need. He's only staying the day and then moving on."

That was good. Father had been busy with Mr. Hill last time. She was eager to have time alone with him.

"We should probably be on our way, Marvella. I don't want to be late picking up our guests." The Judge tossed back the rest of his coffee and got to his feet.

Mrs. Ashbury dabbed her lips with the napkin. "I'm ready."

And without further ado, they bid Ellie good-bye and were gone. She remained at the table looking down at her breakfast and feeling almost as if the encounter had never happened. The Ashburys seemed to be in constant motion.

Ellie finished her breakfast and then made her way to the parlor.

The minutes seemed to creep by and then the hour was gone. Had something happened? After another half hour, she was just about to call for her bicycle when she heard the carriage wheels crunching on the gravel drive.

She hurried to the door and stepped out onto the porch, but as the carriage came to a stop, she found it to be empty, save the driver and luggage.

"Jim, where is my father?"

He jumped down and tipped his hat. "He remained in town. They all did and sent me home with the luggage and the instructions to pick you up and deliver you to the celebration. You are to wait for them at the luncheon table."

"Let me get my hat and gloves."

She hurried back inside. Her things were waiting for her on the foyer table. Ellie settled a simple straw boater on her head and secured it with a hat pin. She was just pulling on her gloves when Jim showed up with the luggage.

"I'll be with you in just a moment, miss." He hurried past her and up the stairs to deliver the suitcases and bags.

Ellie stepped back outside, not bothering to close the front door. Why hadn't Father thought to send for her sooner? It was bad enough that he'd abandoned her for his short trip, but now it seemed that he wasn't even concerned with seeing her right away. It would seem Kalispell had changed them both.

Jim returned, pulling the door closed. He hurried down the steps and awaited Ellie. She let him hand her up into the surrey and settled on the backseat. Her thoughts were a jumble.

She couldn't imagine her father casting her aside, but he had been put out with her when she had questioned Mr. Grinnell about the alterations he wanted in the national park. There had also been other times when she had spoken to her father about other issues, and he had no patience for her views on the matter. Goodness, had they been growing apart all the time, and she hadn't noticed? Would it cause further grief to their relationship when she announced that she wanted to return to the Lord and wanted him to return as well?

It was hard to imagine him shutting her out. She loved her father. He was all she had left in the world. Ellie bit her lower lip. What if they moved into the rambling Hennessy house and simply resigned from each other's company?

People were increasingly present on the walkways, and by the time Ellie reached the city center, the crowds were everywhere. There was an exuberant buzz among the townspeople. They appeared to be more than fervent in their desire to celebrate the Fourth.

Jim slowed the surrey to accommodate the traffic, but finally he managed to maneuver them to a place near where tables for distinguished guests had been set in place by the grandstand. Most of the folks would eat picnic style on the ground unless they brought other means. To the back there were long tables set up with what looked to be hundreds of dishes of food. Ellie had heard from Sarah that several pigs had been roasted for the festivities. It looked like those were being carved up at the far end of the food tables.

Ellie's foot had no sooner touched the ground than she saw her father. He was speaking with several men, and the Judge was at his side. She made her way to them and was relieved when her father looked up and smiled.

"Ellie. How good to see you. I've missed you." He hugged her in an uncharacteristic show of affection.

"I missed you, too. I have been counting the minutes until you returned." She pulled back and looked at his tired face. "You haven't been resting well."

He chuckled. "Ever the worrier." He looked to the other men. "Where would we be without women to take care of us?"

The other men agreed and laughed. Father turned her toward the gathering. "This is Ellie, my daughter." The men tipped their hats and names were given, although she wasn't of a mind to remember them.

She laid her hand on Father's arm. "I was hoping we could talk, but I see the day is much too busy."

Her father leaned close. "Let's go for a walk after the luncheon and speeches. We can talk then."

At least he hadn't dismissed her. She looped her arm through his. "How was the trip?"

"Wonderful. Mr. Hill joined us for a short time and brought us to town on his private train car. We were able to work out many of the details we hope to propose regarding the national park. We've all agreed to head to Washington, DC, in August to meet with the president. It's an election year, however, so he may not have much time to consider our proposal, but we hope by being there he will feel obligated to at least hear us out."

"Washington. Well, that may require new clothes. I'm not sure what we have is fine enough for that."

Her father patted her arm. "I won't be taking you along, Ellie. Louis is providing transportation, and it will just be us gentlemen. I'll explain more when we're alone." The last of this he said in a barely audible voice.

As though he hadn't just stunned her, he walked across the grass, chatting with his companions.

So. It would seem Father had teamed up with his friends and no longer needed her. She pressed a hand to her heart, but the pain there remained.

What was she to do with herself? There was, of course, Mrs. Ashbury and her ladies' club, but that could hardly occupy all of Eleanor's time. She'd gone to school, but how could her studies from Vassar in bookkeeping and history land her a job doing anything but what she'd done for her father? Tears pooled and threatened to spill over onto her cheeks.

She turned from the joyful gathering and walked past the tables. She slipped behind a large tree and wiped at her face.

Letting her thoughts spin out of control wasn't helping anything. Besides, her father said they would talk. Instead of jumping to conclusions, she needed to hear him out. She let out a long breath, no longer on the verge of crying. Though her head was starting to pound.

Straightening her shoulders, Eleanor walked back to the tables in search of a friendly face. Her father and his friends had returned to the tables, chatting with the Judge and Marvella. Conversations were going on all around them, and children seemed to appear from every corner, racing after each other. She pressed her fingertips to her temples. The myriad noises only made her headache worse.

"Have you taken too much sun, Ellie?" Father appeared beside her.

She glanced at him and shook her head. "I'm fine."

He took her elbow and led her to an empty chair. A large tree offered shade and a gentle breeze.

Father pulled out the chair and helped her to sit. Marvella arrived and claimed the seat across from Eleanor, her concern palpable.

"Are you all right, my dear?"

Eleanor nodded. "Just a bit of a headache."

A touch of worry showed in Father's eyes. "She's probably had too much sun. She'll be better here in the shade."

To the left of the grandstand, a band began to take form as musicians with their instruments took their places. After another minute or two, the conductor raised his baton, and the band sounded a call to attention. The mayor stepped up on the grandstand, and the crowd went silent.

"Let us stand for 'Hail Columbia'!"

Everyone rose and the band began to play. Voices were raised from one end of the park area to the other. It was only then that Eleanor really noticed the red, white, and blue buntings fashioned after the American flag. The Montana state flag had been set up in place just a little lower on the grandstand than the Stars and Stripes, and at the tables for the city's important guests, red, white, and blue tablecloths were laid.

Eleanor had never participated in an event like this one. She and Father had never attended parties or such revelry. Generally speaking, Father's work kept them much too busy, and more times than she could count, they were on a train to some new destination when July Fourth came around.

In fact . . . the same could be said of Christmas and birthdays. After Mother died, they had forsaken such things, offering only the slightest attention to those events that demanded action. Father always gave Eleanor a gift for her birthday and Christmas, and she had done the same for him, but there was little celebration.

How could they have let joy escape them?

Last night she'd known such happiness in just reading the Bible and remembering her mother. Could they ever recapture the joy they'd once known without Mother?

The music ended and the mayor again spoke. "We will have the Reverend Brooks offer grace, and then everyone can form a line for the food. Please allow our guests of honor to go first."

The pastor came and prayed while the mayor retook his seat. As soon as the amens were said, the mayor greeted Mr. Hill with a vigorous handshake. He gave a nod to the Ashburys, the Briggses, and Mr. Grinnell. Eleanor allowed her father to maneuver her through the crowd, and the rest were ushered to the front of the line, where Mrs. Ashbury motioned to Nora. The maid immediately took up a stack of plates and handed one to each of them.

"Everyone brings their own plates," Marvella told Eleanor and her father. "Silver and glasses too. It's easier that way. We just pack it all up and take it home afterwards."

Nora handed her and Father a plate, then turned and gave one to Marvella as well.

"Silver and the glasses are being put on the table as we speak. Napkins too." She moved on to Mr. Grinnell and the Judge.

"Seems most efficient." Father smiled at Mrs. Ashbury.

"Oh, it is, and we all just share the load of providing food. The Kalispell Women's Club goes around and gets the help of the various church women. They in turn can reach out to their family members and friends. We never lack for food."

Eleanor glanced down the many tables and marveled at the way everything had come together. No, they wouldn't lack food. That was clear.

"This evening everyone will bring their own food, and we will sit out under the stars, although we won't be able to see them due to the long hours of sun. We'll watch the fireworks and listen to the band play again. It's always such a grand celebration." Marvella's eyes fairly glowed at all she'd arranged.

Eleanor made her food choices and then waited while a big burly man gave her a large piece of roasted pork. It was far more than she'd be able to eat, but she smiled and thanked him for it, nevertheless.

"If you need help with that, just give me a holler."

She turned to find Carter's dad beside her.

"Mr. Brunswick. How nice to see you. I was just thinking that the portion was much bigger than I'd be able to manage."

"Too bad you aren't sitting with us. I know Carter would certainly enjoy that."

She felt her cheeks heat up. Thankfully no one seemed to notice. Even Mr. Brunswick had moved on to greet the others.

Eleanor did her best to calm her nerves. If anyone asked about her cheeks, she would blame the sun. She made her way back to the table only to find Carter waiting there.

"Looks like your eyes may be bigger than your stomach. You sure you can eat all that?"

She smiled. "Your father offered to help."

"That sounds like him." He glanced past her and then returned his gaze to hers. "I see they're all coming back, so I'll be quick about this. I wondered if maybe we could take a walk later."

"Oh . . . well, I'm supposed to take a walk with my father." She hoped he didn't hear the disappointment in her voice. She set the plate on the table, relieving her arms of the weight. My, but she had several important conversations scheduled for the day.

Father was the most important, though a talk with Carter was a close second. Her face warmed. She needed to rein in her thoughts. Even though she had given her life back to the Lord, Carter still might not want anything more than friendship with her. Best to be realistic.

"Maybe after you're done walking with him, you can walk with me. I'm sure you'll still be trying to digest all that." He motioned to her plate as Marvella Ashbury joined them. Her plate was piled even higher.

"I never know how to say no to some of those dishes. Especially that peach pie." She put her plate on the table. "Carter, how nice to see you. I was just speaking to your father."

"Good to see you, Mrs. Ashbury. I was just seeing if maybe Ellie wanted to take a walk with me later."

"Of course she does."

Eleanor rolled her eyes for the first time in Marvella's presence. For goodness' sake, Marvella didn't even look at Eleanor for her approval!

Marvella let out a laugh. She patted Eleanor's arm, ignoring her insolent disposition. "Never you mind. Don't bother giving me any more of your sassy looks. Why don't you join Carter and his family? The men will be busy talking about the railroad and the national park. You should go and enjoy the day and have some fun. There are going to be games after lunch."

Father arrived just then, thank heaven! Eleanor shook her head, doing her best to look disappointed. "No, Father and I plan to take a walk after lunch."

"Oh pshaw!" Mrs. Ashbury waved her words away like a pesky mosquito. "Your father won't mind if you walk instead with a handsome young bachelor. Will you, Stewart?"

Father chuckled. "Not at all. It's only reasonable that Ellie should trade in an old man for a young one."

"It's settled, then." The older woman took her seat. "Now, Carter, you carry that heavy plate of hers."

"Yes, ma'am." Carter grabbed her plate, grinning from ear to ear.

20

Eleanor enjoyed her time with the Brunswicks, despite her being with them because of Marvella's machinations. Sarah and Jacob treated her like a part of their family, and she couldn't have been more welcome. Jacob shared stories of their lives in Kansas. Dramatic tales of prairie fires and tornadic storms and of the two married daughters they left behind when they moved to Montana in 1885. They had come in search of an adventure.

At one point, she dared to ask her question. "So why does one farmer need twenty thousand acres to grow wheat?"

Jacob Brunswick hadn't been the least bit offended, much to her relief. "Because there are millions of hungry people out in the world. Each acre of wheat produces roughly thirty-seven bushels."

Carter jumped in at this. "And each bushel of wheat produces about forty-two pounds of flour. More than that if it's not extra refined."

"And forty-two pounds of flour can make an equal number of one-pound loaves of bread," Sarah added with a smile. "One thing this family knows, is wheat."

"No matter how much I plant, it seems the world always needs more," Jacob finished off. "Wheat keeps the world from starving to death."

It made so much sense. What would the world eat if there wasn't a healthy crop of wheat each year? Some poor families lived almost exclusively on bread and whatever else they could manage to get.

Still . . . "But couldn't the government own the land and keep it public, rather than having a lot of independent farms? Then when storms or insects destroyed the crops, you wouldn't bear the repercussions alone."

Jacob gave a laugh. "Have you ever known anything where the work was done by one person, overseen by another, and owned by a third to ever work well? I know the land like the back of my hand. I tend to it and keep it as healthy as possible. This year part of our acreage will go fallow to rest. Next year another part will be set aside. We even rotate and plant different crops every so often. If we didn't manage the land in a responsible way, we'd end up with nothing. The land wouldn't even grow grass properly."

"What's more," Carter added, "if the government owned the land and leased it out, they might not allow for that kind of responsible management."

They really did know what they were doing. And yet, no one treated her in a hostile manner for her thoughts or questions. These were good people. Maybe they would become friends for a great many year—

Years? Eleanor's mouth dropped open a bit. When had she started thinking in terms of years in Kalispell? She wasn't sure, but these people . . . this place . . .

Yes, she could see herself living here for years.

When lunch was finally over and everyone had had their fill, Eleanor excused herself to return Marvella's dishes and claim her father for their walk. As she approached the table, she was glad to see he was already finished with his meal and sat chatting with the mayor and Mr. Hill. George Grinnell was nowhere in sight.

Father saw her and got to his feet, as did the other men. The courtesy touched her.

"Ellie, I need to put off our walk for a little while. Mr. Hill wants to show me something at the depot. We won't be long." He surprised her with a kiss on her cheek. "Please be patient with me."

So much for them standing out of courtesy. "Of course." She hid her disappointment as Hill and her father headed off and the mayor moved out in the opposite direction.

Mrs. Ashbury was nowhere to be found. Neither was the Judge. Eleanor put Mrs. Ashbury's dishes down with the others just as Nora approached.

"Don't worry about these things, miss." Nora gathered the dishes. "I'll take care of everything."

And just like that, Eleanor was not needed.

Anywhere.

She walked away. What should she do with herself? Oh, wait. There was Carter. She gave him a wave and he was quickly at her side.

"It seems Father is busy for a time, so if you'd like to take that walk now, I'm free."

"I'd be delighted." He offered her his arm, but she refused.

"I'm fine. Thank you." There was really no need for him to support her, and she didn't want people to talk.

They walked past where the band was assembling. They were going to play a tribute to John Philip Sousa and his marches, according to Marvella. Eleanor looked forward to the music. She enjoyed concerts and bands and so seldom heard them.

"Looks like the band is getting ready." Carter nodded toward the gathering of men and instruments."

"Yes. I was just thinking about how much I enjoy hearing bands and orchestras play. We so seldom ever go to concerts. Father is always exhausted at the end of the day. He's never been one to enjoy a lot of society gatherings."

"This town always loves to celebrate Independence Day. It's important to our country, don't you think?"

"I do. I was raised to be patriotic."

Carter hummed, a noncommittal noise if Eleanor had ever heard one. Still, letting silence settle between them wasn't all bad. For the first time in Carter's presence, Eleanor didn't feel stressed out. Or defensive. There was peace between them.

Imagine! Peace!

Of course, it was because there was peace within her now. A wide grin spread across her face. So this was what Mama was talking about when she mentioned "peace that surpassed understanding."

"Now just what is that pretty smile for, Ellie?" Carter's warm voice brought her out of her thoughts.

She blushed and tucked her hands behind her back. Where to begin? Though she had wanted to share her news with Father first, she wanted Carter to know what happened to her, too.

"I read a lot of the Bible last night. I read stories of Jesus healing and of Him raising Lazarus. I read about His kindness to women who sought Him or were brought to Him. Some knew what He could do for them, while others didn't have a clue." She dropped her hands to her sides, her fingers slipping into the folds of her skirt. "My mother knew what Jesus could do for her. She knew that this world was not the end of her life, but that something glorious and wonderful awaited. She told me that."

Eleanor met Carter's gaze. "It was hard for me as a child to understand how she could believe when things were so bad, but now I realize that her belief was all that got her through the pain and suffering. Her faith was so strong that she wasn't afraid of where that pain was leading. I want that kind of faith for myself."

The words slid out and she held her breath.

Carter might have done a flip had he known how! Her words were a balm to his heart. "I'm mighty glad to hear you say that, Ellie."

The rosy color in her cheeks deepened. "Thank you." The words came out low and sweet.

He had a million questions. He could tell something was different. That agitated restlessness was absent. And she didn't seem like she was waiting for a fight to break out between them over . . . something.

Still, he didn't want to rush her. His mother had made it clear that Ellie would need time to figure things out, time for God to impress upon her what she lacked and what He could do for her.

"*Let the Spirit speak to her heart. Let her see the truth of*

Jesus and accept it for herself before you barrel in and impose your charm on her."

Carter smiled. His mother knew him so well.

They walked on in silence, while in the background he could hear the band tuning up. He didn't want to get too far away since Ellie had already commented about looking forward to hearing the band play. "Maybe we should head back."

"I suppose so. Thank you for not trying to push me into getting . . . well . . . saved. Mrs. Ashbury is enthusiastic about it. She was determined I should make everything right over breakfast, but I explained that I wanted to speak to Father about it first."

"Are you afraid he'll be angry?"

"Angry? No." She glanced at the ground and shook her head. "The fact is, with all that seems to be changing in our relationship, I don't know if he will even care. On the other hand, I want him to accept God as well. We've both been so lost since Mother died. She was the center of everything in our family, and when she died, it was as if we died as well. Coming to Montana, I saw a spark of life in Father that I've not seen since she passed. I think Montana has changed us both."

Carter chuckled. "It has a way of doing that."

Grant fidgeted as he waited with the horses. Him and Alvin had eaten lunch with the other men in Alvin's posse, sticking mostly to themselves away from the crowd. Alvin said there was no reason to miss out on the best feast of the year, so they would wait to take Hill until after lunch.

Somehow Alvin had learned that Hill intended to board his private train car that afternoon to head back to Columbia Falls and then onto the new tracks that would head toward Whitefish.

Alvin gave his gang a grin. "We'll take him before he leaves Kalispell."

After lunch Alvin and the others started shadowing Louis Hill, while Grant made his way to collect the horses. He was to take them to the rail yards. Alvin figgered with everyone at the celebration, this would be the perfect place to head out.

Grant had tried one final time to convince Alvin it wouldn't work—that James Hill had dealt with tougher men than Alvin's gang. His brother hadn't cared. He was convinced this would change everything.

Grant didn't believe it. Hill's family would hire guards— maybe even get the Pinkertons looking for the men who took his son. Grant should have left when Alvin first started talking about this scheme. But Grant promised their mother he'd look out for Alvin.

Of course, lately Alvin seemed tougher than Grant. And meaner. He'd never have any trouble taking care of himse—

Grant stiffened. What was that sound? He shushed the mounts and moved them into the shadows between two buildings.

Ah. Alvin and his men. They came toward him . . . and Alvin had a man over his shoulder. The man's head was covered in a hood.

Alvin's grin was triumphant. "We got him at the depot. Come take him while I mount my horse."

The others beat a quick path to take their reins from

Grant. He went to Alvin, who maneuvered Hill onto Grant's shoulder, then snatched his reins and jumped into the saddle.

"Hand him up. Face down in front of me."

Grant followed Alvin's instructions and settled Hill on Alvin's lap. The man didn't move. Must be unconscious. At least . . .

That's what Grant was hoping.

Alvin took up his reins. "We'll head up to the cabin and get him tied up, then the boys will come back to town. Come to the cabin when you have Hill's answer. Don't delay."

"I won't." Delay? He wanted this over as fast as possible.

"We left a note in the pocket of the man Hill was talking to. Knocked 'em both out at the same time." He chuckled. "It was like we'd practiced it. They dropped like flies."

"You didn't kill either one of them, did you?" Grant studied his brother's face.

"Not hardly. Now go send the telegram." Alvin straightened in the saddle. "That note won't be enough. The mayor might not think to send a telegram to the old man."

What choice did he have? "I'll go right now."

"Oh, and Grant . . . don't be the reason this doesn't work." Alvin fixed him with a cold, dead expression.

Had he ever really known his little brother? This man seemed an utter stranger. And a threatening one at that.

"I won't."

They slipped off through the rail yards. They would clear the tracks and buildings and then head north and east toward the river.

Grant shoved his hands in his pockets. Not that there wasn't plenty yet to worry about. Someone might have seen them. Someone might already have found whoever it was Hill was with. Even if they hadn't, it wouldn't take long before someone missed them.

He hurried to the telegraph office and managed to get inside. No one had even bothered to lock up. He sent the message—a very lengthy one—to James Hill, St. Paul, Minnesota.

And then he slipped outside again . . .

And ran.

21

Eleanor and Carter stood with some of the others listening to the music. Some people clapped along to the beat. They were most enthusiastic, and it was clear that the day had brought them great joy. What would her life be like here in Kalispell? With her father working on his book, she would need to find something to keep herself busy. She was qualified to teach school, and yet that wasn't really something she'd ever considered before. Maybe it was time to think about it. Maybe if she found a job she could help with their financ—

Goodness! A man came running across the open area in front of the band, directly at her and Carter! Before Eleanor could say anything to Carter, the man veered away and went directly to the mayor. Soon several men had gathered, and the mayor motioned for them to follow him. Eleanor looked at Carter, who shrugged. He didn't seem overly concerned so she relaxed.

Until Marvella came toward them in a near run.

Something was wrong.

Marvella took hold of Eleanor. "Come with me. You too, Carter."

The band played on even as Eleanor found herself whisked away. "What's happened?"

Marvella slowed a bit, huffing and puffing for air. "It's a terrible thing. Just terrible. But I don't . . . want you to worry. The men . . . will do all they can."

What? All they could about *what*?

Marvella led them past the main body of the crowd to where the mayor and the men who had gone with him were now standing. They surrounded someone who was seated.

The crowd opened as Marvella pushed her way in. "I have his daughter!"

Eleanor's chest tightened. Had Father suffered a spell of some sort? She couldn't see the man at the center of everyone's attention because a man stood in the way—perhaps a doctor? He appeared to be examining the seated man's head. Had the sun gotten to be too much for Father, and he'd passed out . . . hit his head?

She looked at the men. "What has happened?"

The group of men looked at her and then to Marvella.

The older woman shook her head. "I haven't told her anything. There wasn't time. Tell her now."

"Father?" Eleanor tried to peer around the man who blocked her vision. "Are you all right?"

She tried to move forward, but Marvella held her back. Just then the man in front of Eleanor stepped away to reveal Louis Hill seated in the chair.

But . . . where was Father?

Carter came up beside Eleanor. "What's going on?"

"Someone attacked Mr. Hill"—the mayor shifted his glance from Mr. Hill to Eleanor—"and Mr. Briggs."

What? "Where is my father?" Why would someone attack him? And why wasn't he here?

The Judge stepped forward. "I'm so sorry, Eleanor, but someone has taken him. We believe they thought they were taking Mr. Hill, since they look a great deal alike."

"I want some guards immediately!" Mr. Hill sounded like a frightened child. "I'm leaving as soon as the train can be ready. I'm glad the railroad is leaving this town! Such a lawless town is no place for the railroad."

The doctor patted the agitated man's shoulder. "Mr. Hill, you must calm yourself."

"There *is* no calming, Doctor, until I'm away from this wretched town."

The doctor kept his voice soothing. "At least come to my office, where I can stitch your head."

Enough! Where was her father? She opened her mouth to demand an answer, but Mr. Hill cut her off by standing up and shaking off the doctor's hand.

"No. You can tend to me in my private train car. Judge, I need at least a half dozen men to go with me as guards. They will need to accompany me back to St. Paul, where I can hire my own men."

The Judge gave a quick nod. He seemed fed up with Mr. Hill, too. "I will tend to the matter, Louis, but we must explain everything to Miss Briggs first."

Wait . . . was that blood on Mr. Hill's light gray suit coat? She struggled to keep her own voice steady. "Please, where is my father? Is he injured?" She couldn't stop from trembling.

Carter slipped his strong arm around her, steadying her.

The Judge took a step toward her. "The kidnappers left a note saying they were taking Louis. As I said, it seems they mistook your father for him."

"But—"

"My dear." Marvella touched her arm. "Your father and Mr. Hill do bear a remarkable resemblance to each other."

Eleanor managed a nod. It was true, they did.

Carter's tone when he spoke was furious. "Did these fools say what they wanted?"

The Judge nodded. "They are demanding train service be returned to Kalispell."

"That is *not* going to happen." Louis shook his index finger at the group. "Mark my words!"

The Judge ignored him and went on. "They say they've telegraphed James Hill and won't release his son until he agrees to return service to Kalispell."

Mr. Hill looked about to explode. "The very idea that they think they can threaten me and my family. It's beyond the pale."

No, what was beyond the pale was this man ranting about himself when he was safe and Father was not!

She met the Judge's eyes. "Did they strike my father?" *Please, Lord . . . don't let Father be hurt. . . .*

Hill almost growled the answer. "They did. Ruthless cretins. I'll see them all in jail."

Carter's grip around her tightened. "How many of them were there?"

"I don't know." Mr. Hill sat back down and allowed the doctor's ministering, but winced. "They hit Stewart first and he fell. Then me. Got us from behind. I never saw any of their faces. When I awoke, I found myself on my back, a note in my pocket and a horrific pain in my head." He seemed to be calming down and offered Eleanor a regretful look. "Your father was nowhere to be found. Thankfully someone saw me fall and came to my rescue."

How much more could she take? Her stomach roiled. She looked at Carter. "I don't feel well."

How humiliating to admit that she wasn't strong enough to stomach all that had happened.

Marvella nodded to Carter. "Take her back to the house."

Her stomach clenched. "But I need to know what's happening. I—"

"We will all go to the house and plan what is to be done." Marvella was calm and commanding. "Milton, have Jim bring the carriage around. We must get Ellie home."

She didn't fight Carter's hold on her. His arm supported her as he led her to the carriage. Halfway there, her knees gave way. Carter swept her into his arms.

The Judge took a seat with Jim up front, and Carter squeezed into the carriage's second seat next to Marvella, nestling Ellie on his lap.

She couldn't breathe. Could barely think. She was a child again, small and helpless against forces taking away someone she loved . . .

She kept her eyes squeezed shut and turned her face deeper into Carter's solid chest. Father was strong, but a hit on the head could kill a man. Would the brigands who took him care for him if he was injured? Or would he bleed to death?

God, please . . . The prayer came as easy as breathing. The words jumbled in her mind, but He knew. *Please keep him safe. Keep everyone safe. Help us to find him soon.*

Marvella patted her knee. "It will be all right, my dear. We'll get your father back safe and sound. Once the men realize they've taken the wrong man, they're sure to release him."

Would they? Or would their anger make them hurt him? Even kill him? She glanced at Carter's face. His tight lips said he wasn't so confident that they'd let Father go.

They reached the house, and Ellie started to move out of Carter's grasp, but he held her fast. "You just stay where you are, Ellie. I've got you."

And so he did. He lifted her in his arms and carried her out of the carriage and into the house. Marvella was calling orders to the staff and for Nora to bring Ellie tea.

"Have Cook make the special lemon tea. Oh, and put some rosehips in it." She glanced back at Eleanor. "And honey. And be fast about it."

Nora nodded and scrambled from the room.

Marvella's tender smile helped ease Ellie's shaking. "Honey is just the thing to settle your stomach and help you recover from the shock you've had." She patted Carter's arm. "Take her to the sitting room."

Sir Theophilus came at a run. He'd been left behind for the celebration and now barked as if chiding his mistress for the offense. Marvella scooped him up and held him close.

Carter carried Ellie into the large sitting room, then lowered her to a plush couch with plenty of pillows.

She missed his firm grip on her, the solid feel of his chest against her, but at least he sat down beside her. His presence . . . comforted her.

She looked to him and voiced the fear that had been pulling at her. "Do you think they'll kill my father when they realize he's not Louis Hill?"

His gaze was steady, his tone sure. "They'd be fools to kill anyone. It's one thing to assault and take a man, and an entirely different thing to commit murder. I don't think they'll dig themselves in deeper once they know what's happened."

Oh, how she wanted to believe him! "But if he sees them . . . he can identify them."

"They made it clear in the note that they would release Hill when their demands were met. They would have planned to keep their identities secret so they could escape unknown."

That made sense. She drew in a deep breath. "Would you pray with me?"

Their eyes connected. "Of course."

As Carter lifted his heart to the Almighty, her own heart began to calm. She squeezed his hands, and he squeezed hers back.

The house soon filled with men from town. One of them nodded to the Judge as he came into the sitting room. "Mr. Hill is now being guarded by some of the deputy marshals, so we came along to offer our help finding Mr. Briggs."

In mere moments, Marvella had them settled into the sitting room. She seemed to understand Ellie's need to know the details, even if they were difficult to hear.

Marshal Shelton drew everyone's attention. "We'll form a posse and go after them. I've already got my deputies checking out tracks and seeing what evidence they've left behind. We'll be ready to head out as soon as we're done here."

Carter put his hand over Ellie's, where it rested on the

couch, and gave it a squeeze. Then he let go and nodded to the marshal. "I want to join the posse."

"I want to go as well."

The men all stared at her. She didn't care. They might not want a woman along, but if her father was hurt, she would be there to help—

"I'm awful sorry, Miss Briggs, but you can't go. I wouldn't be comfortable putting a woman in danger." The marshal gave her a sympathetic nod. "But I do understand."

She lifted her chin. "I can't just sit here! I couldn't live with myself knowing that my father was out there hurt, maybe even dying, and I just . . . sat. I *must* go. I can take care of myself. I can read a map and use a compass. I'm capable in every way of surviving out there."

Marvella came to her and sat beside her, lifting Ellie's hand and giving it a squeeze. "My dear, this is something we must leave to the men. They would only have their attention divided between worrying over you and trying to hunt down dangerous criminals. You wouldn't want their attention taken from rescuing your father, would you?"

"Of course not, but . . ." Tears stung at her eyes. "I can't just sit here."

"Then we will get some of the women together and pray." Marvella smiled. "It's the most powerful thing any of us can do to help."

"She's right, Ellie."

She glared at Carter. Him jumping into the matter just made her all the more frustrated. "*No one* understands. I've been with Father on many dangerous trips. I'm not a liability. I can hold my own."

"The answer is no." Marshal Shelton's tone brooked no

further debate. "And that's final. Now here's what I plan to do. We're going to see if any of our men who are good at tracking can locate signs of their trail. If not, Grant Wallace is in town, and he's the best tracker I've ever known. I'll get him to come help us."

The conversation continued until the butler entered and announced that the marshal was needed in the foyer.

"That will be my man. Let's go." Several of the men followed him from the room.

Carter turned to Ellie. "I'll do everything I can, and when we find your father, I'll take care of him as if he were my own father."

She gave him a nod. But if he thought she'd given up, he was sorely mistaken. Her father needed her. *Her.* Not Eleanor, with all her social skills and pride. But his Ellie, with all her creativity and strength and determination and whatever else she could muster to find and save him.

Let the others go. She'd bide her time and slip out once they were on their way. Follow them at a distance. She lifted her chin. They'd never know she was there. After all, their focus would be on the road ahead of them . . . not behind.

And Ellie's focus would be on Father.

And God.

What Carter wouldn't give to stay at Ellie's side. She was so scared. So worried about her father. He was worried too. He didn't trust that the men would just turn Briggs loose once they realized they didn't have Hill.

Of course, he couldn't tell Ellie that. No need to make

her worry even more, not when he was concerned enough for them both.

Lord, please guard Ellie's dad and keep him in Your care. You know the situation and know his condition. Lord, I pray that he wasn't hurt when they took him, but figure they hit him same as they did Mr. Hill. Please don't let the man suffer or die. Ellie needs him so much.

"You got your horse, Carter?"

He looked at the marshal. "No, but it won't take me long. Which way are you going? I'll catch up."

"My men found activity around the rail yards. We'll head out from there and go north."

"I'll find you." Carter did a quick step down the Ashburys' drive and then ran all the way to the livery downtown. Ellie had seemed so fragile when she heard her father was taken. What would it do to her if something terrible happened to him? She was a strong woman in some ways, but if her father didn't survive this, she'd be alone.

Could she survive that?

She needs you so much, Lord. She knows that. She remembers her mama telling her as much, but the world and the devil have done their best to convince her otherwise. Please help her to see the truth and embrace it. Help her father to accept it too.

He reached the livery stables and gave a wave to the boy who was mucking the stalls. "I'll saddle Mercury myself." He went through the building and out into the pen outside. There were a couple dozen horses in the corral, but when Mercury saw Carter, he pushed his way through and came to his master.

"You're a good boy, Merc. I hope you've had your feed because we're going on a little trip."

Carter had the horse nearly saddled when his father showed up out of the blue. He was carrying a bulging bag, canteen, and bedroll.

He'd never been so grateful to see him. "Dad, I was hoping to get word to you and Mother. I'm sure you've heard about what happened."

"Everyone has. That's how I knew I'd find you here. I figure you plan to help with the search."

"I do." Carter tightened the cinch. "I have to."

"Figured you might need some things, then."

Carter nodded and took the canteen to fill at the nearby pump. "Thanks for thinking of these."

"Partly your mother's doing." Dad set the bag down for a moment, then tied the bedroll onto the back of the saddle. "Didn't figure you'd have time to get things together and we had this stuff in the wagon box." Given the farm's distance from town, Dad was always insistent they pack a few items for survival just in case a blizzard or other problem arose.

Carter finished filling the canteen. "Ellie's back at the Ashburys', but she wanted to come too. We persuaded her to stay, but you might ask Mother to check up on her." He slipped the canteen strap around the horn of his saddle.

His father handed him a bag. "I wish I could join you, but this is a young man's job. This food your mother packed should be enough to share."

Carter smiled. "Leave it to her to think of such things. The men will know to take canteens, but probably forget about food."

"They'll be glad of her thoughtfulness. She got them to wrap up a bunch of the leftover roasted pork. She also included a bunch of other stuff."

Carter secured the bag to his saddle. "Tell her thanks. I don't know when we'll be back." He stopped directly in front of his father. He'd never been more thankful for his dad's steady presence. "I love you, Dad."

Dad wrapped his arms around his shoulders, giving him a tight hug.

"I love you too, Carter. Please be careful. We'll be praying for you."

When Ellie went to Marvella and said she needed to go to her room to rest, Marvella hadn't suspected a thing. In fact, she told Ellie it was a good idea.

Now if she could just get away without being seen.

A split skirt would be best for this venture. Especially if it took longer than Ellie hoped. The posse could find the men right away, but it was also possible they'd be searching for Father for days. She glanced around her room. She needed her camping things from the carriage house. And food. It was risky to slip into the kitchen, but she had to try.

She penned a short note for the Judge and Marvella and propped it against the plush pillows on her bed.

Please, God. Help them understand and not be angry.

Funny how it was getting easier and easier to pray.

She grabbed her heaviest coat and riding gloves as protection against the cold nights. Now . . . how to get a horse? The liveryman would probably not want to lend her a horse without the Ashburys' approval, and once they were notified, she wouldn't stand a chance of leaving.

Making her way down the servants' stairs, Ellie paused to listen. Everything was quiet. It was nearly four o'clock.

Marvella had given most of the staff the day off to celebrate so hopefully she would remain unseen.

Ellie reached the bottom step and glanced around the corner of the wall into the kitchen. It was empty. She grabbed what she needed and headed toward the back.

The back porch was empty as well. So far things were going her way. The carriage house was quiet, but Jim was there somewhere. Of course, he might have taken the Judge and Mr. Grinnell back to town so they could be on hand to help Mr. Hill.

Please . . . let that be the case.

She glanced outside to where the riding horses grazed in a small, fenced pasture. The horses might be skittish despite the times she'd petted them at the fence, so she grabbed a handful of oats along with a bridle and made her way through the gate.

22

S tewart Briggs has been kidnapped!"

Grant stopped what he was doing, as did everyone else at the rail yard. "Stewart Briggs? Why?" What had his brother done? Mr. Briggs couldn't do anything about the railroad.

The man shook his head. "Someone said the kidnappers thought they was takin' Louis Hill."

The wrong man. They'd taken the wrong man.

Grant went to an isolated area and punched the wall. What in the world would Alvin do when he realized the truth of the situation?

"They's formin' up a posse," a man called out as he passed Grant. "They gonna head out in two groups to scout out where the men went."

Grant clenched his teeth. Marshal Shelton was a pretty good tracker. If he got on to Alvin's tracks, the posse would find them.

Eventually.

He'd better see what was going on. He left the rail yard and went to where the posse was forming. They were loading up their horses with supplies for several days. Other men gathered around to watch them as well.

So much for the holiday celebration.

Grant's boss, Collin Hoffman, came to stand beside him. "Someone said James Hill was hurt too, but he wasn't taken."

Of course not. Why should things go right for Alvin? What a stupid idea this had been.

"He okay?"

Hoffman shook his head. "He's hired on about a dozen guards. Maybe more. And he's locked himself into his private rail car and posted guards all around." Hoffman gave a dry chuckle. "Guess he's heading out of town as soon as he can."

This was a disaster! If he was ever gonna hightail it outta town, now was the—

"Wallace!"

Grant turned—and froze. The marshal was coming toward him. Did he already know?

"We need your tracking skills and will pay you two dollars a day."

He opened his mouth to refuse but stopped. How could he? The marshal would want to know why, and he didn't have a good reason. "I'll get ready."

Things moved fast after that. Maybe by agreeing so quickly to help, Grant had thrown any suspicion off himself. Or Alvin, for that matter.

The marshal mounted his horse. "Wallace, I'll take these eight men and head north and west. The boys found that the trail split up northeast of town. Looked like more men took to the west, so we'll take eight men and go that way. You take the other six and head northeast." He looked at Grant for confirmation that he'd heard.

"Sure thing." His teeth clenched so hard his jaw ached. If he knew Alvin, and he did, the route the marshal just gave him was the one Alvin took. Odds were good his brother went off to the cabin with one other man, maybe two, while the rest of the group went west as a diversion for the posse.

If so, it was working.

Grant did his best to sound relaxed. "Marshal, I'll need to grab some gear and a horse."

The marshal nodded. "Tell Jeb at the livery to give you a good strong mount and charge it to my office. I've got an extra bedroll and canteen at my office. Just come back here when you have the horse, and I'll have the rest of the stuff. I'll loan you a rifle as well, so you don't have to go home to get yours."

Grant did as he was told. With any luck at all he would be able to lead the posse in circles and take them far from the river cabin. Of course, these men weren't stupid. Most could find their way around these parts even if they couldn't track. He'd have to be careful, or someone would figure out what he was doing.

How in blazes did Alvin take the wrong man?

He was such a fool to put this plan together in the first place. If they weren't careful, they'd all end up dangling from a rope.

Tonight, when they made camp for the evening, Grant would slip away on the pretext of searching for tracks. With any luck, though why he'd expect luck now was beyond him, Grant would make a wide circle and then head to the cabin. He'd warn Alvin. Tell him to leave Briggs there and git. Grant would lead the posse to find the man on the next day.

Seemed a reasonable plan. Alvin could get himself somewhere where he could have an alibi just in case someone tied him to the crime. His girlfriend would surely cover for him. The other men, well, they knew what Alvin would do to them if they talked.

He stepped up into the saddle. "It'll work."

It had to.

Ellie kept out of sight, riding around the outskirts of town. She'd heard the marshal say they would start at the rail yard and head north. However, when she arrived near the depot, she spotted the marshal giving instructions to the dozen or more men mounted on their horses, ready for action. Ellie guided the horse behind one of the tool shops and waited. As the men rode out, she grimaced. They had split into two groups. How was she to know whom to follow?

Carter's group had that man she'd met at the outfitter's store weeks back. What was his name? Grant, wasn't it? Grant Wallace. Hadn't he said he took people into the wilderness . . . that he was a tracker? She nodded.

That was the group she'd follow.

They were nearly out of sight, so she eased her mount from their hiding place. It was almost five thirty, so they'd still have a few hours of sunlight. She'd have to hang back a ways to avoid being spotted. She would *not* let them send her back.

She grimaced again. It didn't bear thinking about how upset Carter would be with her if they caught her. There was a time when that wouldn't have bothered her in the least, but now . . .

I should go back. Carter and the posse needed to focus on finding her father, not worrying about her.

She lifted her chin. "Piffle! I'm fully capable of taking care of myself."

Carter would just have to understand. And if he didn't . . . well . . . then he didn't. She would deal with that later.

For the next few hours, she managed to stay far enough back that she was out of sight. The horse was a good mount. He was well-trained and not at all skittish like some horses she'd ridden. He seemed to anticipate her moves and plodded along at the slow pace she set without demanding to have his head.

By the time the posse stopped to make camp, the skies were still dimly lit, and although the air had cooled considerably, it had been a hot day and the evening felt pleasant.

Ellie glanced around for a place to camp. She needed to remain hidden from the posse and yet protected from wildlife. She shifted in the saddle, ready to dismount and scout out the area—

"Augh!"

Her scream rent the air as she went flying. Her horse had spooked and reared. Ellie hit the ground hard.

"Oohh . . ." She gasped for breath, then froze. What was that sound? Oh no! Pounding hooves.

Her docile, well-trained horse was running for home.

She lay on the ground, not ready to move and see what hurt. She stared up at the darkening sky. Maybe her horse would just go a short distance and then stop to graze. She could catch up to him on foot.

All she had to do was stand. She had just pushed to her feet when a horse and rider came crashing through the brush.

One look was all she needed.

Carter.

"Somehow I just knew that scream was yours." Carter jumped from the back of his mount and was at her side before Ellie could even dust off her backside.

"What happened?"

She crossed her arms over her chest. "My horse spooked and took off."

Carter started to speak, and she halted him with a lifted hand.

"I'm fine. I will catch him and bring him back."

Carter shook his head. "One of the men has already ridden after him."

What? How did they . . . ? She narrowed her gaze at him. "Did you know I was following you?"

"No, not until this happened." He took hold of her arm and looked her up and down. "Is anything hurt?"

For some reason his concern made her grin. "Just my pride. I was doing all right following you, but I wasn't prepared for my horse to rear." His brow was still creased, but not with anger. He was concerned about her. She sighed. "Sorry to worry you."

He let go of her just as Grant Wallace returned with her horse. He handed the reins to Carter but smiled at Ellie. "I met you a while back. Are you out here camping by yourself?"

Carter answered. "No, it's her father who was taken. She was supposed to stay home and wait for word from us, but she figured she could be useful in the search."

Grant's brows drew together, but then his features relaxed, and he tipped his hat. "You might as well have her come set her camp with ours. No sense in staying out here alone."

TUESDAY, JULY 5, 1904

Early the next morning, the men readied to pick up the trail again. Ellie longed to go with them, but she was moving slow. Her backside ached from her fall the night before. And a night of restless sleep on lumpy dirt hadn't helped anything.

"We're heading out!" Grant Wallace yelled to the group.

Panic clawed at Ellie's chest. She wasn't near ready. Carter strode over to her, picked up her saddle, and placed it on the horse.

A man nodded at Carter. "Brunswick, Wallace said to get on your horse and follow him."

Ellie looked at Carter. He wouldn't just leave her here, right? What a silly thought. Hadn't she touted her riding and survival skills yesterday? Now the thought of Carter leaving her side made her nervous.

"I'll stay with Ellie."

"No." The man shook his head and dismounted. "He needs your knowledge about this area. Something about caves and whatnot."

Carter glanced at her, his expression softening. "Are you all right if I go? Wilbur here is a decent man. He'll help you catch up."

Ellie glanced between the two men and nodded. Father needed Carter in the search party more than she needed him with her.

347

Carter grabbed her hand and gave it a squeeze. "I'm gonna give you my rifle, okay? I have my pistol, but now that you're officially on the posse, it will be helpful for you to have a weapon."

He went to his horse and grabbed the gun. He brought it back and handed it to Ellie. "I'll see you shortly. Stay safe." He brushed his finger down her cheek, then ran to his horse and jumped on, racing to close the distance between him and the trackers.

Wilbur cinched the saddle around the horse, then threw Ellie's saddle bags on the back. When those were secure, he led the horse to a small stump. Ellie followed him, exhaustion making every step laborious.

She stepped on the block, grabbed the pommel with one hand, and slipped her right foot in the stirrup. With a deep breath and a prayer heavenward, she swung her left leg over the saddle and settled on the horse. After this whole ordeal was over, she was going to take a nice long soak in a steaming hot tub of water.

But they had to locate Father first.

With slow, plodding steps, Wilbur led her out of the clearing and up the trail where the men had disappeared twenty minutes before. Ellie was grateful the man wasn't a talker. She needed the silence to process everything that had happened.

Had Marvella found her note? *Please, Lord, don't let them be angry with me.* Her throat tightened at the thought. *Lord, I really love the Ashburys and want to continue to count them as dear friends.*

Especially now that she and her father would be living in Kalispell.

That was, if her father made it through all of this alive.

At the loud screech of a hawk, Ellie jumped and glanced around. Where was Wilbur? Where was *she*? How on earth had she lost the man who was supposed to keep her safe and lead her to Carter?

The pounding of hooves drew her to the present. Her horse's ears twitched, and Ellie prayed he wouldn't unseat her again. She reached to pull Carter's rifle out of the scabbard attached to the saddle bag. Her fingers met nothing but air.

Oh, Lord Jesus, please help me. Her throat tightened as the hooves got closer. She had nowhere to turn—the dense brush was difficult to maneuver in. She was vulnerable and alone.

"It's me, Miss Briggs."

She sighed her relief as Grant Wallace rode up.

"I've come back for you, miss. Carter said you're to come with me, and I'll take you to your pa."

Ellie drew her hand over her heart. "Then Father's alive?"

His broad smile sent her heart soaring. "He is and he wants to see you."

She let go of the breath she'd been holding. "Thank you so much, Grant. Please, take me to him."

23

Carter and the others returned to camp. He wanted to hit something. They'd found no sign of Mr. Briggs or his kidnappers. They'd fanned out in pairs, which had disappointed Carter. He'd wanted to be paired with Ellie but knew Wilbur would make sure she stayed safe. They'd returned to camp with nothing to show for the day's search, but now their attention was focused on getting supper and turning in.

One of them looked at Carter as he pulled his saddle off his horse. "Have you seen Wilbur? Or Grant?"

Dismounting, Carter looked around at the riders filing back into camp. Not only did he not see those men, there was no sign of Ellie.

He fought the concern clawing at him. The campfire was still burning, and everything they'd unpacked was still there on the ground, but Ellie was . . . gone.

Calm down, man. You know Ellie. She probably trekked out a little farther to see if she could find her father. He clenched his jaw. That woman was going to be the death of him. She'd probably separated from Wilbur and got herself lost. Well, he should just leave her to wander around. When was she going to learn?

Of course, with all she'd gone through, it was no wonder she felt she had to do something. At least he'd left her his rifl—

Hang on. His rifle was still leaning against the tree by the small mounting stump he'd set up for Ellie that morning. She hadn't even bothered to take it with her! What was she thinking? Her willfulness and stubborn streak were going to get her killed if she wasn't careful.

"I ain't seen nobody but you fellas." Shorty, a young fella who'd proven himself a solid rider, piped up. "Where's that gal that was here earlier?"

Good question. Carter shook his head.

"Maybe she's with Wilbur and Grant."

Carter seriously doubted it, but said nothing. He couldn't just leave her out there by herself. He prepared to mount his horse again. "I'll go look for them."

Shorty angled him a look. "You want help?"

"No. You fellas deserve a rest. Ellie's my problem." He climbed into the saddle. "I'll find her."

Just then, Wilbur came into the camp. He was more than a little bit excited. "I lost track of you guys and ended up on the river south of here. I found a place . . . a cabin. I think it's our place. It's not very big and right on the river. I slipped up close to the window and heard a man talking about waiting to hear from Mr. Hill. There was at least one person with him. Maybe two. I couldn't see in so I can't say for sure, but it seems promising."

"Are you sure you can lead us back there?" another of the posse members asked.

"Pretty sure. It's not all that far away."

Great. Carter shook his head. Should he go with Wilbur and the others, or go find Ellie? "Where's Ellie?" Panic started to bubble in his chest. "Did you see her after you left camp?"

Wilbur shook his head. "No. We got separated early. I thought she was behind me, but when I looked, suddenly, she was gone."

Carter let out a groan and swiped a hand down his face. That woman was going to be the end of him.

Shorty looked from Wilbur to Carter. "What about Grant Wallace?"

Again, Wilbur shook his head. "I didn't see nobody. Like I said, I got lost. But I think we ought to go right away and check out that cabin."

Blast! He wanted to find Ellie first and make sure she was safe, but she'd never forgive him if something happened to her father because he'd gone looking for her. Besides, the men in the posse needed him to fulfill his obligations.

Please, God, guide her back to safety.

The others mounted up, and when everyone was ready, one of them called out, "Show us the way, Wilbur."

Carter urged his horse forward. Why had Ellie gone out on her own? She knew it wasn't saf—

For a moment, his breath left his body. What if . . .

What if she *didn't* go off on her own? What if she'd been discovered and taken by the men who'd taken her father?

He spurred his horse into action. "Let's go, Wilbur! Now!"

"Are we lost?" Ellie looked around them.

Grant didn't seem all that concerned. "No, I left the others up by the river. We'll be there in just a few minutes."

"Did you see my father? Is he all right?"

"I didn't get a chance to see him, but the fellas were sure this was the right place to come."

Just then a light appeared in a clearing directly in front of them. Ellie strained against the darkness to see what was up ahead. "Is that a cabin?"

"It is. That's the place where I left the others."

She felt her heart pick up its pace. *Please God, let Father be all right. Don't let him be dead.*

"We need to be careful so we don't get shot." Grant stopped his mount. "Climb down, and we'll lead the horses the rest of the way."

What? That didn't make any sense. "Why would we get shot? They know you came back for me, don't they? If Carter told you to get me, surely the others expect us to show up."

Even so, Ellie climbed down from her horse, since Grant had dismounted and reached out to take hold of her gelding.

"They won't know it's us, necessarily. They could think some of the men who took your pa were coming back to the cabin."

She hadn't thought about that. She fell into step beside Grant. "Do you think Carter and the other men have already gone in and taken control?"

"Could be. If they saw an opportunity, I'm sure they'd try it. Come on, we'll get a little closer, and I'll tie the horses off."

They walked about twenty feet, and Grant found a small

tree and tied the horses to it. "Come on." He took hold of Ellie's arm.

Ellie pulled away. "I don't need help."

"I don't want to risk you falling and letting out another scream. You nearly split the sky with the last one."

She smiled. "I didn't mean to scare everyone."

They were nearly upon the cabin. "Hey, Alvin, it's me, Grant."

Alvin? She didn't recall anyone on the posse with that name. The door opened. Her eyes widened. Grant's brother! The angry one from the store. Tremors crawled up her spine. What was going on?

Alvin seemed just as surprised as Ellie. "What's going on, Grant? Why are you here? Did you get word from James Hill?"

Grant pushed his way inside, Ellie in tow. "No, I joined the posse that's looking for you so I could get to you first. You know you don't have Louis Hill, right?"

Ellie looked from Grant to the other man, trying to follow the rapid-fire conversation. Where was Carter? The rest of the tracking group?

"He keeps telling me he's not Hill. I thought he was lying to fool us."

Ellie looked around the cabin and saw a man tied to a chair. No, not just a man . . .

"Father!" She yanked her arm free from Grant's grip and rushed to his side. "Are you all right? Why haven't they cut you loose yet?"

Her father moaned. "Oh, Ellie, how did they capture you too?"

Capture her? There was a bandage on the side of his

head. Perhaps the blow he'd sustained had left him confused.

Enough! Father needed to lie down. She went to work on the ropes, but Grant came and took hold of her, pulling her away.

She spun on him. "*What* is happening here? My father is injured. Why are you stopping me?"

Grant's gaze hardened. "Because you're our prisoner now."

Prisoner? Had they all gone mad?

"Why did you bring her here?" Alvin sounded, and looked, furious.

Grant shook his head and pulled Ellie to a chair. "Sit there and be quiet." He grabbed a piece of rope hanging on the wall and came back to her chair. He wrapped it around her midsection and the chair.

"No! What are you doing?" Ellie grabbed at the offending rope and tried to slip out of it—

And saw stars.

Someone had struck her! In the face!

"No! Leave her alone!" Father's weakened voice came to her as she tried to blink away the stars. When her vision cleared, Alvin stood in front of her, ready to strike her again.

Grant grabbed his arm and shoved him away. "There's no need for that." His words to his brother were low and ominous. He turned to Ellie, and his eyes locked onto hers. "*Is* there?"

She swallowed hard and managed a small shake of her head, which sent it pounding. She put a hand to her aching face. "Why are you doing this?" She fought against the ropes tightening around her wrists, flailing her legs, rocking the chair from side to side. "Let me go!"

"Alvin, grab her legs!" Grant glared at his brother. "But don't hurt her."

The bulky man caught her ankles in his strong grip and pushed until her legs met those of the chair.

Grant secured her to the chair and stepped back to face his brother. "I came by this way earlier and saw you out getting wood. Without a mask." He looked at Father. "So your prisoner knows what you look like."

Alvin stiffened. "So what?"

"I brought the woman here for a little more insurance. As soon as the posse knows she's been taken, they won't be so inclined to come shooting their way in."

Grant's brother eyed her, then turned away. "The posse will never find us."

"Of course they will!"

The desperation in Grant's voice sent a chill through her. Desperate men did awful things.

"Alvin, they're *close*. We gotta ride. Get clear out of Montana. If we get out of here before that posse arrives, we should be able to get clean away."

Grant's brother motioned to her and Father. "But they know our names now."

God, help us!

Grant grabbed Alvin's arm. "It doesn't matter. We can disappear. Plenty of good places to hide, but we don't have time to argue about it. Look, we've got some money and gear. Let's just ride."

Alvin's features darkened. "So who's the man we took, and who is she?"

Grant waved a hand at them. "He's nobody! He's not worth a dime! The only person who would care that we have him is *her*. She's his daughter."

"Where did Hill get off to?" Alvin paced the room. "Maybe we can go there and take him after all."

"No! Listen to me. Hill left on his private car hours ago. He did exactly as we figured and hired himself a team of guards. We'll never get close to him again. We need to just give up on this and go. Right now."

Alvin's dark gaze came back to Eleanor. "I don't know. *They're* hearing all of this. They'll tell the marshal what our plan is."

Grant rubbed a hand through his hair. "We haven't said anything yet that will give us away."

"I say we kill them and then go." Alvin narrowed his eyes as he studied Eleanor's face.

A shiver jolted up her back. It was as if she were staring into the face of death. Alvin's cold blue eyes were void of feeling. He seemed completely at ease with the thought of killing. Had he done it before?

"Kill me, but please, spare my Ellie!"

At Father's pleading words, Grant gritted his teeth.

What time I am afraid, I will trust in thee. . . . In God I have put my trust; I will not fear what flesh can do unto me.

Ellie caught her breath. She'd read those verses from Psalm 56 just a few nights ago. Now they sang through her, calming her racing heart. *I will not fear . . .*

"It's all right, Father." Was that her voice? That confident tone? "I'm not afraid. God is with us. I trust Him to protect us."

And she did. With all her heart.

Grant groaned. "*Forget* about them, Alvin. I'm telling you we don't have time. Come on. At least come outside with me in case the posse shows up. We can figure the details out as we go. We can go find the boys and make another plan. They're probably already back in town, snug in their beds."

Alvin hesitated—

I trust You, Lord.

—then nodded and turned to Grant. "Let's get out of here."

Thank You, Lord! Thank You!

Alvin grabbed his stuff, and he and Grant hurried out the door.

Ellie looked at her father. "Are you all right?"

He managed a shaky smile. "Scared. I have to admit, I've never been more scared."

If only they'd untied her! She needed to find out how bad his injury was. "Are you hurt badly?"

"I don't think so." Father shifted in the chair as if testing his body for pain. "Somebody hit me on the side of the head. I was knocked out, and when I woke up, I was tied to this chair."

She nodded. "They hit Mr. Hill over the head too. They thought they had him when they took you."

Father shook his head, then grimaced. "Ouch. Not ready to move my head much yet. I figured out their mistake when that fella kept insisting I was Louis."

Ellie was torn between tears and laughter. "They left a note with Mr. Hill. Apparently, they thought they could force his father's hand with the railroad and keep the train coming into Kalispell." Ellie strained against the ropes. Grant had tied them too tight. She wasn't getting free.

Father closed his eyes, as though keeping them open was painful. "Louis's father, Mr. Hill, has already invested the money to move the line. He wasn't going to just stop that work and return here."

His voice seemed to weaken as he talked. *Lord, please help me get free.*

A gunshot sounded not far from the cabin, followed by several more. Ellie looked at her father. They weren't safe yet.

She drew a deep breath. "I need to tell you something. I've returned to Jesus, Father. Returned to the faith that Mother taught me when I was young. All those things she used to say came back to me as I started reading the Bible." Tears blurred her vision. Ellie blinked rapidly so she could see her father's face as she shared her joy with him. "I wanted to talk to you. I've . . . I've turned back to the Lord, Father. I've asked Jesus to save me, just like Mother taught me all those years ago. That's why I wanted to talk to you at the picnic. I want so much for you to not be upset with me."

Father opened his eyes and smiled. "Upset with you? Of course not. When you said God was with us, that you trust Him, I knew what had happened. And I'm glad."

He was glad! "Oh, Father . . ."

"Sitting here, a prisoner, I admitted I might be facing my death. I didn't want to do that alone."

Were those tears in his eyes?

"I prayed, Ellie. For the first time in my life, I really prayed, and I asked God to help me—to save me not only from these men who had taken me, but from my life of ignoring Him."

The gunfire sounded again. This time closer to the house.

I trust You, God. Whatever happens, I trust You.

"Father, no matter what happens here tonight, we'll be all right. God truly is watching over us both."

The door to the cabin flew back, and Ellie screamed—Carter stood in the doorway.

She'd never been happier to see anyone in her life!

"Ellie, are you okay?"

She met his worried expression and smiled. "I'm better than okay. My Father accepted Jesus. We both belong to God now."

He'd never heard anything so wonderful as Ellie's happy words. In two steps he was at her side and cut her loose. She jumped to her feet and threw her arms around him, hugging him like she'd never let go.

His arms closed around her for one delicious moment, then he let go—until he saw the red mark on her face. Heat boiled as he cupped her face. His fingers brushed the small welt rising on her cheek. "They *hurt* you?"

"That scoundrel Alvin hit her."

She winced, both at her father's angry words and at Carter's touch where she'd been struck. But she placed her hand over his. "I'm fine, Carter. I promise."

After a moment, he nodded and knelt next to Ellie's father. But he directed a firm look at Ellie. "Are you sure you're all right? Why did you leave Wilbur?"

Her face turned red. "I got lost in my thoughts. I wasn't paying attention to my surroundings, and all of a sudden, he was gone. Please don't be angry," she whispered, then darted around him to her father. With deft movements, she examined his head injury. After all she'd been through, her first thought was for her father. Just one more thing to love about this woman.

"Grant found me on the trail and told me you wanted me to join you. I rode out with him only to have him take me captive."

If ever a man deserved killing . . . Carter pushed the dark thought away. "But you aren't hurt?"

"No, I'm fine." She moved the cloth they'd wrapped around her father's head. "At least the wound doesn't seem to be bleeding."

Her father reached up to touch her hand. "I'm all right. Don't either of you worry. I have a headache, but nothing all that bad."

Carter removed the last of Mr. Briggs's bonds. The older man rubbed his wrists where the rope had irritated the skin.

"Mr. Briggs, how many men were here?"

Ellie's father shook his head. "All I saw was the one called Alvin."

Ellie nodded. "Grant and Alvin are brothers." She looked back at Carter. "There wasn't anybody else here."

Ellie's father stretched his legs in front of him. "But the one called Alvin talked about 'the boys.' Apparently, part of their gang headed west of town to throw off the trackers."

Carter helped Mr. Briggs stand. He wasn't exactly steady. "Do you think you can walk to the horses?"

"I believe so."

Carter held on to him as they walked.

Ellie supported her father on the other side but glanced at Carter. "Where are Grant and his brother?"

He hated to tell her, but he had no choice. "Dead. They

saw us and started shooting. We returned fire. They didn't survive. Come on. Let me take you both home."

"You guys all right in there?" Wilbur was at the door, then came in to take hold of Mr. Briggs. "Let me help him."

Carter moved next to Ellie and put his arm around her shoulders.

Wilbur looked over his shoulder at them—and grinned at the sight of Carter holding on to Ellie.

She pulled away. "We're fine. God was watching over us."

Carter motioned to Wilbur. "I think it would be best if you get Ellie to her horse, and *I'll* help Mr. Briggs." Miracle of miracles, Ellie didn't protest. She just moved ahead of Wilbur and out of the cabin.

Good. Carter looked at Mr. Briggs and smiled. "I wonder if I can ask you something important? I realize it might seem like poor timing, but given the events of the night, I want to say this before anything else happens."

Mr. Briggs's smile was broad. He patted Carter's arm. "You want to marry my daughter, don't you?"

24

Days later, Ellie and her father sat in the Ashburys' large sitting room reiterating all that they had experienced to Marshal Shelton and the mayor. Father seemed no worse for the wear. Even so, Ellie never wanted to have an "adventure" like that again.

"We tracked the rest of them to the west and then back to town." Marshal Shelton leaned back in his chair. "One of them had a lame horse and had to walk the last mile or so. I tracked him right to the place where he lived with his folks. It was Jimmy Hutchins."

"Jimmy?" The Judge frowned. "I've had him in my court a couple of times on petty thefts, but that was when he was just twelve or thirteen. I'd hoped since I hadn't seen him in years that maybe he got in with the right bunch and was doing better."

The sadness in the Judge's voice touched Ellie. If only the young man had realized he had such a wonderful friend in his corner, how different his life might have been.

The marshal shrugged. "He's not a bad fella, but easily influenced. I told him it would go better on him if he'd say who else was involved. His father demanded he do so, and Jimmy told me the whole story."

"So they really thought they could change James Hill's decision on the railroad by taking his son?" Marvella gave a little huff and shook her head. "Madness!"

Sir Theophilus perked his ears at this and gave a yip.

Ellie laughed. Sir Theophilus was as determined to put in his two cents as his mistress was.

Father put down his cup of coffee. "I think their fears just got the better of them."

That he could be so understanding of those who had treated him so ill was wonderful. He'd softened in so many ways since coming to faith in God. Ellie didn't even try to hide her pride in him.

Father's tone was gentle as he went on. "When faced with losing their livelihoods and having to move away, they grew desperate to find another answer."

"Breaking the law is never the answer." The marshal crossed his arms over his chest. "We've rounded everybody up and put them in jail. It was Alvin Wallace who hit Louis Hill over the head. A man named Clarence Woodbury hit you, Mr. Briggs. He's no older than Jimmy. Just eighteen. Never been in trouble before and cried when he told me what he'd done. Asked if you were all right."

"I don't want to press charges against anyone," Father told them. "Especially given it's the boy's first offense."

"I would advise we address it in court and show mercy there." The Judge nodded to the marshal. "He needs to be frightened enough to never do anything like this again."

Father seemed to consider this for a moment, then nodded. "I trust that you know best, Judge."

"In this matter, I do. I've seen many a young man let off with warnings only to return to nefarious deeds. We'll let him sit in jail, see what it's like without his freedom, and ponder what he did. He's not the type to take it lightly. I taught his Sunday school class when he was just a boy. He can be saved. I feel confident of this."

"The Judge is an excellent discerner of people's character." Marvella held up the silver coffee pot. "As I am an excellent discerner of empty coffee cups. Marshal, would you care for more?"

The marshal put his cup forward. "The best coffee in the world can be had at this house. Even better than that served at the Conrad's."

Marvella beamed. "Thank you, Marshal." She poured him a cup and looked to Ellie. "What of you, my dear? More tea?"

Ellie shook her head. "No, I'm fine."

"I do hope you learned your lesson about sneaking off as you did." Marvella shook her head. "You worried the life out of me. I was so afraid of what might happen to you."

"As was I."

Ellie looked to find Carter in the doorway.

The butler stood at his side. "Mr. Brunswick, ma'am."

"Oh, Carter, do come in." Mrs. Ashbury waved him forward.

Father sighed. "I think Ellie knows the worry she caused everyone."

Was he upset with her? But no. One look at his face told her he was teasing.

He looked at those gathered there. "She isn't generally so willful, but given the situation, I think she can be excused."

Laughter echoed in the room.

"Well, before she decides to run off and do something else entirely too dangerous"—Carter dropped to one knee in front of her—"I want to ask her something."

What . . . ? Was this what she thought it was? One look at Carter's face told her it was exactly what she thought it was. Giddiness filled her, and it was all she could do to just sit there and not jump into his arms. "I'm listening."

He grinned and produced a ring from his pocket. "Miss Briggs—"

"Ellie." *Oh, Lord . . . this man. This wonderful man . . .* "Call me Ellie."

His smile lit up her insides. "*Ellie,* I've long prayed for a wife knowing that God had the perfect woman out there somewhere. We might have had a rocky start, but the longer I am in your presence, the more I love you. Will you marry me?"

Before she could answer, Sir Theophilus jumped from the sofa and began dancing around Carter. Barking, the little scamp raced back and forth in the short space between Ellie and Carter.

Marvella drew her hands together over her heart. "I think he's encouraging you to say yes, my dear. He loves to see people happy, as do I."

Ellie laughed and met Carter's gaze. The love there took her breath away. She gave him a teasing look. "Well, it just so happens I've fallen in love with you as well, Mr. Brunswick."

"Carter."

Oh, what that man's grin did to her!

"*Carter.* I would be happy to marry you."

He slipped the ring on her finger, and the others applauded. Marvella, of course, launched into a lecture.

"You must both always put God at the center of your marriage. Seek Him first, and everything else will fall into place. The Judge and I have found this to be of the utmost importance. It never fails when something goes wrong. If we don't seek God on the matter first, things only become more difficult."

Ellie caught Carter's eye. He looked as ready as she was to burst into laughter.

As though Marvella sensed the impending hilarity, she pinned Ellie's fiancé with a firm look. "Carter, you know exactly what I'm talking about. I trust that your mother and father have taught you this very secret. Although calling it a secret really isn't the right word."

"Marvella." The Judge gave her a stern look, a single brow raised. "I believe Carter is entitled to kiss his fiancée before receiving your chastisement."

Marvella sniffed. "I'm not *chastising*, but advising, Milton. I just want them to . . ." She pursed her lips, gave her husband a nod, then turned to Carter. "Go ahead, if you must." Her lips twitched. "Kiss her."

Carter rose and drew Ellie up with him, pulling her into his arms and kissing her gently. Ellie wrapped her arms around his neck, not caring that they had an audience. Carter made her feel such joy that she could hardly contain herself.

The kiss ended almost as soon as it had begun, but Ellie had no desire to leave Carter's arms. She pulled back just enough to meet his gaze. "I love you, Carter. I felt it coming on gradually, and it terrified me. So many things weren't what they needed to be. Not the least of all, me. But now, by God's grace, I will be a good wife to you."

"And I'm seeking God's direction to be a good husband to you. We'll have our share of arguments and troubles, I'm sure. However, like Mrs. Ashbury pointed out, if we put God at the center of our lives, there shouldn't be anything we can't overcome."

"Agreed." Ellie stretched up on tiptoe, and Carter, seeing what she was doing, bent his lips to hers. She kissed him, not caring that it was a brazen thing to do in front of her father and the others.

She could have remained there in his arms, but Sir Theophilus was jumping up against her skirt. She broke her hold on Carter and reached down to pick up the little dog. "You, sir, have very poor timing."

The others laughed as Ellie took a seat with the dog in her lap. "However, I have come to enjoy your company." She scratched the pup under the chin and then let him bounce back to Marvella.

"Well, you two have many things to discuss." Marvella picked up Sir Theophilus and snuggled him close. "Wedding plans are not easy to master, but I'm sure I speak for the Judge when I say that we are at your disposal. Carter's mother will want to be a part of the planning as well."

"Mother already managed weddings for my two sisters." Carter took a seat beside Ellie. "She told me she would abide by whatever we decided."

Marvella put on her best regal look. "Well, it will take at least six months to plan out a grand wedding. Of course, that will put us into the winter months, which can completely alter even the tiniest of details. My roses, for example, won't be available for your bouquet, and the wedding carriages will have to be enclosed."

"I don't believe I want to wait six months." Ellie looked to Carter. "Do you?"

He shook his head. "Not on your life."

"Well, you need to find a place to live." Marvella was not to be deterred. "That is always of the utmost concern."

Carter grinned. "Father is gifting me land for my birthday. I kind of figured we'd build our own house. Ellie can plan out what she wants that way."

Marvella inclined her head. "But again, that will take time."

Father piped up. "We're about to move into that very large Hennessy house. I see no reason you two newlyweds couldn't live there until you figure out what you want and build your own house."

What a wonderful idea! Ellie squeezed Carter's hand. "How would that suit you, Carter? We could have the entire west wing to ourselves."

"Sounds accommodating." He smiled. "As long as you're there, I can be happy."

Ellie gave a firm nod. "I really don't have much interest in waiting long at all. As you know, I'm a woman who likes to get things accomplished."

"What are you suggesting, Ellie?" Carter's expression and tone betrayed his amusement.

"Well, it's just that the roses are in full bloom in Marvella's garden. It would be the perfect spot in which to get married. And the Judge is right here. Perhaps he could marry us right away." She looked to the Judge and smiled. "Is that possible, Judge Ashbury?"

"More than possible. I'd be honored to unite the two of you."

"Oh, this is so very exciting!" Marvella clapped. "I can put it all together immediately. Just tell me what you would like and who you want here. I'll send my staff out with the invitations and get Cook a list of foods for the wedding breakfast."

Ellie laughed. "I thought I might be able to count on you, Mrs. Ashbury." She looked back to the Judge. "When might you have a free day, Judge?"

"I have nothing on the docket for Monday the eighteenth. Would that be soon enough?"

Returning her gaze to Carter's blue eyes, so full of love, Ellie smiled. "Well? What say you?"

"I say a week from Monday sounds perfect."

"I'll figure out all of the particulars with Mrs. Ashbury and let you know the details." Ellie turned back to the gathering. "Now if you'll excuse me, I need to find a wedding dress."

Saturday, July 16, 1904

On the Saturday before the wedding, Ellie and her father officially took possession of the Hennessy house. Mrs. Ashbury had paid her staff to clean the place from top to bottom and arrange things in such a way as to accommodate the newlyweds, as well as Mr. Briggs and his conservation work.

Marvella even surprised them by putting a staff in place after sending word to her friends that she had immediate need for a cook, a housekeeper, a lady's maid, and a butler. She assured Ellie that if she didn't like the people chosen, Marvella would arrange for their dismissal and the hiring of others.

The final surprise was a partial remodeling of the room Ellie had chosen for her and Carter. When Marvella learned which room it was, she sent workers in to remake the room into a fitting bridal suite. Ellie had to admit, she was impressed. Even now as she walked into the massive room, she marveled at all that had been accomplished in just a few days.

How had Marvella done it? She'd had the walls papered and the trim painted, as well as the floor polished, the marble fireplace cleaned, and new draperies hung. There was a large, four-poster bed with new bedding and pillows, homey and inviting. She'd also arranged some of the left-behind furniture in the room so that there was a sitting area in front of the fire and a desk and chair in the corner.

It all suited Ellie's tastes perfectly. She wasn't at all sure what Carter would think of it, but as Marvella had told her, it could always be changed to suit any desires they might have.

The older woman hadn't excluded Ellie's father either. She had refreshed his room as well as the library. He was pleased with the house and tried to insist Marvella allow him to pay her. But, as they both were learning, Marvella was not one to be insisted into anything she didn't want to do.

Why, she'd even provided Ellie's wedding dress. Having

no daughter of her own, Marvella gave Ellie *her* wedding gown. True, Marvella and the Judge had married in 1864, when he came home on a Christmas pass during the war, so it was very much out of fashion. But Marvella called in her dressmaker.

The woman altered the dress, creating something elegant.

Ellie had been very touched that Marvella would gift her the dress. The ivory satin-and-lace creation must have been very dear to her, as she had seen to its meticulous care all these years.

A knock sounded on her open door. Ellie found her father gazing in. "I'm sure you're readying yourself for bed, but I wondered if you had a moment."

"Of course, Father. What do you need?"

"I wanted to tell you that I've made some plans. I hope you won't mind." He stepped into the room. "I tend to think you won't."

She smiled and went to him. "Whatever have you been up to now?"

"I'm going back to New York after the wedding. George invited me to come and stay with him prior to our trip to Washington. He has a group of wealthy friends he thinks we should speak to about the national park. I thought how appropriate it would be to do so following the wedding. It will allow you and Carter to have nearly two months on your own before I return from the East. So that is going to be my wedding gift to you."

Two months? On their own? "That is very generous. Are you sure you want to do this?"

"George and I talked about it before I was taken. I was

trying to come up with a way to tell you that wouldn't cause you to feel abandoned."

Ellie took his hands in hers. "I'm sorry I made you feel that you had to take me with you everywhere. It truly never dawned on me that you might like to be among your friends without your daughter traipsing behind you. What a bother."

"No, you were never a bother. After your mother died, you were all that kept me going. Now, however, I believe we are both able to see our individual ways. God has done that for us."

"I agree, and I will be just fine. You go and enjoy your trip. Do the things that are important to you. I'll be here."

He smiled. "You have always been here. No daughter has been more cherished or loved." He hugged her close and kissed the top of her head.

MONDAY, JULY 18, 1904

It was actually happening!

Ellie peered through her veil, gaze fixed on Carter as she walked beside her father. She couldn't hold back the tears as Father lifted her veil and kissed her forehead, then placed her hand in Carter's.

Stepping back, Father stood with the other guests.

Ellie gripped Carter's hand and turned to face Judge Ashbury. He gave her a grandfatherly smile and opened his Bible. His rich voice rang out. "Dear friends, we have come here together to join Eleanor and Carter in holy matrimony . . ."

A lump formed in her throat. What a wonder God was. What a blessing He'd given her in Carter. And all these people who had become a part of her. So many wonderful changes had come to her life. She would have a home instead of being on the road, wandering from one place to another. She would have a husband to love and cherish. And the greatest change of all, she was now a child of God. The God of the universe had chosen *her* for His own, and for the first time since her mother died, Ellie felt whole again.

The Judge cleared his throat. "Carter, repeat after me. I, Carter, take thee, Eleanor—"

"Ellie."

The Judge stopped and she gave him a smile. "Not Eleanor"—she met Carter's loving gaze—"Ellie."

The Judge smiled, nodded, and began again. "Carter, repeat after me. I, Carter, take thee, Ellie, to be my lawfully wedded wife."

Carter's grin widened, and Ellie couldn't hold back a laugh. He gave her fingers a gentle squeeze. "I, Carter, take thee, Ellie . . ."

Epilogue

Carter gripped Ellie's hand as they stood at the top of their favorite lookout in the national park. "The older I get, the more I realize I won't be able to make this climb forever, but I sure do love it."

She wrapped her arms around his waist. "I'm glad your parents don't mind taking the kids off our hands for a few days each year so we can do this."

"Me too." He kissed the top of her head. He held her in his arms, and they stared out at the glaciers and mountains before them.

Thank You, God. "You know. I was an idiot when I met you. That whole summer, I said and did some pretty dumb things. But I sure am thankful that God took a flawed mess of a man like me and gave me the greatest gift ever." He looked into those eyes he loved so dearly. "The woman who completes me. My helpmeet."

375

She pulled back a few inches and looked up at him. "I had no idea how lackluster my life was until I came to Kalispell. God used that journey to bring me back to Him. And in the process, He brought me to you."

He kissed her on the forehead and then trailed his kisses down her cheek and neck. He pulled her into his arms. No need to worry about being disturbed. There was no one else around for miles.

After several moments of heart-pounding kisses, Ellie pulled back, breathless. "Carter Brunswick"—she stepped away and put a hand to her stomach—"you still know how to take my breath away."

"Good." He winked. "I hope it's always that way."

"Oh, believe me, I don't think there will be any trouble with that." She dashed away down the trail to another look-out point.

Carter gave chase, knowing the trail almost as well as she did. These times when they were able to get away from the hubbub of life with four children were a refreshment for them both. Heart, mind, body, and soul.

She stopped at the next spot and gazed at the waterfall gushing over the cliff.

He stepped up behind her and wrapped his arms around her. "What are you thinking?"

"I'm thinking about how much I love you. With each tomorrow, it grows stronger as we grow closer together and to the Lord."

"I love you too, Ellie."

She swayed back and forth. "I keep thinking of a few verses from the Psalms. 'The heavens declare the glory of God; and the firmament sheweth his handywork.' And 'In his hand are the deep places of the earth: the strength of the hills is his also.'"

He shared the next part. "'The sea is his, and he made it: and his hands formed the dry land.'"

They spoke the last verse together. "'O come, let us worship and bow down: let us kneel before the LORD our maker.'"

He turned her to face him and kissed her. Then took her hand and led her over to a large boulder. He got down on his knees and she joined him.

"That should be our family's guiding principal from here on out."

Her lips tipped up in a smile. "With each tomorrow, let us worship and bow down."

If you enjoyed *With Each Tomorrow*,
read on
for an excerpt from

A

LOVE DISCOVERED

by

TRACIE PETERSON

Marybeth and Edward are compelled by their circumstances to marry as they trek west to the newly formed
railroad town of Cheyenne. But life in Cheyenne is fraught
with danger, and they find that they need each other more
than ever. Despite the trials they face, will happiness await
them in this arrangement of convenience?

AVAILABLE NOW WHEREVER
BOOKS ARE SOLD.

1

NOVEMBER 1867
INDEPENDENCE, INDIANA

It seems all I ever do is attend funerals," Marybeth Kruger murmured as the cemetery caretakers began shoveling dirt over her father's casket.

Just days ago, all had been well. She and Papa had been talking about the coming of Christmas. Papa had agreed to freight a load of grain to Evansville from a farm thirty miles out. A snowstorm blew in and made the conditions worse than anyone had seen in years. The sheriff told Marybeth that Klaus Kruger was nearly to his destination just beyond Pigeon Creek when tragedy struck. The horses got spooked by the wind and snow, and the wagon ended up upside down at the end of the bridge. The doctor said Papa had broken his neck and died instantly. Marybeth supposed that was better than lingering in pain and suffering. But best would have been if he hadn't had the accident at all. Her little sister, Carrie, wasn't even two years old, and at the age of twenty with no husband or living relatives, Marybeth had no means to support her. What were either of them to do?

She felt someone touch her shoulder and turned. It was Edward Vogel. Her dearest friend in all the world. She saw the dampness in his eyes. He and her father had been close. She and Edward's wife, Janey, had been lifelong friends, but Janey's was another tragic death that weighed heavy on Marybeth.

"You ready to go home?" Edward asked her.

"I feel like I have no home." She looked across the cemetery. "I keep thinking of all the dead. There are so many. Our lives have been short moments of joy encompassed by sorrow and death."

He looked toward where Janey and his son were buried, and Marybeth couldn't help but follow his gaze. He'd married Janey after returning from the war. And then Janey had delivered a stillborn son and died herself shortly after. Marybeth had been devastated by Janey's death. They had been so very close.

They were surrounded by the graves of their departed loved ones. Marybeth's mother had died seven years earlier. Marybeth's stepmother, Sarah, had died after giving life to Carrie. Now her father was gone as well. For Edward, there was Janey and his son, his mother, and two brothers who'd died in the war.

"Marybeth, I was hoping to have a word with you."

She turned to find their pastor. She gave a nod. "Thank you for such a nice service, Pastor Orton."

"Your father was a good man and trusted friend, Marybeth. We were blessed to have him as an elder."

"Yes. He loved our church." She didn't know what else to say. A neighbor had offered to have Carrie over to play with her children while Marybeth attended the funeral, but she still needed to get home.

"I know this is a delicate matter and perhaps a poor time to bring up such a subject, but have you considered what you will do about your sister?"

Marybeth frowned. "What do you mean?"

The pastor's expression was one of compassion. "Well, you and she are alone now, and you have no means of supporting her, much less yourself."

"I'm sure there must be a better time to talk about all this," Edward piped up. "The grave isn't even covered."

"Yes, I know. I feel terrible for it, but on the other hand, I cannot allow for a babe to go hungry," the pastor replied.

Marybeth looked at the older man. He had been pastoring at the little Methodist church for as long as she had memory. He had presided over her mother's funeral and her stepmother's.

"Carrie isn't going hungry," Marybeth said in a barely audible voice. "The house is full of food. People haven't stopped bringing food since the accident."

"But that will only last a few days. In time she may well starve," the man said. "That is why I'm suggesting you give her up. Let her be raised by a family who can provide for her. I've been speaking with Thomas and Martha Wandless. They're quite well-off, as you know, and would be happy to take Carrie as their own."

"But she's not their own. She's mine. I've raised her from birth and done a good job, if I do say so myself." Marybeth's ire grew. People always seemed to think they knew what was best for other folks, but Pastor Orton was the worst of all for trying to arrange people's lives.

"Now, Marybeth, no one is trying to suggest you haven't taken good care of your sister, and while your father was alive and providing for the both of you, no one would have suggested things go on any other way."

"I should say not. Papa would have torn into the man who suggested he divide his family." She fixed the pastor with a glare. "He would have despised the interference or suggestion that he couldn't take care of his own."

"And would have well been within his rights. But, child, you have no husband and no other relative to provide a living for you and your sister. Winter is upon us, and you'll need money for heating and food. Where will you come by it?"

"I'll help her." Edward's voice was reassuring. "I'm sure others will as well."

"For a time," the pastor said, nodding, "as good Christian folks should do, but it won't be possible to continue forever."

"I'm sure it won't need to continue forever," Edward replied.

"Edward!" They all glanced up at his name being called. It was his sister, Inga Weber. She waved and called out again. "Edward, could I speak to you for a minute?"

He turned to Marybeth. "I'll be right back."

He moved toward Inga, leaving Marybeth feeling deserted. How was she to fight for her sister without his support? Pastor Orton had always intimidated her, and she was sure he knew it. She glanced back at him and squared her shoulders. She would just have to be strong.

Pastor Orton shook his head. "You must think of poor

Carrie. She has now lost her mother and father. The Wandless couple could provide her with that and give her a life of ease. They have plenty of money, and Carrie would live a life without want."

Marybeth finally found her voice. "I'm her sister and the only mother she's ever known. I could never give her away as if she were a doll I'd grown bored with. I pledged to my stepmother and my father that I would always care for her."

"Marybeth, you need to see reason. You have no way to provide for Carrie. I'm sure you wouldn't want the law to be involved."

"What are you saying?" Marybeth fixed the older man with narrowed eyes.

"I'm saying that those who know better might become involved and take matters out of your hands legally. After all, we just want what's best for your sister. She's only a babe."

"I'm what's best for her, and she's what's best for me. We belong together. We've lost everything else. How could you be so cruel?"

"It's not meant to be cruel, Marybeth. If you were to calm a moment, you would see that for yourself." He reached out to take hold of her arm, but Marybeth pulled back. "Please, I'm only trying to help. Soon you'll have to find a job, and you won't be able to do that and care for your sister. There's a family with the will and means to provide for Carrie. They can give her what you cannot, Marybeth. I'm sure they'd allow you to visit."

Edward returned just then. "We need to be going." He took hold of Marybeth and turned her from the pastor's intense face. "Afternoon, Pastor."

He led Marybeth to where the wagon stood, horses

stomping in the snow and blowing out great clouds of breath.

"Are you all right?"

"He wants to take my sister from me. After everyone else I've lost. He wants to take her as well." A sob broke from her throat, and Marybeth pulled her woolen scarf to her face. "Why did God allow this to happen?"

"I've asked myself that over and over about a lot of things." He helped Marybeth up onto the wagon and then followed her. "He still hasn't answered me."

"It's not my fault or Carrie's that Mrs. Wandless is barren. I've long felt sorry for her, knowing that she wanted children. I've even prayed for her. People have suggested they adopt before now, but she's always put that off, hoping to have her own baby. I don't know why she suddenly feels the need to rob me of a sister."

Edward picked up the lines and released the brake. "Busybodies. That's what they are. Pastor Orton has always stuck his nose in where it wasn't wanted. He thinks just because he pastors a church that he has the right to be in all the details of his flock's life."

"I know what he's saying makes sense to him." Marybeth let the tears run down her cheeks. The cold air stung, but she didn't care. "He's right that I don't have any way to provide. Once the money Papa saved is gone, I honestly don't know what we'll do. At least he owned the house outright."

"Then that will come to you and Carrie. I'll talk to my brother-in-law, if you like. He can handle legal stuff for you since he's a lawyer. I don't know if your pa had debts, but I doubt it. He was pretty firm on paying cash."

"Yes, he was, and I know of nothing that he owed. He

wouldn't even let me run a tab at the grocers.'" Marybeth wiped her face with her scarf. "Oh, Edward, I know you're hurting too. Pa always said you were like the son he never had."

"He was always good to me. My pa said he was the best man in Independence."

"They were good friends. Right to the end," Marybeth admitted. "I appreciated that you and your pa were pall-bearers. I appreciate even more the way you helped Pa when he was alive."

"He was easy to work with and good to teach me about things I didn't know." Edward shook his head. "He always understood my desire to work as an officer of the law. He encouraged me when my pa started nagging me about quitting that work and coming back to help him with the horse farm."

"Pa had a talent for seeing what a man was cut out to do. He often spoke of what a great deputy you made."

"I wish my pa could understand like yours did. Raising horses is just not my calling. Inga loves it. Her boys love it too, so there will be someone to continue the family business. But I intend to go on working in law enforcement. I like being a part of the police department in Evansville."

"That's because you're good at it." Marybeth sighed and huddled down in her woolen coat. "I was sure hoping it wouldn't turn so cold so soon."

"Me too. People get mean when it gets cold. You'd think they'd go find a place to stay warm and keep inside, but instead it seems to make them seek attention out of boredom. We arrested three different groups of folks yesterday for fighting."

They turned down the street where Marybeth's father had purchased the family house over twenty-two years ago. Back then, the town of Lamasco, as it was called, was only about eight years old. Situated on the west side of Pigeon Creek across from Evansville, Indiana, this community had attracted a vast number of German immigrants, including Marybeth's mother and father. Marybeth had been the first of their family to be born in America. Her first six years of school had been given in English and German, so she spoke both fluently.

In 1857, the parts of Lamasco that had overflowed to the east side of Pigeon Creek had been incorporated into Evansville, but on the west side of the creek, folks had decided to remain independent of Evansville and changed their name to Independence. Some of the older folks still called it Lamasco, but no one seemed to mind much.

Marybeth remembered when their house had been only one of a handful. Now houses were built side by side, block after block. It had been a wonderful place to grow up, and she'd hoped to give that life to Carrie, but now she wondered if that could still happen.

She looked over at Edward. Their talk of the horse farm seemed to have brought him even lower. "I'm sure your father will understand in time. He loves you."

Edward brought the horses to a stop and glanced her way. "It's of no matter right now. You've just lost your pa, and it's not right to focus on anything but that. Look, I'll be by tomorrow to bring you some more wood. Do you have plenty for tonight?"

Marybeth nodded and jumped down from the wagon. "I do. I'm gonna go stir up the stove and get a fire going in the fireplace before I head over to pick up Carrie. Thanks again for standing by me at the funeral. I know Pa would have been grateful for your support and all that you're doing for me and Carrie."

He smiled for the first time that day. "I'm honored to help. You and your pa got me through the worst of it when Janey and the boy died." He always referred to his son as "the boy," since he and Janey hadn't picked out a name for him. Edward had buried them together, with the boy safely tucked in Janey's arms. The gravestone simply read *Jane Vogel and Son.*

"That's why God gave us to each other," Marybeth said, letting the finality of the moment settle on her. Papa was really and truly gone. She glanced at the house and trembled.

"Best get in out of the cold. I'll see you in the morning." Edward slapped the reins and headed on down the street.

Marybeth had never felt so alone.

Edward made sure the horses had adequate feed, then went into the house. He and Janey had rented this place at the edge of town when they'd married. That was shortly after he'd come home from the war. Of course, he'd needed time to finish recovering from a wound he'd taken at the Siege of Savannah. A ball cored a hole through his side and out the back in the blink of an eye. Loss of blood had nearly killed him, but thankfully nothing vital had been hit. Little by little, Edward had recovered enough to be sent home just after the first of the year in 1865.

Inga had been his nurse since their mother had mourned

herself to death over the loss of his two brothers. She had died that September after news that Jacob had been killed in August at the Battle of Atlanta. Their brother Gunther had taken a minié ball two years prior to that at Shiloh. Mother had been convinced that she would lose all three when the brothers had enlisted to join Evansville's Twenty-Fifth Regiment of the Indiana Infantry. And she'd nearly been right. Edward might have died but for the fact that after being wounded, he'd mistakenly been transferred with some special patients—sons of congressmen and senators—to a hospital in Washington. There, he'd received quality care that wouldn't have been available on the battlefield. Most likely it had saved his life. Inga called it God's provision. Edward sometimes wondered, however, if he had cheated death and that was why Janey and the boy had to die.

Once inside the cold house, Edward made a fire in the hearth and sat down to enjoy the warmth before heading out for his night shift. They'd been outside for far too long in the growing cold. He probably should have talked Marybeth into canceling the graveside services, but it hadn't occurred to him at the time. Thankfully the wind hadn't been blowing.

Catching sight of the letter he'd left unopened on the table, Edward got up and grabbed it before settling back down in front of the fire. It was from his former commanding officer, Major Henderson. The man had written only once before. That letter had come to congratulate Edward on his marriage and to offer hope that Edward was fully recovered.

Edward looked at the letter for a moment. Major Henderson had always had plans to go out west after the war. Like Edward, he was a law enforcement officer with a strong desire to keep the law and order of a frontier town. Edward had always figured to get enough experience in Evansville that one day he could go west and take up a position standing guard over an entire community. He and Henderson had discussed it quite thoroughly once.

He opened the letter and read the contents. Henderson was a man of few words, always getting straight to the point. This letter was no exception.

I'm sure this letter takes you by surprise, but I have an offer to make.

Tracie Peterson (TraciePeterson.com) is the bestselling author of more than one hundred novels, both historical and contemporary, with nearly six million copies sold. She has won the ACFW Lifetime Achievement Award and the *Romantic Times* Career Achievement Award. Her avid research resonates in her many bestselling series. Tracie and her family make their home in Montana.

Kimberley Woodhouse (KimberleyWoodhouse.com) is an award-winning, bestselling author of more than 40 fiction and nonfiction books. Kim and her incredible husband of 30-plus years live in Colorado, where they play golf together, spend time with their kids and grandbaby, and research all the history around them.

Sign Up for Tracie's & Kimberley's Newsletters

Keep up to date with Tracie's and Kimberley's latest news on book releases and events by signing up for their email lists at the links below.

TraciePetersonBooks.com
KimberleyWoodhouse.com

FOLLOW TRACIE AND KIMBERLEY ON SOCIAL MEDIA

[f] Tracie Peterson

[o] @AuthorTraciePeterson

[f] Kimberley Woodhouse

[o] @KimberleyWoodhouse

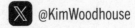 @KimWoodhouse

More from Tracie Peterson and Kimberley Woodhouse

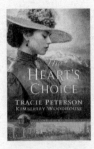

Rebecca Whitman is the first female court reporter in Montana. During a murder trial, she's convinced that the defendant is innocent, but no one except the handsome new Carnegie librarian, Mark Andrews, will listen to her. In a race against time, will they be able to find the evidence they need—and open their hearts to love—before it's too late?

The Heart's Choice
THE JEWELS OF KALISPELL #1

Set in the 1904 gold-rush boomtown of Nome, Alaska, three sisters grapple with personal challenges amid a backdrop of family bonds and burgeoning romances. You will be swept away by Tracie Peterson and Kimberley Woodhouse's seamlessly woven historical romances of strength found amidst adversity in a remote, unforgiving landscape.

THE TREASURES OF NOME:
Forever Hidden, Endless Mercy, Ever Constant